Critical Praise for Chuck Logan

Hunter's Moon

"Hold tight for a memorable ride…"

> —*Publishers Weekly* *Starred Review*

The Price of Blood

"This darkly entertaining novel . . . sustains Logan's promise as one of the best of the new thriller breed."

> —*Publishers Weekly* *Starred Review*

The Big Law

"The ingenious plot and cast of well-fleshed out characters . . . continue to mark Logan as a standout in the genre."

> —*Publishers Weekly* *Starred Review*

Absolute Zero

"Logan is a new maestro of suspense."

> —*Publishers Weekly* *Starred Review*

"Good writing, a colorful cast and a thoroughly appealing protagonist."

> —*Kirkus* *Starred Review*

Vapor Trail

"A hot read."

> —*People Magazine*

BROKER

Chuck Logan

Conquill Press

This book is a work of fiction. Names, characters, places and incidents either are products of the author's imagination or are used fictitiously. Certain liberties have been taken in portraying regional settings and their institutions. This is wholly intentional. Any resemblance to actual events, or to actual persons living or dead, is entirely coincidental.

For information about special discounts for bulk purchases, contact conquillpress@comcast.net.

BROKER

Cover Design: Rebecca Treadway

Library of Congress Control Number: 2016952194

Logan, Chuck

Broker/ by Chuck Logan – 1st edition

ISBN: 978-0-9908461-6-1

Conquill Press/March 2017

Printed in the United States of America

10 9 8 7 6 5 4 3 2 1

For Jeannie, Sofie, Brother Bill, Kelly and Kevin, who had my back during the rough spots.

Also by Chuck Logan

The world is a beautiful place
to be born into
if you don't mind some people dying
all the time...

LAWRENCE FERLINGHETTI

Chapter One

Saturday, November 17, 1979

The news continued to be bad. Vietnam and Watergate rustled in the gutter like soiled gum wrappers and money was tight and mortgage rates hit close to 15% and lines backed up at the gas pumps. Fucking Carter put on a sweater and dialed down the thermostat and proposed canceling the White House Christmas tree lights. And now an Iranian mob had seized the U.S. Embassy and Americans were paraded as hostages in Tehran. The days got shorter. The shadows lengthened toward winter. In Minnesota, people turned up their collars against the chill as the seductive bass beat and ominous lyrics of Pink Floyd's "Another Brick in the Wall, Part Two" blasted from boom boxes and echoed down the slushy streets.

They looked up and wondered, What else can go wrong?

*　　　*　　　*

"Aw shit!" grumbled J.T. Merriweather when he spotted his boss, St. Paul Narco Lieutenant Joe Desmond, walk through the door, dusting snow off his curly red hair. Desmond's quick China-blue eyes paused briefly on J.T. and kept moving as he grinned automatically and began working the crowd, shaking hands and acting totally oblivious about the perfect storm of gossip and innuendo that swirled around him. Word was out. He'd hit his wife, and she had filed papers on him.

The building was full of cops who—even in party mode — were a hard sell when it came to wiggling out of thumping your

1

wife. Desmond was an Irish cop of the old St. Paul pedigree: choirboy, Eagle Scout, a St. Thomas grad who studied law, nights, at William Mitchell. A faction of traditionalists in the department put him on the short list for deputy chief.

Now all that was on hold.

"Damn." J.T. sagged.

"The Man of the Hour, huh? What the hell's he doing here?" quipped an FBI agent standing next to Merriweather as they watched Desmond wade into the crowd. Then, maybe in an attempt to lighten the mood, the agent said, "Looks pretty casual for a guy with a price on his head, especially out here in Soap Turrie territory."

"Oh yeah, *that*, right," Merriweather mumbled as they watched Desmond finesse his way through the jostling bodies.

It was billed as a party, a Saturday break in the two-week Mid-states Organized Crime Workshop put on by the Minnesota Sheriff's Association and specifically hosted here, in Stillwater, by Arnie Grunwald, the Washington County sheriff. Grunwald had welcomed the outstate attendees with a folksy speech about the charms of the old river town, popularly known as the "birthplace of Minnesota" and which was located on the Wisconsin border twenty miles east of the Twin Cities of St. Paul and Minneapolis. He suggested they look over the remains of the state territorial prison where Cole Younger, of the Jesse James gang, had been the prison librarian after his capture during the abortive Northfield bank robbery.

The touch football game had just been cancelled due to a fitful whiteout. And now sixty cops from all over Minnesota and several adjoining states were clustered at the entrance to the county shooting range. They kicked snow off their boots as they sipped coffee and hot cider and kibitzed about the surveillance techniques offered in the course, as well as the array of useful technology set out on display. Another fifty local cops had shown up for the free feed and to get a look at the vintage

Thompson machine gun one of the DEA trainers had brought as a conversation piece. The predominantly male crowd milled in street clothes, shoulder to shoulder, and spanned a cross section of working law enforcement from crew-cut state patrol types to shaggy undercover narcs. Here and there a bold, trailblazing female cop broke up the monotonous testosterone. Merriweather's black face drifted in a sea of Norwegian, Irish and German extraction.

The cement block building was a former bus garage with a less-than-snug tin roof, so the atmosphere seeped up from the cement floor all drafty, damp and poorly heated. The closeness of over-dressed men in sweaty wool mingled with the smoke of grilled chicken and pork chops that wafted in from the parking lot through the ajar doors. Tubs of slaw, trays of baked beans and other hot dishes were being set out. The banquet tables and folding chairs had been arranged. Booze wasn't on the menu because the cooking smells mixed with the nitro-aftertaste of gunfire drifting from the shooting line at the far end of the structure. Masked by heavy plastic sound curtains, gunshots popped by ones, semi-automatic twos and threes, and one ripsaw racket of full auto rock and roll. A variety of weapons were laid out to play with, and now the workshop had been transformed into a dry tailgate party for cops, with at least one antique machine gun in attendance. Later, when they put the guns away, there would be beer.

J.T. turned back to the FBI agent, who was saying, "You were there, right? When Turrie did his famous face plant at Alary's? Nothing really to it, I heard. Just a drunken piss-off."

"Pretty much," J.T. said as he tracked Desmond's progress through the throng. In fact, Desmond wore the threat like a laurel.

It was a standing joke. Desmond had led the Metro Area Narcotics Squad that dismantled the Others Motorcycle Gang drug operation. Now the gang's leadership resided not far away, in the Stillwater state prison. The case earned Desmond the vengeance of local legend Russell "Soap" Turrie, who claimed deep roots in the Stillwater community. His notorious younger brother, Danny T, was the gang honcho. But what really pissed old Soap off was that his nephew, Jo Jo, had drawn a harsh sentence for drug possession in the juvenile detention center at Totem Town.

"It got a little rough, I heard," the agent said.

"Oh yeah." J.T. was clearly tired of the story.

Alary's was a cop bar in St. Paul. The last week of September, Soap Turrie had famously fallen off the wagon and made the death threat against Desmond. But the agent was waiting for more, so he gave him the brief version. "He barged in totally loaded and bad-mouthed the whole crowd. Tossed a cop I work with, Terry Connor, over the bar when Terry tried to calm him down. Then he informed everyone, as we wrestled him into the cuffs, that Desmond was a dead man, that the call had been made."

"So not real smart, everything considered, Desmond being out here," the agent added circumspectly.

"You think?" J.T. allowed, tight-lipped. Soap Turrie famously operated a car repair shop in town and occasionally employed ex-felons who'd cleaned up in "The Program."

Changing the subject, J.T. asked, "So that thing I asked you about, something big that went missing?"

"Straight up, J.T.?" The agent leaned in. "Folks in my shop are leery about this story Desmond's putting out. What we heard is his wife caught him fooling around with Miss Annie O'Neil again. They argued, and Lilly Desmond wound up with a black eye. Word on the bricks is he floated the idea about Annie being into some big drug shipment to cover his ass. So Annie dropped out of sight to duck the gossip. Appreciate you being loyal and all, but he's got you out here chasing unicorns."

"Look past the gossip, man. I asked you a question." J.T. was showing signs of the strain.

The agent appreciated J.T.'s dilemma and relented. "Nothing special's going on. Talked to DEA, ATF and the marshals; zip with them too."

"Don't add up. Desmond might bullshit about his personal life, but I've never known him to blow smoke about the job," J.T. said evenly.

The agent tugged his sleeve and moved closer. "And Desmond's wife filing the domestic abuse complaint, that's just bullshit too, huh?"

"Check you later," J.T. said when he spied Terry Conner, of Alary's tossed-over-the-bar fame, coming through the press of bodies.

Terry pulled him aside and yelled, "What's Des doing here? He isn't supposed to be here."

"I think he's lost it. We have to get him out, right now," J.T. yelled back to be heard over the chatter from the overdressed cops coming in from the cold. Gunfire from the far end of the building added to the din.

"Yeah, well, Des is only half the problem because Wilson just showed up."

"Christ! I thought he was in Wisconsin, hunting."

"Got his deer this morning and came back for this thing. He's on the firing line, last I saw." Terry tapped his teeth together. "What's the plan?"

"You grab Wilson and drag his dumb ass out to the parking lot. I'll slow down Des. Meet up after you get asshole clear."

Forty-two on his last birthday, Desmond was still built like a young bull, with a square, ruddy face that was pebbled with acne scars and freckles. When J.T. appeared in front of him, blocking his way, he worked up a grin and angled up and

5

spoke into the taller man's ear. "So you come up with anything talking to your fed buddy?"

J.T. shook his head. "He says nothing out of the ordinary's going on." Then it was J.T.'s turn to speak into Desmond's ear. "Like everyone else, he's into the gossip, Des. He says you have me tracking down your missing girlfriend on company time— that you made up this talk about a big missing dope shipment as a distraction."

Desmond's smile bit down on it: "We find Annie O'Neil, we find out what's going on."

"Christ sake, Des, why wouldn't she lay low with all the talk going around?"

Desmond's face stiffened; the tender spot being poked, his eyes flashed. "Hey, J.T., cut me some slack. It's my day off."

Undeterred, J.T. drilled in because passive didn't cut it on Desmond's squad. "Be advised, Des; if that complaint your wife filed about you knocking her around holds up, you could have a lot of days off."

Desmond stopped and turned. Several creases transformed his face into a condescending frown. He patted J.T. on the arm. "She was pissed off. She lied. I'll get it sorted out first thing Monday morning."

"Bets are running two to one you get suspended Monday morning. You should get your ass out of here."

Finally Desmond acknowledged J.T.'s unblinking gaze with a fatalistic shrug. "All right. It could get a little bumpy." He allowed a modest grimace as he looked around. "Listen, J.T., I've been cultivating a new source out there, got him look-ing for Annie. If I get caught up in Internal Affairs red tape, he's going to need a new connect, so I gave him your pager."

"Who's that?" J.T. asked.

Desmond affected a mysterious grin. "Probably won't come to that, but if it does, you'll see," he said, showing more of his new dental work.

"Des, man, you aren't making sense," J.T. said. "I think you should get out of here and spend some time with a police union lawyer."

"Been nice talking to you, J.T." Desmond winked and started moving again because he saw Sheriff Grunwald and ambled over to shake hands.

J.T. gritted his teeth. The man was definitely out of touch. Like forget a bunch of white people and their dirty laundry. But Desmond was his rabbi in the department and had had his back on more than one occasion. And the only thing Des and Wilson shared in common—other than apparently now Desmond's wife—was a tendency to flash anger. So it was time to hit his give-a-shit button. This was not the place for Des and Wilson to collide. Uh uh. So he set his jaw and shouldered through the crowd, hovering just behind Desmond.

A few feet away Sheriff Grunwald was giving Desmond one of his cooler political handshakes. "Didn't know you signed up for this course. Don't recall seeing you during my great welcoming speech," he said carefully.

"Nah, just dropped by. Heard you had a machine gun," Desmond said, cracking a smile.

To Grunwald's practiced eye the smile looked slightly forced. But he warmed a little. "Anybody can get a machine gun. We got an old Eliot Ness Special, a Thompson with a drum magazine just like in the movies."

"Want to have a look at that," Desmond said.

The conversation stalled awkwardly, and Grunwald pulled on a wool cap. "Sorry. Have to go. Got another speech to prepare. Lions Club."

"Perils of elected office," Desmond said.

Grunwald detected a wistful hint of envy in Des' voice. He had the big case, law school and, of course, a very ambitious wife. And now the wife had become a problem.

"You okay, Des?"

Desmond shrugged it off. "Don't believe everything you hear."

"Watch yourself," Grunwald said. He bid Desmond good-bye and watched him disappear into the raucous crowd. Then he turned and found himself face to face with J.T.

"Merriweather," Grunwald bit off the words, "get your boss the hell out of this building. These guys are all laughing behind his back."

"I'm working on it," J.T. said. Then he left the sheriff and continued to ride shotgun on Joe Desmond until Terry relocated Wilson.

*   *   *

It was a burden. J.T. was the newest member of the Narco Squad—just a year out of patrol. But he was the only cop in whom Desmond had confided the entire story, which had started last Wednesday night when one of Desmond's confidential informants, Annie O'Neil, called him at home and his wife, Lilly, picked up the phone and recognized the caller's voice. Here's how it went.

"For you," Lilly said with acid in her voice. "That peroxide-blonde whore you got caught sleeping with. The one you promised Father Murray you would never see again." Then she tossed the receiver at Desmond's face like a brush back pitch.

Blindsided, Desmond fielded the phone and blurted, "Jesus, Annie, what're you doing calling me at home?"

Annie blurted back, "I'm scared, Des. You gotta come over here right now."

Which, according to Desmond, wasn't like Annie one bit. She owned a bar on St. Paul's West Seventh Street that was a clearinghouse for information and sometimes stolen goods. She didn't spook easily. She'd made herself available as an informant in the biker case. And she'd made herself available in other ways to a tired cop with problems at home who didn't object when she poured one last drink after closing. Hence, in the middle of the task force investigation, Desmond had strayed with one of his snitches and had been found out and confessed and wound up in couples counseling with the parish priest.

"What's going on?" Desmond said.

"This guy came to me who's into something so hot he's scared shitless and wants a private meet with you," she said.

"What guy?" he said.

"I'm not passing any names on the phone. Thing is, Des, he's so freaked he dumped it all on me and split," she said.

"Dumped what?" he said.

"Jesus, Des, you're not hearing me. This is way too touchy to say on the phone. You got to come over to the bar right now."

And Desmond told J.T. that the palpable fear that over-powered Annie's usually husky voice had brought on a tingle of early cop Christmas. Jesus, what's it take to get Annie hyper-ventilating? And why would she be talking to him if it didn't involve cargo coming into the metro? And talk about lousy timing. Lilly, arms folded, tapping her foot, dressed for a night out. An early dinner, theater tickets. Fresh coffee brewed.

"I'll be right there." Desmond just had to find out.

*   *   *

J.T. watched Desmond stumble into a guy wearing Sorel boots and a hunting jacket with a spray of dried blood on the blaze orange sleeve. Desmond recovered and started glad-handing a Ramsey County deputy that J.T. vaguely remem-bered was named Halvorsen. *Not good, Des.* The room was full of watchful eyes, suspicious eyes. Cops' eyes. No way Desmond didn't know they were whispering behind his back, tracking him, like everyone had been ever since the bar talk started, about how his erstwhile protégé, Sergeant Al Wilson, had been observed by three tipsy, off-duty patrol guys going at it with Desmond's wife, Lilly, in the parking lot of Mancini's Restaurant last Wednesday night. And damned if that wasn't tied right back to Annie O'Neil, too.

Because right after Des hung up the phone, Lilly Desmond delivered an ultimatum in the middle of pouring coffee. If he ever saw Annie O'Neil again, she was calling a lawyer. And Desmond, who was getting testy at being wrongly accused—this time—told his wife that she was out of line because Annie was a source and this was The Job.

J.T. gathered that something in Lilly gave way when Des said that. A lot of cops who'd worked with Des were not reluctant to say she was too ambitious and good-looking for him. And way too high strung. They said maybe he should have paid more attention to her depression after the last miscarriage, when she couldn't even return to her job as a paralegal in the Ramsey County Attorney's office. The meds barely took the edge off the insecurities. He probably should have spent more time at home with her.

But he didn't.

"I got your job," Lilly had hissed, and then she'd snapped and, coming around the table, she'd flung the coffee pot.

According to Desmond, he'd reacted to a chestful of scalding liquid by instinctively throwing a backhand to deflect the glass decanter. He missed and accidently caught Lilly a glancing blow alongside the head, splitting her eyebrow and swelling her right eye. The glass coffee pot bounced off his chest and shattered on the table. The hot liquid stung. The damage on his wife's face hurt more. Wincing, gritting his teeth, he'd said, "Christ, I'm sorry. Lilly, you okay? Come on, we should put ice on that, get you to Emergency."

Staggering back, she'd snarled, "You come near me, I swear I'll call the cops." Then she grabbed the keys to the station wagon and bolted from the house. Stunned, Desmond followed her in his car. By the time two officers took Lilly's statement in the emergency room at St. Paul Ramsey, her right eyebrow was puffed up like a stitched eggplant.

"I caught the sonofabitch cheating on me with one of his snitches, that slut Annie O'Neil. I confronted him and he hit me is what happened," she'd stated.

And so Annie, a confidential informant, had her name entered on the public record.

The patrol cops dutifully interviewed Desmond, who was pacing in the waiting room, to get his side of the story. He pulled his drenched coffee-stained shirt up to show the scorch marks on his chest and reported accurately what had happened. In the meantime, Lilly checked herself out and, according to the gossip, returned home, touched up her hair and put on her best catch-me-fuck-me-dress, the black one that showcased the cleavage topside and the marathon runner's thighs down below. She removed the bandage and wore the puffy eye like a badge of scorn as she stalked into Mancini's Restaurant, where she knew Al Wilson would be drinking at the bar.

It had to be Wilson, the story went, because Joe, her husband, had been Wilson's mentor on the Narcotics Unit, and because Al loved to brag about his prowess with the ladies. With a relentless forward motion fueled by Chivas on top of downers, she ran right over Wilson's common sense. After a brief struggle, he lost to his whiskey-addled hormones, and they wound up in the front seat of his Mustang in a dark corner of the back parking lot. Lilly's strawberry curls were bobbing in Wilson's lap when the off-duty patrol cops stopped to blink in shocked fascination through the windshield.

Desmond returned to a deserted house, made a concerned call to Lilly's sister, and came up empty. Then he drove to O'Neil's Bar to follow up on the tip from Annie. "Left in a real hurry," the bartender said. "Didn't say where. Called a cab. Her car's still out back in the lot."

Lilly did not return that night, and Desmond went into the office the next morning and sought refuge in routine. But before lunch, word had leaked out from the Patrol Division about the scene at Mancini's, and a seismic eye roll shook the cop shop. Then the calls started coming in about the domestic abuse complaint that had been filed by his wife. Desmond protested to his boss—like, hey, I might be on to something really major here if I can track down Annie O'Neil. The boss said maybe he could play Internal Affairs about the abuse complaint, but he couldn't do anything about the gossip coming down from the street cops—and now the first inquisitive calls were coming in from the *Pioneer Press* cop reporter. So in the end Desmond took the tight-lipped advice to disappear until things got sorted out. Wilson received the same guidance and slipped off to hunt in Wisconsin, but not before he lived up to his reputation as an asshole and managed to drop a few droll remarks about his conquest. So Desmond bought a bottle, went home to his empty house, and worked the phone, putting J.T. on the street to track down Annie O'Neil.

The bottle remained unopened. J.T. squeezed his snitches and came up empty. Now what had started as some exciting talk on the street had taken an absurd bounce and exploded into an X-rated cop soap opera. Lilly had disappeared into a humiliated funk, probably at her sister's—who wasn't answering the phone. Annie O'Neil was nowhere in sight, and her cryptic phone call now echoed like a snicker behind Desmond's back.

J.T. exhaled, bumping shoulders in the crowd, pacing Desmond, who had apparently decided to come up for air and push back against the gossip and show his face someplace outside of town, like the workshop shindig in Stillwater.

And now they'd run out of crowd, and Desmond plodded toward the sound of the firing with J.T. trailing him. He parted the sound curtain and stepped into the range area where maybe twenty cops were clustered around the shooting stations. A few county deputies in uniform stood around, keeping an eye out. But for the workshop, the discipline was relaxed. An exotic variety of firearms was displayed along with corresponding boxes of ammunition and bulbous ear protectors. The atmosphere was less that of a police firing range than of a convivial gun show with live ammo. Twenty-five yards downrange a line of posters had been tacked up—each featuring the turbaned face of the Ayatollah Khomeini, who glowered through a cheesecloth of bullet holes. A red light glowed on the overhead video camera so they could add some footage to a workshop commemorative tape.

J.T. shifted on the balls of his feet. The Thompson aficionados created a traffic jam mid-range, and Desmond paused briefly at the edge of the group. So there was a line for the main toy. Desmond drifted to the right, ignored an Uzi and the Kalashnikov AK-47, and picked up an old-fashioned snub-nosed .38 revolver, loaded six rounds in the cylinder, and squinted down the range at the old Iranian cleric's bearded face.

So Desmond was off to the right. Terry addressed Wilson on the left. J.T. figured there was time. The crowd around the machine gun created a brief buffer zone that separated Desmond from Terry Conner, who was tugging on Al Wilson's jacket, trying to ease him from the shooting tables. Wilson, being an asshole, obviously had other ideas. Fresh from the woods in blaze orange—and always the hotdog—he was shoving Terry away because he had removed his ear protectors and was showing off this long-barreled, antique six-shooter to one of the few female cops at the workshop, a not-bad-looking blonde wearing a snow jacket with an outstate county patch on the shoulder.

J.T. decided his best option was to help Terry stiff-arm Wilson off the premises and then deal with Desmond. So he pushed through the scrum of cops around the Thompson as an automatic burst battered his unprotected eardrums and a shower of twinkling cartridges clattered on the cement floor.

Then the Thompson stopped firing, apparently jammed. The man holding it yanked out the drum magazine and stared. One of the range officers walked over.

The guy standing next to Desmond pulled his earmuffs down around his neck and held up an automatic pistol with a silencer attachment. Desmond lowered the unfired pistol and likewise doffed his ear protection. The guy said, "You know, in the movies they go 'phsst,' but in fact the action makes this ga-chung sound."

That's when the knot of cops around the Thompson stepped back to let the range officer clear the jam, and Desmond caught a flurry of activity beyond the Thompson kerfuffle. He recognized J.T. with Conner, another detective from the unit, shifting bodies, hard to see, some kind of grab ass it looked like.

Fifty feet and a dozen cops away, J.T. said, "C'mon, Al, time to leave," as he and Terry Conner crowded Wilson away from the firing line. Wilson's eyes drifted past the Thompson gaggle and stopped on Desmond. "Back off, Merriweather," he said. "Go find another apple to polish. Check it out. Desmond has fallen off his fucking pedestal, and he won't be getting back on any time soon."

J.T. was running out of patience, because Wilson was apparently very into enjoying his fifteen minutes of notoriety. So J.T. and Conner exchanged a fast glance that signaled it was time to quit screwing around and get physical and manhandle Wilson from the building. J.T. stuffed a flash of pique. He had better things to do on his day off than babysit a smart ass, pop-corn cop who watched too many police shows on TV and who spent more on clothes than he could afford.

The outstate female cop read the back and forth with wary eyes and took a sensible step backwards. Wilson predictably braced and resisted. He pushed Conner aside, then confronted J.T. "Fuck him, let him leave. I was here first," he snorted.

"I about had enough of this playground strut," J.T. muttered to Terry as they poised to wrap Wilson up. But just then the swarm of bodies around the Thompson drifted apart, the sight lines opened up, and in a single, dizzy moment Wilson and Desmond locked eyes in the eye-tickling powder haze, and J.T. saw it all.

Like it was supposed to happen.

Walking away wasn't a choice anymore. All the people watching were cops.

If Desmond didn't address it, he'd look like a pussy.

The close air reeked of gunpowder and bodies sweating in too much clothing, and a scented curl of hot-dish normalcy— macaroni and cheese, plates of grilled chicken— circulated over the sound curtain. Very clearly, in the gaps between the gunfire, the sound of people laughing out there carried to the firing line.

And J.T. saw it all come to an instant boil on Desmond's face. Humiliation. Shame. Then anger.

Wilson pushed away from J.T. and Conner and smiled down the range, a youthful raffish grin that ended in a smirk. For emphasis, he raised his left hand and made an elaborate production out of sniffing his fingers in an unmistakably lewd gesture.

And J.T. witnessed everything that Desmond had been, would ever be, close in and trap him in a red rushing spiral.

Minnesota Bureau of Criminal Apprehension Detective Harold Cantrell, lead investigator on the incident, would comment in his private notes: *"We should keep in mind that a problem arises with revolvers under certain conditions, even for trained men. The weapons lack a safety. Reflex and adrenaline can take over, and it's just like pointing your finger. This is especially relevant in this case, where an officer was blindsided by flash anger, shame and insult surrounded by his peers. Most police officers, like most soldiers, never fire their weapons at anything more threatening than paper. Neither Desmond nor Wilson had ever actually fired a gun at a human being, but they both had a street rep for never backing down and being fierce with their fists. Except, when they started toward each other, they both had revolvers in those fists."*

What the . . .? For a split second J.T. thought that Wilson experienced a moment of sober calculation, like this macho posturing could really go over the edge. He skidded and raised his hands. Like whoa. There was time. Ten or twelve yards separated them. But in doing so, the big Colt in his right hand swung in line with Desmond's face, and that only upped the ante because a surge of cuckold fury had blurred the stop signs in Desmond's usually orderly mind. And it looked like it was right there happening.

No! J.T. blinked, stunned, when the .38 bucked in Desmond's hand.

Wilson took the first round in the left hip and spun down, getting off two wild shots as he fell. Desmond, ducking, fired again, twice. Wilson thrashed on the floor and the blonde female cop standing behind him reeled back, clutching her knee. Up and down the line faces froze in a tableaux of disbelief as Wilson feebly tried to return fire. The blonde crumpled into the man at the end of the range, who up until now, crouched, aiming at the Ayatollah—walled off in his ear protection—had not noticed what was happening next to him.

J.T., frozen in mid stride, saw the man spin, shake off his ear protection, and note the blood welling up through the denim on the female cop's knee. In one icy, suspended beat of time, the man took in Wilson sprawled on the floor and Desmond continuing his charge, aiming. The blonde screamed, and the raw pain in her voice broke the stranglehold of shock. People blinked, their eyes wide and startled—this wasn't supposed to happen here! Desmond jerked the trigger again, and the wild round zipped past the man's ear.

The last thing Joe Desmond saw was the man's green eyes tighten and focus as he instantly dropped to one knee. In a continuous, smooth motion he planted his left elbow on his cocked left knee, placed his left palm under his right elbow, extended his right arm, and fired two .45 caliber slugs an inch apart into Joe Desmond's heart.

Eight shots in less than four seconds. Three people down. Time came unstuck, and the reaction reflexes kicked in. Terry Conner yanked out his personal weapon and instinctively covered the man who'd shot Desmond. J.T. balanced on the balls of his feet, willing his thoughts to synchronize with what his eyes had just witnessed. He raised a hand to steady Conner. "Easy, Terry," he cautioned as he stared first at Des' crumpled body and then at the shooter, who slowly rose to his feet and made a point of carefully reversing the pistol in a practiced move, finger off the trigger, so he held it muzzle down by the handle.

The shooter was late twenties, maybe thirty, with a rugged outdoor varnish to his regular features. J.T. recognized the raw physical bearing of someone who'd started out as an athlete or a soldier and had gone on to something rougher. He wore jeans and a gray wool surplus West German Army sweater. Dark hair snarled over his ears, and his thick eyebrows seemed to blend in a shaggy line over the unflinching eyes. J.T.'s first thought was, undercover narc maybe? Not local.

"Put down the weapon, back off and get your hands up!" Terry Conner yelled to control the tremor in his voice. Then he demanded, "Who the hell are you?"

Slowly the man with the eyebrows lowered his pistol to the floor, stepped away and held up his empty hands, palms out.

"Broker. Phil Broker. I came down from Cook County."

Terry Conner blinked rapidly, getting a slippery handle on the swirling shouts for help, the crackling radios, the first aid kits ripping open. He dry swallowed and quickly looked into the stunned faces up and down the line. "You're a cop, right?" he said as J.T. moved in and slowly depressed the muzzle of Terry's weapon with his hand.

"Not exactly," Broker said. Then he slowly pointed to the female officer writhing in pain in front of him. "Better put some pressure on that knee and get a medic over here," he said in a steady voice.

Terry shook his head to sort out the blurred impressions and the echo of the gunshots. Des sprawled there like a pile of bloody laundry. Guys feeling for a pulse. Wilson groaning, surrounded by cops who tore open his sopping clothing and who screamed above the chaos for EMTs. "Who shot first?" he muttered to J.T. "You see who shot first?"

"Yeah," J.T. said, kneeling to attend to the prone deputy. "I saw the whole thing go down." Then in a lower tone of voice, he added, "Went down fast." One look at Conner's wide expression and he could see the thoughts forming. So as J.T. wadded a handkerchief and applied pressure to the ashen-faced deputy's knee, he appraised Broker through half-lidded eyes, and he flashed back to his casual banter earlier with his FBI contact, who'd asked him about the famous night at Alary's when Soap Turrie had drunkenly spilled the cold promise that Des was a dead man. That the call had been made.

Chapter Two

Hands raised shoulder high, Broker inhaled deeply to slow down the confusion. The old machinery had automatically kicked in the instant he'd turned and felt the round snap past his ear. Years ago, the machinery had originated from an icy baptism in the facts of survival. Now the machinery just ruthlessly removed clutter from his thoughts, from his reflexes, and from his field of vision.

And from his illusions. This was the last thing in the world he needed.

He exhaled slowly, never taking his eyes off the lowered pistol that, despite the black guy's intervention, was still wavering in the other cop's hand. Guy was having trouble with processing the psychic judo, having just seen a man's face go from warm and animated to sudden cold dead meat, because Joe Desmond's blank open eyes now stared at the ceiling with all the personality of a pork chop.

Up and down the line the shock dissipated and the yelling started and the running back and forth. Broker watched cops do what cops do, which is play catch-up and assert control and try to figure out what happened as the cozy workshop disintegrated past mere bedlam into nightmare. And it was all hello chaos my old friend and other riffs from good music that went with real bad times.

At least the second cop, the big spade dude, had some sea legs and was moving in to calm down his freaked-out pal, and now the pistol had lowered and the muzzle pointed at the floor.

Just go down, take some notes, John Lucht, the Cook County Sheriff, had said when he handed Broker the Special Deputy ID. No big deal. That way we get credit for the workshop and the federal funding that goes with it. You get to put the workshop on your work history. And you get exposed to the life and the people. We're going to build you some credentials in slow, easy stages.

Another deep inhale. Old John had this long-term plan to eventually employ Broker as a full-time deputy. Attending the workshop was a first step meant to finesse around certain questions the Cook County board had about this huge gap in his background.

He expelled the breath. Probably shouldn't have wandered over to the range and picked up the Colt. Shoulda, woulda, road not taken. So much for laying low up north with a small sheriff's department. Kicking back with his folks. Figuring out what came next in his life.

Now it was clear that what came next was a man stretched out flat on the cold cement. The machinery was swift to point out: *It won't help to think about it. So don't*. Sheer reflex—absolutely necessary in another life not so long ago—might be construed to be inappropriate here and now, in the slower world of Officer Friendly. Talk about Murphy's Law. Even with the grim circumstances, Broker almost laughed out loud. Quickly he checked himself. *Just let it play out. Procedure will set in. Somebody has to be in charge.* All of which cycled through his head in about three seconds, because the wounded female cop hissed, "Hurts like hell," through gritted teeth as another guy, who'd spelled the black cop, now pressed a dressing to her knee and kept yelling for a paramedic. Two more cops knelt with her and were discussing whether to put on a tourniquet. Bleeding wasn't her problem, more like the smashed nerves and architecture of her knee. But Broker knew his best response right now was to say absolutely nothing until someone who wasn't waving a gun in his face informed him as to his status. Because nutcase was back swinging the nine-millimeter around despite his buddy's efforts to restrain him.

"What do you mean you're not a cop *exactly*?" the excited cop shouted, and dots of spittle hit Broker's cheek.

"Stand down, man," the black cop growled.

The excited cop took a look at the corpse lying six yards away and ranted, "Wake up, J.T. We cuffed Soap Turrie together at Alary's that night. Now this guy fuckin' shot Des!"

"You're outta line! Des went nuts, shooting at Wilson. He hit her." The black cop pointed at the tight-lipped female cop now being given professional first aid on the floor.

"Bullshit," the excited cop spat, his face working. "Des was just defending himself."

Broker decided that Terry was having a tantrum and probably wouldn't shoot him, so he tracked his eyes down the range. The man he'd dropped, who apparently was named Des, now lay unattended because the cops had called it and determined he was past saving. They'd moved on to the second man, whom Broker gathered was named Wilson, and who had been the target in the attack—Broker breathed out—and who was still alive.

And now a leader in a uniform had emerged to stalk through the mayhem, shouting orders and sorting out the spectators and making room for paramedics who rushed in with a gurney to load up Wilson. The female cop with the knee wound hobbled behind the gurney, hanging on the shoulders of two deputies. More uniformed deputies, pouring in now from other towns, formed a cordon in an attempt to block access to the sound curtain, which was not an easy task because the overlapping sheets easily moved aside and were a totally permeable barrier. On the other side of the plastic, backlit by the lights in the dining area, a swarm of shapes surged like blurry hornets.

Then a pack of those super-curious shapes pushed through the sheeting and attempted to get past the deputies trying to establish the cordon. There were heated words, fingers were pointed and a few fists were cocked, but the cordon managed to shove most of the intruders back. It was touchy going because they were all cops, like everybody here, *except*, Broker thought, *me*. One of the interlopers managed to barge through and huffed up, a beefy guy with the dimensions of a weightlifter gone to seed on a donut diet. Clearly a buddy to the overwrought Terry.

Great. Broker shifted from one foot to the other.

"Freeze, asshole. Don't fuckin' move." Terry was bringing the pistol back up, which clearly pushed J.T. over the edge.

"Aw, fuck this!" he muttered as he moved in and twisted the weapon from Terry's hand. Then he pointed, no nonsense, at Broker. "Put your hands down but stay put." Broker gladly did.

"What the hell?" the slightly porcine friend of Terry blurted as his eyes shifted from his pal being disarmed by J.T. to Desmond's body amid the blood and strewn bandages, then back to Broker, who noticed he had barbecue sauce on his chin.

"Don't know, like, this guy shot Des. I saw it," Terry said too loud.

"Hold on, goddammit," J.T. protested.

"J.T., don't go wimping out on us," Barbecue Face sneered.

Broker watched the guy they called J.T. scowl and—deceptively light on his feet for a big man—close the distance and knife the rigid fingers of his left hand into Barbecue Face's ample stomach. The recently seized pistol hung casually in his right hand. Barbecue Face backed up, stumbling.

And that caught the attention of the senior uniform who was crouched over Desmond's body. He grabbed at a guy in street clothes and sent him running over. The new arrival inserted his considerable physique between J.T. and Barbecue Face and glared at J.T. "Holster that weapon. Now!"

"Belongs to this dummy," J.T. muttered as he handed the pistol back to Terry.

"You fire your weapon?" the man asked Terry, who shook his head. "Then get it out of sight."

"Who are you ordering us around?" Barbecue Face bristled.

"Sergeant Duffy, Washington County." Duffy's large knuckles tapped on Barbecue's shirt. "And according to my captain over there, you are standing in our crime scene, so shut up and back off." He addressed Terry. "Get rid of the weapon before I cuff your ass."

After Terry reluctantly holstered the pistol, he pointed to Broker and said, "This guy shot Des. We all saw it."

J.T. hung his head and moved it slowly back and forth. "Terry, man, that's bullshit. Des fired on Wilson first."

"It was a confusing situation," Terry countered.

Duffy held up a hand and turned to Broker. "You fire a weapon in this?"

Broker pointed to the Colt .45 lying on the cement several feet away.

"He's not a cop," Terry insisted. "That's what he said."

Duffy's eyes clicked back on Broker. "ID."

Broker removed his wallet and handed over the Cook County Special Deputy ID along with his Minnesota driver's license.

Duffy perused the cards, handed them back and wondered out loud, "Somebody want to tell me what the hell happened here?"

When he was certain he had full eye contact with Duffy, Broker slowly raised his hand and pointed to the video camera bolted to an overhead girder in a position to sweep the entire firing line. The red camera light was on.

"Got it," said Duffy.

A few minutes later the harried senior cop on site walked over and, radio set pressed to his ear, said to Duffy, "Sheriff's on the way. Comm center is calling cops from all over to help ride herd on this clusterfuck." Then Duffy motioned the commander aside and pulled back his vest to reveal the VHS tape he'd retrieved from the range camera. They conferred quickly, heads close. Duffy pointed at Broker.

They returned and the senior cop said, "Okay, listen up. I'm Investigations Captain Dennis Mordant. You guys come with me." He nodded toward the St. Paul cops. "Let's relocate over there. I'll have someone take your statements." After the St. Paul faction drifted away and briefly talked with Mordant, he broke away, came back and addressed Broker with a controlled eye roll. "Okay, seems we got us an extra snafu situation here." He stopped in mid-sentence when an older, uniformed deputy limped up. He had sergeant's chevrons on his sleeve, and his left pant leg flapped, ripped open above the knee to accommodate a bloody dressing on his calf.

"Christ, Johnny," Mordant grimaced, "you okay?"

"Nothin', just a fragment, ricochet," the sergeant said. "Look, Denny." He raised his hand and pointed. "I was standing right there. I saw it all. If this guy wouldn't have reacted, there'd be more bodies on the ground, believe me." He nodded at the corpse and winced. "Joe Desmond, right? Guy was way out of line."

Mordant nodded. "We'll get a statement, but right now—if you're up for it—we really need to separate these assholes. Get everybody who wasn't on the line the hell out of the building." His lips pursed in a tight smile. "There's a hundred guys milling around out there, most of whom are armed, and some of them are starting to talk crazy shit to each other."

"Gotcha," said the injured sergeant. He turned and stumped toward the sound curtain, where he summoned a crew to speed up clearing the dining area and stow the curtain.

Then Mordant leaned more intently into the radio set and held up a finger to Duffy and Broker. Wait one.

"Right. Paramedics from Lakeview Emergency arrived within minutes. It's a real mess, Arnie. We got one dead. Yeah. Joe Desmond from St. Paul Narcotics was pronounced on the scene. Depending who you talk to, Desmond went ape shit on a cop named Wilson, also from St. Paul Narco. They met up on the firing line and all hell broke loose . . . Yep. I know, we all heard the wife thing. Wilson's on his way to surgery at Lakeview along with a female deputy, Marcy Hanson, from Cass County. She caught a bad one in the knee. Maybe a couple other minor wounds. We're getting a count.

"We're taking statements, but we don't know what we have here exactly." He watched his cops scramble to isolate witnesses at separate tables. Eisenhower was herding the last of the rubberneckers out into the cold. Two more cops were stringing yellow tape down the length of the range now that the sound curtain had been walked back. Briefly he stared at the wad of dressings on Desmond's motionless chest; then he glanced at the .45 that Broker had placed on the floor. "Yeah, guy from Cook, up north. Name's Broker. Eisenhower was acting range officer. He got nicked by a ricochet . . . Nah, just a flesh wound in the leg. Ike swears Desmond fired first on Wilson, then hit the female deputy, and this Broker stepped in and ended it before Desmond could finish Wilson off. We checked; there's still two rounds in Desmond's gun."

Mordant grimaced, listening, then went on, "Yeah, but a witness from Desmond's unit is yelling that Broker used the argument as an excuse to gun down Desmond. It's a complete cluster. He says, she says, *Rashomon* bullshit. Only hook to hang it on is Pat Duffy secured the range tape. That might give us a narrative to go by."

This time Mordant barely listened before he cut in. "Boss. Be advised. There's wild stories already flying all over the place. I got a crowd of Desmond's pals from St. Paul and Ramsey County who are seriously worked up, which brings up a local angle. Remember the famous biker contract on Desmond that Soap Turrie shot his mouth off about? Some St. Paul cops don't think it's a joke anymore, uh uh; they sound like they want to lynch this Broker guy. Doesn't help he's not even a real cop. He's a reserve deputy sent down from Cook to attend the workshop. Right, he's a flashpoint. Hey, boss? We have the Crime Scene from Hell here. I mean, the victims, the shooters and witnesses are all coppers."

After listening for a full thirty seconds, Mordant sighed and clicked off the radio transmission. "Okay," he said. "The sheriff is not exactly in a hurry to get back."

Duffy's lips flicked a bad cop smile. "Press. Arnie doesn't want to be the first face they see on TV associated with this stinker."

"Whatever," Mordant said. "Okay. Pat, move Broker someplace out of the way, like my office, and sit on him. No questions, no statement. Just keep him on ice. Make sure you keep that tape quiet. Media's gonna smell blood and be on this like vampires. Sheriff already called BCA, and they're sending an investigation team, their crime lab, the works. We'll do our best to keep the lid on, but the state boys are going to have to sort this out."

"So there it is," Duffy said.

"BCA's case," said Mordant. "We cover our ass." He nodded at Broker. "Now get him out of here."

Chapter Three

*D*on't overthink it. Deal with what's in front of you.
And what was in front of Phil Broker was the burly Washington County deputy, Duffy, who had just whisked him out a side exit from the shooting range and then escorted him into an office in the nearby Government Center. "Dennis Mordant, Investigations" was printed on the small plaque on the door.

"We'll wait here for Captain Mordant," said Duffy, who was casual in a flannel shirt, jeans, trail boots, and a hideout holster under his leather vest. Except for the general "can you believe this shit" ambiance that was going around, he showed no overt signs of strain about the cop horror show that had just erupted next door. The tape from the overhead camera now sat on Mordant's desk in a labeled evidence bag.

There was a chair in front of the desk and another along the wall. Broker chose the chair that backed against the wall and sat down. The deputy stood by the door with his hands clasped behind his back.

NOW WHAT?

It hung like a silent flashing neon sign in the air between them for two, three minutes. Then the door opened and Mordant walked in. "I got a call in to John Lucht up in Cook to confirm you, but I have no reason to doubt your ID. And since you're not a sworn officer, I called the county attorney at home because he's going to have to get with BCA to determine your status. Now. Like I said, the BCA is on the way, and they are

27

taking over investigating this." Mordant shook his head. "Whatever this is." Mordant regarded Broker for a full five seconds, then said, "There's a lot of wild talk going on out there about what happened. Right now, technically, this is not headed for a custodial interrogation. You are under no constraints, you're not being charged, but obviously you have to be interviewed. My advice is you stay put, here. You save anything you have to say for the BCA. We have you pretty sequestered, but if a rat reporter squeezes in through the cracks, the last thing in the world you want to do is talk to any of them. We clear?"

Broker nodded.

"Who's BCA sending?" Duffy asked.

"Sounds like that damn Cantrell."

Duffy nodded. "Figures. He catches the real dirty ones."

"Whatever," Mordant said again, like the expression had become his signature response. He seemed glad to finish his talk and immediately left the room.

Broker removed a battered pack of Lucky Strikes from his jeans pocket and lit one with a beat-up Zippo. "So I'm under no constraints, huh?"

"That's what the man said."

"So I can just get up and walk out?"

Duffy repositioned himself in front of the door and smiled.

Chapter Four

A few cops—the ones who'd been up dark stairways with him —respected Harold J. Cantrell. It would be a stretch to say they liked him. Most cops throughout Minnesota felt their guts tighten up when Cantrell worked a case in their city or county. They disliked the southern twang—straight out of Selmer, Tennessee—that sometimes insinuated into his sarcasm. They regretted his choice to migrate up north, after the Marines, to attend the University of Minnesota. They didn't appreciate his contempt for their traditions or his self-deprecating humor —like his often repeated remark that cops were just a bigger violent gang with pretty good political connections and, as such, needed that much more policing. He'd come up meteor fast in Minneapolis, where he'd found a home in Internal Affairs until he'd pushed cases against one too many coppers and was advised to move on before there was a bounty on his head. He wound up carving a niche for himself at the state crime agency.

Cops objected to the way he dressed, in cowboy boots, black denim jeans, a dark T-shirt, and a gray leather trench coat —not a proper Bogey-type trench coat, but this European job with no buttons, just a belt—like some faggy Hollywood producer might wear. Plus he never wore a hat, regardless of how cold it got. And he swept his longish blond hair back in a fifties duck butt.

Mostly they resented that his flamboyance was tolerated because he got results. Cantrell came on relentless, and a lot of cops in Minnesota wished he'd just go off and die.

An hour after the last shot had been fired in the Washington County garage, snowflakes stuck to Cantrell's uncovered hair as he pushed his way through a scrum of print and TV journalists who crowded the yellow tape cordoning off the ambulance that served as Joe Desmond's hearse. He badged a deputy, who admitted him through the tape line. After he watched the ambulance pull away, he entered the garage and took a moment to shake off the snow and absorb the askew shooting range at the far end of the building. He raised his chin and sniffed the troubled air, then took a Camel straight from his trench coat pocket along with a Blue Tip match, which he flicked into flame with a thumbnail. After he lit up, he took a second look. The sound barrier had been stowed away, and the once festive bus garage was now a solemn cavern. Cantrell threaded his way through groups of witnesses being interviewed at widely-spaced banquet tables until he breasted the yellow tape.

The coroner had left a chalk outline marred by only a small, unreadable Rorschach blot of blood. Hit twice in the heart, the call said. Very little bleeding.

Guy could shoot.

All the weapons, including the Thompson, were still laid out on the firing range tables exactly where they'd been placed or dropped when the lethal bullets started flying. The handguns involved in the shooting still lay where they'd fallen or, in the case of the Colt used by Broker, remained where it had been placed on the floor. Along with coagulating blood and bandages and wrappers, the concrete was littered with dozens of expended cartridge casings. Several local techs were gingerly searching out which two casings had come from the .45 fired by Broker. The state crime lab guys, along with two other state investigators, marched in a minute after Cantrell made his entrance and started connecting with the county cops.

"Hey Cantrell," said Mordant, walking up. "Let me show you something." Cantrell ducked under the yellow tape and followed Mordant to the target at the end of the firing line. "This is where the shooter, Broker, was located when the shit hit the fan. We interviewed the guy who was on this shooting station just before Broker, and he saw him put up a clean target so he could mark the fall of the rounds." Mordant tapped the paper with a ballpoint where there was a hole at four o'clock in the Ayatollah's beard. The pen tapped again. Another hole, at a diagonal angle from the first one, in the Ayatollah's cheek. Last tap. Two holes touching where the bridge of the caricature's nose met the eyebrows. Mordant tucked the pen back in his pocket. "Not saying it goes to intent or motive."

"Uh huh." Cantrell nodded. "Just that he picked up a cold, 1911 Colt off the table and figured out exactly where it shot in four rounds."

"Yep." Then Mordant handed over the VHS tape from the range camera that was sealed in a plastic evidence bag.

"You look at it yet?" Cantrell asked.

"Nope," said Mordant.

"Don't want to go anywhere nearer this thing, huh, Denny?"

"Nope."

Cantrell slipped the tape into a roomy trench coat pocket. "I need a staging area and three interrogation rooms for me and my guys. Any preliminary statements I can look over?"

"I put together a rough summary." Mordant led Cantrell over to a table where a crammed, single-spaced sheet lay next to a thermos and a cup. Cantrell sat, poured some coffee, and read for two minutes. Then he stood up and said, "First I want to watch the tape. After that I need to use a private phone. Then I want to see him."

Broker had been moved to an interrogation room that contained only a bare table, two simple folding chairs, and recessed ceiling lights. No cameras or recording devices were apparent.

The room had cork soundproofing on the walls and ceiling. A single two-prong electrical outlet was set in one wall with an empty phone jack to the side. The only ornament in the windowless room was a large wall-mounted clock.

He checked the clock. Two and a half hours had passed since he'd shot Joe Desmond. There was a knock on the door, and then it opened and a lean man—mid-thirties—walked in wearing a gray leather trench coat, dark clothing, and hand-tooled western boots. He had his blond hair combed back like a '50s hoodlum and the kind of face that attracts shadows, with lots of concavity and clefts. He had these mercurial blue eyes and in their prisms Broker caught hints of charm, mischief and pure menace. He carried a phone with a cord in one hand.

"Harold Cantrell, Special Investigator, State Bureau of Criminal Apprehension. And you're the guy who screwed up my Saturday afternoon poker game. Broker, right?" The voice was easy with an undercurrent of sly. It was from way south of here and reminded Broker of certain dangerous, foxy rednecks he'd encountered. Airborne sergeants mostly.

Cantrell plugged in the phone, placed it on the table, then took a moment to study Broker. Broker studied back. Like looking into a mirror. The guy didn't give anything away except alert, wary poise.

"You okay?" Cantrell asked.

"What do you think?" Broker said back.

Cantrell merely nodded and said, "Ask a silly question . . ." Then he picked up the phone and dialed a number. After several beats he said, "Yep, got him right here." He handed the receiver to Broker. "For you. John Lucht."

Showing no reaction to this opening gambit, Broker took the phone. "Yeah, John, you heard?"

The old sheriff drew in a whistling breath. "Looks like I sent you into a shit storm. How you doin'?"

"Don't know yet."

"You can trust Cantrell; we go back a ways. I told him some about you."

Broker didn't like the sound of that. "Okay," he said.

"Bottom line, once they get past the public relations catastrophe, this is going to shake out as simple third party self-defense. That's what he said. They have two solid preliminary witness statements, and more important, they have the whole thing on tape. Cantrell just watched it."

Broker exhaled. "If you say so, John."

"Hang in there. Don't worry. Right now they want you to stick around while they comb through the interviews. I already talked to the county board, and we'll foot your per diem since we put you in this. Now I have to prepare your folks because it's all over the radio, even up here. Take care, kid. I'll be in touch."

"Tell them I'll call as soon as I can." Broker returned the receiver to the phone cradle, glanced at Cantrell and said, "Just like that?"

"John said you're a project of his, that he's been recruiting you for his department. Sending you down here was an initial step. Sort of getting you to dip your toe in to test the water, huh?" Cantrell's eyebrows arched in an ironic expression. "He also said you were a handy guy to have around. If Al Wilson makes it through surgery, he's going to agree with that assessment."

"The guy Desmond shot."

"Yeah," Cantrell said, taking a seat. Broker took the other chair and arched his back. Cantrell noted the faint tremor as a load of tension released. Then Broker stretched and finished by hiking up the sleeves on his wool sweater. Cantrell's eyes flicked on the scar that blemished Broker's left forearm, where a tattoo had been removed. He said nothing. After an interval, Cantrell continued, "Okay, so Mordant told you this is a non-custodial interview?"

"Like no Miranda?"

"Right. But if we get uncomfortable?" Cantrell shrugged. "Well, the rules will apply. We good?"

Broker nodded.

"The names Soap Turrie or Danny T or the Others Motorcycle Gang mean anything to you?"

Broker shook his head.

"Did you ever see Joe Desmond before he pointed a revolver at you today?"

"No."

"Same for the guy whose life you saved, Wilson?"

"I never saw anybody who was in that building before the workshop."

"And you have no idea what you ran into this afternoon?"

"You going to tell me?"

"It's like this. It isn't your normal situation, so they yanked my chain because I'm not your normal cop."

"Say again, slower."

"A scandal just blew up in St. Paul Narcotics. It appears Wilson got caught banging Desmond's wife. Plus there's a messy back story. They both were given leave to avoid being in the same room, to clear the air—and then they bump into each other here, and it blows up in public. You get the picture?"

Broker nodded slowly, all the while engaging Cantrell's changeable blue eyes. "So what should have been a fistfight in the parking lot goes south because they collide on the firing line," he said.

"Classic poor impulse control. Exactly what cops are not supposed to do. But there it is. Desmond lost it and pulled the trigger. You know the rest." Cantrell paused. "But there's a couple flags on the play."

"I figured there'd be a punch line," Broker said.

"The guy who went off on you, waving his gun around."

"Terry," said Broker.

Cantrell took a moment. This Broker was a cool, quick study. On top of all the players. "Right," he said. "Terry Conner, St. Paul detective, was on Desmond's squad. He's telling everybody you took advantage of the tiff between his boss and Wilson to fire on Desmond."

"You said flags, plural?"

"Well, this goes to the messy back story. Terry's fantasy plays into a street rumor that a wannabe biker gang put a contract on Desmond after he sent their leadership away. Put two and two together, you get the IQ of the idiots talking up this shit."

"What are you saying exactly?"

Cantrell gave another casual shrug. "There's gossip brewing that you executed the biker contract on Desmond, and it's bound to get in the media. It doesn't help that a local character named Soap Turrie is publicly linked to the contract talk. But don't sweat it. There's a sharp St. Paul cop and a sergeant in this department who saw the whole thing. Their statements back up the self-defense story." Cantrell lifted the bag containing a VHS tape from his pocket, "And there's this. I just had a serious look at it, and it's all right there."

"So, what?"

"So we've got to observe the forms, go through the motions. You keep yourself available, like stay in town. After we interview everybody, I take it to the county prosecutor. It's Saturday, so tonight everybody in the St. Paul and Stillwater cop shops will be getting hammered, believe me. So it won't be until Monday I sit down with Pete Yerbich. Like I told John. It's going to be open and shut. No Miranda. You're not a sworn officer, no Federation lawyer involvement. You react to an imminent threat, you save a guy's life. Good shoot. No bill. No grand jury. You being a reserve deputy shouldn't even be a factor in a regrettable tragedy that spun out of control. Blah blah blah. And I'm the poor slob they brought in to play shit catcher, who has to go out there and give a suitably vague statement to the fuck-ing press weasels."

"So just hang out over the weekend?"

"Yeah, and keep a low profile. There's some St. Paul cops sound like they want to waste you. They get to drinking and run into you, it could be nasty. So be sensible. Where you stay-ing?"

"American Inn, off Highway 36. Room 114."

"Okay then. On your way out, tell Mordant where he can find you. Get the comm center direct number. He's got a plan to scoot you out around the press, get your car to you. Probably send a squad around to check you're okay."

Broker cocked his head and narrowed his eyes as he ab-sorbed Cantrell's speech.

"Relax," Cantrell said. "It's a shit sandwich, right? Best not dwell on it. Like I said. John Lucht's word carries a lot of weight, and we have witnesses and a tape."

With that Cantrell walked him to the door and into the hall, where two dour but game guys in slacks and sports coats were waiting with sheaves of paper in their hands. Broker could feel Cantrell's attention erase him and refocus on his two col-leagues.

"You want me to start dividing up the witnesses?" one of them said.

"Oh yeah," Cantrell said. "It's gonna be a long Saturday night."

After Broker handed over the keys to his aging Jeep Wag-oneer, he was given the comm center direct number and then led into the garage, tucked into the back seat of a van, and driven out the back to avoid the press. Duffy was waiting with a deputy in an unmarked squad next to Broker's Jeep on the frontage road next to Highway 36. The hefty deputy advised him to grab some takeout and eat in tonight and generally stay down low till Monday. He'd ride shotgun to the motel, and then a car would be on the prowl around his room to keep an eye out.

An hour later Broker was sitting in his motel room poking at chicken and cole slaw from Kentucky Fried and talking to his dad on the phone.

Dad was a die-hard North Woods Savage who'd served a term as Cook County Sheriff after retiring from the Army. Now he and Broker's mom, Irene, ran Broker's Beach, a small cabin resort on the Superior shore in Devil's Rock, on Highway 61 north of Lutsen.

Broker Senior ended up a general harangue by growling, "Nothing good ever comes from going down to the goddamn Cities."

Broker evaluated the extra edge in his dad's voice and figured he was hearing the shrapnel coming off his most recent bladder surgery at the Minneapolis VA. Stage one cancer. Waiting on the path report. Again. He'd come home trussed in a catheter and leg bag. Again.

"They didn't read you your rights?" his dad was saying.

"No Dad, the BCA guy asked me a few squirrelly questions. And, like I said, he talked to John, who vouched for me. Plus they have the tape. So they take statements and it goes to the local prosecutor and he makes the call."

"Guy just started blasting away, huh?"

"Sounds like a civilian soap opera that got out of hand, and live ammo was involved. I get the impression they want to squash the smell on this thing quick. Nobody wants it aired in public."

"Good luck. Press is going to have a field day," his dad grumbled.

"No doubt."

"But no lawyer?"

"Don't think so."

"Just saying, Phil; you've been off the grid for a while, and another set of eyes can't hurt."

"I'm okay, Dad. Anything comes up, there's time."

"All right then. Ah, Irene, the witch nurse, wants to talk to you."

"Yeah, Ma, so how's the old man?" Broker asked when Irene came on the line.

"Ornery. He's not good at being sick," Irene said.

"I can hear that on the phone just talking to him."

"He'll eventually stop his whining," she said with a dramatic rise to her voice, for her husband's benefit. Then she mused, "So much for our plan to ease you into law enforcement up here on little cat feet, eh?"

"Coulda been worse," Broker said.

"My son, the optimist," she said. "Now Phillip, I want you to exercise caution, because your moon in Scorpio makes you prone to trust your gut too much."

Broker had to grin. "We should've had this talk yesterday."

"Don't mock an ancient science, son."

"Roger that, Ma. I hear you."

Irene Broker raised her voice slightly. "Your father and I don't agree on a lot of things, but we're definitely on the same page when it comes to the Cities being a den of devious jam tarts. We clear?"

"Clear, Ma."

"Okay then, watch yourself."

After exchanging a few more diplomatic pleasantries, Broker rang off and sat for a moment, staring into the middle distance. The diagnosis had come down last June, in the busiest part of the season. During a month of rushing back and forth to the Minneapolis VA, plumbing problems plagued the two most popular units, and Dad, who excelled at jury-rigging those problems, was off the clock. Friends tried to fill the gaps. But it wasn't enough. Renters politely demanded their deposits back and took their business elsewhere. Complications from surgery —infections, blood clots, midnight runs to the Grand Marais ER —eroded the time that should have been spent repairing nagging roofing problems on most of the cabins. They lost the season. Then, at the beginning of November, they got hit with the early freeze, and ice attacked all the structural weak points of Broker's Beach. Eaves buckled, pipes froze.

Broker caught himself in another long stare at the remains of his dinner he had just tossed into the trash basket. John Lucht had made a valiant effort to bring him on as a full-time reserve deputy to add a semblance of financial stability to the family's shaky economy. Broker exhaled. And attending this workshop was a centerpiece of that Samaritan gesture.

Don't overthink it. Do the tricks.

He took a long, hot shower. A pillow and blanket were still arranged on the carpet from this morning. So he sat down on the floor and folded his legs easily into a half lotus position. He'd spent a lot of the last ten years around folks who didn't own chairs and had come to understand this was the most natural way to sit. He'd also picked up the rudiments of meditation, so he sank into the technique and let the day's events untangle and drift away, his breathing going one way, his heart beat another, and his thoughts trailing off like underwater bubbles.

Briefly he visualized the angry force of Joe Desmond's life wandering lost in the Big City of Death, then let it pass.

Half an hour later he got up, took a can of Bud from the room's small fridge, and stacked a pile of pillows against the bed headboard. Then he settled back and opened the thick third volume of Shelby Foote's Civil War trilogy to the place where Ulysses Grant had his wakeup call with Bobby Lee in the thickets of the wilderness.

Chapter Five

Five minutes after J.T. Merriweather finally finished giving his detailed statement with one of the BCA investigators, he was searching for an open phone to call the date he had stood up because of the outrage on the shooting range earlier in the afternoon. Damn cops were worse than gossiping high school girls, still hanging out, hogging the phone lines. That's when the bulky, newfangled pager clipped to his belt buzzed.

He didn't recognize the number.

So screw gossip; this was work.

"Make a hole, police business," he growled, pushing through a gang of cops lined up for the pay phone in the government center lobby. The guy using the phone took one look at J.T.'s eyes, dropped the receiver on the cradle, and stepped back.

"Thank you much," J.T. said as he dropped a dime and dialed in the number from his pager.

"Who's this?" said a deep voice before the third ring.

"Merriweather, St. Paul Narcotics. Who am I talking to?"

"Merriweather, right; Desmond's new soul brother narc who pushed my face through the floor at Alary's last September."

J.T. cleared his throat to cover the flutter in his chest, because he had connected the rumbling voice to a face. After a pause he said, "Russell Turrie. How'd you get my number?"

"Call me Soap. Desmond gave it to me for backup. If it's true what they're saying on the radio, you're it. So is it true?"

"Saw it myself." J.T. bit off the words.

"I've already had three calls congratulating me. Can you believe that shit?"

"Is there a reason we're talking?" J.T. said, his voice going cold.

"Just thought you'd see the irony, or is irony above your pay grade?"

"You have five seconds to say something real," J.T. said.

"Just thought Desmond let you in on it."

"Let me in on what?" J.T. said evenly.

Silence. "Okay, I'll explain later. Look, I've got a situation that calls for a delicate touch. Desmond had you looking for Annie O'Neil, right? I might have found something. Now Des's out, so you're up. Where are you?"

J.T. debated for a beat, then decided to go with it. "I'm still in town, your town," he said.

"You know where my car shop is?"

"I can find it." J.T. had once been on stakeout around Turrie's home, north of town, and his place of business. But he'd check the street address on the shop to be sure.

"You aren't driving an unmarked or anything that'll scream cop?"

"Burgundy Chevy Blazer."

"Alone."

"Alone," J.T. said.

As he hung up the phone, J.T. reflected that he'd been doing post-graduate work in irony all his life. You'd have to be a really stupid American black man not to. So why should getting a call out of deep space from Russell Turrie six hours after seeing his boss shot dead be any different? Turrie was apparently Desmond's mysterious new source, death threat and all.

He looked up the shop address in the local phone book, finally left the still-bewildered atmosphere of the Government

Center, got in his car, then spent a minute hunting in his Hudson's map under the dome light, found the location of Soap's Shop off Curve Crest Drive, and then squeezed between two TV vans and pulled out of the Washington County Government Center parking lot.

The snow had stopped. Back inside the workshop site the blood had barely dried on the cement floor. Out here, Stillwater wore a sparkling, small-town communion dress. Some houses blinked with early Christmas lights, and the contrast worked on J.T.'s head. Joe Desmond died over and over in memory as he drove past plastic Middle Eastern shepherds kneeling before a manger, marooned in the snow.

The plows hadn't been out yet, so as he fishtailed getting traction at a light, he reviewed what he knew about the man he was about to see, whom he'd handcuffed last September.

"Soap" Turrie was the eldest son of a once-prominent local family, and he exemplified the use of the adjective "checkered" when applied to one's biography. Older members of law enforcement, and their counterparts in the criminal subculture, still held Turrie in minor awe. His reputation derived primarily from an incident years back, in the early sixties, when Turrie liked to spend his weekends running his Harley on the open road. Unlike his outlaw younger brother, Turrie was always a loner, with no club affiliation. He'd been swept up in a biker brawl at a roadhouse outside of Madison, Wisconsin, on a summer Friday night, and the local sheriff decided to let "the bunch of biker assholes" stew in county for the weekend.

Turrie was on his way to the shower carrying nothing but a towel and a bar of Lava when two amped-up Hell's Angels prospects decided to carve him up with makeshift shivs. According to the story, Turrie brained the first one in the temple with the bar of soap—Neanderthal hand hatchet style. Then he snapped the wrist on the second one and stepped back and let the deputies clean up the mess. The first guy was pronounced dead on the shower floor, hence the street name: Soap. Turrie walked on self-defense, and J.T. had never heard a cop call it any different.

Later, Turrie, a master mechanic, ran a Standard station franchise with a garage back in downtown Stillwater. He saw the self-serve pumps coming, arranged a loan with the help of an old war buddy, equally colorful St. Paul raconteur and bar owner Tommy O'Neil, and opened his own repair shop. It was getting to be a small world. Tommy O'Neil's widow, Annie, who now ran the tavern that her husband had made famous, was who he had been looking for. And apparently still was.

Everybody trusted Soap to fix their cars, especially crooks throughout the Metro who liked to show him off at their parties. So he had evolved the ceremonial status of elder underworld counselor who was sometimes brought in to mediate disputes between warring factions. His name floated through investigations, but nothing ever stuck.

J.T. turned in at the tall SOAP'S SHOP sign and paused to take in the layout. Roomy garage bays flanked the two-story shop office. The property extended in back, where a chain-link fence enclosed a large Quonset garage and what looked like stacks of snow-covered building materials. He wheeled into the blacked-out parking lot and stopped at the office door. A figure stepped from behind an evergreen next to the entry, moving stiffly because he had what appeared to be a .12-gauge shotgun pressed tight to his right leg. A hooded sweatshirt and a black watch cap hid his features as he squinted in the faint light through the driver's side window. Then he nodded and motioned to J.T. and pointed to the door. J.T. got out and followed the sentry, who tapped on the door while J.T. made out the silhouette of another man squirreled down in the cab of a tow truck at the edge of the building.

For a moment J.T.'s hand hovered inside his overcoat, near the nine automatic holstered on his side.

Then the door opened and he entered the dark interior, making out a customer counter, lobby chairs and couch to the side. Turrie stood in the shadows, his craggy face chiseled in ambient light spilling in from the road. Seeing him again, J.T. recalled the night of the altercation at Alary's and decided that, if he'd wanted to, Turrie could have tossed him over the bar along with Terry Conner.

J.T. jerked his head back toward the guard at the entrance. "You expecting company?" he asked.

"I don't know what to expect. That's why I called you." Turrie's deep voice was part low thunder, part cement mixer, with shiny pearls of Irish lilt tumbling with the dirt and gravel. It sounded bored with the fact that it could command a room. "This way."

J.T. followed Soap down a short corridor through a doorway into another dark room. The door closed. Soap flipped on the light. The room contained file cabinets, shelves, a work counter, and the all-too-familiar smell of fresh blood. A narrow-shouldered young man sat on a chair in the center of the room. He was trembling despite wearing a winter jacket, and his left knee pumped like a piston. His eyes flitted, his sparse beard was scraggly, and he cradled his bandaged left hand in his lap. J.T. noted the mopped red swirl on the floor and several bloody gauze dressings strewn next to a waste can in the corner. The blood still glistened. Fresh.

J.T. cleared his throat and took a moment to assess Soap Turrie, who regarded him with unflappable gray eyes that managed to be bottomless and bluff at the same time and suggested that he could handle anything that walked in through the door. Axle grease. Blood. The Apocalypse.

Turrie favored denim, large belt buckles, and western boots. The unbuttoned, flannel-lined Levi's jacket displayed a black Wall Drug, South Dakota T-shirt. When he removed the jacket and tossed it aside, J.T. saw the rawboned frame of a well-preserved man pushing sixty. His salt-and-pepper hair was still thick, combed back and gathered in a modest ponytail. The taut angles of his face were subtly scarred with reminders of a misspent youth and were clean-shaven except for a meticulously groomed soul patch. The nicks and cuts on his thick fingers, along with begrimed fingernails, suggested he was still a working mechanic. A fading Screaming Eagle tattoo on his muscular right forearm anchored him in time and identity and could serve as his obituary. Beneath the division icon J.T. noted the stacked type:

First Sergeant
506 PIR

"This is Norman Bolin," Soap explained as J.T. removed his overcoat and folded it over the back of a chair. "Norman is a dispatcher at the Summit Warehouse on the East Side of St. Paul, off Arcade. We collected him about an hour ago, and I patched up his hand as best I could. We have to make this quick because he needs surgical attention."

"Fucker cut me," Norman blurted. "Worked on my fingers."

J.T. focused on Norman as Soap explained, "They cut the tendons and ligaments of his little and ring finger. Methodically."

That commanded J.T.'s attention. "When did this happen?" he asked.

Norman's watery brown eyes jerked to Soap. "Shit, man, he's a cop."

"Norman, I'm going to find the guys who did this to you. But I can't do it alone. So it's okay. Tell him," Soap said. Norman bit his thin lips and stared, so Soap turned to J.T. "If this was me and Desmond, it'd be off the record. Right?"

"Sure, absolutely," J.T., intrigued, said a little too readily.

"So the quicker you talk, the sooner I have Joey run you into St. Paul to Ramsey, where they can repair your hand," Soap said.

"Shit, okay." Norman stared at the bandage, then started to speak in a rush. "So last week this shipment comes in from the Port of Duluth, these four big crates for the big-ass Sports Center store in Roseville, the one by Har Mar. Thing is, the manifest only listed three crates. The fourth one was an erratic, delivered by mistake. Just was a stencil on the side from some Eye-talian bicycle company. No paperwork. Must have been misloaded. So I got a dead end box. Big sucker, weighed over a ton. I move it in back of the yard and pry it open. It's packed with these expensive bicycle parts. That's a lot of bicycle parts."

Soap inclined his head, grimaced, shut his eyes, and scratched his forehead.

"So," Norman said, "in situations like this, sometimes I call my buddy, Leper."

"Travis Diggs, he works for the landscaping company I run out of the back. I've been trying to train him in as a mechanic off-season. He has this birthmark on his cheek, so when he was in the joint they called him Leper," Soap explained.

"In the joint," J.T. repeated.

"Travis is a petty thief right down to his toenails. An inept petty thief—just can't help himself," Soap said. "I was trying to break him, but as you see, no luck." Soap and J.T. turned their attention back to Norman.

Norman went on, "So Leper gets a truck big enough to cart the thing and comes in at two a.m. last Wednesday morning through the back gate, so no one's around. I leave a forklift for him, he loads, and off he goes. Idea was, he lays it off and we split whatever he gets. Simple, huh?" Norman managed a sallow grin.

"I take it no initial complaint report was filed, like for theft," J.T. said slowly.

Norman shrugged, and despite his situation, actually grinned. "No reason; the box wasn't on the manifest. It was a dead end."

"Except it was my dump truck Travis borrowed, with my business address stenciled on the door." Soap exhaled. "No one has seen Travis or my truck since last Tuesday night. His Chevy is still sitting out there in the lot."

Speculative tendrils twined in J.T.'s imagination like speeded-up stop-action photography; Des to Soap, now the timing of Norman's story. Des's obsession that something big was missing that was connected to Annie O'Neil, who was also missing and who, in the past, like her husband, had a rep for dealing in contraband. His eyes swung to Soap, who, clearly reading his thoughts, lowered his gaze with a slight shake of his head. Like, *not in front of this guy.* Instead Soap turned to Norman. "But here's the thing. Tell him about the guys who cut you."

Norman's attempt to shrug came off as a bone-deep shiver. "It's Saturday night, right? I was going to order a pizza, smoke a number and watch *SNL*. There's a knock on the door. I crack it thinking it's the pizza delivery and—boom—they're in. Two guys, both wearing these thin black ski masks."

Patiently, Soap said, "Norman, you see their faces, maybe we aren't having this conversation."

"No shit," Norman gulped. "But, hey. These guys were different, absolutely cool—no," he paused. "Wrong word. They were strictly business. They knew what I did at Summit, they knew I was on the clock the night the box disappeared, and they wanted to know who took it and where it was. Period."

Norman did manage an almost normal shrug. "I thought they were some kind of special cops, like feds maybe, only worse. Until the one took out the knife." He bit his lip. "Guy explains what he's going to do, starting with the little finger of my left hand. Tells me, real calm-like, as long as I have my pointer, middle finger and thumb I'll still have a decent grip."

When Norman looked up at Soap, his face cringed. "I made it through the little finger, but then . . ."

47

Soap turned to J.T. "Norman gave him where Travis worked, where he lived, even the name of the black chick, Charlene, he likes to get high with over at Selby Dale." He reached over and patted Norman's shoulder. "It's okay, kid; you're just a civilian who got caught in between." Turning toward the door, he said, "I'll get Joey to run you to Ramsey."

"Shit, man," Norman whined. "Gotta be a closer ER."

"Listen, Norman. Joey's going to give you some money to tide you over. He'll give you an address in Hastings where you can stay in one of my properties when you get out of the hospital. So lay low and stay in touch. And you have to absolutely forget about this conversation. You hear me?"

"I hear you, Soap, but I need a hospital right now."

"You need a level one trauma center, believe me," Soap said.

After Soap left the room, J.T. asked Norman, "What will you tell them at the ER?"

Norman stared into the middle distance. "The guy who cut me said to tell the police some Mexicans from the West Side had me confused with someone owes them money. Said I tell the docs or the cops any different, they'd know and be back."

"How are they going to know?" J.T. wondered, now intrigued. "Could you tell anything about their voices? Did they sound like locals?" J.T. tilted his head, sussing it.

"Nah, man. Like Joe Friday, you dig? They was going 'just the facts,' nothing extra," Norman said.

J.T. nodded and said, "Efficient." No wasted motion. Like operators.

After Norman trundled out, Soap and J.T. sat in the darkened lobby and peered across Curve Crest at the lights in a row of apartments, where normal life was going on. Finally Soap expelled a long breath and said, "Some night."

After a moment, J.T. asked slowly, "You said people were calling about Desmond, congratulating you? What did you mean?"

"I guess they went for the line of bullshit Desmond and I concocted after the Others' bust. How after my brother and nephew were sentenced—in other words, when push came to shove—I had to be seen to side with Danny and his biker assholes. The Alary's scene was Desmond's idea of a cover story."

"Wait. Let me get this straight. You were informing for Desmond on the gang bust?" J.T. said, now even more pleasantly alert.

Soap seemed to loom in the darkness, but his deep voice was unhurried, patient. "We made a *deal* on that. This thing now? When Annie dropped out of sight, he asked me for a *favor*."

"How about you do me a favor and back up and start at the beginning?" J.T. said.

Soap expended his second long breath. "Last summer my moron brother came to me wanting a loan to finance going West Coast, from speed, to this new meth bullshit. Look, Merriweather—I know you're drug police and all, but I have no quarrel with people smoking or dealing small amounts of pot. I've been off booze—mostly—for ten years, but the wife and I sometimes take a few tokes before hitting the sack, if you know what I mean."

J.T. held his tongue, so Soap continued, "But this meth stuff is a dirty business, and I told him as much."

"Give me a fucking break." J.T. laughed, marveling that he was having this conversation. "You sound like Don Corleone telling Solotzo to take a hike in *The Godfather*."

Sitting two feet apart, they studied each other across a vast, complicated chasm. Then, calmly, Soap said, "You're right-handed, but you wear the gun cross draw on your left hip, because ever since you took off your overcoat I've noticed the sag to your left pant leg. You should consider getting a shoulder rig." After a few beats he said evenly, "Merriweather, I'll let what you just said pass because you're just starting out as a baby cop." Another pause. "You want to hear this or not?"

J.T. accepted the affront because he wanted to hear it. He suspected the two of them would let a lot of things pass before the night was through. "Your dime, you talk," he said.

"It came down to family. My sister-in-law's a lost cause, pills and booze. I tried to intervene with her but got nowhere. Jo Jo, her son, was turning wild. So I got involved. My wife and I took him a couple nights a week. I was breaking him in here, odd jobs around the shop, after school. To spite me, after I turned him down, Danny put me and the shop off limits and stuck his son on the street slinging that shit."

Soap paused, then continued very deliberately. "So I asked around and nobody sounded like they'd shed a tear if my crazy, vicious brother went away. It was all right there in the name of his wacko, pickup outfit. The Others? Means guys who couldn't get into a regular club. So I went to Annie O'Neil—who was screwing Desmond at the time—and she arranged a quiet meet with Des, and I gave him Danny's whole operation: his lab, his distribution, the guys on his crew who'd flip about home invasions and robberies that financed his bullshit. Danny put me off limits to my nephew, so I put his psycho ass in Stillwater. End of story and end of my deal with Desmond."

"So revenge?" J.T. asked.

"Not exactly." Soap shook his head. "The deal was, Des assured me that Jo Jo would get a stiff bit in Totem Town with some extra trimmings to scare his young ass straight. The Alary's charade was window dressing."

"Some charade." J.T. coughed lightly. "There's cops in St. Paul Narco who are believing it. So was there really a contract on Des?"

Soap shook his head. "It was his idea. What they call grandiose in AA. I mean, you were there, right? Was there any way Desmond could have been deliberately targeted?"

"No way." J.T. paused. "But it was a phone call from Annie O'Neil that set the whole mess in motion."

Soap fingered the soul patch briefly. "I talked to the guy just this morning, and this afternoon he's dead."

"It was pretty crazy. Rounds started flying, and everybody —everybody," J.T. repeated, "was caught flat-footed. Except this one guy nobody knew, this wild card from up north. He stepped in fast and stopped Desmond before he did any more damage." Efficient, J.T. reflected. No wasted motion.

"So suddenly there's a lot of weird shit flying around that could be connected." Soap grimaced and kneaded his forehead. "At first, like everybody, I thought Desmond was covering his ass, floating a big lie to excuse his wife catching him back playing footsie with Annie."

"You tell me," J.T. said slowly.

"But then Leper disappears. Annie disappears the next day. Which begs the question, did he lay the box off on her? So it started making sense, what Desmond was saying. And you heard Norman. Now somebody wants their box back. It's getting to be a tight shot group."

"We agree that a ton of bicycle parts wouldn't bring them out of the woodwork," J.T. said. "So what's in the box?"

Soap shrugged. "Guns, I'd say Travis would go to a biker connect. Dope, West Side or the black gangs. If it was pricey electronics, TVs, stereos, he might have gone to Annie." Soap tilted his head back and forth, thinking out loud.

"But Annie wouldn't freak out and call Des over a bunch of TV sets. So it has to be somebody's dope; why else call a narcotics officer?" J.T. speculated.

"Hey, Merriweather—I spent a good amount of hours on the phone, and over coffee, with a number of people you'd love to bust. In the process of asking about Annie—" he held up his hand and made a circle out of his thumb and index finger "—I heard zero chatter about a big dope transaction. That's a lot of sharks. None of them are smelling blood."

"So? What's your take?"

"Maybe a Colombian pipeline sprung a leak and a box didn't get to Miami? There's a good chance this isn't local, which could make it very scary." Soap came forward in the chair. "All this cops and robber talk is fine, but where's that leave us? I need some kind of help here if they come after me next because their box was last seen in my truck. Some quiet kind of help. You saw Norman's hand. Those guys are either psycho or they're highly trained. I don't have the resources to hunt people like that."

"Pot's light," J.T. said. "You saying we're supposed to help you out of kindness?"

Soap took a moment, weighing it in his quiet eyes. "Look," he said finally, "this isn't just gossip anymore about Desmond tripping on his dick. Let's say I might have an idea where she is —Annie—where she might go in a situation like this. If she's in danger behind this shit, I definitely want to get her clear. But I can't go after her until I know who these guys are. And I can't be seen bringing her in with the help of the cops."

J.T. took a long, heady minute to think about going way the hell out on a limb—hell, clear off the tree. Then he leaned forward and lowered his voice, even though they were alone in the dark. "The kind of help you need I can't provide without putting your arrangement with Desmond in the street." J.T. paused. "An arrangement which I have apparently inherited."

"I called you, didn't I? Are you hard of hearing? This isn't shaking out like something I can put right by knocking a few heads or convening a meeting to get a ruling. Something weird is going on."

"I hear you, and the only way I can help is by painting you all over with cops, which isn't what you need. Right? But there might be another way. No cops up front."

"I'm listening."

"It'd be a real long shot, and I'd have to bring in an investigator from BCA who knows how to run situations like this. You'd owe us."

"How much? I don't want my name written in a snitch book so I come out in discovery during a trial."

"What about we help each other solve this problem, discreetly; then maybe we negotiate where we stand?" J.T. said softly, setting the hook. "You got eyes?"

"No cops, right?"

"No cops. Not up front. So where can I reach you?"

"Home or here at the shop." Soap heaved to his feet, went to the counter, and wrote a number on the back of a business card. "Okay then, we have a tentative deal. See what you can do. And run some checks. See if anybody heavy is leaving footprints around town."

Chapter Six

At 11:00 p.m. Saturday night, Joe Desmond's body stiffened under an ice-cold sheet in the Washington County Morgue. A mile away Phil Broker was down in deep, dreamless sleep in his motel room. At the Washington County Government Center, Cantrell arranged the witness statements in separate piles along with the crime scene photos and a preliminary forensic report. He sent his two investigators home to get some rest; then he got on the phone and made his checks. Wilson, minus a kidney, had moved off the critical list and was charted in serious but stable condition in intensive care at St. Paul Ramsey, where he'd been moved for surgery after being stabilized at Lakeview Hospital in Stillwater. Cass Deputy Hanson had also been moved to Ramsey, where they were performing a second procedure on her knee. Sergeant Eisenhower had been sent home with a few stitches and a bottle of Vicodin.

Cantrell stepped into the deserted corridor with a sheet of paper in his hand. The almost deserted corridor. The tall detective from St. Paul Narcotics sat in a chair, staring intently into an empty white Styrofoam cup.

The only black guy at the workshop, the only guy who'd been wearing a suit. He still had it on, but now the tie was loosened and he'd sweated through his collar. Cantrell's gut told him the guy—even considering he was a narc—was a reliable witness. One of two guys who'd seen it all happen in real time. He squinted as he pulled the name from memory. "Merriweather, right?" he inquired as he held two opposing ideas in his head: his thoroughly racist upbringing in Tennessee and the fact that to rise in law enforcement, a black or a woman had to be twice as good as the next guy.

"Yeah, call me J.T.," Merriweather said, getting to his feet.

"So?" Cantrell opened his hands to indicate the empty hall.

"So we should talk," J.T. said.

"Talk after everybody else goes home?"

"Uh huh."

Cantrell jerked his thumb at the lunchroom he was using as his office. "Be right back after I give a statement to the fuckin' press."

Then he walked to the front door of the Government Center and looked with satisfaction at the practically empty parking lot. His plan had been to wait the weasels out, so he'd timed his appearance to fall past the evening news and the deadlines of both metro daily papers. Wind-whipped snow slung sideways, and the icy desolation matched the mood that hung over the incident that had ruined his weekend. Only a cop reporter from the *St. Paul Pioneer Press* and a crew from Channel Four had dug in for the long haul.

He read the brief statement and took no questions:

"BCA investigators have confirmed that St. Paul narcotics Detective Joseph Desmond died as a result of gunshot wounds suffered on the Washington County shooting range at approximately three p.m. on the afternoon of November seventeenth during a training workshop. Also seriously injured in this incident were St. Paul Detective Alfred Wilson and Cass County Deputy Marcy Hanson. Washington County deputy John Eisenhower suffered minor wounds. The incident is under investigation, and due to the large number of officers being deposed, no definitive cause of the incident has been established at this point. No one has been charged. No one is in custody. The Washington County Prosecutor's Office will make a determination once the investigation is concluded."

Cantrell handed the sheet of paper to the print reporter, then turned and walked back inside.

*   *   *

"You have something to add to your statement?" Cantrell asked when he reentered the office. He crossed to the sideboard, took the glass pot off the Mr. Coffee, and offered it to J.T., who held out his Styrofoam cup. Cantrell poured, then returned the pot to the counter.

"Well?" Cantrell said as he assessed the taller man, early thirties, with his very dark skin and his dark gray suit and lighter gray shirt and his black tie. Highly polished black shoes probably rounded out the ensemble, but they were hidden in galoshes. A narc who wore galoshes? He noted the intelligent smolder that informed the focused brown eyes. Now he'd met two guys today he'd never want to fight.

"You run this Broker in the system?" J.T. asked.

"Sit." Cantrell indicated a chair next to the lunchroom table on which he'd assembled his notes. J.T. sat. Cantrell took the chair across from him and briefly massaged his eyes. The hour was late, and the day's procedure had been lockstep gloomy. "No need, man; I caught a shit clean-up detail. I have your statement along with Sergeant Eisenhower's. I've viewed the range tape and checked him out with Sheriff John Lucht up in Cook. It's not pretty, but it's got a bow on it."

J.T. removed a cigar from his suit coat inner pocket, stripped off the cellophane, bit off the end, deposited the plug in an ashtray, then put the stogie, unlit, in his mouth. As he rolled it across his lips, he said, "You know what guys in St. Paul are saying? They're wondering if Broker—" he paused and struck air quotes with his fingers, "—acted alone."

Cantrell pitched forward and moved some sheets of paper around, selected one, and held it up. "Right. Your colleague,

56

Terry Conner. The famous Alary's wipeout. Says he personally arrested Soap Turrie on a drunk and disorderly during which Soap made certain threats."

He dropped the paper, leaned back, and smacked his fingers to his forehead in a Road to Damascus moment. "Stupid of me not to see it right off. So this broken down, ex-biker legend is pissed at Desmond about his scumbag little brother, and about sending his nephew to juvee. He hires a contract killer. He falls off the wagon—first time in ten years, I checked—gets shit-faced, bulls into a cop bar and publicly announces—wait a sec—" Cantrell ran a finger along the scrawled note taking, "'—that the call had been made.' Then he arranges for Desmond and Wilson to get embroiled in a love triangle with Desmond's wife that will explode this afternoon at the workshop, where Broker, the random guy from the North Woods, is cleverly positioned to step in and blow Desmond away?" Cantrell closed his eyes tightly. When he opened them he said, "J.T., it's late."

"Just saying. It's gossip, right?" Now J.T. leaned forward across the table. "And what happens when you dangle selective gossip to hungry reporters under color of law?"

Cantrell leaned his elbow on the table, settled his chin into his upraised palm, and thought about it. Slowly he answered, "They smell headlines, so they troll around and try to confirm it."

"And it gathers momentum, huh?" J.T. leaned back. "Humor me. Run Broker in the system."

"At nearly midnight? Now why should I do that?"

"Because I was there, man. I saw him react faster than everybody else. I've seen guys like him before."

"Oh yeah?"

"Yeah. And so have you, maybe?"

They studied each other for five long seconds. Then Cantrell gnawed his lip and said slowly under his breath, "In that war we aren't supposed to talk about because it upsets people."

"Run Broker in the system," said J.T.

"You fucking narcs. Always holding back shit, working angles—" Cantrell squinted across the table.

"Run Broker in the system."

Chapter Seven

It was 12:30 a.m. when the first faxes started trickling in from the jangled night watch at BCA headquarters. Cantrell had faxed them copies of Broker's Cook County Special Deputy ID and his Minnesota license and told them to run him in every data stream they had access to, including Interpol. He further told them to wake up the FBI comm center in Minneapolis, tell them they owed him, and have them pull everything on the guy: military records, employment, IRS, the works. Hubba hubba.

In the meantime, Cantrell put on a fresh pot of coffee, and then he and J.T. went down to the basement locker room for a shower. J.T. had set aside his soiled undershirt and dress shirt, and now his athletic-cropped hair was at odds with the baggy, but clean, purple Buddy Holly T-shirt Cantrell had found in his overnight bag. With a fresh cup of coffee in hand, Cantrell slit the cellophane on a new pack of Camels while J.T. spread the faxes out on the table.

"*Nada.* Not a thing," J.T. said, not real surprised, still chewing on the unlit stogie.

The single military records coversheet was stamped with the intriguing but useless header: FILE CLASSIFIED; ACCESS DENIED. No discharge paper, no DD214. Nothing. They exchanged raised eyebrows.

"Well, John Lucht did say that Broker had, ah, some military background, and that he was a handy guy to have around,"

Cantrell mused as J.T. thumbed through the sparse sheets. Their eyes met again, and they laughed out loud.

"He was born in March 1949 in Grand Marais. He graduated Cook County High School in June 1966. Smart. Skipped junior year. Drops out his first semester at UMD, then nothing for eleven years!"

"Nothing?"

"Zilch, until he shows up with the Montana Department of Natural Resources being disqualified from applying for a smoke jumper job in 1977—" J.T. looked up, "—for false statements on his job application. Two 1040s prepared by H&R Block in Grand Marais, minimal payment for part time work with the Cook County Sheriff's Department last year and this year. One credit card, no real credit history. Checking account with a Grand Marais bank, only a couple hundred bucks. He could be driving without insurance."

They left the table and were drawn to the picture window that overlooked a bleak, empty side parking lot. They could just see one corner of the garage-cum-gun range that was now marked off by flapping yellow crime scene tape. For a few moments they engaged the random patterns in the wind-whipped snow as light from swaying sodium vapor lamps flickered on their faces. Then Cantrell asked with mock formality, "So what do you detect, Detective Merriweather?"

"Well, Detective Cantrell, I think we may have us a ghost."

"So maybe we have to look someplace else, off the grid, where they write stuff down with invisible ink," Cantrell speculated.

"You know somebody like that, excluding the local feds?"

"I might—that is, if you tell me what you got up your sleeve about Broker," Cantrell said.

A weary smile pulsed on J.T.'s lips, but his eyes were steady as he looked Cantrell up and down. "Straight up, soul brother to cracker?"

"Try me."

"I want to put Broker next to Soap Turrie."

At first Cantrell bridled. "You guys in narco are always coming up with the snaky angles. You go out there and roll around in bottomless shit, money and scumbags." The rant made no impression on J.T.'s carved expression. So Cantrell took a breath, and a tiny jolt of alert energy drew his features to a point. "You're serious," he said.

J.T. shrugged. "Just following up on what Desmond had going, man. He was developing Turrie as a deep background source. The Alary's scene where he got arrested? Desmond and Turrie dreamed that up to give Turrie cover for handing over the entire OMG dope operation."

Cantrell sat more erect, catching up. He gnawed on it back and forth behind his lips.

After J.T. recounted a detailed report on his visit to Soap's car shop, and the back story that went with it, he had Cantrell's full attention. Then he said, "Des wanted me to come to this workshop to meet a number of people—from the FBI office, sergeants from Ramsey and Hennepin, a guy from Minneapolis Intelligence. I asked them all the same question about Annie O'Neil's tip: is anything big and hot moving through the Metro? All of them said no clue. So it could be that something *huge* fell off the beaten path and it accidentally wound up in Annie O'Neil's lap. She freaked and ran. And now it seems there's some ice cold pros in town wanting their box back."

J.T. leaned forward across the table. "And there's a chance Soap knows where she is, but he won't cooperate if we wheel in the regular machinery, which might implicate him with—you know—us. Now, if there was another way to get these guys off his back . . ." J.T.'s voice trailed off.

"Take a breath." Cantrell's right hand made a palm-down, calming motion. "We're out in Washington County on a Saturday night, which is usually strictly kitten in a tree."

J.T. ignored the remark and plunged on. "I mean, we already have the gossip starting to bubble. There's otherwise smart guys in St. Paul already blowing smoke that Broker carried out Soap Turrie's contract. You have to admit, coincidence and all, there's a certain emotional logic there. There has to be some way to dirty him up and fuel the gossip that he killed a cop and walked."

Cantrell was impressed. "Pretty cold, J.T.; I thought you and Desmond were pals."

"Not cold, man; it's smart. Des's last wish was that I find Annie O'Neil, and that's what we're going to do, and Broker could help us. Your whole agency could spend its entire budget and never manufacture a chance like this. We help Soap now, maybe we can get a deep undercover asset in his world, in his connections. And the cool part is, Broker isn't even a cop."

"Even if we could make that fly, why would Broker agree?"

"That's your department. I've only run street snitches. This is over my head. There must be something he wants."

"Something he wants." Cantrell mulled it, turning it over in his mind. "The Cook County sheriff is trying to recruit him. Thinks he could clean up into a good cop."

"With those gaps in his CV? That's a stretch," said J.T. "Guy like him—he'll never put up with a big belly patrol sergeant pestering him at a roll call. All the paperwork. Uh uh."

"It's early in the morning, and we've been drinking way too much coffee—" Cantrell gave him the "time out" sign. "Let's get some rest. I'll call my guy when the sun comes up."

He went to the lobby of the tomb-like cop shop and told the graveyard deputy manning the phones to wake them at six a.m. Then they flopped on the nearest couches to grab some sleep.

Sunday

Cantrell waited until six a.m. so it'd be seven a.m. in the Washington, DC suburbs. Then he dialed the number of an old Marine buddy. Jerry Proskin answered, groggy, on the third ring. "Proskin."

"Hey, Jere. It's Harry Cantrell in Minnesota. How you been?"

"Jeez, Harry, hi. It's ah, seven in the fuckin' morning, man."

"So how's the federal marshal business? How's the wife and kids, and does your wife's brother still work as an analyst for you know who?"

"Forget it, Harry; that old buddy bullshit has limits. Somebody could lose their job if I do that again."

"What do they call that place, No Such Agency, something like that?"

"I mean it, Harry. You gotta stop doing this."

"Hey, Jere, buddy, you owe me."

"On hindsight, it's highly debatable you actually saved my ass that time in Chu Lai, and even so, that was only once, and that's one favor. That ship done sailed. Now you're asking for two."

"I'm really jammed up here. I could use a little assist."

"I don't know."

"I can tell you're weakening. C'mon man, help me catch some bad guys. It's what we do, ain't it? You have something to write on?"

"Aw shit, wait a minute. Okay, what do you need?"

"Anything interesting on a dude named Phillip A. Broker, DOB March eighteen, nineteen forty-nine, Grand Marais, Minnesota. I'm asking because his record is totally erased, and I'm curious why." Then he gave the Social Security number off the last tax return. "That's all I can find on him. And I need this ASAP."

"I'll see what I can do. He your bad guy?"

"Can't say."

"Get back to you."

After J.T. went home for a change of clothes, Cantrell spent Sunday morning in a caffeinated nicotine cloud, working the phones and checking the news. Wilson was making guarded progress, and it looked like he was out of danger. Hanson's life was never in doubt, but she was looking at a lot of surgery to restore function in her knee.

Then he clicked through all the channels and scanned the Sunday *St. Paul Pioneer Press* and the *Minneapolis Star Tribune*. The coverage was sketchy, but the outlines of the love triangle gossip were starting to emerge. WCCO had already wrangled a copy of the domestic abuse report Desmond's wife had filed. The TV stations had crews camped outside the Desmond house, trying to get an interview with the wife, and generally, the shooting was frothing up like a cesspool and the press smelled gangbang; they were going to sell a lot of newspapers.

And then there it was, J.T.'s voodoo, in plain sight. They'd pulled Broker's face and his prominent eyebrows off his driver's license photo and splashed it on the screen. "Mystery surrounds this man who allegedly ended St. Paul Narcotics Lieutenant Joe Desmond's bizarre shooting spree in Stillwater yesterday. Sources in the St. Paul police have revealed that although Broker, a reserve Cook County deputy, was enrolled at the Stillwater training workshop, he is not a sworn police officer."

Then a skewed, grizzled visage appeared on the screen, hair awry. Turrie's mug shot from the Alary's arrest.

The photo was positioned next to Broker's, and they remained onscreen as the anchor's voiceover stated, not without a hint of provocation, "St. Paul police arrested this man, Stillwater resident Russell 'Soap' Turrie, on September twentieth during a brawl at Alary's Bar in St. Paul, during which he bragged that a murder for hire contract had been taken out on Lieutenant Joe Desmond. Police sources speculate that Turrie was angry about his juvenile nephew's stiff sentencing for possession of narcotics in connection with a biker drug case last summer. Deceased St. Paul cop Desmond headed the Metro Area Narcotics Squad that dismantled the OMG biker gang."

Cantrell turned and saw J.T. standing next to him, Sunday casual in a heavy, hooded U of M maroon sweat suit. Snow melted off his Sorel boots. He winced slightly and said, "Just assure me you aren't as straight as you look. Okay?"

"Rest your mind," J.T. said, "just as long as you assure me you aren't as fucked up as you look."

"Deal. Now, you have anything to do with this?" Cantrell pointed at the screen.

"Nah, man. Seeing it here for the first time, but like I told you. It's in the wind," J.T said.

Before Cantrell could respond, the phone rang.

"Now you're the one owes me big time, you sonofabitch," Proskin grumbled. "I had to drive to Ft. Meade and wait at this icy rest stop in the woods off the parkway and miss Sunday with my kids. This is just word of mouth, and it isn't much. No way my brother-in-law can take files out of the building."

"Lay it on me," said Cantrell.

After eight intense hours of phone conversations and brainstorming, Cantrell and J.T. took a moment to get their pitch laid out in simple terms. Cantrell grimaced, rubbed his bleary eyes, and blinked at an overflowing ashtray where he'd burned up a whole pack of Camels going back and forth with his boss, the Minnesota Director of Public Safety, and with John Lucht up in Cook County.

J.T., his cigar chewed down to a stump, had been on the phone to Soap Turrie at home. He'd also wrangled a speed of light favor out of a Minneapolis Narcotics contact, who ran an informant in Stillwater Prison, who could get close to Danny T, Soap's younger brother.

"How well do you know Yerbich?" J.T. asked.

"He was in the prosecutor's office when I was in Minneapolis." Cantrell coughed, then cleared his throat. "We did some cases together."

"But he has a rep for thinking outside the box, right?"

Cantrell probed his eye sockets with his thumb and forefinger and said, "You could say that." He took a deep breath, blinked his red eyes, and then reached for the phone. Yerbich answered, at home, on the third ring.

"Pete, it's Cantrell; I've been up all night with this St. Paul detective, and we have this idea that our shooter, Broker, would make the perfect deep undercover."

"Huh?" said Pete Yerbich.

Chapter Eight

In keeping with the clandestine nature of this little war council, and because, J.T. surmised, Cantrell and Yerbich shared a minor weakness for showmanship, they wound up standing, stamping their feet, in the snow at the edge of Pioneer Park on the bluff overlooking the St. Croix River Valley. Stillwater twinkled below them and could have been lifted straight off a frayed Currier and Ives postcard, with the snow trickling on shabby Victorian gingerbread and church steeples and the Italianate cupola of the old courthouse. Only the spidery girders of the antique railroad lift bridge that spanned the river suggested the iron resolve that now shackled Harold J. Cantrell and J.T. Merriweather together in an act of pure will.

To keep the drama going, they were drinking from chilly cans of Grain Belt beer. Yerbich had come out of Eveleth, where he played hockey, and where he and his gentle high school teammates would load up a pickup full of firewood on a Friday night, drive out onto a frozen lake, and light a huge bonfire to keep them company while they drained a keg. Some foreign Iron Ranger ritual, J.T. figured, to tempt the ice to melt and swallow them whole.

Pete Yerbich fingered his chin with a gloved hand as he listened to J.T. recount his meeting with Norman Bolin and Soap Turrie. "Desmond dreamed up the death threat talk as a smoke screen for Soap's cooperation? Tell me more." Then, as he listened to Cantrell and J.T. start to unpack their plan, his forehead wrinkled, and he stepped up to Cantrell so their noses were just inches apart. "You are pulling this straight out of your ass."

"I am, absolutely. What's called grabbing a passing advantage." Cantrell didn't even flinch.

"Put this guy next to Soap Turrie? *Our* Soap Turrie?"

"Hey, Pete? I didn't dream this up on my own," Cantrell protested. "It all started with Annie O'Neil calling Desmond, and then . . ."

"I get it." Yerbich nodded. "You think it's linked. Soap's guy goes missing. Then Annie vanishes. All with a mysterious box mixed in. And Turrie might be able to cough her up—if we get some scary bad guys off his back, in a highly devious way." He turned, his cheeks shiny in the crisp night air, and scrutinized Cantrell. "And you think this Broker can spar with said scary bad guys and find Annie O'Neil?"

Cantrell shrugged. "Yeah. If he'll go for it."

"What if Annie's dumped in a snowbank? Then what?"

"Soap knows where she is, Pete. He said as much," J.T. said.

"Uh huh. So give me one reason why this particular Bozo from up north would sign on for this? After what just happened?" Yerbich asked.

"John Lucht told me he has a highly developed sense of integrity—it's just covered up by some real rough edges," Cantrell said.

"Everyone respects Old John, but that's still clear as mud," Yerbich said.

"Well, John said he'd call Broker to prepare the way. And I, ah, kind of like the rough edges part. Okay, how about this? I just had someone—can't say who—run a discreet check on him through NSA."

"Oh boy." Yerbich exhaled.

"Yeah. Try this on. Except for some reporters who stayed behind, the last American left Vietnam on April twenty-ninth of seventy-five. Famous picture of the helicopter lifting off the roof?"

"Yeah, so?"

"According to my source, Broker was on the ground in the northern provinces until the end of May. He smuggled out Vietnamese assets who worked for us, people the mission abandoned. Snuck them out to a clandestine flotilla off the coast, all stuff that absolutely nobody has heard of. Pete, man—he was the last guy to leave Vietnam. Amateurs don't pull stunts like that."

"I'm listening. What else?"

J.T. said, "No records of any kind are on file for Phillip Broker. Just rumors with a bunch of creepy CIA alphabet soup, acronyms like MACV/SOG, PRU, Phoenix. So he's some kind of spook who got erased."

Yerbich turned to Cantrell. "Say that's true. He's not a scumbag informant you can lean on, and he's not a cop you can order around. How do you control a guy like that?"

Cantrell put on his down-home grin. "We can provide something he needs. With his background, Broker should be sneaking around in Iran. But he's working day labor for chicken feed up on the North Shore. So he's on the outs, a non-person. And now he doesn't have the credentials to even get hired by the small sheriff's department up where he lives in Cook, where the sheriff is pulling for him."

"So he needs a job." Yerbich weighed it, his lips canted sideways.

Cantrell moved a step closer. "We vet him with a legit paper background, so John Lucht can hire him. We phony up a certificate from the police academy, credit him with a year working with my shop, and throw in a letter of recommendation from my boss." Cantrell turned up the collar of his trench coat and hunched his shoulders. "Another thing: his folks run this resort on Superior. The father's sick, and the place is more than Mom can handle. So I think—and Sheriff Lucht agrees—the prospect of scoring some quick cash might be a powerful incentive."

"And you've got that covered?" Yerbich asked.

"I do," Cantrell said. "So all he has to do is be himself and agree to go on a contract, you know, a mission."

Yerbich coughed and lowered his can of beer. "A mission?"

"Exactly. For starters, his job is to hang with Soap and find out who these finger-carving fucks are—and where we can find them," Cantrell explained.

J.T. interjected, "If we can dial down the heat, Soap will bring Annie, and her package, in from the cold. Desmond already had him on a string. We help him now, off the record, we can braid the string into a chain," Cantrell said.

"Pete, there's already talk on the street," Cantrell added. "They're running Broker's picture alongside Soap Turrie's on TV."

"I saw," said Yerbich, "the contract thing. Lotta ifs, Cantrell, lotta ifs. Put Broker next to Soap Turrie, hmmmm." Yerbich mulled it. "You know that people like to have their cars repaired in his shop because of who they might rub shoulders with." He looked at J.T. "You know Heywood Tyrell, right?"

J.T. nodded. "Chicago front man in St. Paul for the Southside Disciples."

"Heywood drives his hog out to Soap's to have it serviced." Yerbich slowly shook his head. "Soap's our celebrity black sheep, just enough edgy coloration from the past to give him that criminal allure, something he might have been in but not of. So when the Alary's stink happened, it saddened a lot of people, at first—you know, local redemption story, orphaned rich kid to war hero to outlaw to solid citizen." Pete paused. "But then they said, 'Of course, he's a Turrie. Blood will tell.'"

"The father," Cantrell offered.

Yerbich nodded. "Billie Turrie shot himself in the basement of that big house on the North Hill after the crash of twenty-nine. He'd cashed in on the tail end of the logging boom, then made bad investments on the Iron Range. Soap was nine years old. The mother split, and he and his baby brother wound up with shirt-tail relatives. He went from maids and nannies to coming up hard in the middle of the Depression, then the European Theatre. That had to twist him up."

"Well, he didn't sound nutty when I talked to him. Far from it," J.T. said.

"C'mon, Pete; I have a feeling it's the kind of thing Broker knows how to do," Cantrell urged.

"Along with killing people." Yerbich cleared his throat.

"Well, yeah. Here's the thing: maybe Soap Turrie is dirty. Maybe he isn't," J.T. said. "But one thing I know after talking to him last night is he's nervous about something big being in play that we have no intelligence on."

"Something that could have a Colombian return address," Cantrell said.

"That got lost and found in our backyard," J.T. said.

Yerbich thought about it, then said, "And Soap don't scare easy."

Briefly, an enticing vision of the Big Sparkly Collar insinuated in the chill air: a big case with their names on it.

Harry said, "If nothing else, getting Broker next to him would be the perfect listening post out there. And Pete, we need to do this quick. Like tomorrow morning."

"Jesus. I don't know. If I were him I'd head back up north and never come to the Cities again," Yerbich said.

Cantrell shrugged. "John Lucht thinks he might go for the beefing up the resume part, and he definitely needs a payday. He says it's getting old for Broker up north cutting firewood and repairing the roofs on his dad's cabins. You know, like he needs to get out of the house."

Yerbich hunched his shoulders and sipped from the freezing can. "Hmmmm. You're talking about winging it. No time to convene—anything. We'd have to keep this one off the books."

"Amen," Cantrell said. "Telephone, telegraph, telecop."

"So we're talking secret cowboy shit," Yerbich said. "Where's the bread come from to bankroll this thing?"

"There's discretionary BCA money. I've negotiated a tentative green light from the Director of Public Safety," Cantrell said.

"How much money?" Pete asked.

"Twenty grand to start. Comes with a condition: Broker has to submit to a psych eval. C'mon, Pete. It's all right there in front of us on the TV news. We have some pissed-off St. Paul cops telling the whole world that Broker somehow executed Turrie's contract on Desmond. Hell, we got Soap Turrie getting calls of congratulation."

"You know that for a fact?" Yerbich asked.

"Direct quote, last night," J.T. said. "And tonight he received another call—from his brother in prison, like atta boy, big brother. I moved the earth off its axis to get confirmation from an informant in Stillwater. Danny T apparently is basking in the media hype."

"Soap's all in. All we have to do is get them linked in the public eye and frame Broker with a false arrest to pump up the badass hype," Cantrell said.

"Arrest?" Yerbich narrowed his eyes.

"For assault. Except it won't hold up. Tomorrow morning I bring in Soap for questioning about the contract gossip," Cantrell said.

J.T. said, "Broker's there too, to be interviewed back to back with Soap. They're standing around waiting, and I walk in with the chief conspiracy theorist in St. Paul Narco, Terry Conner. He doesn't have to be an insider. He's already on a hair trigger. We see them together—"

"So with all the publicity and gossip, it'll be tense, you dig?" Cantrell said. "Words will be exchanged. Punches thrown. I'll make sure there's wall-to-wall TV cameras."

"Harry, somebody has to take a hit for a public brawl in the lobby of my goddamn Government Center," Yerbich glowered.

J.T. raised his hand. "Your Honor, I worked with Joe Desmond, and when I saw those two together I guess my emotions just got the best of me."

Cantrell said, "We talked it over. It'll probably mean pleading down an assault charge and suspension from St. Paul. I'm thinking, after a decent interval, J.T. might have more of a future with me over at BCA. With Desmond gone, he's left with no joy in a squad full of Irish rednecks."

"You fuck this up, you're on your own. You pull it off?" Yerbich paused to evaluate the play. "I'll be the cooler head that prevails. I'll soberly examine the facts, the witness statements and the TV video. If they reveal that Broker only resisted to defend himself, I will wisely decide to cut my losses. A fast confidential settlement follows. Real fast."

"BCA money laundered through your shop," Cantrell said. "In the meantime we sequester him in county, brief him on Soap and Annie, and bring in a shrink who's willing to moonlight off the record to sign off on him. To keep my boss happy."

"Where are you going to find a shrink like that on short notice?" Yerbich asked.

Cantrell tossed off Pete's question. "I placed a call to Andrea Sabic's answering machine. She owes me."

"Christ, Andrea?" Yerbich said. "Is there anybody in this who isn't a maverick?" But he couldn't stop the droll lilt from coloring his voice. "Boy, you two have been up all night."

Undeterred, Cantrell said, "And we put him in play. Boom!"

J.T. nodded. "Soap plays it cool, no wild talk, except now he has a famous cop-killer for backup to help him find Annie, his lost employee, his truck, and the famous missing crate. And we'll see how good Broker really is, if he can eyeball the opposition."

Cantrell shrugged. "C'mon, Pete; we spin Broker the right way in the press, the bad folks will invite him to their parties along with Soap. Like we drop some hints he worked for Operation Phoenix in Nam. After the Church hearings, everybody thinks Phoenix was an assassination program, right? The newsies will do the rest. When they get done, it'll smell like he blew away one of the most hated coppers in the Cities and got away with it. How's that for street cred?"

"This I have to see," said Yerbich, crushing his beer can.

"He's over at the American Inn. We're on our way over to run it by him." Cantrell looked up. Big, dizzy, spinning snowflakes had appeared magically in the night air.

"I didn't mean see personally," Yerbich said with an appropriate touch of feigned probity. "I can't be anywhere near this thing." He cocked his head. "Think he'll go for it?"

Cantrell shrugged. "Like I said, John Lucht thinks it might fly. Guy like this? Been hiding out in the North Woods after God knows what. You think he's going to suddenly go back to school, put on a tie and sit in a cubicle?"

Chapter Nine

It was never going to stop snowing. Phil Broker sat at the tiny desk in his motel room where he'd spent most of the day with a phone receiver stuck to his ear, staring out the window. When he was a kid he'd fancied that he could decipher patterns in swirling snow, in the sway of waves on the Big Lake. Tonight all he saw were bone-white gobs hitting the glass pane and cold memories of shoveling. He took a deep breath, then shifted on the chair and looked over the cramped room where he had essentially been hiding since yesterday afternoon. Unnatural TV light flickered on his face. The evening news, sound turned off, nevertheless blaring a bold banner across the screen: *Iranian Hostage Crisis, Day Fourteen.*

He exhaled, turned and looked back out the window. One edge of the motel sign was visible: glowing, lonely red neon cutting in and out of the spitting flakes. *American* it said. *Vacancy* it said.

In the phone receiver, John Lucht's voice was saying, "They're on the way over, so you'll have to let them know one way or another."

The old sheriff's persistent voice came through the connection, not unlike, Broker surmised, the waves of Lake Superior banging on the slowly freezing bedrock shore a few blocks away from the Cook County Sheriff's Office that was located in a brick cubbyhole next to the municipal liquor store on the Grand Marais waterfront. John ran six full-time deputies for one of the biggest, emptiest counties in the state. And one of them was getting ready to retire.

"When it comes down to auditions, Phil," John said, "you did announce yourself with a bang. Sorta got everybody's attention."

"C'mon, John, you make it sound like I owe them," Broker said.

"Just saying, this could be a hell of an introduction into police work. And face it, you need the jing. Hey, kid, this could be a way to write your own ticket, avoid all the Mickey Mouse. He's offering a diploma from the academy, no questions asked, and a year's credit on the job with BCA. Throw in a reference from the BCA director. I'm pretty sure that'll swing my county board. And Nagel is getting ready to collect his pension. There'll be an opening down the line."

"You trust this Cantrell?" Broker asked.

"He's all right, I guess, for a city guy. He could have mislaid the tape that exonerated you," John speculated. "Jacked you around, tried to get a lock on you. Least he's being upfront about it."

"You trust him, John?" Broker repeated.

"Far as it goes."

"That's my read too," said Broker.

"So what are you going to say to them?"

"You really think I could get hired behind this?"

"With a letter of recommendation from the Director of Public Safety? I think so. And you get the front end state money, twenty grand for starters. Renegotiate in six months."

"You're right about needing the money," Broker admitted, entertaining a fast vision of frozen, busted pipes and the damaged roofing. "A year undercover max, right?"

"If it works. It falls apart from the git, I think you still keep the down payment and you come home with enough to fix those cabins and extra. Keep you in beer and bar whiskey. Just sit on the rocks and stare at the horizon line, huh?" John chuckled.

Broker briefly appreciated how the bullets he'd fired into Joe Desmond had not stopped in his body. They had now set this chain of events in motion. He had to laugh.

"What's so funny?" John asked.

"And here I was trying to find a way to live where I never had to lie about anything ever again."

"Ah, is that a yes or a no?" John asked.

Broker weighed it a final time. The fast money was impossible to pass up. His folks were in a bind. And it wasn't like he had anything else going on. "Okay, what the hell. A year."

"There you go kid." John Lucht's voice swelled with satisfaction, like he'd finally set his hook in a trophy lake trout after trying out many, many lures.

Less than a minute after he hung up the phone, Broker heard the knock on the door.

They stood in the motel room doorway, two men who'd remained gaunt in a country going to flab. Their eyes glittering with exhaustion, unable to suppress conspiratorial hangdog grins. The black one wore a maroon Gophers sweat suit and a ridiculous, tasseled wool cap. He held a folder full of paperwork under his arm, like he'd dropped over to do his homework. Snowflakes melted in Cantrell's piss blond hair. Three cans of beer dangled in a plastic webbing in his hand.

"We thought you might want a nightcap," Cantrell said with the narrow smile.

Broker nodded at the other guy. "You were there yesterday."

"J.T. Merriweather. And yes I was."

Cantrell cut in, "He means *Detective* Merriweather from St. Paul Narco."

Broker, lacking title or credentials, stood barefoot and wore an old pair of sweatpants and a threadbare black T-shirt with a big red five-pointed star on the chest. Not sure if it was appropriate to shake hands, he didn't. "Uh huh. Well, you might as well come in out of the cold."

After Cantrell closed the door, he offered Broker an icy can of beer. Three pop tops popped. Cantrell said casually, "By the way, we know where you spent May seventy-five."

Now where'd he get that so quick? Broker revised his opinion of Cantrell from tricky redneck up to smart, tricky redneck and showed the barest smile. "How'd a guy like you wind up in Minnesota?" he asked.

"Had to go somewhere to learn to stop saying 'ain't,'" Cantrell replied in that easy voice. He could detect no reaction in Broker's quiet green eyes, and he noted that the corners of his low-key smile showed slightly pronounced canines. The heavy eyebrows, the spring-loaded musculature, and the shaggy hair lent him the aspect of a totally relaxed predator passing for tame.

Then Cantrell tilted his chin up slightly and added, "But, on the other hand, we don't have a clue as to why your entire records sheet, since high school, has been wiped clean. I'd sure like to know why."

"That's fair," Broker said slowly. "So, yeah, down the line." Then he held up his hand. "But right here and now we're talking about a specific deal and twenty thousand bucks."

"Done," Cantrell said.

"Cool. You can skip the foreplay, because I've been on the horn with John Lucht all day." Broker moved his beer can in a welcoming gesture. "So take a seat."

The spare room was cramped. An open suitcase, along with a folder of notes from the workshop, filled the one comfortable chair. Cantrell sat on the bed. J.T. took the desk chair. Broker had no problem with lowering himself to the carpet between them, where he folded his legs casually into a half-lotus and said, "So I'll be flying wingman for Soap Turrie, who allegedly took a hit out on Desmond but turns out to be an undercover asset. That's more of a back story than you ran down in the first interview at the range."

"A hit," J.T. said, "that some people think you carried out."

"And that's what I play into." Broker faced Cantrell. "So whose side is Turrie on?"

"His own. And he goes by Soap," Cantrell said. "The irony here being that Desmond was the author of this scenario. He concocted the death threat against himself to give Soap cover for his informant work on a big, recent case—" Cantrell's voice caught, and the two cops looked away for just a beat. *They're exhausted,* Broker thought. *Maybe, despite their forced, upbeat bravado, they suddenly felt a creepy pull in their guts—even I do—that we're dealing cards on a dead man's eyes.*

After an interval, Broker sketched what John Lucht had told him about people vanishing behind a lost dope shipment and nasty folks showing up, looking for their missing shit. "And they think it all connects back to Tur—ah, Soap," he finished.

"Uh huh," J.T. said, "and we want you to find out who those guys are so we can take them off the board."

"And hopefully keep Soap in one piece," Cantrell added.

"Okay, where do I start?" Broker asked, looking far cooler than the competing red-hot cautions and attractions that flared back and forth in his mind.

Spontaneously Cantrell and J.T. left their seats and scooted down on the carpet. When they all three were hunkered cross-legged in a circle with their knees touching, J.T. leaned in close and placed his dossier on the carpet.

Cantrell said, "You'll have more time to study this file tomorrow, in county, after we pose you with Soap."

"Pose me where?"

"Nine in the morning in the lobby of the Government Center, in front of the sheriff's office. We're going to stage a little reverse-police-brutality sting to stoke up the hype. A similar gambit worked for Desmond and Soap with the Alary's scene. So we'll just keep it going. It's like this: I will execute an unprovoked attack on your ass because some of my colleagues in St. Paul Narcotics think you're a paid killer who offed our boss." J.T.'s hands conjured, fingers spread wide. "Working off that premise, an arrest will follow for assaulting me. There will be a lot of witnesses. I'll wind up being the one who goes to court, and you'll walk with a payday." J.T.'s smile was natural, unaffected. "All part of the game. I'll coach you through stage positions later."

"Okaaay." Broker kept his face and voice expressionless. His eyebrows did go up slightly.

"Hey, it's cool," J.T. said. "We have it all worked out. But you will get roughed up a little."

"Gotta keep it real," Broker said in a neutral tone.

Cantrell said, "Tomorrow night, Turrie will get a couple threatening phone calls that will sound like vigilante cops. He'll report the threats to Washington County. Given that you both will get rousted by angry cops, what better way, after we spring you, to needle law enforcement than bringing you on as a bodyguard to protect him from said cops, huh?" He plucked a black-and-white photo from the file and placed it on the carpet. "Soap Turrie."

The picture captured a durable glint of Depression kid toughness that lingered in Turrie's eyes and in his seamed features. The thick neck tapered up from swamp buck shoulders. Okay. This is a guy who is not good at retreat.

J.T. said, "We put you in his life. You help him squirm out of his fix, he owes us."

Cantrell said, "And he agrees to let you hang in his world, which happens to intersect with every organized criminal circle in the state—at least on a social level. Could be more."

"Okaay." Broker drew it out.

"Yeah, now." J.T. added another black-and-white picture of a striking woman, late forties, whose short, edgy hair was styled with a deliberate wildness and whose face might be plain if her knowing eyes and full lips weren't composed in an expression of jaded but electric energy.

"That looks like trouble," Broker observed.

"Yep. That's Annie O'Neil."

"Uh huh. And these guys tracking her aren't your typical Minnesota crooks," Broker said.

"Well, we don't know, do we?" Cantrell said. "So we could be in this sort of gray area." After a pause he added, "Your kind of territory, maybe?"

The remark produced another silence that dragged on a beat too long, so Cantrell slowly rose to his feet. "I'll leave you guys to it; there's something I have to do." As he turned toward the door, he pointed to the way Broker was sitting and asked, in an attempt to lighten the mood, "What's that, yoga?"

Broker took a sip of beer. "Ambushes. First tour I carried the radio. You lay down, you fall asleep. You lean on something, you fall asleep. This way you wake up when you start to fall over."

"Right," Cantrell said. Then he left.

*　　*　　*

Thirty fast minutes later, after pushing his cherry '57 Chevy on slick freeways, Cantrell parked on the bottom level of the Victory Ramp off Wabasha Street in downtown St. Paul. He checked his wristwatch, exited the car, and stared past the concrete pillars down the empty cement stalls that surrounded him with all the cheer of a catacomb. As usual, St. Paul was a graveyard on Sunday night.

Right on time he heard a squeal of tires as a Ford station wagon wheeled down the ramp and parked next to him. A prematurely white-haired, fidgety man in his mid-thirties got out. There was a looseness to his face and to his body, but his blue eyes were slash, bang, pointy as typewriter keys. *Pioneer Press* columnist Johnny Lager was Cantrell's favorite press weasel because the guy was just so damn hungry. Lager would dig like crazy for the right story, the story he could craft into a template for a Pulitzer, that would pave his way out of journalism into writing novels. It was a work ethic that infused the feisty St. Paul newsroom, in contrast, say, to the fat and sassy *Minneapolis Star Tribune* across the river. In Cantrell's experience, some of the *Strib* reporters suffered from a geographic anomaly. When they exited their building onto Portland Avenue, they acted like they'd just smacked their wingtips down in mid-Manhattan. Cantrell did not consider TV faces real journalists.

"So you caught the shooting in Stillwater, right?" Lager said, taking out a spiral notebook. His breath made little puffs in the air. White. Curved. Commas maybe.

"Yeah. And put that scribble pad away." Cantrell deliberately looked around at the desolate parking ramp, then lowered his voice. "Down and dirty. I'm going to ask you for a favor. You give me a hand, I'll put you in front of the shooting, but you can't quote me directly. But I'll give you enough to own the story."

Lager failed in an attempt to look hard to get. "Define 'enough,'" he said.

"We've been holding back a video tape that captured the whole incident. The tape exonerates Broker—"

"And he's not a real cop, right? He's part time out of Bumfuck, Egypt North?"

"Cook County. And he was enough of a cop to get enrolled in the workshop," Cantrell said in a tight voice, raising his hand. "But that isn't the point. You don't print this until you get it, official, from Wash Co. We still cool?"

"We're cool."

"The tape clearly shows that he shot Desmond in self-defense. I watched it five times, and there's no other explanation."

"What about some St. Paul cops linking Broker to a biker contract on Desmond?"

"Sober St. Paul cops?" Cantrell raised an eyebrow. "Look, the tape tells the story. Quite a story, actually. Right now Pete Yerbich has it. Maybe I can get him to give you a look." Cantrell paused for effect, initiating the dance. "Maybe it tells more than one story."

Lager and Cantrell measured each other. "What have you got, Harry?" Lager spread his hands.

Cantrell reached in his trench coat pocket, withdrew a rumpled stack of paper, and handed it to Lager. "Don't know for sure what I got. We ran Broker in the system. That's what came back."

Lager angled his head in the weak overhead light, then looked up. "Access denied, classified." He paged through the other sheets and pursed his restless lips in a smile, like he'd just found something shiny. "There's nothing here."

"Yeah. And however weird the way he bounced in, when a cat like this shows up," Cantrell said with a straight face, "you want a bio on him. All I could find were rumors from somebody in DC—" Cantrell paused again. "Can't say who."

"What kind of rumors?" Lager asked, and Cantrell could see the way he subtly, but firmly, now gripped the sheets to his chest in both hands.

Cantrell hunched his shoulders. "Could be Broker's under some kind of cloud connected with his military service." He paused, then continued, "There's some gobbledegook acronyms jotted there on the top page: SOG, PRU, Phoenix."

"That's Vietnam spook shit." Lager's eyes clicked. "So where's Broker now? He isn't in custody. Last night you said nobody was being charged."

"Johnny, buddy, a guy like this is never going to talk to somebody like you." Cantrell gave the signature thin smile. "Unless you find the right can opener. Like who erased his background? And why? Like who the hell is he?" Cantrell stepped in closer to the columnist. "And nobody has it but you. Only thing I ask is—you scare something up, you call me first. Deal?"

"Deal." Lager carefully folded the pages, inserted them in his parka pocket, said goodnight, and walked to his car. As he drove away, Cantrell made a mark next to a box in his mental checklist. Okay. Next thing, call some TV stations.

Chapter Ten

At quarter to nine in the morning, Broker, unshaven and bleary-eyed, was working off three hours' sleep when he eased his rusty Jeep to the side of the access road that led to the Washington County Government Center and put the shift in neutral. He cranked down the driver's side window, and with a fresh Lucky and a travel cup full of bad motel coffee for breakfast, he contemplated the cut-glass solitude that had descended on Stillwater following two full days of snow. Then his eyes stopped at a lank yellow ribbon tied around a bare box elder on the edge of a playing field and small playground. His sight line shifted to the strip of public housing that ran along the access road. He watched a woman in a blue parka appear between two of the housing units. She led a group of children dressed in colorful snowsuits who bobbled behind her, roped together, like enslaved cartoons.

Broker took a drag on the cigarette, and then he took a sip of the raw coffee. In about half an hour he was going to get punched out by a tall black dude he'd just met last night and who looked like he could go a full three-minute round with Muhammad Ali without breaking a sweat.

Perhaps Cantrell would be watching from a safe remove, with that sly grin on his mournful face, indulging his fantasy to play case officer. He'd be moving money around as his fingers pulled strings that ran to the county prosecutor, the press, Soap Turrie.

Broker exhaled. Depending on how his collision with Turrie and J.T. Merriweather unfolded, he might visit the emergency room at Lakeview Hospital. "Some stuff you can't fake," J.T. had said. Then he'd be taken into custody, manhandled through the county jail, and booked for assaulting an officer. So it was all wired. Up to a point.

They'd sideline him from the main population, and he'd cloister with a ringer psychologist named Andrea Sabic who, according to J.T., was a real piece of work. Bored with treating routine trauma, she had an itch to get into the FBI's Behavioral Science unit so she could catch, and then study, serial killers. If she decided he was minimally sane enough, he'd get the job and the state money that would be filtered through Washington County. They'd drop the assault charges in exchange for a fast, on the spot, non-disclosure settlement promising that he would not seek legal remedy, etc. After a decent interval, the shooting investigation would be ruled self-defense, based on the range tape. Or so he gathered from the chain-smoking, marathon cram session he'd been through with J.T. until 4:30 this morning.

After they cut him free, he'd head back up north, where John Lucht would take him off the Cook County payroll so he could return to the Cities and hook up with his assignment, Soap Turrie. Details to come.

So they were also making it up as they went along.

Briefly he searched his memory for an appropriate metaphor to embrace what came next. Orpheus entering the Underworld? Could be worse. Could be Detroit, where he'd spent a couple years attending Wayne State after he'd left the Army. Here the crooks probably went back to addressing Hallmark cards after they dumped you in a snow bank. Well, he'd promised his mom he'd get a real job. And they needed the money.

He put the Jeep in gear and motored down the access road toward the parking lot in front of the Government Center. He parked and plodded toward the entrance, looking scruffy in his blaze orange knit cap and his frayed, stained Carhartt jacket that smelled faintly of chain and bar oil from cutting winter firewood in the forest above the North Shore.

Broker's experience with the Washington County Sheriff's Department was limited to being escorted in through a side door and being snuck out the back. The workshop classes had been held across the complex, in the court services area. This was his first look at the lobby. Someone had already placed a Christmas tree in the middle of the far wall. Panels of county sheriff patches from all over the country flanked the winking red and white lights. A long wooden bench ran along the right wall and ended at a glassed-in cubicle where a deputy managed the traffic through the secure door that led, Broker presumed, to the offices. Right now the deputy was engaged in a patient conversation with a woman who held a squalling infant in her arms while a toddler clutched her skirt.

"If you'll have a seat, ma'am," the deputy said, "I'll try to find out the courtroom where he'll be arraigned." When the woman sulked toward the bench, the deputy looked up. "Next?"

"Phil Broker. I have a nine o'clock with Detective Harold Cantrell."

"Right, take a seat. We'll call you."

Soap Turrie was already in position, sitting at the end of the long bench in jeans and a heavy Levi's jacket. This muted signal came off him, like lights and flashers, no siren. People naturally moved to the side.

Turrie casually refused eye contact with Broker and kept checking his wristwatch, like he was expecting someone who was tardy.

First the film crew from Channel Four walked in. Channel Eleven appeared just minutes later. They proceeded to mill around, getting their bearings, and then spotted Soap sitting on the bench and Broker at the other end. There was a quick whispered conference over a copy of this morning's St. Paul paper, where Broker's and Turrie's pictures appeared side by side, grabbed from yesterday's TV. A column by Johnny Lager ran alongside the pictures and recounted how a preliminary records search on Broker's military background had come back suspiciously vacant. The headline read: *Rumor Ties Stillwater Shooter to Special Forces Black Ops.*

Then. Camera. Lights.

Cue up the mic on J.T.'s booming, thoroughly disgusted voice. "What is this shit, these two here together for the cameras?" He came striding across the lobby, with stubble on his chin and cheeks and his face harrowed gray with fatigue. He wore rumpled street clothes: jeans, a parka, and a red USMC sweatshirt with yellow symbol and type. The garment was artfully stained with spilled beer.

Action.

J.T. nosed up, in his face, doing his best junk yard dog so Broker got the direct blast, but none of the reporters crowded around missed the reek of alcohol. "What you gonna do now, mystery man?" J.T. sneered in Broker's face as he slapped a rolled-up newspaper across Broker's chest. "Give them some Green Beret bullshit about jumping out of airplanes?" For emphasis, his knuckles thumped Broker's sternum. Terry Conner was at J.T.'s side, looking hungover but definitely up for following J.T.'s lead.

Broker shot J.T. a guarded look, but he stepped back and raised his hands defensively, which was important because the gathering witnesses and the cameras had to see him attempt to avoid a fight.

J.T. closed the distance with a stiff, two-handed shove. As Broker staggered back, J.T. hissed, "Fuck you, asshole."

As Broker bounced back in an attempt to regain his stance, he smirked and pointed at J.T.'s sweatshirt. "Marines, huh? Oh yeah, you're the guys who jump out of boats—"

Maybe Broker caught a peripheral flash of a grin on Soap Turrie's face just before J.T. suggested a feint with his right and then sizzled a lightning, left hook sucker punch into Broker's right cheek. On the flailing way to the floor, Broker glimpsed Soap trying to step in and being mobbed by Terry Conner and two uniforms. By then J.T. was straddling his chest, and Conner, having cordoned off Turrie, now piled on, along with the deputies. J.T. pulled his punches. Conner and the deputies did not, obviously not in on the plan. They jumped in just to pummel another scofflaw asshole. When they pulled him to his feet, he'd been roughly handcuffed, and his nose was bleeding copiously down the front of his sweater.

And the cameras caught it all.

Chapter Eleven

Tuesday

Yesterday, prior to booking, Broker had been given first aid and was cleaned up by a pair of paramedics. Then they'd tossed him in a solitary cell, where J.T.'s files on Turrie and Annie O'Neil were waiting. At suppertime a trustee delivered a folder with his meal that contained a copy of the Minnesota Multiphasic Personality Inventory and a felt tip pen. Later in the evening the trustee returned and collected the completed multiple choice test.

This morning, wearing a blue denim jumpsuit with WASH CO stenciled on the back to replace his bloodied clothes, they moved him to another room down a corridor several partitions removed from the hum of the inmates. Whitewashed cement block walls crowded in. No windows. The floor tile smelled of disinfectant. Two industrial oak chairs and a matching table were bolted to the floor. As he sat down, his lips tightened. His ribs hurt. His kidneys hurt. The mere act of grimacing hurt.

J.T.'s knuckles had turned his right cheek into a purple-yellow ooze of swelling that snaked below the eye and blended into the damage from other fists that had thickened the bridge of his nose. A wide strip of adhesive disfigured the middle of his face like a sideways nasal piece.

The door opened, and Broker automatically defaulted to the machinery. His pulse slowed, and his concentration downshifted to uncluttered and alert. This would be the shrink who, despite J.T.'s advance warning, was a surprise.

No makeup distracted from her clean features that were molded around intensity this morning, more than mere, hard good health. The name placed her south of the normal Minnesota Scandinavian/German gene pool. Somewhere in her early thirties and almost religiously fit, her medium gold hair was styled a bit too long and carefree for the strict brown pants suit and practical low quarter snow boots. A hint of departing outdoor cold burnished her cheekbones, and Broker suspected she'd have defined hip bones, too. When she leaned across the table to offer her hand, her jacket puckered and, in the heave of her silk blouse, he caught a hint that she wasn't wearing a bra. And that could be a subtle poke in the eye, or perhaps a lingering stamp of feminist audacity? Broker didn't have enough information to tell. He looked past the tawny blond, beige and honey window-dressing and studied her bold gray eyes. Andrea Sabic's eyes suggested that she was in a hurry, under pressure, and taking a chance. And she was enjoying it, like she'd had a sip of the Saint Joan Kool-Aid, along with Cantrell and Merriweather, and had embarked on a secret mission.

"Mr. Broker, I'm Dr. Andrea Sabic." Her handshake lasted a beat too long, like a probe. "This is strictly off the record, between us. Cantrell brought me in to do a pro forma psych eval on you. He explained that, right?"

Broker nodded. "Part of the deal."

"Correct." She sat down and flipped open a spiral notebook, then pressed the plunger on her ballpoint pen with an audible click. "And so far so good; you test within an acceptable range on MMPI. Just short of anti-social. Except for this one scale."

"Really?" Broker was suddenly extra present in the moment.

"Really, and if I were a male test grader, I might say you have a deviant male personality," she said with a hint of a smile.

"Why's that?"

"Because your sensitivity scales normal for a woman."

Broker experienced a slight chirp in the machinery, like a belt slipping. Their eyes were suddenly sticky, catching on each other. Involuntarily her hand floated up to her hair, and now Broker couldn't read her. Was she for real, or was she just real good? This bothered him, because indecision about reading people was not one of his weak points. For a full five seconds he looked directly into Andrea's eyes. And she looked back. Not a stare-down; more like a mutual stare-in.

When it came to quick studies on women, he relied on acquired instinct. Not unlike a healthy predator, he assumed he'd learned to pass on diseased quarry. But with Andrea he couldn't tell. Was she healthy? Or was she infected with the New American Me Disease of seeing the world through her own aggressive self-interest? Certainly she felt a need to project a tough edge, but that could just be defensive callus built up from working with hyper-masculine, horn dog cops.

Locked eye to eye with this particular psychologist, he entertained, very indirectly, the fleeting idea that, yes, he might have a few weak points. But what he said, slowly, was, "So, do I get the job?"

"You get the job, on two conditions. First, you have to fill Cantrell in on some background. I believe that you and he have discussed this. So he wants to know what you did to get black-balled. It's a legitimate concern. He's sticking his neck out."

Broker smiled. "Undercover asset for the BCA?" he chuckled, genuinely amused, not a scratch of cynicism in it. "Doctor, ah, Sabic—"

"Andrea," she clarified. "And what's so funny?"

"Andrea—" Broker spoke slowly, almost to himself. His hands came up and moved back and forth, fingers conjuring as he visualized untying a ribbon. The bow on his personal Pandora's box. *Be mindful, Broker; you haven't talked to an outsider about this for four years.* "I once swore I'd never again work for another goddamn three-letter organization. You have to appreciate, it's pretty funny, me being here, having this conversation with you."

He was now getting the full frontal Andrea eye treatment, and he still could not goddamn tell. Was she real or not? Didn't matter. "Okay, what the hell." Then he pointed across the table. "But no notes, nothing written down." As she closed her notebook and slid it into her purse, he continued, "I've got some ground rules, not just for me. There's other people who—" He thought about it, then said, "Just be better if nothing is written down."

Andrea opened her hands, to show they were empty but also in anticipation.

"I'm going to tell you a story with no names in it but mine," Broker said. "If that's not good enough for Cantrell . . ." His voice trailed off.

"We don't need chapter and verse. Cantrell just wants a credible explanation."

Broker shrugged. "I stole something. Me and another guy. But it was my idea—and I was still, technically, an officer, so I was the one they blamed."

"So what did you steal?"

Broker grinned fondly. "Oh, it was this *really big* helicopter. A Chinook, actually, painted gray, and it had this type along the side—" He raised his hand and drew letters in the air "— that spelled *Air America.*"

Andrea leaned back in her chair, arched her spine, and shoved her hands deep into the pockets of her pants suit jacket. A purr crept into her voice. "You stole a CIA chopper?"

"Yes, ma'am, and it was absolutely packed to the gunnels with glassine bags full of the best heroin in Southeast Asia at the time—which was late April of seventy-five."

Andrea sat up straight and leaned forward as the fingers of her right hand fluttered out, questioning. "I applaud the bravo, I guess. But . . ."

"*Tai sao,*" Broker said under his breath. "Why?" Without drama, he said, "Real simple. We needed barter material. We had more than a thousand people on the beach north of Hue and more coming in by the hour. The NVA were on the rampage all around, and we had a flotilla of Malay pirates off shore for transport. But we had no way to pay them. Plan A, our financing arrangement, had fallen through."

"Which was?"

Broker just shook his head, then went on. "So, the thing about being in the middle of South Vietnam as it collapsed around our ears was that for a moment there, everything was up for grabs. And I happened to know the location of some primo trading material: this little heroin processing lab that a certain Laotian general ran in cahoots with the Agency and the Saigon ruling clique. So we took a quick trip to the Laotian border with a pilot we trusted. After some minor fireworks, we got away with enough loot to keep the pirates coming back for load after load right through May."

"How many did you get out?" Andrea asked.

"Around two thousand, counting dependents. People I'd worked with back when I was in the Army—well, in the Army but detailed to the Agency. But I'd had it with the war and mustered out. I was going to school in Detroit when the call went out to assemble the gang for this crash plan to go back in and pull out our old assets. There was a lot of that going on under the radar at the time."

"So basically you pissed off some important people," Andrea speculated.

"Pretty much. So take it or leave it; that's the story."

"Works for me, with some reservations," Andrea said.

"And the second condition?" Broker asked.

"That'll come later." She cocked her head and fixed him with a maybe sincere look. "You do a real psych evaluation with me. Not this rubber stamp version."

Broker sat up. "Say again?"

"Look around; we're winging it here. That's why I'm giving you your marching orders and not Cantrell. When I leave this room, an assistant county attorney and notary come in and you sign a non-disclosure agreement attached to the settlement about the fight yesterday morning. They agree to eventually rule the death of Joe Desmond a case of self-defense. Full stop. Then they give you a check as compensation for being assaulted by officers in their Government Center. You get out of Dodge and drive directly to Grand Marais, where John Lucht will diplomatically fire your ass because of all the crazy stuff that will start blowing through the media."

"More crazy publicity?"

"Trust me," Andrea said as she withdrew a business card from her jacket pocket and handed it over.

Dr. Andrea Sabic
Forensic Psychologist
Specialist in Trauma

"I'm teaching at the U this semester, but I still see a select group of clients," she said. "John Lucht will recommend that you leave the county until the media stink wears off. He'll give you that same card and suggest that if you get down to the Cities—wink wink—you should look me up. Idea being that if you ever want to work in Cook County, you need to get a psych eval from a pro."

"Okaaay." Broker was blindsided but impressed. "So when do I hook up with Turrie?"

"No idea. He'll make the move. He made two angry calls last night to 911 about people sounding suspiciously like cops phoning in threats on his life. So that part's on the record and will be leaked to the press to stoke the gossip. So when you show up with him, it plays into the idea he's retained you for

95

protection. Once you get launched out there, you'll be totally on your own. It's not like you'll be ringing up Cantrell every day on a pay phone. You'll have no contact with law enforcement, period. But you will have a maybe plausible reason to talk to me. So, until you settle in, I'm your connect with Cantrell."

"Doesn't this put you a bit off the reservation?" Broker asked.

"No kidding," she chuckled. "My professional association would censure me, if not worse." She leaned forward. "But we're in a gray area. I don't think the American Psychological Association has specific ethical language to cover recruiting ex-spooks for unofficial undercover operations."

"So why risk losing your license?"

Dead pan, she held up three fingers of her right hand and recited, " 'On my honor I will try to serve God and my country and help people at all times.' Except it gets old, shoveling sewage through the system, bucking the bureaucracy. So this is a change of pace. But we all have an agenda. You need a job. I need a job reference. Cantrell and J.T. want to catch some bad guys. And, let's say, I have a professional interest in someone like you."

A silence followed during which Broker tried to engage the range finder in her eyes. The moment timed out, and her hand floated across the table and touched the scar on his left forearm. "Looks like you had a tattoo removed there. I'm curious what it was."

"That part of the test?" he asked.

"Not really, just context."

"Looks like you aren't wearing a bra. I'm curious why you'd parade that in a county jail?"

She cocked her head, appraising. "Maybe I dressed in a hurry this morning."

Another silence ensued, during which she planted both elbows on the table, clasping her hands, and curled her interlaced fingers under her chin. The gray eyes studied him, not aloof exactly, but as if from high up, riding a thermal. It occurred to Broker that, since she'd entered the room, her gaze had never lingered on his damaged face. Just his eyes. "So do I take more tests or what?" he asked.

"No. We're done here. I came in to take a look at you. The MMPI was just fluff to assure the Director of Public Safety you won't throw the cat through the screen door and wipe your ass on the drapes." She shrugged. "Not worth trying to find you in MMPI or the standard psychopathy checklists. Your test comes every week, with me."

"Ongoing evaluation?"

"That's right. Harry Cantrell wants to know who you are. And he sees the world in fairly simple terms. There's sheep, there's dogs that guard the sheep, and there's wolves. He knows you aren't a sheep."

Andrea stood up, shouldered her purse, walked to the door, turned and fixed him with the eyes, full intensity. "Shooting Desmond: you think about it?" she asked.

"I remember it," Broker said.

For a moment she seemed to savor his answer; then she knocked on the door. Just before it opened, she turned and said, "Call me as soon as you get back in town."

"Yes, ma'am," Broker said to the vacant doorway and the echo of her boot heels.

*   *   *

An hour later Andrea Sabic walked into the county attorney's office on the second floor of the Washington County Government Center. A secretary ushered her down a corridor into a room where Pete Yerbich and Harry Cantrell stood at a window, watching more snow sputter down from the gray, exhausted cloud cover.

"So how'd it go?" Yerbich asked.

Andrea composed her features in a Gallic shrug. "He gave some vague background: he was Army, seconded to the Agency in-country. Perhaps he was an officer?" Then she related Broker's abbreviated back story about the helicopter and the evacuation that had resulted in the reprisal scrub of his bio.

Cantrell and Yerbich exchanged sidelong glances.

"I can live with that. I think. Sounds like our boy may come with his own shark tank," Cantrell finally said.

Andrea continued, rapid fire. "I watched the tape twice and graded MMPI. I read all the witness statements taken at the range. I looked over the stuff you pulled on him—or rather, what you weren't able to get on him. Then I spent fifteen minutes in a room with him an hour ago. After that I had to make a stop to pick up my report." Andrea shook off her coat, reached in her purse, removed a plastic bag, and tossed it on the conference table. *Johnny's TV* was printed on the side.

"Huh?" said Yerbich.

Cantrell upended the bag. A VHS tape of the movie *Jeremiah Johnson* and a receipt fell out. "What's this?" he asked.

"My psychological assessment of Phil Broker. File the receipt under my expenses."

"You think he's Robert Redford?" Yerbich said experimentally.

"No, I think he spent way too much time downrange, where he picked up a bunch of snappy skills along with lots of psychic numbing. Now he's a traumatized romantic who thinks he can leave civilization and hide out in the woods. Us? The rules? Just so much more bullshit that he's tired of. Well, the North Woods are remote, but they aren't the Rockies circa 1850. At some point he'll realize the folly of playing hermit, and he'll have to come in from the frontier and learn to compromise. Like the rest of us. And I'm going to help him negotiate that transition. In the meantime, he won't be able to resist going out there and stirring things up for you. Just watch."

The two men stared at her with cautious expressions.

Andrea allowed a brief laugh. "What? You want a bunch of shrink jargon? He's perfect." She took a few steps past them, faced the window that framed a potentially turbulent sky, and said softly, "He's a fugitive from an adventure book for boys."

"But, ah," Cantrell cleared his throat, "can we rely on him not to, ah—?"

"Kill somebody," Yerbich interjected.

Andrea turned and allowed a modest smile. "Well, you know what we say on my end of the building: the best predictor of whether someone will kill is whether they've done it before."

"Short of killing someone, can we trust him?" Cantrell said.

"You mean, to not embarrass us, blow back on us, screw up our careers?" Andrea asked with a droll expression.

"Well, yeah."

Andrea waffled her palm. "I suspect he's smarter than he lets on, that he's highly functional within a narrow range. But without his records, we can only speculate. We do know he's competent, has good reflexes, and he can obviously keep his mouth shut. My take is he's cool. But not cold."

Yerbich squinted at her. "You're enjoying this."

"We have an understanding, right?" Andrea said. "I agreed to sign off on your hair-brained scheme and play go-between until he settles in. My end is simple." She looked pointedly at Cantrell. "Your boss gives me a solid, platinum recommendation, right?"

"Right," Cantrell echoed.

Andrea said, "Another thing. There's a big debate going on in American psychology circles about whether to include Combat Stress Syndrome in the new DSM III. Access to Broker is like Pasteur having that flap in a patient's belly to look into his stomach." She ended with a satisfied smile.

"I guess," Cantrell said finally.

"There's something else," Andrea said. "He has a scar on his arm where a tattoo was removed."

"I noticed that. So?" Cantrell said.

Andrea turned back to the window. "I suspect this guy's sworn NDAs to keep everything he's done secret for the last ten years. Maybe the tattoo is his non-disclosure agreement with himself," she speculated. "Just might be the crack in his armor."

"But can we control the sonofabitch?" Yerbich asked.

"Something like this is never going to come along again, so I guess we just have to find out," Andrea said, still looking out and beyond.

After Andrea left the room, Yerbich pursed his lips as he placed a wall phone back in its cradle. "Well, he's out-processing right now. It's on the rails."

"I already called J.T., had him alert Turrie," Cantrell said. "And remember, you have to toss Lager an interview, give him a peek at the tape."

"Right. And mention the threats against Turrie. He'll be here this afternoon," Yerbich said. "Another thing. You saw the news last night. Merriweather is out of a job for sure. No way I can't charge him with assault."

"He's cool, all part of the script. I'm arranging a soft landing in my shop."

After a pause, Yerbich asked in a lighter tone. "So Andrea? She's really going for this thing."

"She's angling for a slot with the Bureau in Behavioral Science. She figures working Broker could give her an edge," Cantrell said.

Yerbich chewed on it for a moment, then asked, "So, ah, you ever get anywhere with her?"

Cantrell squirmed in his chair. "Nah. But you know, I thought I had a chance because she has this obvious interest in really fucked-up, violent men."

Yerbich chuckled. "What's that say about you?"

Cantrell turned and looked out the window. "What's that say about Broker?"

Chapter Twelve

Broker cleared Washington County at 10:30 A.M. He tossed the bloody sweater from yesterday morning into the back of his rusted green Jeep, pulled on a fresh woolen shirt, turned the key, and immediately started working his way toward 35E, the road north. For company he had a check in his pocket for twenty thousand dollars, along with a travel cup full of bad deputy sheriff coffee. He did not turn on the radio, but he could feel the media cloudburst massing behind him about the lurid love triangle that had erupted Saturday afternoon on the shooting range. He could imagine the headlines from tabloid heaven and the pictures of the scorned wife next to Wilson, the one-night revenge-fuck, and then the dead husband, and finally Annie, the brassy bar owner who had mysteriously vanished. There was the hot TV footage about the "police brutality" excesses in the Wash Co lobby yesterday morning. Coming soon was gossip about a renegade group in St. Paul Narcotics bent on vengeance, fueled by Turrie's calls reporting threats. Plus whatever twisted bullshit Cantrell was leaking to the press about him. He shook himself to dispel the distractions.

Just step on the gas and do the tricks.

Deal with what's in front of you. Wall the rest off.

But now, Post-Andrea, there was a definite quaver in the machinery. He could actually visualize the defensive mechanism he kept between himself and the outside world threaten to dissolve right before his eyes. A tangible sensation turned in his chest, and for one dark, musty moment he caught a tiny whiff and shiver of it. Then it was gone. Almost like a tease, like the thing he kept at a comfortable distance was pacing just off stage, getting set to lope right up close and sniff in his face.

Wow.

Been awhile. Remember fear, Broker.

In more concrete terms, by the time he hit his turn indicator to pull off on the Hinckley exit to get a coffee refill at Tobie's Restaurant, he was certain he had company. This gray Plymouth town car, tinted windows, was hanging back, pacing him, at six car lengths. The car did not take the exit. After getting his coffee and removing the patch of adhesive from his nose in the men's room, he got back on the road. Sure enough, after the next on-ramp, the Plymouth was back in position behind him.

Cantrell monitoring him? Press? Soap Turrie? Worse? Guess he'd find out.

He stopped at the rest stop overlooking Duluth and Superior to void the morning's coffee. Then he threaded his way through the Twin Port City's hills and high bridges and finally pulled on to North Highway 61 and saw the Big Water brooding on his right. Superior's horizon laid down a plumb line that was his first stable memory, along with the lullaby of the breaking surf. But he'd logged some miles since then. So when he rolled down the window and listened to the breaking waves that carried on the bitter wind, they crashed, not crooned. He'd been all over and he always came back here, to this primitive shoreline that celebrated ancient winters of forest, snow, ice, and stone. Where the wilderness started just across the highway and stretched all the way up through Canada.

Where you could touch raw ledge rock that was two billion years old.

North of Two Harbors the tail made its move, the dark windows passing him at ninety miles an hour. He automatically memorized the rental plates as the Plymouth accelerated and disappeared around a turn. Okaay.

Past mid-afternoon he cleared Tofte, then Lutsen and then slowed, tires crunching in the snow crust, as he turned onto the shoulder that dropped off sharply to a narrow cobble beach that curled around a tidal pool of boulders.

He got out and faced the lake and listened to his own heartbeat in the icy rhythm of the surf. Then he peered at the beach for a long time as his breath puffed white and faded in the thin, frigid afternoon light. Stepping carefully, he descended to the beach and picked his way to a long, flat granite slab. It lay as if posed, like a ceremonial rune that his Norwegian or German ancestors might have fancied and decided to drag somewhere. Two uniquely large cobbles were placed, medium on huge, at the foot of the plinth stone.

Broker spied the pieces of driftwood and then saw what had happened. He bent and picked up the third distinctive cobble, smaller but hefty enough that lifting it required both hands. He placed it, cairn-like, on the other two.

He stepped back. *There.*

A few minutes later he slowed at the sign that announced Devil's Rock, population 86. He turned at another sign on which Irene had daubed a realistic bouquet of devil's paint-brush: *Welcome to Broker's Beach Resort.*

Seven log cabins hugged the rocky shoreline, within spitting distance of the water. The ice dammed up under the eaves gleamed in the thin light and had the look of too much upper gum. The dock was still in the water, and Dad was counting on him to haul it in. Not this trip, Dad.

Two pickups were parked at an end cabin. Number Seven. Broker had worked alongside his father building it, the entire summer after his sophomore year in high school. The name place, Freya, was cold-chiseled into the lintel. Irene had originally wanted to name the cabins after constellations, but Dad had put his foot down, so they compromised on Norse gods. The tenants were probably late season deer hunters, locals who overlooked the cranky plumbing to throw a few bucks Dad's way. He stopped the Jeep in front of the more substantial, two-story red cedar residence where Irene Broker sat atop the old Ford 9N tractor with snow bucket attached. She wore a jacket cut from a red Hudson's Bay blanket, and her still mostly-dark hair was braided in youthful pigtails. She was arguing with Dad, who shuffled on the porch, parka over his bathrobe, with the catheter leg bag half full of pink liquid strapped to his bare calf that disappeared into an untied Sorel boot.

Broker got out of the Jeep and gathered they were quibbling about snow removal. His way. Her way. But Dad was a shrunken, singed version of himself at the moment. And she had the tractor.

"Hey guys," he called out, "take a break."

Irene climbed down and said, "I'll heat up the coffee." Neither she nor her husband were the least surprised when their son just nodded and walked off between the cabins toward the imposing rock formation that anchored the north end of the property.

Slowly, minding the icy footing, Broker clambered up the fissured gabbro face, using the gnarled trunk of an ancient, rock-hugging cedar for handholds.

The Devil's Rock was the landmark that gave this little settlement its name. Brooding two hundred feet above the shore, it was so named by Northern European immigrants who displaced the Ojibwe, to whom this stand-alone crag was *Man-didowish*—sacred. Broker's Christian ancestors—who saw Satan behind every birch tree—crossed out *sacred* and wrote in *The Devil*.

At the top, he settled back into a rough, well-worn cranny of stone and looked out over the rocky shore. He could almost be a kid again up here, visualizing geologic time and the fire and ice that had shaped this place. Here and now he took out his cigarettes, stripped off the paper, and sprinkled the shreds of tobacco to the wind. A small, private gesture. As a boy, his favorite forest spirit had been Naniboujou the Trickster, who was said to frequent this overlook when he was contemplating the folly of men. *So what do you think?* No machinery for back-up. The machinery wasn't allowed up here. "A year," Broker said under his breath. *I can swim with these reef sharks for a year.*

When Broker entered the kitchen, Irene deftly did not mention recent events or his ragged face. She set out the coffee cups and brightened. "So, are you home for Thanksgiving?"

"More important, you have to winch in the dock. People are worrying about early freeze up," Broker Senior grumbled. He got a mild raise of the eyebrows from Broker for his trouble.

Son and father studied each other for several seconds. It was jarring for Broker to see the strength ebb from his father's face and his robust body. Twenty years an airborne NCO, two jumps in Europe and one in Korea. A turn in law enforcement. During that time he had dealt with all manner of threats that sought to destroy him, ranging from the Waffen SS to a deranged, armed hermit barricaded in a cabin up the Gunflint. But now his own body was trying to kill him, and that was a new experience for them both.

"Yeah, right, you've been busy," his father said as he shoved the outstate editions of the *Star Tribune* and the *Pioneer Press* across the kitchen table. "Congratulations. Your beat-up face is on the front page of both papers. Above the fold. Probably Duluth, too. John already called. The county board is shitting a brick."

"Yeah, well, it got kind of hectic down in the Cities," Broker explained as he turned both papers upside down on the table. "John's my next stop." As he accepted a cup of coffee from Irene, he said, "And I may have to take a rain check on Thanksgiving. I might be headed back."

For a long silent minute the three Brokers sipped their coffee. Broker doubted that John Lucht would put them in the loop, but he'd had enough of these opaque conversations with the folks for them to sense that—after his enforced exile—their son was "working" again.

"So." Broker withdrew the Washington County settlement check from his pocket, along with a pen. He endorsed the check and pushed it across the table to Irene. "Stick that in the bank to tide things over till Grumpy here gets back on his feet. I'll talk to Davey over at the Loon to round up a crew to stow the dock. Then you guys contract with him to steam out the ice dams on the cabins and rig some kind of cover on the roofs—that'll hold until I line up a roofing crew in the spring."

After a crowded silence, his dad read the type on the upper corner of the check. "Washington County Treasurer's Office? That was quick."

"Hey, Pa, I don't think it's going to bounce. And the cops who jumped me were recorded on tape by two television stations." Then Broker took a last sip of coffee, got up from the table, walked to the sink, and dumped the rest of the coffee down the drain. Reaching for his coat, he said, "Just don't talk to any reporters. And don't believe everything you read in the papers or see on the TV."

Twenty minutes later Broker walked into the Cook County Sheriff's Office in Grand Marais. Doris, the receptionist, pursed her lips and lowered her eyes when he appeared. She hit a button on her phone console and said, "He's here."

Chief Deputy Craig Nagel was standing against the wall in John's office, his thick forearms folded across his crisp khaki uniform shirt. They nodded to each other. Civil. Clearly John hadn't told him, either.

John sat behind his desk in a plaid wool hunting vest that matched his folksy, incipient jowls. But his owl's eyes were all business. Nagel was present to witness him take out the garbage.

"Your face looks like shit. People gonna see it a mile away," John said.

"Not as bad as it looks, actually," Broker said.

John slid a check across the table. "Five hundred ten bucks, what you're owed, to include per diem at the workshop and later. That clears you off our books." Broker picked up the check. John said, "It is what it is. You're all over the media, and we think it's best you lay low for a while, preferably in another county." He handed Broker a business card, Andrea's business card. "If you're in the Cities, you might call up this psychologist. She specializes in officer-related shootings. An evaluation from her might go down favorably with the county board, for future reference. That's it, Phil; now I'll need your Special Deputy ID card."

Broker took out his wallet, inserted Andrea's card, and then handed over his deputy ID. There were no parting words as he turned and walked out of the office. Doris did not raise her eyes from the paperwork on her desk.

No parting words and no further instructions, either.

He allotted a few minutes to motoring slowly along the harbor front, constantly checking the angles and the mirrors. No pursuit Plymouth. Idling at a light, he looked out over the lake, where he saw lots of snow but no artists on Artist Point. The wind had completely calmed. The gray harbor was motionless as the afternoon turned still and seriously cold. A faint tincture of arctic rose bled into the ice water sky, and smoke from the Coast Guard station chimney trickled straight up.

On the way out of town he checked the streets and his mirrors again. No gray Plymouth.

*　　*　　*

The Last Loon, a roadhouse that sold groceries on the side, was located on the north edge of Devil's Rock. In the off season, the joint drew a certain local clientele, mainly guys who logged, outfitters killing time between snowshoe trips, and late in the evening, the more hard-core, leftover sixties crowd from Grand Marais. But it was early, with only a few trucks in the lot. As he went in, he inhaled a winter broth of sweaty wool and wood chips and reminded himself that, this time of year, a stranger walking in would glow like neon.

"Hey, hey, hey!" Davey the bartender crowed, inspecting Broker's face. "Our favorite lost pilgrim has returned home again after his latest adventure."

A couple loggers down the bar thumped their glasses, then went back to talking, heads close.

Davey slapped down the front section of the *Pioneer Press* on which Broker's disheveled booking picture occupied two columns, complete with bruised cheek, thickened nose, and blood-rimmed nostrils. Judging by the four-column headline, Johnny Lager was pushing the columnist's leeway all the way to hype: *Speculation Rife in St. Paul Narcotics Unit That Stillwater Shooter Was Special Forces Assassin.*

Broker reached for the paper, but Davey placed his hand on it and held up a pen. "Autograph it, and the first drink is on the house," he said.

Broker snatched the pen, took out his severance check, signed the back, and pushed it across the bar. "How about I autograph this, and you cash it and take enough for you and a gang of guys to haul my dad's dock in for the season. And he might have a few more paying jobs before freeze up."

"Bite me, Phil; we were planning to pull the dock anyway. Do it tomorrow," Davey grumbled on his way to the cash register. In the middle of counting out bills, he pursed his lips and just stared.

Broker smelled her—with a pleasurable chill of *déjà vu*—before he turned and saw her. This damp musk of fresh-turned earth from an open grave, like an olfactory echo of the sensation that swooped through his chest as he was leaving the Cities. But it wasn't fear he scented. It was perfume. *Patchouli.*

She had crow-black hair and an alert mocking twinkle in her green eyes, and she moved with the kind of lean athleticism you get from hard work, not the gym. At five ten she was tall enough that most men wouldn't look down on her. Dark freckles dusted her pale skin, and her lips were composed in a game smile, anchored on either side by Celtic cross earrings. A silver clasp held her long hair in an artful coil around her head. Broker found her slim face as refined as the jewelry she wore, but he didn't buy her from the neck down: the motorcycle jacket with an excess of zippers and buckles, the tight–fitting black T-shirt, tight-fitting jeans, and dark leather boots. *Uh uh.*

But she definitely had the attention of everyone else in the bar.

"Gee," she said as she reached for the newspaper on the bar. Briefly she held it up as she looked from the front page to his face. "I've never been with a guy who killed a cop before. What's that like, I wonder?"

"Let me guess. You came all this way to find out?" Broker said, continuing to size her up. Coincidence was out of the question.

"No, actually, I came to check out the cross country skiing," she said.

Broker smiled. "I doubt you've ever been off the main roads."

"You ever heard of Title Nine, Cowboy?" she said. "I was co-captain of the Stillwater High girls' cross country ski team."

Their eyes glanced, hers catnip and cool clover, his narrowing slightly. When she reached up to remove the clasp from her hair, he noted a silver Claddagh ring on the little finger of her left hand. She shook her hair loose in a practiced move so it tumbled in a black cascade around her leather-studded shoulders. Broker noted the touch of theatricality, but also a clean kinetic energy to her. He placed her age in the mid-twenties.

Okaaay. "Cross-country must have been before you majored in motorcycle jackets, huh?" Broker played along.

"Afterwards, actually," she said with a touch of smirk in her smile. She unsnapped the top button of her jeans and peeled the denim down far enough to reveal a red Harley logo tattoo that stretched hip to hip on her flat tummy below her belly button.

The only sound was Davey's breathing as he hovered, wiping his hands on his apron, eager to take an order.

"It's okay, nothing at the moment," she said as she rearranged her jeans. "We just need some privacy."

"We do?" Broker asked as Davey retreated down the back bar, grumbling for the second time in three minutes.

"We do," she said. "It's like this. My dad, Russell Turrie, would like a word with you. On account of he thinks you maybe got that," she said pointing to his face, "because of him. And now he's getting calls at the house—from cops, he thinks—making threats."

"What kind of threats?" Broker kept his tone neutral as he processed the cloak and daggery of Cantrell and Merriweather.

"The kind he takes serious enough to send my mom out of town. Basically, he'll pay you to hang around with him until these threats blow over. And he wants to talk to you tonight, and we don't have a lot of time because, well, things just got a little urgent."

"And if I say no?" Broker asked.

"Would you step outside? There's somebody I want you to meet," she said.

Broker gathered up the pile of cash on the bar, stuffed it in his jeans, and followed her out the front door. The gray Plymouth was parked on the shoulder. A squat, comic but also ferocious figure stood next to it in a white snowmobile suit and bulbous, white, arctic pack snow boots. White mutton chop whiskers edged his square impassive face, sweeping up into a nimbus of white-blond hair. At fifty yards Broker could clearly mark the startling blue of his eyes. The figure opened the Plymouth's trunk and held up a five-gallon can of gasoline.

"That's Joey," she said. "He dislikes the cold; maybe that's why he overdresses and tends to be an expert at starting fires." She inclined her head. "Your folks' resort is built of wood, correct?"

Broker kept his eyes on Joey, whom he decided was muscled like a Morlock out of H.G. Wells' *Time Machine*. With a face copied off a bust of Socrates. "How'd you find me here, at the Loon?" he asked, genuinely curious. "I didn't see the Plymouth when I left Grand Marais."

"I'm in the blue Avis Civic over there," she said. "Was a little tricky but—*voila*—here we are."

"Pretty sure of yourself, aren't you?" Broker said.

She cocked her head. "Not me. My dad. His theory is you'll go for it because you both been screwed over by the cops."

Broker shrugged, nodded at Joey standing next to the Plymouth, and said, "I guess I have to yield to superior force, huh?"

"Don't be coy, Broker. I suspect there's a lot more going on than I'm privy to. And it's been going on for some time. But it's no girls allowed. I'm just the messenger," she said as she extended her hand, which was surprisingly firm, sinewy and edged with callus. "Rita Turrie, glad to meet you. Now let's go get your stuff."

Broker knew how to totally ignore his folks' worried shadows in the window of the residence as the Plymouth and the Civic followed his Jeep to the resort and stopped at the small cabin where he'd been staying. Joey remained outside. Rita followed him in.

"So what do I pack: toothbrush, dental floss?" Broker said as he tossed a down mountain parka, underwear, socks, a spare sets of jeans, and some sweaters into an overnight grip. As an afterthought he added Foote's thick history volume.

Rita's eyes inspected the Spartan one-room cabin and rested on the gun cases stacked in the corner by the narrow bed. "I think maybe you bring those." She pointed.

"Getting dramatic?" Broker said.

"Don't think so," Rita said. Then she nodded to the phone on the desk. "Can I get an outside line on that?"

"Sure."

She went to the phone, dialed, waited a moment, then said, "We're good. We're getting on the road as soon as I hang up." She returned the phone to its cradle and said, "Let's go."

On the way out through the mudroom, she paused to look over Broker's extensive carpentry and woodworking tools. She picked up an antique wood chisel and tested the edge for sharpness. "Are you any good with these?" she asked.

"I do all right."

"Uh huh." She returned the chisel to the shelf next to the big Jonsered chainsaw, which she touched lightly. "Nah," she said with the twinkle in her eye. "Don't think we're there yet."

Back out front Broker carried three gun cases and his grip. Rita followed with a 50 cal. ammo can full of rounds and a small briefcase that held Broker's .45 automatic pistol. He started for his Jeep.

"Uh uh," she said and jerked her head toward the Plymouth, where Joey had popped the trunk. "Your truck's known in the Cities. We'll fix you up with wheels."

Broker went back into the cabin and left his car keys on the desk. Then he came out and, as he loaded his gear into the Plymouth's trunk, he tapped the gas can, which was empty.

Up close, Joey's troll smile was warm despite the tug of a hair lip. "Just messin' with you," he said.

When the gear was loaded, Broker looked his two new traveling companions up and down. Were they in the loop? Did it matter? The connect had been made. But he had to ask. "You going to give me a clue about what happens next?"

"We lose the Civic at the first Avis we find open on the road," Rita said. "Then I ride shotgun to keep Joey awake. You ride in the back and try to get some sleep. I have a feeling it's going to be a long night."

"Ain't no big thing," Joey said softly, "but it says in the newspapers you're some kind of gunfighter?"

Rita shrugged. "So I guess my dad is in the market for a gunfighter. C'mon, we're burning time."

Broker stretched out on the Plymouth's back seat with his coat bundled for a pillow. After Rita turned in the Civic in Two Harbors, she and Joey were using up what was left of Highway 61 to discuss whether Bob Dylan's decision to go electric was spontaneous and creative or calculating and spiteful. They conversed in low tones and, as if under orders, said not a word to their passenger. *So roll with it and get some rack.*

Dozing in the fanciful zone before sleep, he was reminded that Superior had frozen and thawed twice since he'd been involved, on a regular basis, with a woman. And now—starting this morning—he'd met two of them on the same day. Andrea Sabic came on fast and straight ahead, not above flirting with harm's way, if, he figured, she could strike the right alignment of excitement, ambition and duty. Soap Turrie's low-key daughter was the darker flip side, with hard hands edged with callus. And where did she get that grip?

Onward. Do the tricks; breathe to relax. As the reds and grays behind his eyelids flickered off to black, he recalled Cantrell's Serve and Protect metaphor, as relayed by Andrea, about the sheep and the dogs and the wolves, which begged the open question of where he fell on their moral spectrum. Briefly, he pictured winter silence in the empty northern forest. Where wolves leave their tracks. Where sheep and dogs never go.

Cantrell's metaphor wouldn't be his first choice for a job description, because he hadn't been raised with the notion that evil resides in Nature, or with the spiritual cosmology that went with it. His lips curved in a tiny smile. *What would Naniboujou say? Maybe that wolves tended to mind their own business unless provoked. And people weren't sheep. And shepherds guarded sheep only until it was time for shearing or slaughter.*

As the Plymouth hurtled through the dark, ferrying Broker to meet Soap Turrie and earn his pay, his last conscious thought before he fell asleep was to wonder: *And now where do I fit in?*

Chapter Thirteen

Coming to the junction of south 35E and 694, Broker roused when the tires briefly lost traction. His eyes popped open to snow streaking at the windshield like a display on *Star Trek* when the *Enterprise* switched to warp speed. Joey accelerated to pass a train of snowplows that were cutting a trail through blowing drifts. Slowing back down, he said to Rita, "You know, they send snowplow drivers from all over the world here to study under the Minnesota Department of Transportation."

"C'mon, all over the world, like from Russia?" Rita wasn't buying it.

"Yep, Norway too." Joey jerked a thumb back toward the plows. "Check it out. We got the biggest, harshest functioning winter road net on the planet."

Twenty minutes later they turned off Highway 36, and Broker made a note to acquire a local road map to get up to speed. Growing up on the North Shore, the only regular trips he'd made to the Cities had been to attend the high school hockey tournament. He was more familiar with the territory between the Laotian Highlands and the Tonkin Gulf than this part of his home state.

A moment later they pulled into Soap Turrie's car repair shop. Joey stopped in front of the two-story office, reached down and pulled the latch to pop the trunk. Rita turned to Broker and said, "I'm going to take your stuff inside. Dad's around back." She hopped out, collected the gun cases and travel bag, slammed the trunk, and hiked through the blowing snow to the office door. A guy with a black beard, in mechanic overalls, opened the door for her. He made no effort to conceal the shotgun he cradled in the crook of his arm.

As Joey drove past the shop along a chain-link fence, Broker asked, trying to keep it light, "You guys expecting an attack?"

"Already had one," Joey said evenly.

The night abruptly turned a bit darker and colder. Broker raised his hand and scrubbed the remaining sleep from his eyes as Joey stopped at the gate to the fenced enclosure. A gate guard carrying a shotgun left the warmth of a pickup parked across the entrance, came to the driver's side window, and grunted, "Hey Joey."

"Hey Tony."

Tony returned to his vehicle and moved it aside to let them through.

Inside the wire, Joey stopped in front of a huge Quonset-shaped garage. "In there," he said.

As he headed for the smaller entrance next to the wide garage door, Broker passed bins of snow-covered landscaping material: different grades of rock and timbers and railroad ties, in addition to a sizable cache of lumber, shingles, and sheet plywood. He opened the door and looked down an aisle of more materials. A front loader, a backhoe and several Bobcats, whiskered with frost, were hunkered up like a family of yellow steel oxen. And finally, there was Soap Turrie, who stood at the far end of the building in the same flannel-lined denim jacket he'd worn yesterday morning, minus the black T-shirt that he'd exchanged for a red fleece. As Broker approached, Turrie kept his big mitts at his side, clenching and unclenching his fingers.

A glass-walled office with a lean-to roof was built into the back end of the huge shed. Next to the office a cement pad was raised off the frozen gravel. A large, top-door meat freezer sat on the pad and emitted a faint electric buzz.

They stood for a moment, face to face, with their breath merging in a crystalline cloud. "So you're the guy I hired to kill Joe Desmond. Practically says so in the newspaper." Soap's faint laugh rumbled off the curved metal walls.

"Yesterday's headlines," Broker said.

"Yeah, well, Desmond was always a cop, you understand, but an okay guy to have a beer with. I'm told," Soap said.

"I wouldn't know."

During a span of silence, Broker discovered that, up close, Soap's gray poker eyes gave away nothing. So he looked directly into those eyes and said, "Joey said there'd been trouble, and I see two guys with .12 gauges outside."

"Yep." Turrie's face remained expressionless. "Your pal Merriweather's undercover bullshit just busted a gut. Joey found this. I haven't shown it to Rita yet." He reached in his jacket pocket, removed a wrinkled sheet of paper, and handed it to Broker. The ragged, typed note was smeared with brownish stains. Broker raised his eyebrows.

"Meat juice," Soap explained. "Was wrapped around a package of venison brats. It showed up in my mailbox sometime last night at my place north of town. Joey found it when he went out to check the house. I've been forted up here at the shop since I called in the alleged death threats—as per the agreement."

Broker angled around to see better by the meager overhead light:

We know she's got our stuff.
We think you know where she is.
You have till Friday at noon.
NO COPS. WE'LL KNOW.
We also know you have a wife and kid.

Soap said, "I keep the brats here, in the freezer, for the guys on my crew." He walked to the freezer and lifted the lid.

Broker was more familiar with death in the tropics, where the maggots and the heat got to work, than with what he saw in the long, rectangular freezer.

The naked corpse of a young man lay in a tight curl on a hard white bed of packages wrapped in freezer paper. Frost cushioned the surrounding walls. Beneath a stiff fringe of tangled dark hair, the dead man had a deep-purple-going-to-black birthmark on his upturned left cheek. Duct tape clamped his mouth, and his clouded eyes were bugged out, stuck wide open. The wrists and ankles were viciously bound in rusty barbed wire, and the fingers of both hands were flayed to the bone, several bare joints showing through lumps of crystallized tissue and blood. Deep, red-etched claw marks gouged into the frosted walls.

"Leper," Broker said slowly. "Travis Diggs, your missing employee." He tapped his cheek. "Merriweather takes good notes. I read them last night."

"So?" Soap asked slowly, deliberately, drawing it out in a controlled voice. They moved side-by-side, shoulders touching, like two men viewing a casket.

"So he was still alive when they put him in there," Broker said.

"I can see *that*," Soap said as a burst of frustration blew past his grated face. "They were here, man. They put him in there when my wife, my kid and I were sleeping upstairs in the shop no more'n a hundred yards away. I had two of my guys up all night playing sentry to protect me from imaginary cops. They didn't see shit. With all the snow, we can't find any tracks. Nothing. So are you ready for *this*?"

"Not exactly what we agreed to," Broker said, staring at the frozen corpse. "But here we are."

"You think?" Soap paused, literally looking Broker up and down before he continued. "So in my line of work, solving a problem requires using the correct tool. I gotta ask: Are you still the right guy for this job?"

Broker took a moment to appreciate the here-we-go-again shadow that tiptoed through his chest. *Plans collapse. People mill around in circles. Now what?*

The words—the challenge of it—came almost too easily. "You have a choice," he said, nodding toward the phone on the desk in the glass-walled office. "You make the call, and Washington County is here in five minutes."

"And this becomes a crime scene?"

"Be advised, Soap; this *is* a crime scene."

Another cloud of breath mingled in the chilly air. Soap said, "And the other choice?"

"If they *do* mean Friday, you have three days to flush out these assholes before they come after your family."

"Hmmm." Soap caressed the triangular patch of beard on his chin with a thumb and forefinger. "I sent Jan to Illinois; I don't even know where. Some Castaways owe me a favor, and they agreed to look after her. No questions asked. Actually, they're kind of flattered I'd ask them to shield my wife from 'vigilante' cops."

"They the guys outside with the shotguns?"

Soap shook his head. "Tony and Duke? They're two of my mechanics. They know about this, along with Rita and Joey. And now you. Except for Joey, they think Leper got in over his head with somebody local. I don't buy that. And I have no clue what we're up against." He toyed again with the patch of chin whiskers. "So the Castaways will protect my wife, but they won't go to war over Leper. Nobody I know would go the distance for the guy because he stiffed so many people with his dumb-ass heists. If word about this got out, nobody'd be surprised. And Tony and Duke? They're loyal, but they're, ah—"

"Stand up guys, but this is a stretch," Broker said, and all the while he was processing the scene before his eyes in terms of his job, which was to assist Soap Turrie in making his problem go away, and now the problem had just gone nuclear. It would be perfectly acceptable to walk away and hand it over to Cantrell, like a good sheep dog. But if the threat to Soap's family was real—and judging by the way Leper had met his end, it definitely was—calling in a standard police intervention could amount to signing their death warrants. And he couldn't help wondering, if he made the call to Cantrell, would they pull the plug on his undercover role? Would they stop payment on the check he'd given to Irene earlier today? He glanced back at the note in his hand, the cryptic two words, in all caps for emphasis: *WE'LL KNOW.*

Briefly he visualized Rita Turrie, eyes locked wide open, twisted on an icy bed of freezer paper.

And there was something about the way the body had been tortured that nagged him, this compelling puzzle piece that clearly fit with nothing in Soap Turrie's world.

Quietly the machinery gave him permission. *I can do this.*

But not alone.

"Why's Rita still here?" he asked as he studied the coils of rusted wire cinched tight around the corpse's wrists and ankles.

"You met my twenty-four-year-old daughter," Soap said.

"I did."

"And you think I could *make* her go? Nah. She's going to fill in, to run the office. If I sent her into hiding, I'd have to put Joey with her for security, and that would leave me with nobody really solid." Soap paused, then fixed Broker with a direct stare. "Except maybe you." More silence, more comingling of frosted breath. "So we've gone all of a sudden from nickel-dime to Big Casino. What do you think?" Soap asked.

"Two things," Broker said. "This is way bigger than a misstep by an inept thief. And whoever did this were pros. Maybe that buys us a little latitude. Second—and I'm not positive about this—but I think it's damn near impossible to establish time of death on a frozen body."

Soap judiciously digested Broker's remarks, then said, "And it looks to be a cold winter." As Broker absorbed Soap's scrutiny, he had the distinct impression the older mechanic was evaluating him like a potentially useful instrument. To figure out how he worked, if he could go the distance. Soap said, "So you're in? Just like that?"

"You, me, the BCA—we all want to know who's breathing down your neck and what they're after. And whatever Leper's failings, he didn't deserve this," Broker said. Then he stooped, flexed his cold fingers, and plucked up a round of barbed wire, rusty except for the bright, snipped ends.

"I didn't keep a lock on the freezer. They crimped that wire in the hasp to keep the lid closed after they dumped him," Soap said.

Broker held up the wire and studied it in the weak light. "I doubt these assholes carry rusty barbed wire around with them. More likely they used something that was close to hand. That you'd find around, say, an old farmhouse. Someplace remote."

Soap nodded at the freezer. "Who could stand up to that? He worked for me. He was driving my fuckin' truck. I'm next on their list."

"Too late for Leper. So where's Annie O'Neil?" Broker asked.

Soap thought about it for a few beats. "I have a pretty good idea. There's a hideout only me and her know about."

"I say again: Where is she?"

Soap exhaled. "Okay. I keep a cabin, off the books, back in the woods near Hinckley. Annie's former husband and I used it to stash certain items back in the day. That's where she ran to."

"You're sure?"

"Yes, I'm sure. We checked. You met Joey, right?" Broker nodded. Soap continued, "He doesn't normally run around dressed like an Eskimo. First thing after we found Leper, way early, I sent him north with a detailed map to go in the back way through the woods, creep the cabin real low key. There was smoke coming from the chimney. There were still signs of heavy duty tire tracks going into the pole barn."

"Did he talk to her?"

"Nope."

"Bullshit. Go all that way and not talk to her?"

Soap didn't even flinch. "Told him to stay hidden until we get a handle on what we're dealing with. I've been on the paranoid side since this morning, since I bundled off my wife. So Joey spent more time looking to see if he was being followed. He gets out and calls in. I tell him Rita missed you at the courthouse. J.T. told me you had to touch base with the sheriff's office in Grand Marais before we collected you. And he gave us your Jeep. Joey was watching for it from an on ramp south of Hinckley. Spotted you. I sent Rita straight to Grand Marais to stake out the sheriff's office. That's a lot of ground to cover, them on pay phones relaying through me at the office. Not like we do this stuff every day."

Broker searched the older man's lined face for a sign of dissembling. Nothing showed. *Make a note; never play cards with Soap Turrie.* He didn't believe for a second that Joey made that trip and didn't check on Annie's physical well-being, or on the contents of that shipping crate. *So why's he finessing it?* "You're doing fine." Broker decided not to push it, for now. "If you located Annie, we don't have to track her down. We can concentrate on the opposition," Broker said.

"Concentrate how?"

Broker sifted through possibilities, all the time overruling the gut check that kept nagging him, like rust gumming up the machinery. "Pretty simple, really," he said. "We have three days to get them before they get us."

"How the hell do we pull that off?"

"We'll need help."

"What? Cops?"

"Deal was no cops. So we'll try that way first. But if we come up empty, you might have to bring in BCA to protect your family, and that'll pretty much blow our arrangement. But we aren't there yet. If we can ID these guys, find where they live . . ." Broker's voice faded as he walked toward the enclosed office. "I need to use your phone."

Soap closed the freezer top and patted it once with a gesture that was part finality, part affection; then he removed a Yale padlock from his jacket pocket and snapped it shut on the hasp. "Okay then. Let's go use the phone in the shop where it isn't so damn cold," he said.

Chapter Fourteen

As they walked to the shop, Broker rubbed the snip of barbed wire between his thumb and forefinger like a prayer bead, as if it were trying to tell him something about the killers. Like maybe they could afford to be sloppy with Soap Turrie because he was an amateur out in the sticks who'd stumbled into something way over his head and now they had him running scared.

Which could give them a slim advantage.

Walking toward the office door, he suggested to Soap, "We should send your mechanics home to get some sleep. They have to work normal shifts, right?"

"Okay, but I'm keeping an eye on you," Soap said.

Entering the stuffy office, they were met by Rita, who sat behind the desk puffing on a joint. Seeing Broker and her dad, she set her mouth in a stubborn straight line and turned up the volume on a cassette player. Ordinarily, Broker was not immune to hearing/feeling Rosemary Butler's breakout riff on Jackson Browne's "Stay Just a Little Bit Longer" right down to his testicles.

Soap leaned over the counter, snatched the reefer from his daughter's lips, and ground it under his heel. Then he smashed off the music. He swiveled his head and glared at Joey, who sat on the sofa and just calmly held up his hands, palms out. *Not by me.*

"We have rules in the shop," Soap growled.

"Hey, Dad. What the hell's going on?" She jumped to her feet and pointed an accusing finger at Broker. "And just who is he, anyway? And don't tell me he's just another stray coming into Soap's Tough Love Ashram for Lost Boys to get his shit straight. That approach worked real good for Leper."

"Take a breath," Soap cautioned.

Rita stood her ground with her knuckles planted on her hips as her voice cut the ripe air: "This isn't some macho fist-fight at a biker picnic. Or some drunk cops making bullshit phone threats about the lame shooting all over the news. Not my favorite idea, but why aren't we calling some real cops about Leper being murdered?"

Soap made a grumbling sound deep in his throat and thrust his hand, palm open, at Broker. "Note," he said. Broker dug it out of his pocket and handed it over. "Excuse us," Soap said as he wrapped an arm over his daughter's shoulder and steered her into the back room. The door closed.

After a moment Joey said, unperturbed, "She'll be okay. She just wants to be kept in the loop."

Three minutes later the door opened and Rita entered the lobby with the note in her hand. Her eyes came at Broker like two emerald drills. "Let me get this straight: whatever Leper ripped off and gave to Annie now involves us, and if we go to the cops, they'll kill my mom?"

"Probably you first," Broker said. "And we know they don't make idle threats."

"What do they mean, 'no cops, we'll know'?" Rita asked.

"Probably they have eyes on the shop, specifically the garage out back. If a squad and an ambulance show up, they'll know. Maybe they have a scanner to monitor traffic in the county. If they have more than that, it's too damn scary to contemplate," Broker said.

"So we're going to fight them," Rita said, her eyes unwavering.

"No. We're going to identify them and then try to deal our way out of this, before anyone else gets hurt," Broker said with a patience he did not feel.

Rita glanced back at her dad, then at Joey, taking the temperature of their eyes. Then she thrust the note at Broker. "Yeah, bullshit," she said. "We're gonna fight them." Broker could detect nothing in her body language or her voice that suggested impulse or bravado.

Then she walked to the front door, opened it, and with a tiny roll of her eyes, pulled it to and fro. As she aired out the lobby, Broker took a look around to get oriented. Plate glass windows on either side opened on the dimly lit garage bays, where shadowy hydraulic lifts and dangling cables occupied the gloom like fixtures in adjoining aquariums. Soap stood in one of the entry doors with his two sentry-mechanics. He motioned Broker over.

The mechanics wore winter jackets over blue overalls, and the long night clearly showed in their faces. Their shotguns were visible, leaning against a tool caddy, deeper in the garage. Soap said, "Duke, Tony, this is Phil Broker, like we talked about." Fast handshakes; Duke, the bigger one with the beard, had a vice grip for a hand. Tony was shorter, tight-knit. Soap continued, "From now on, Broker, Joey and I will handle the nights. We'll try to run the shop as usual unless it gets too crazy. And we keep what's in that freezer on the quiet side—for now."

The two men nodded. "We need to tidy up some stuff," Tony said; then he turned and pointed toward the shotguns. "They're still loaded. Where do you want them?"

"Leave them. I'll put them in the office," Soap said. Then as they turned to leave, he added, "And boys, I won't forget this."

When they were alone, Soap walked into the dark garage to retrieve the shotguns, sweeping his hand along a wall panel of switches. The overhead lights popped on, bringing the tool stations and overhead girders and ducts into sharp relief.

"Huh." Broker stopped in mid-stride. The far wall jumped into focus and became a wide, vibrant, floor-to-ceiling mural. For two seconds he stared, pleasantly dumfounded. Then he laughed because it was fun, as the sharks gathered, to experience being amazed.

"Yeah." Soap suppressed a smile at Broker's reaction. "That's our conversation piece."

Broker was looking at a pretty damn good recreation of a 1930s Socialist Realist masterpiece. And not for the first time. The forceful industrial palette—gray of muscle and steel, chemical yellows in the steam—portrayed men and machines intertwined in the stolid fury of mass-producing automobiles. Fords, actually—a perfect backdrop for turning wrenches and pulling transmissions. "That's the production line at River Rouge, in Dearborn, Michigan," he said.

"Correct." Soap sounded a bit surprised. "Rita's idea of classing up the joint," he minimized in a breezy voice to conceal a lump of pride. "Merit Project. Took her four months, her senior year in high school, up on a scaffold every night."

Broker inclined his head toward the mural. "Rita did that?"

"Yep. It's taken from a famous mural."

"Uh huh, Diego Rivera's Court at the Detroit Institute of Arts. I've seen the original," said Broker, fighting an urge to take it as *a sign*. He'd viewed those murals over numerous Sunday mornings when he lived in Motown. They'd sit in that court and nurse hangovers, him and a guy he hoped like hell still shot pool on Tuesday night. So don't overthink it; but still, you know, it added an elusive shiver of fate. *We don't believe in shit like that*, the machinery was quick to point out.

Soap picked up the shotguns and called to Broker over his shoulder, "Catch the lights on the way out."

Broker hit the switches, and the mural vanished. Soap stowed the shotguns behind the counter. Joey and Rita were waiting. "So after Tony and Duke go home, it's the four of us," Rita said.

Broker took a moment to re-evaluate her rough-tough veneer now that he'd been schooled about the casual talent she packed in her hip pocket. "I'm going to try to bring in a trained guy I know," he said.

"A mercenary? Like you?" she asked.

"I wouldn't say that. He's picky who he works for."

Unconvinced, she shot a glance at her dad, who acknowledged with a subtle nod.

"Okay? We good?" Broker checked their faces. Joey showed no reaction. Rita remained watchful. He continued, "Things could get intense. Might not be a lot of sleep the next few days, so we need some go-pills. Speed. The cleaner the better. Can you handle that?"

Rita glanced at Soap, who merely raised his eyebrows. "I can do that," she said.

After an interval, Broker lowered his voice. "And Rita, that's some mural you put up in there."

"That was high school," Rita said with a hint of her dad's ineffable expression coming to her eyes. "Look around; *school's out*." She turned and walked through the doorway beyond the counter.

Broker faced Joey. "Stick around. I'm going to need a ride a little later, to this address." He took out his wallet and handed Andrea Sabic's card to Joey.

"East Sixth, that's in Minneapolis, student housing near the university," Joey said, his eyes flitting from Soap back to Broker, who pointed to the snowmobile suit and outsized boots.

"You'll need to lose the astronaut outfit," Broker said.

Joey handed back the card and said, "I have some street clothes upstairs."

After Joey left, Broker sat down behind the counter and placed the twisted piece of barbed wire on the desktop. His eyes caught on a framed photo propped in the corner: a younger Soap in a garish Hawaiian shirt, palm trees in the background, poolside, it looked like. A handsome, dark-haired woman in a bikini top leaned against him, and that would be Jan, the absent wife. They were hugging a ten- or eleven-year-old Rita, who tin-grinned through braces.

Okaay. He cleared away the workaday office clutter: a scheduling book, handwritten carbon invoices, a credit card swipe machine. Then he folded over the top sheet of the desk blotter to a clean page. He thumbed through the meager contents of his wallet and placed Andrea's card beside the phone. Next, he removed another card: The Alcove Lounge, on Woodward Avenue in Detroit, just off the Wayne State campus. He looked up at the wall clock: 10:05 pm. Detroit was an hour ahead.

"Of course you know what you're doing?" Soap asked, resting his heavy forearms over the counter.

"Old Vietnamese proverb," Broker said. "To charge Hell with a bucket of water, you need a dude named Harry Griffin. Cross your fucking fingers."

He dialed the number, reminding himself not to mention his intriguing encounter with the Rivera mural. Harry, while fascinated with magic as metaphor, had little faith in it out in the real world. *C'mon.* He counted under his breath because Harry—part time PI, sometime freelance photographer and full time Merry Trickster—kept a low profile and only took phone calls at the bar. No other way to reach him. Two thousand. Three thousand. "Alcove." A female voice picked up. He visualized Paulette, the night manager, quick behind the bar in her signature blue dress and white nurse's shoes. As usual, she sounded harried but efficient.

"Hey Paulette, it's Phil Broker. Been awhile."

The Alcove was superficially a college hangout, but back in the day, it had come with a deep bench of cops, ex-cops, lawyers and scarred veterans from the early, bloody days of the UAW and Teamsters. Only the most jaded of that crowd still ventured out, to knock back shots and shells and to transact quiet, mostly legal, business on the solitary pool table at the back of the establishment. Paulette, adept at reading the score-cards of all her customers, dispensed with pleasantries and immediately put it together.

"You're in luck. He's here, shooting pool," she said.

"Nine ball?"

"Yep. Money game."

Broker breathed a little easier. "So he's drinking . . ."

"Yep. Black coffee. Hold tight and I'll grab his skinny ass."

Broker engaged Soap's impassive face as he took a moment to savor the background bar chatter coming through the connection. The same retro jukebox still throbbed the same oldies. "Stop in the Name of Love" ending. Kenny Rogers, "Ruby, Don't Take Your Love to Town" starting up. The bar was Harry's nostalgia fortress while outside, on the street, the Fall of Detroit was fueled by white flight, closing factories and gangbanger turf wars. Harry had this theory that if he stayed in that bar and played that old juke long enough, he could drink his way back to the early sixties.

"Shit, man, I thought you'd been eaten by bears up in the fuckin' woods." The voice came on the line equal parts flawed and fearless: pure, upbeat, in-your-face Detroit. Broker had to grin. They were two cats down to their ninth lives.

"Detroit Harry. What it is." Broker put a little juice into his flat, upper Midwest accent.

"You get lonely on your exile up in the sticks? Your night light burn out or what?" Harry said.

"I've got a situation, man. I need to call in a marker."

"So this isn't a social call? You never were any good at foreplay, you know that," Harry said. "Or so say a long list of women who gave up on you and came to me for relief." After a pause, Harry turned serious. "So how bad?"

"I'm real jammed up on a real short time line."

"This involve trans-Pacific flights and a gray helicopter full of Double O Globe?"

"Nah, nothing like that. I'm in St. Paul, the eastern suburbs actually."

"You, in the suburbs? That I gotta see. And?"

"Long story. Best not explained on the phone. I need somebody from the outside who can be invisible to track some folks, snap some pictures."

"Uh huh."

"Except I don't know who they are."

"I see. So when's this supposed to happen?"

"I need you to catch the first thing smoking and be here like tomorrow. Drive or grab a plane, whatever's quickest."

Long exhale in Detroit. "And you want me to bring my shit." Pause. "All my shit, right?"

"I assume you still keep your hand in."

"Yeah, I still job out off and on. Okay. Got it. So you're working again?"

"Something like that. Take a couple numbers."

"Roger. Wait one. Okay, send it."

Broker gave Harry the business number off the front of Soap's office phone. Then he read off Andrea Sabic's home office phone. "Call the first number when you get your travel arrangements figured out and have an ETA. You can trust whoever answers."

"And the second number?"

"That's who'll be driving you around." *Except she doesn't know it yet.* "Neither of us knows the territory; we need the locals."

"Uh huh, so no idea who's the target?"

"Could be the Colombian bobsled team."

"Never a dull moment." Harry paused. "Okay. This is going to cost me big time. I have to call in a major favor on short notice. But I'll get on the horn to a guy I know who owes me, and he has a private plane. No way I can bring all my stuff through baggage check at a commercial airline. I'll call when I have an ETA." Harry hung up.

*　　*　　*

After he placed the receiver back on the cradle, Broker said, "He's on his way." Then he stood up, grabbed his jacket, pulled on his cap and gloves, and said, "We need to take a walk."

"Sure. Look, Rita's cool. Just sometimes she overplays the tough stuff. Maybe 'cause she's scared."

"She's fine," Broker said, not unkindly. "We just need to dial down the murder in her eyes."

"Okay. I'm on it. So tell me about the guy you called."

Broker chuckled. "Harry? He's a low-rent version of the End of the World."

"Just what we need, huh?" Soap sighed.

When Joey came back into the lobby dressed in a Navy-issue winter parka and a black watch cap, Broker asked him to cover the phone. Then Broker and Soap stepped out into the still-blowing snow and turned up their collars.

Broker scanned the apartment units across the way that looked like low-income housing. An office complex rose on higher ground to the west across a snow-beaten field. Empty lots to the east ended at a Standard station on the corner of Greeley.

"They probably have eyes in those buildings across the street. I would," Broker said as he watched Tony and Duke start their cars and brush snow off their windshields. *Good,* he thought; *when Joey pulls out, with him down in the back seat, it'll look like another guy heading home.*

But he was getting ahead of himself. As they plodded along the chain-link fence, Broker said, "I assume, after you found Leper, you made some calls?"

"I did, of an indirect nature," Soap said. "Mainly I talked to Hector Garza over on the west side of St Paul. He runs a restaurant where your more discerning Mexican gangsters hang out. Leper had a bad run-in with those guys last year on a gun deal that went south. It cost me some, to straighten that mess out. He said he'd ask around to see if anybody has seen Leper or my truck."

"You think the Mexicans had it in for Leper?"

"They're the only folks in the metro who sometimes add extra flourishes to killing people. But it feels off. Hector would have dumped the body in my driveway, not a meat locker. And he wouldn't have returned my call."

"You tell him about finding the body?"

"No, man; I told him Leper had disappeared with my dump truck and I wanted it back."

Broker nodded. With Harry in the mix, he evolved the plan out of thin air. "You need to call him again and set a meet. We need someplace remote, in the open, with good sight lines and only one road in. Be good if it also had a pay phone. We're also going to need somebody who can develop film and make prints anytime, day or night."

"Let me think," Soap drew it out. "What's the play?"

"We may have an edge if these assholes think we're small town rubes. So we give them what they want, we act suitably scared shitless, follow their instructions, drop everything and start looking for Annie. So you line up people to meet you in a location where you feel safe talking, so it looks like you're following through, beating the bushes with the usual suspects."

"And your Detroit buddy sets up to see who's watching us," Soap said slowly.

"Correct. We get their cars, their faces, and follow them back to their nest. We get the info to Cantrell at BCA. He runs interference. You bring in Annie."

Soap considered it for a moment, then asked, "So what do you need?"

"At least three cars linked by commo. That's Harry's department."

"You and me can take a car. We'll put Joey in another. I'm not comfortable with putting Duke or Tony in the third car, and I assume you want to keep your Detroit guy walled off from us, right? That leaves him blind. He won't know the road grid."

"I'm working on that, but we're pretty thin on the ground," Broker said.

"Sorry to disappoint you and your cop pals, but my guys are top line mechanics, not gangsters. They have families."

Except for maybe Joey, who seemed to be a big cut above the rest, Broker reflected. "So where's Rita fit in?"

"She runs the shop. I'll bring in some temp mechanics with me and Joey off the clock."

"You know, she has quite a grip, even for an athletic, ah, painter."

Soap shrugged. "For a day job, she manages some real estate I own. In a pinch she fills in as a spare mechanic. She's been turning wrenches since she was twelve."

"Uh huh. So just how legit is the car shop, the landscaping? How much is a front for something else?"

Soap's face reacted with the first spontaneous expression of the night, somewhere in the range of an indignant reformed pirate and prodigal son. "Hey, my shop and other ventures? They're ninety-nine percent straight up." Then he actually relaxed and grinned. "But I do supplement my inventory from time to time with moonlight packing."

Broker stopped and peered through the snow-clogged chain links. "And these other ventures involve building materials." He pointed through the fence. "That's a pile of really fancy shingles, along with plywood decking and lumber."

Soap's demeanor changed subtly, and Broker could imagine him exchanging his denim for a sport jacket and standing in front of a microphone, addressing a roomful of people in that deep voice. "Well, I am involved in some real estate. I have a partner, and we plan to restore old homes here in town. There's this theory I subscribe to that development is going to shift from the west metro and spread out our way. Ten years from now Stillwater is going to be a tourist destination. Plus, people are figuring out that they can live out here, where they don't have to drive east to work in the Cities, with the sun in their eyes. Things are kind of on hold—the inflation, the high interest rates on mortgages—but I'm betting it'll settle down."

"That's great. We'll have a chat sometime about the relative merits of interest rates and the free market. But right now, do me a favor. Don't give that speech to Merriweather, because he'll mistake you for a gung ho taxpayer and end our association. But the thing is," Broker said, "I'm calling in a major chit reaching out to Harry, to ah, help you with your situation."

"Yeah," Soap said cautiously, his sanguine developer façade resetting to the immediate world of death threats and frozen bodies.

"In Merriweather's bio, it says you were in the 506th Parachute Infantry at Bastogne. What battalion?"

Soap's eyes narrowed to a squint. "Charlie company, Third Bat."

"Uh huh." After taking a pull on his smoke, Broker said, "My dad was in the second battalion, same time, same place."

"Where are you going with this?"

"Well, the old man has a tube jammed up his dick attached to a leg bag after surgery for bladder cancer. So he's not real spry at the moment, and he and Mom run these seven cabins up on the north shore. I've been meaning to repair the roofs on those cabins, but now I'm down here with you."

"Seven cabins."

"Yeah, not real big cabins either. They could all use new roofs."

Soap cleared his throat. "Well, it so happens those shingles you're eyeing were one of Leper's few successful jobs, so you could say I acquired them at a considerable discount."

"So, if we come out of this alive—" Broker speculated.

"We come out of this alive, I'll come up to do an estimate, and we'll talk about bringing in a crew in the spring," Soap said.

"Those cabins are going to need decking, too."

"Of course, with Leper's midnight plywood," Soap chuckled. He removed his glove, and they shook on it.

Chapter Fifteen

At 11:15 Broker was back on the office phone calling Andrea Sabic's home number. Five rings. Six. Joey was pulling a different car, a Ford Bronco, into one of the garage bays so Broker could climb in the back seat unobserved, if, in fact, they were being watched. Six rings. Seven.

C'mon.

Eight. Finally she picked up, sounding foggy. "Andrea Sabic."

"Hey, Andrea, how are you doing?"

"Who is this?"

"Phil Broker. We talked this morning. You said to call as soon as I hit town."

"I didn't mean at midnight."

"It's a good forty minutes until midnight," Broker said. "Look, I'm jammed up and I need to see you."

"Ah, okay; let me check my calendar. I might have an opening tomorrow afternoon."

"I was thinking more like half an hour at your place."

"Ah—wait a minute." Her voice tightened.

"Andrea, you can't have it both ways—come off like a hard ass in a holding cell at Washington County, then get cold feet out on the street."

"Get cold feet?" The sharp edge to her voice told Broker she was now all the way awake.

"Put on some coffee. I'll be right over."

"I'm in the upstairs apartment," she said after a long silence that Broker worried could go either way. As he hung up the receiver, he let his eyes go wide for a beat. J.T. and Cantrell were grabbing at straws. Now he was too. *Just that I have this hunch about her . . .*

Soap asked, "How'd it go?"

Broker grinned. "She's my shrink. I think I can get her to chauffeur Harry around, give him a place to lay low. Like you said, we don't want him anywhere near this place, linked to us."

"Wait a minute—*your what?*"

"It's not that complicated. She's my off-the-record connect with BCA, and I wouldn't be here if she didn't sign off on basically a secret operation. And now we're in a secret jam. Involve too many outsiders, it ain't a secret anymore." Broker took the note from his pocket, smoothed it on the blotter, and pointed to the words NO COPS. WE'LL KNOW. He looked directly at Soap. "Eventually you're going to tell me what's in that damn box. Question is whether it's big enough to buy cops and judges?"

When Soap maintained his impassive expression and remained silent, Broker pocketed the note and said, "She's not in the operational loop. She's just a relay station. If things get dicey I want her close, to call in the dogs direct, on our terms, our timing; not theirs."

"A relay station," Soap repeated.

"That's right, so let's make her *our* relay station." Broker stood up and pocketed the note. "And line up somebody with a darkroom. Make sure Rita scores those go pills, and find me that stakeout location." He tapped Andrea's number on the blotter. "Call me if Harry gets back with an ETA in the next hour." Then he opened the door to the darkened shop area where Joey was waiting in the Bronco.

It didn't surprise Broker that Joey was an accomplished wheel man, to include working jigsaws and keeping an eye out for a tail. When he was sure they weren't being followed, he told Broker to climb into the front seat. Quietly Joey explained the route: Highway 36 to Interstate 35, where they turned off on the 4th Street/University exit. Moments later they were creeping along poorly lit, unplowed, residential side streets to the west side of the University of Minnesota.

Andrea was located in a green, wood frame Victorian that had a security door and two mailboxes. The windows on the lower floor were dark, but the upstairs lights were on, and Broker glimpsed a shadow patrolling behind the curtains.

"Probably there's a porch and stairs around back," Joey said. "If we're being snooped, be best to avoid the street and go up that way. I'll drop you up the block, and you can work your way back through the yards." Clearly, in addition to being a reliable driver, Joey had some experience with casing houses.

Around the corner, as he got out of the car, Broker handed Andrea's card to Joey and told him, "Find a pay phone and call me in half an hour about a ride back." Then he was out on the street, where he paused to let his eyes adjust to the dark. And to let the machinery finish its lecture: *You know she's too risky. You're rolling those self-destructive bones again. You think you see a handle. You think you can* recruit *her?*

Broker ranged his eyes over the dark street and nodded. *Yes, I do.* Then he picked his way through the backyards, skirting garages and fences until he came to the rear of the house. Joey had guessed right: there was a porch with a stairway leading up to the second story. Broker padded up the steps and rapped his knuckles on the rear door.

First, the curtain inside the window to the left of the door parted as she made sure of the identity of her late night visitor. Broker heard the chain security lock release, and then Andrea opened the door. Backlit by an overhead ring of fluorescent lights, she stood in the doorway wearing a green terrycloth robe and slippers. Head cocked to the side, her face was still slightly puffy, and her hair was hand-combed, not quite in place. But she was awake enough to narrow her eyes and plant her fists on her hips in an unmistakable statement:

It's midnight.

This is where I live.

It better be good!

"I really need your help," Broker said through the ajar storm door.

She pushed open the outer door and scrutinized him as he entered the kitchen. "As a general rule, I don't bring my work home with me," she said, tart and to the point.

"Sorry. Couldn't wait."

"Your beat-up face is all over the papers. And you look like you slept in those clothes," she said.

"Guilty," he said as he closed the door behind him and stamped snow off his boots on the doormat. The kitchen was minimal and efficient: a small table, two chairs, clean Formica counters, a scrubbed stainless steel sink, and a dish drainer that held one upturned wine glass. She hadn't moved when he entered the room, so now they stood close enough to feel each other's breath.

"And you still smell like the Washington County Jail," she said as she removed her fists from her hips and crossed her arms tightly across her chest. One slipper tapped on the varnished hardwood floor. She smelled like toothpaste, Listerine and a faint under scent of wine. But the other aroma in the kitchen was encouraging, brewing up from an electric percolator.

And their faces were six inches apart.

The hour was late. He fairly pulsed with urgency. The sheer physical proximity amped the kitchen with enough electricity to jolt Frankenstein to a sitting position. They reflexively stepped back. *Interesting,* the machinery reflected, *you both mistrust spontaneity.*

141

And Broker wasn't sure. Did a kiss *really* almost threaten to erupt like a shiver with no place else to go? But he *was* sure that their faces would fit together. She'd taste like toothpaste, mouthwash, wine and tongue.

Andrea unfolded her arms, placed her palm on Broker's chest, and used the pressure to push herself away. He watched her eyes briefly savor this new cushion of physical tension between them.

Broker's eyes went up in an apologetic head shrug. "We were standing too close. Charged particles. Opposites attract."

"So now you're a physicist? Where're you going with this?"

"Not sure," he fumbled. "A buddy reminded me just an hour ago I'm not real good at foreplay."

"Very funny. So what do you want at twelve midnight? A call to Cantrell?"

Broker's smile came out on the tight side. "Actually, what I need from you sort of skirts the realm of law enforcement."

Her eyes braced, and her voice took on some of the neutral whetstone buffing the professional edge. "I don't recall that being part of the deal."

Now it all depended on playing one card, and his gut. "You're a trauma specialist, right? But there's something important missing from your resume," he said.

Seconds passed as they fell into that exploratory eye contact that had set all this in motion. After an interval, she asked slowly, "And that is?"

"The personal sharing of danger," he said. "You walk a couple miles in my shoes, it might fill in some blanks."

A very expressive "Huh?" came from her lips, equal parts startle and quick study. She stared at him. "You're not kidding."

"No, ma'am."

Her eyes flared ever so slightly, and the faintest crimson crept in her cheeks. She sidestepped to the sink and spit into it. Then she took three stylized steps backwards.

"Is that a yes or a no?" Broker was impressed.

"Old Serbian custom I learned from my Nona when I was a kid. If a black cat crosses your path, you spit and take three steps back to ward off a curse."

Broker smiled. *So far so good.*

Chapter Sixteen

"Jesus, Broker, first day on the job and you're in trouble already?" Andrea recovered quickly.

"Not me. Soap Turrie. And I thought you might find the trouble part worth observing."

Andrea laughed. "Don't presume. And don't flatter yourself. You were doing better with the stuff missing from the resume." She paused and affected a wry smile. "You're right about that, you know. We really don't know what we're talking about downrange. We just sit in our safe little offices under our framed degrees."

It was more than boldness he witnessed in her eyes. *She really wants to know what's out there. Like an analyst who yearns for a whiff of the field.* So he watched her think about it and maybe re-arrange a goalpost or two. *Yes.*

"You're really up shit creek?" she asked.

"Big time."

"What do you have in mind?"

"I really appreciate this," Broker said.

"No, you really need this," she said. "Needing falls short of appreciation." She took a step closer. "So why my doorstep?"

"This showed up in Soap's mailbox." Broker removed the note from his pocket and handed it to her.

Her brow furrowed as she read. She looked up. "What do they mean? 'No cops, we'll know'?"

"Not sure. Could mean they're monitoring police traffic. Probably they're watching Soap, and that includes me. Soap's worried enough to send his wife out of town."

"But you think it could be more?" she asked slowly, handing the note back.

"It's a possibility. So going to law isn't my first thought."

"But you're talking to me." Their eyes locked.

"Yes I am. And I came over here hiding in the back seat, and I don't know anybody south of Duluth. So I'm bringing in a friend from the outside, unconnected to Soap or anybody else. He's good, but he needs a driver. It wouldn't be anything heavy. Low-key surveillance."

"Like a stakeout." She mulled it. "I've been on stakeouts." She was back to the wry smile.

"Thing is, Harry won't know the roads. Hell. I don't know the roads."

"Harry?"

"Yeah. One day, two days max." Broker's forced Cheshire smile brought Andrea to the brink of laughter.

"Christ, Broker, you're tap dancing."

"Yes, ma'am. On a razor blade. Fast as I can."

"So drop everything, clear my calendar and call in sick? Jesus, my folks are expecting me for Thanksgiving in Alexandria." She paused and inclined her head. "And what's *Harry* doing while I'm driving him around?"

"Getting into position to take pictures of the people who are pressuring Soap Turrie about their missing stuff. So we can ID them for Cantrell."

"So it's already going," she said, more serious, as she moved to the counter, opened a cupboard door, selected two cups, and poured coffee from the percolator. Then she handed him a steaming mug, turned and nodded toward the living room.

He unzipped his jacket but didn't remove it. Then he put his coffee on the table and, in deference to her spotless housekeeping, unlaced his beat-up winter boots and placed them near her neatly lined-up footwear next to the back door.

"How long has it been since you've done that, I wonder?" she said, looking back.

"Hey, I always leave my boots at the door. But usually not in a place like this," he added as he followed her into the main room that was Zen-spare, with lots of hardwood floor, a small Oriental carpet, a dark leather couch, and one comfortable matching chair. The color scheme ran to subtle grays with accents of black and ornate red twining through the rug. A portable telephone attached to a long cord sat on the low table in front of the couch. Broker noted the album cover, Miles Davis, *Kind of Blue*, propped against the low table that held the stereo.

An alcove opened off the main room and held a desk, file cabinets, and a Selectric typewriter on a side table. Tall snake plants hedged the alcove like a spiked perimeter, and Broker recalled that Irene had told him that snake plants were damn near indestructible. They'd grow in the dark.

A hallway led, Broker suspected, to the bathroom and the bedroom. He turned his attention back to her office space, where two black-and-white posters faced each other on the walls to either side of the desk. One was Sigmund Freud. The other was B.F. Skinner.

He raised his cup at the posters. "Jung didn't make the cut into your fan club? Probably a little too hippy-dippy for you. So whose side do you come down on? Freud or Skinner?"

Andrea perked up. "I'm surprised you know Skinner," she said.

Broker shrugged. "I was one of his guinea pigs. Basic training, sixty-six; every other word they had us scream was 'kill.'"

"Not bad. So you're into psychology?" she asked.

Broker shook his head. "Not me. I've just spent a lot of time watching people. Mom was the psychology major. Sometime after her master's she switched to a sister pseudoscience, astrology."

"Must be where the Jung comes from." Andrea saluted with her cup as she deftly took a seat on the couch and primly tucked her legs under her. Broker sat in the comfy chair across from her. "So," she said, "you usually take girls on a clandestine op for a first date?" Playing it sardonic, the bemused, improbable gun moll.

"I need you to listen carefully," Broker said, his tone downshifting, the machinery kicking in, metal on metal. "The guys after Soap aren't local. *They're—real—dangerous—people.* You know what they did to Norman Bolin."

"I do. And you don't think it's Cantrell time?" she asked, watching him carefully as she blew steam from her cup.

Broker took a moment and considered whether a shrink licensed to testify for state and county police agencies was an officer of the court. If he told her about the contents of Soap's freezer, would she be compelled, by more than ethics, to immediately report it? Carefully he parsed his reply. "They haven't made a move directly on Soap personally yet, just sent him the ultimatum."

Full frontal Andrea eyes: "Have you done anything like this before?"

Broker shrugged. "It's recon 101. But we don't know the area, the road net. That's where you come in."

Andrea leaned forward on the couch, placing the cup on the table with one hand, instinctively gathering the front of her robe with the other. "Okay, but I have one condition," she said, extending her hand and summoning him closer with a curl of her fingers.

Broker came forward and was reminded that rural Vietnamese summoned animals—and Americans—with that palm up gesture. People were signaled palm down. "Yeah?" he said.

She eased the sleeve of his jacket and sweater up on his forearm and gently tapped the whitish scar tissue. "You tell me what this is all about."

Broker continued to be impressed with her inside moves. "Deal," he said, "but when it cools down. After."

Andrea exhaled and settled back into the couch, now holding her cup with both hands. "So threats against family, and you still want to keep Cantrell out of the loop?"

Broker held out mollifying hands. "We're just going to work the edges. Get pictures. Soap had a deal. No cops up front. That was my deal, too."

"Oh, yes," Andrea said slowly. "I was there when we went out on a limb to put you in play. Wouldn't do if you fell on your ass right out of the gate. We all rise and fall together in this little adventure." Then she rallied and said, "So who's this Harry you're sticking me with?"

"Harry Griffin. He's flying in from Detroit."

"Detroit? Do I have to worry about my major appliances disappearing?"

"Not if he's sober," Broker said.

"Great. So who is he?"

"Remember the story about the helicopter?"

"Yes."

"Harry's the other guy who helped me swipe it."

"Riiight." She drew it out. "So what's he like?"

Broker couldn't resist a merry twitch to his eyebrows. "Harry and I are opposites. You might say he's vulgar and erratic and, ah, brilliant."

Now amusement replaced the doubt in her eyes. "Which makes you?" she asked.

Broker tried for gravitas as he held his right hand chest level, palm down, absolutely steady. About two seconds into Andrea's fit of nervous laughter, the phone on the coffee table rang, and Broker immediately snatched it up.

Chapter Seventeen

Broker gestured for writing materials that Andrea immediately provided from her desk. He wrote while Soap talked. "He'll be coming in on a private plane, a Cessna 210. In fact, everything about it sounds private. He's going to land at the Lake Elmo strip, runway 33. Shit, Broker, that's just down the road from me. I thought you wanted to keep him at a distance."

"Probably the pilot has an arrangement with somebody at that airport."

"What kind of arrangement?"

"Your kind of arrangement, the kind that involves contraband and no paperwork."

"Wonderful. He expects to touch down at five a.m. our time."

"Got it."

"And Rita has a line on an old high school buddy who's a hobby photographer. He has a home darkroom here in town. And I have a location that might work."

Broker said, "I'll be back as soon as Joey picks me up." He hung up the phone and handed Andrea the flight information. "You're collecting him up at the Lake Elmo Airport. You know it?"

"Lake Elmo? Sure. But, Christ, Broker, that's clear across town, right next door to Stillwater."

Broker actually sighed. "I'm sure Harry will have a reason that probably involves calling in a favor from a pilot." He blew out the bottom of the sigh. "Who makes selective contraband runs."

"I guess. So how will I ID him?"

"He'll recognize you. You'll be wearing a beret, sunglasses and this big name tag that says 'Natasha.'" Broker managed to keep a straight face for about two seconds before he gave her his best dead-pan grin. Then he went to the side of the couch where she kept old newspapers in a wire caddy. He plucked up the front section of yesterday's *Star Tribune*, the one with his booking picture above the fold. "Just tuck that in the crook of your arm. And give him a head start on the background."

A moment later he was at her back door, pulling on and tying his boots. "In a few minutes a soft-spoken man named Joey will call your number. Tell him to pick me up on the street where he dropped me off." Then he opened the back door and zipped up his jacket. "Try to grab a few hours' sleep before you leave for the airstrip. I'll be back around six thirty."

She reached out and tugged the shoulder of his jacket. "You know what you're doing, right?" she asked.

"I missed that part of the job description you and Cantrell dreamed up for me." He grinned. Andrea didn't conceal the concern that washed across her eyes, so Broker dropped the loose tone. "Andrea, we're going to keep Soap and his wife and daughter alive. We call Cantrell in before we figure out who's after Soap, there's a good chance they're dead. Can you abide with that?"

"Abide." Andrea repeated the word like she'd never heard it before.

Broker squeezed her elbow. "Hang in there," he said, then pulled the door shut behind him. "Phew." He sagged momentarily at the top of the stairs. *Congratulations. Your plan's made out of bubble gum and fucking Popsicle sticks,* the machinery opined. Which was true. But it was also true that a tornado can blow a Popsicle stick clear through a brick wall.

Phil Broker turned up his collar and went down the stairs and disappeared into the night.

Ten minutes from Stillwater he climbed into the back seat. Joey pulled the Bronco into an open garage bay, and Broker exited the car in darkness.

When he entered the lobby, Soap was bent over the phone at the counter, the blotter under his elbows chicken-tracked with phone numbers and rough sketches. Eyeing Broker, he ended the call and pointed to a box of take-out pizza on the counter. Munching on cold pepperoni and cheese, Broker came around to Soap's side. As he did, Soap rapped a knuckle on a hand drawn diagram. "Pine Point" labeled a square set in a web of lines marked with numbers—55, Co. 7—that looked like county roads.

"This is Pine Point Park, about four miles north of town," Soap explained. "A state hiking trail starts there and runs all the way to St. Paul. The parking lot only has one entrance. There's a restroom and a pay phone." He scrawled wooly circles around the perimeter of the square. "Tree lines for cover. Cross country ski trails you can move on unseen behind the trees." He looked up expectantly.

Broker studied the sketch. A hand drawn map was not the terrain. "I'd like to go out and have a look, but there's a chance we might be followed. You sure of the layout?"

"Taught Rita to ski there. I'm sure," said Soap. He reached down and opened a desk drawer and removed a plastic pill bottle that contained black capsules. "And this is some power-ful shit: pharmaceutically pure Dexedrine." He snapped the pills down on the counter.

Broker, suddenly ravenous, reached for another piece of pizza. He crossed to the water cooler, drew a cup and drained it. *Keep an eye on dehydration,* he reminded himself. "So who's going to show up at the park?" he asked.

"I'm thinking Hector Garza from the west side. And a dude named Heywood Tyrell from St. Paul. But we have to stagger them. Heywood runs the Disciples franchise in St. Paul, and they tend to start shooting at Hector's colleagues when they don't have the Mississippi separating them. Plus Heywood's sister, Charlene, runs an after-hours joint where she and Leper used to meet up. Heywood strongly suggested she knows something." Soap paused and probed his bloodshot eyes with his fingers.

"You've been busy," Broker said.

"Yeah. The meets are set at two thirty and four in the afternoon. That way your guy can scout the location in the morning and set in. I just talked to a contact in the Castaways, but he begged off. Said something doesn't feel right. Like he didn't want to talk on the phone. I'm not sure what that means." After a pause, Soap said, "So what about the morning?"

Broker grimaced and rubbed his fingers against the thick stubble on his cheek, getting a whiff of three days unwashed. "We're kind of dependent on Harry and what he brings, commo wise. We'll need time to get organized."

"Look, man, it's your plan, but it's my ground, my people," Soap said. "So, after you settle your boy in, I suggest that you and me drive over to St. Paul, head up West Seventh Street, and have a face to face with Murph, Annie O'Neil's bar manager. It's the logical first move for somebody who's panicked and looking for her. Joey can trail us and keep an eye out."

Broker shrugged. "Sure. Might get lucky."

The lobby lights switched off as Soap said, "Take a load off; grab a seat." Broker flopped into a leather chair next to the window. Soap appeared, holding out a bottle of beer; then he sat in the adjoining chair with a can of ginger ale.

"Saturday night I was sitting right here with J.T. Merriweather," Soap mused. "They took his badge and gun, suspended him for jumping you. Said on the news he'll be charged out here. Wilson's off critical and is listed in serious but stable condition. Don't know about the female deputy with the knee. And I read in the paper they're burying Desmond Friday. I doubt he'll get the cathedral and the bagpipes." Soap shook his head. "And Norman Bolin made the Sunday's paper, this teeny news brief. 'Mutilated fingers, gang related.'"

They sipped their drinks. Shadows cast by snow streaming past the parking lot lights crawled on their faces.

Soap finished his can of soda and said, "Should try to grab some Z's before the Detroit guy's plane comes in. There's cots upstairs in the lunchroom. I'll take the first watch, then hand it over to Joey." But Broker only half heard. His mind had wandered back to the freezer, to the methodical sadism that had ended Leper's life. Was the puzzle piece becoming clearer? Or was he reaching? Because he'd seen people cut like that before.

When Broker finished his beer, Soap directed him to the stairs to the upper level, where a lunchroom on one end and an office on the other anchored the layout. In between, rows of shelving held motor manuals. Fan belts and other equipage hung from pegboard walls. The table had been removed from the lunchroom and now leaned against the pegboard to create space for a crash pad. Inside, a subdued Rita sat on an Army cot wearing a black armless T-shirt and yoga shorts. More cots were jammed in a U-shape around the walls in a jumble of blankets, pillows and sleeping bags. A stack of bath towels and a small TV sat on a counter next to the refrigerator. His gun cases and travel bag were stowed under the cot across from her.

Twirling an unlit cigarette in her fingers, she contemplated the static sizzle of a test pattern on the TV screen. As Broker entered, she hopped up and turned off the TV. Lithe definition rippled in her bare arms and thighs.

"Hope you don't mind the co-ed dorm, but we're kind of cramped for space. I tried to talk Dad into getting mattresses, like in *The Godfather*. But he went for cots."

And it occurred to Broker that, with Andrea, there was the suggestion of hidden softness that intimacy might reveal. Rita looked like she'd rather make mud pies.

"You're staring," she said with an impish, freckled smile. "Maybe because you're tired. Maybe because I'm not bad looking."

Broker went with number two. She looked like she could break your heart or just as easily knock you down. "Tired," he said, and flopped on an unused cot and began unlacing his boots.

His fingers fumbled in a spasm of fatigue, and she was there, graceful and efficient, kneeling, removing his boots. "Take a break. Lay down and I'll work out some of the kinks," she commanded.

Won't argue. He fell facedown onto the canvas cot, and a moment later she was removing his sweater and then his undershirt. She repositioned and sat, crowding his hips as her fingers pressed into the muscles of his back. Her touch paused on scar tissue, exploring hieroglyphics from another world. "This'll knock you out, guaranteed five minutes," she said.

In the close air Broker could smell her musky patchouli now mixed with raw burrs of nervous sweat. He felt the warmth radiate from her bare thigh as she leaned her whole weight into kneading the tension in his neck, the occipital ridge.

Rita said, "Don't get any ideas, Cowboy. I'm off men this season. All you bastards want is one thing these days."

"Huh?" Broker attempted to lift his head, but he had given himself permission to relax and he was already drifting off.

"Problem with giving good head is you never get laid anymore."

Broker didn't hear; her knowing fingers had sunk him into oblivion.

Chapter Eighteen

A t six a.m. Broker and Joey were bumper to bumper on 35E in an icy fog of auto exhaust. Blinking red taillights and pale headlights formed the scales of a sluggish serpent winding to and from the vague spires of Minneapolis. All around them the planet's biggest functioning winter road net was going to work. Broker had a travel cup of Soap's bitter motor oil coffee in his hand and Soap's rough map in his pocket. He took a deep steadying breath. Leaving the shop had involved the usual hide and seek in the back seat. Once on the freeway, Joey had finessed some abrupt lane changes that set horns to blaring, and now they were satisfied that the gridlock would work against anyone trying to tail them. But Joey's flair behind the wheel didn't alter the fact that it was still amateur hour.

Traffic halted, and Broker peered at gray, lockstep commuter faces sealed inside their frosted car windows: a woman busy with cosmetics and a comb, fixing her face in a rearview mirror. Any one of them could be the sadist that had carved up Leper and then left him to suffocate. *These are guys with skills. What are they looking for?* Having no idea only reminded him how alone he was, operating in mid-air. And now Harry Griffin waited for him just up the road. Harry was absolutely the guy you wanted on point.

If he was sober.

Broker let it all out in a long exhale. Change the subject.

"So what were you doing before you signed on with Soap?" Broker asked.

155

"I was a dope fiend, man; barely made it out of Miami after the Colombians came in," Joey said. "Soap helped me straighten out. Before that I was a squid. Sixth Fleet out on Yankee Station." Joey took his eyes off traffic and added a spark of menace to his wise, stolid face. "Armorer's mate. Dig it, we'd drop acid and go below decks on the *Ticonderoga* and mix up vats of napalm."

Definitely a Morlock, Broker figured, but a smart, disciplined Morlock. Soap's Morlock. No mention of his scouting trip up north. Broker didn't believe for a minute that Joey had set eyes on that cabin without talking to Annie O'Neil. Soap was holding a hole card close to his vest. He knew what was in the famous box.

He glanced away from Joey's steady blue eyes and watched the faint skyline emerge from the gloom. They turned off on University.

Ten minutes later he was trudging up the back steps to Andrea's apartment. Joey would circle the block. Andrea was waiting, looking suitably anonymous in faded jeans, a hooded gray sweatshirt, and a wary expression. When she opened the kitchen door, Broker smelled fresh coffee mixed with the old, familiar perfume of solvent and gun oil.

A lean, deceptively relaxed man, around Broker's age, sat at the kitchen table wearing a fleece pullover, cargo pants and winter boots. He exuded a prickly sharpness, suggesting metal filings barely under magnetic control. If Broker's shaggy demeanor suggested lupine comparisons, then Harry, with his short razor-cut brown hair and sometimes too-quiet brown eyes, had the deft grooming and alertness of a big cat. He didn't look up from threading a bore brush into the barrel of a dissembled Sig-Sauer P220. The slide housing, guide rod and spring rested on the front page of yesterday's *Star Tribune* that he'd spread on Andrea's table. Next to the weapon's magazine a smear of gun solvent blotted Broker's mug shot on the newsprint. Broker recognized the rounds in the magazine as .22 long rifle, explosive hollow points.

"Took you long enough. Where you been?" Harry's voice was a staccato, muted snare drum. He quickly reassembled the pistol, threaded on a silencer, pointed it up, and pulled the trigger. The bolt clicked on the empty chamber, and he set the pistol aside. Then Harry gave Broker his full attention, studying the stained jacket, the Levi's still stippled with blood from the courthouse incident, and the down-at-the-heels boots. "Broker, man, I have to take you shopping," he said softly.

Andrea watched them carefully with curious eyes, like a kid sizing up her first scary carnival ride. Clearly she was deep into information overload, and Broker hoped, as he sat down, that he hadn't made a mistake. Across the table, Harry grinned, revealing slightly crooked teeth that skewed his spare features. When drunk, Harry's smile could come across as crazy; sober and alert, it gave him a minor key brooding aspect that accented the dead spaces that sometimes floated in his eyes.

He tapped his index finger on the newsprint. "Andrea's been bringing me up to speed. Only you could turn blowing a cop away into a job with the state crime agency. You're so deep undercover you're reporting to a shrink?"

"It's a temporary arrangement," Broker said.

"For me, too," Andrea added.

"Uh huh. So we're taking her on a field trip?" Harry's face tightened a fraction. "You really think that's a good idea?"

"Andrea, could you excuse us for a moment?" Broker jerked his head toward the kitchen door. Harry rose and grabbed the gray mountain parka from the back of his chair. Broker, who hadn't removed his soiled Carhartt, led him onto the back porch. Once the door was firmly shut, they stood at the railing and watched a thin dawn creep over the rooftops and yards.

"Andrea's a little shaky, so lay off. Go with it. She was the only choice I had," Broker said.

"Do tell. I get a feeling this is all a little shaky," Harry said with a crooked, doomed smile. "You really decided to scurry up into some high branches this time." The smile widened into the signature grin. "But hey, you know me. I'm cool with crash and burn."

Broker ignored the remark and said, "She explain the set-up? I'm supposed to be playing bodyguard to this police asset."

"And one of his guys broke the Eleventh Detroit Commandment: Thou shalt not steal thy neighbor's dope." Harry grinned. "Special Forces assassin, it says in the papers. You were never in Special Forces, except for that off-the-books course on Okie. You went straight from the ranks into SOG, like me."

"Yeah, well, don't tell Andrea. She thinks I'm some kind of badass."

"*Cuc bo,*" Harry chuckled. Vietnamese for bullshit.

Broker frowned. "Listen up. Turrie's missing guy just turned up suffocated in a meat freezer. Andrea doesn't know that, and neither do the cops. I want to keep it that way, for now."

"Uh huh," Harry said with a touch more gravity. "So how far up in this tree are you planning to scramble?"

Broker shrugged. "Far enough to get a line on these assholes. Set them up for the cops to clobber later, when we're clear."

Harry's grin widened. "So now we're the UN peacekeepers, huh?"

"Listen. Turrie's guy was worked over pretty good. They took their time, very deliberately cutting the tendons on his fingers. Does that ring any bells?"

Harry fingered a Camel from his jacket and thumbed a Zippo. "Interrogation technique favored by Provincial Reconnaissance Units." Briefly their eyes met. "And some of their agency handlers."

"Yeah, that occurred to me," Broker said.

"Pretty thin, Broker. Every army in the field has its share of torturers."

"What isn't thin is they gave Turrie three days to return the missing item or they start killing his family. Assume they have eyes on around the clock."

"Cool. So what's the plan?"

"Let's go back inside," Broker said. He started toward the door, but Harry remained, smoking, staring across the snow-covered rooftops. "Harry?"

"Give me a second to work out the change of scenery," Harry quipped. "I just came in on a midnight run from the 313. This place is kinda monochromatic, all snow banks and white bread."

Back inside, Andrea was leaning against her kitchen counter with her arms crossed over her chest, brow furrowed, feeling left out.

"Just catching up," Broker said, resuming his seat at the table as Harry came in. "I was telling Harry how you've got your sights set on getting into the FBI. How you want to profile serial killers."

Harry grinned. "Cool. As long as you understand that governments are the real serial killers."

"She's also interested in head-shrinking guys who came back from the war," Broker said.

"That's easy, Andrea," Harry said, off hand. "All you need to remember is that Vietnam vets have muscles in their ass and they can eat pussy all night long."

Andrea smiled sweetly and asked in her best saccharine voice, "Broker, would you like a cup of coffee?"

"Hey, that'd be great," Broker said as he took out Soap's hand-drawn map and spread it on the table.

"You know where the cups are," Andrea said, pulling up a stool.

"Touché." Harry grinned as Broker got up and poured a cup of coffee. Then he resumed his seat and explained the set-up, as far as it went, with no eyes on.

"Pine Point. I run there sometimes," Andrea said. "This time of year, you get off the trails and it'll be pretty rough going in the woods with a foot of snow, lots of hills."

"We'll need to measure the ground," Harry said to Broker, "but I want to stay no more than a hundred yards from you, ideally with some elevation, where I can cover the road, the lot and see into the woods."

"You'll have the rest of the morning and early afternoon to check out the tree lines and road grid. Soap's main guy, Joey, will show around one p.m. and link up with you." Broker paused and then said, "You can't miss him. Soap and I will be there by two. One party will show up at two thirty, the other around four." Broker caught himself in mid-sentence, seeing Harry's grin. He looked at Andrea. "Shit, what are you driving?"

"Maroon '78 Audi Fox," Andrea said.

"Of course," Broker said. "Wish we had a van."

A minute later they were standing in the living room looking at Harry's gear spread out on the couch. "Real simple: two camera bodies, two lenses," he explained. "The 500mm f/8 Reflex Nikkor sets up on a tripod for longer distance; the other's for close in with a wide angle. Throw in a flash attachment for kicks." He turned to Broker. "You find me a darkroom?"

Broker nodded. "Twenty-four-hour access."

"Might have to push the film, depending on the light conditions."

Broker knelt and rifled through the duffel. He ignored the separate barrel and stock sections of a disassembled mini Car 15 assault rifle along with four loaded magazines. He was looking for a bottle.

"We're working, remember," Harry said softly in a joking voice. "I'm good for at least three days before I get the shakes."

Broker thought he heard Andrea audibly swallow.

Then Harry pointed to three olive drab radio units about the size of skinny shoeboxes. "Motorola military prototype walkie talkies; they're testing them with the Marines. New batteries, spare batteries, preset primary and alternate channels. Motorola's bullshit propaganda says these sets have a planning range of ten to twelve miles. Real world, they might work out to a mile, line of sight, depending on the terrain."

"One with you two, one with me in the park with Turrie, and one for Joey, who'll hang in the woods to back you up," Broker said.

"Good. Now, this park is used for cross country skiing?" Harry asked.

"Pretty much," Andrea said. "Rest of the year it's a hiking and bike trail."

"Forget skis," Harry said. "How are you in the woods?" he asked Andrea.

"I grew up in Minnesota, not in a city," she said evenly.

"So you can look all outdoorsy. Cool. Do you own a pair of snowshoes?"

Andrea shook her head.

"That's our first stop. We'll pick up some Bear Paws at a sporting goods shop. Then we'll look like Mr. and Mrs. Natural tramping around taking pictures. Wholesome gal like you—I get some good snaps, maybe I can sell them to *Outdoor Life,* huh?" Then he said to Broker, "Don't worry; I'll have you covered."

"With cameras or with that silenced pistol? Are you licensed to carry in Minnesota?" Andrea asked.

Harry smiled patiently. "The pistol's just a close range conceit. If push comes to shove, there's a CAR 15 broken down, reconfigured to mount a two-power scope, fits in my camera bag. But the way this works, there's no record of me landing in Lake Elmo. I'm not here, Andrea. And we aren't doing what we're about to do."

Andrea tossed Broker a measured look. "He's not talking about mere stealth, is he?"

"No, ma'am," Broker said.

"That's why, when your records came back blank, they knew they had a 'ghost.'"

Broker didn't care to respond. He stood up. "I'll take the two radios. Got stuff with Soap. See you in the park."

Chapter Nineteen

The décor at O'Neil's Tavern on St. Paul's West Seventh Street tended toward dark hardwood floors smelling of sawdust and walls dripping with more Druidic trim and wainscoting. Booths lined the walls, and heavy oak tables were scattered beneath an antique, silver, patterned tin ceiling. There were Jameson's posters and kegs embossed with the Guinness logo and "*Slainte*" set in green tile on the wall over the long polished bar. A photo prominently displayed over the service counter showed a younger, prettier Annie O'Neil sitting at a table, smiling, next to Minnesota senator Eugene McCarthy and a broad-shouldered eminence he assumed was her former husband. More pictures graced the walls with broken-hearted nostalgia: Michael Collins. Bobby. JFK.

Broker speculated that an after-image of Scott Fitzgerald probably emerged from the mirrors after you'd downed your fourth double Scotch. The ambience was no doubt magic for the faithful after dark. But at ten a.m., with baleful morning light flooding through the plate glass windows, creatures of the night like vampires and hardcore Irish drinkers were nowhere in sight.

Murph was a chunky barkeep with a misleading cushion of fat fitting loosely over a heavyweight's physique that came with a broken nose, split eyebrows and thick, jammed knuckles. He skipped the small talk, just looked Broker up and down and then pointed to the last stool at the end of the bar. "Joe Desmond used to sit right there, with his back to the corner, where he could see the door."

"Cut the shit, Murph," Soap said. "Just take us through it."

Murph's sigh was a phlegmy grumble in his throat. "Been all over cops since your friend here dropped Desmond. Before even. That big nigger worked with Desmond? He come in here Thursday night after she disappeared."

"Just vanished?" Soap asked.

"Wednesday, late afternoon, she's in the office going over accounts. Says she has to step out. No big deal. An hour later she's back in the office, door closed. Then she's pacing, not talking to customers, waiting like. Then alla sudden—Poof. She's gone. Her Beamer's still out back. Later that night Desmond drops by looking for her. Same as I told the coppers."

Broker and Soap exchanged glances.

Murph said, "Look, I took whatshisname—Merriweather—over to her house on Goodrich when he came back Friday, let him in with my key. The cat had torn open the food bag. Plants weren't watered. Ain't like her, man. I'm paying the neighbor kid to come in and look after the cat and the ferns and shit."

"So what's the word on the street?" Soap asked.

"People think Desmond gave her a heads up about his wife going ballistic, putting her name in that complaint. So she ducked out ahead of the questions and the publicity." Murph's pug ugly eyes briefly dusted Broker's face. "Then *he* plugged Desmond, and the media went crazy. She booked, man. Word is she grabbed a male stripper and went on a cruise."

"Nothing extra going on, any side deals?" Soap pressed.

"*Nada.* She's been a regular Girl Scout since she got caught in her last fling with Desmond, before this latest shit went down. We've been running a totally clean operation."

"You know Travis Diggs. He been around?"

"Fuckin' Leper? I barred his ass months ago. He tried to peddle us some rotgut labeled as Canadian Club." Murph was emphatic.

Soap squared up, leaned over the bar, and looked Murph directly in the eye. "You have anything else to add, now'd be the time."

"Don't be selling me wolf tickets, Soap. I got no reason to bullshit you," Murph said, holding his ground with conviction.

On the street, heading for Soap's Suburban, Broker paused, picking up the rushed energy of people scurrying in and out of storefronts where Christmas displays were appearing in the windows. Then he remembered: tomorrow was Thanksgiving. A few minutes later he scrunched down in the passenger seat while Soap drove and pressed the talk switch on the Motorola. "Joey, Broker; how do you hear? Over."

The squat mechanic was circling the area, staying in motion. His voice came back medium strength, scratchy: "Got you three by three. Negative on a tail, over."

Broker signed off by pushing the squelch twice. Soap said, "Maybe nobody's following us."

"Or maybe they're just real good," Broker said.

Back in Stillwater, coming down Curve Crest toward the shop, Soap braked suddenly when a flash of flame and a billow of black oily smoke erupted in front of one of the garage bays. As the roiling cloud engulfed the parking lot, Soap jerked erect behind the wheel and shouted, "What the hell?"

Broker already had his .45 out, thumb on the safety, head swiveling. "Keep driving," he said.

"Wait," Soap said. Then, "Aw shit." They watched his mechanic, Tony, dance around a car's flaming engine with an industrial fire extinguisher. Another mechanic and Rita pushed it out of the bay into the lot.

"Goddamn Oldsmobile. Fuckin' GM," Soap rumbled as he whipped into the lot, skidded to a stop and jumped out. Broker returned his sidearm to the waistband of his jeans under his coat. For a moment he watched Soap, Tony and Rita have a wildly gesticulating discussion amid the clouds of oily smoke. Figuring he could add nothing to the fire-fighting, which was now under control, he retreated to the office, where a new guy he'd never seen before stood behind the counter. One of the temps Soap brought in.

Broker checked the time: 12:20 p.m. Two hours until the first meet at the park. Then he rubbed the three-day stubble on his chin and asked the temp, "There's an employee shower, right?"

"Yeah," the guy said, "left through the door, past the stairs."

Ignoring the smoke still drifting across the parking lot, Broker went up the stairs into the bunkhouse-lunch room and reached in his duffel for his travel toilet kit. Then he spotted the stack of bath towels on the counter next to the sink. Quickly he stripped off his grubby clothes, wrapped a towel around his waist, and padded, barefoot, back down the stairs. He was just lining up his shaving gear and setting shampoo and conditioner on the shower stall ledge when the door burst open. The harsh reek of burning oil preceded Rita Turrie, who was swearing at the top of her voice.

"Goddamn GM and their goddamn diesel engines," she vented as she peeled off first her sweatshirt, then her shoes, socks and jeans. "They got the conversion from gas to diesel all wrong. Way too much compression." She lifted a lank strand of her hair, sniffed and made an ugly, sooty Leprechaun face. "So what happens is—" She unclipped her bra and flung it to the floor on top of her other clothes and then leaned into the shower stall to test the temperature of the water Broker had started to run. "—the fucking piston rings can't contain the fucking compression, so it forces the oil out of the crankcase—"

Lastly she stepped out of her underpants and confronted Broker, Harley tattoo and all. "The engine gets slathered with oil, and the tiniest spark—Whoosh!" She tossed up her grimy hands.

After a few beats, seeing Broker's neutral expression, she ejected, "What? You never see a girl before?" With that, Rita stepped into the shower and pulled the curtain.

Broker exited the shower room. He may have been off the grid and generally out of touch the last few years, but he understood it would take her a while to get her hair back to normal. In the lobby he was met by Joey, who now wore wool trousers, wool sweater, a green windbreaker and cross-country ski boots. A backpack hung from his shoulders.

"You see the oil fire?" he asked, jerking his head out the window at the charred chassis of the Oldsmobile that sat, still smoking, in black rings of trampled snow. "Fucking GM diesels, huh?"

"Spare me. I just got it from Rita," Broker said.

"Uh huh. Well, I, ah, got my skis in the Bronco. To blend in while I scout around," Joey said. "I'll go meet up with the other crew, then start working the trails, set up a pattern in back of where you and Soap will be." Then he zipped open the pack and revealed Harry's Motorola and a .45 automatic.

"Be careful with that pistol," Broker said.

"Stand by, Broker; this isn't my first cookout." Then he eyed Broker's bare feet and the towel wrapped around his waist.

"Don't ask," Broker said.

Almost fifteen minutes later Rita exited the shower room in a cloud of steam, her hair glistening and her pale freckled face, neck and shoulders showing a well-scrubbed blush above the towel wrapped around her midsection. "All yours," she said as she skipped up the stairs.

After a quick scrub and shampoo and shave, Broker inspected his face in a fist-rubbed porthole on the steamed mirror. Yellows and grays were edging out the purple bruising under his eye and on the still-thickened bridge of his nose. Then he took a few moments to comb the snarls out of his hair and slick it back.

When he entered the bunkroom, Rita, now wearing a terry-cloth robe, was sitting cross-legged on his cot. With one hand she ran a big-toothed comb through her hair. The other hand held the bulky Civil War history she had evidently picked out of his open duffel. Seeing him, she held up the volume.

"At the U I was in this women's history course that mentioned there were gals in the ranks in the Civil War, disguised as men. They were discovered when they got wounded or killed," she said.

"Or became pregnant," Broker said.

Rita set the book down. "So don't get shot and don't get pregnant."

Broker crossed the room, drawn to a framed photo that hung on the wall over the counter. In faded sepia under glass stood three hollow-cheeked men in uniform and Corcoran jump boots, a suggestion of Georgia pines in the background. Soap Turrie was in the middle, looking scary young.

Seeing his interest, Rita said, "Tommy O'Neil, Dad and Jimmy Briggs. They graduated in the same class at Stillwater High, enlisted together, served in the same platoon, jumped into Normandy and Holland, and froze at Bastogne. Jimmy's still around. He and Dad do real estate deals."

"When did Annie's husband pass?" Broker peered at the faces from 1943.

"Ten years ago, about the time Dad's wild phase ended and he embraced family life." A corner of her mouth crinkled in a wry smile.

"A friend's funeral can do that."

"Among other things. More likely it was Mom threatening to leave after she caught him sleeping with the widow. He quit the life on the spot. Things improved at home, and I went from tatted-up delinquent to art student."

"You set me up," Broker said.

"Don't be so quick to reach for clichés," Rita replied, and the wry grin broadened as she collected a folded pile of fresh jeans, a top and under accessories from the cot next to her. She stood up and said, "Broker, don't worry. I'm not going to mess with you helping Dad." As she passed him, she said, "You know, you look better with your hair combed." At the doorway she paused and studied him with more woman than imp in her eyes. "Eyebrows," she said thoughtfully. "I think that's your street name."

The door closed, and Broker quickly changed into a silk under layer, a heavier mid layer, a fleece, and fresh jeans. Then he laid out his mini-arsenal. He'd brought a .12 gauge, riot pump shotgun, his .257 Roberts deer rifle, and the AR 15, along with an ammo can full of rounds for them all. Might as well throw the whole caboodle in Soap's Suburban as props, if nothing else, for the benefit of the people Soap was going to meet. Five minutes later he was downstairs stacking the gun cases in the corner of the lobby. He'd added a fast draw holster for the .45, positioned butt out on his left hip. Outside, the burned vehicle had been pushed off to the back of the parking lot, where it leaked black wisps of smoke. Rita, composed and cleanly attired, was at her station behind the counter. Quiet background jazz trickled from a radio at her side. Normal work routine had returned.

Soap, in his flannel-lined Levi's jacket and cowboy boots, was in the lobby as Broker shouldered his gun cases. Soap opened a desk drawer behind the counter. Another Colt .45 appeared, which he stuffed into his waistband. Rita followed them out the door and handed her father a windbreaker. "Just said on the radio that another winter storm's heading for the east metro. You guys watch yourself, okay?" she said.

Getting into the truck, Soap said, "So we just go out there and hope someone is following us? Here goes nothing."

"We have Harry watching over us," Broker said. As he got into the passenger seat, he reflected, *And Harry is a lot of things, but nothing ain't one of them.*

Chapter Twenty

F at, random flakes drifted. The sky clumped like yesterday's oatmeal. The temperature hovered at 30 degrees,
and Soap turned up the heater as they sat in the nearly empty
lot, close to the outbuilding. The trailhead T-boned at the parking lot; a groomed trail descended a slight hill to the north, par-
alleled the lot and ran south into the trees, while another
branched at a right angle and followed the flat path of the hiking trail due west. Seven vehicles were parked in the lot, all
empty. Joey's Bronco, Andrea's Audi and Soap's Suburban
made three. So not many civilians were cluttering up the land-
scape. But Broker didn't like how close the pine forest en-
croached on the restroom building and the lot.

"Radio check," he said to Soap, then exited the truck and
stepped around the rear of the outbuilding and went a few paces
into the cover of the trees. He removed the Motorola from the
inner web pocket of his parka and pressed the talk button.
"Harry, Joey; how do you hear, over."

Harry's voice came back immediately. "Got you Lima
Charlie. We hooked up with Joey—who is a real trip—and he
has our location. I have a clear line of sight on you back in the
trees. We're about eighty yards off your two o'clock, up the hill,
across the trail that skirts the parking lot."

"See anything?" Broker scoured the tree line in the direction Harry indicated. They were totally hidden.

"One guy doing loops, looks like he's training for the
Olympics. Rest is just parents with their kids, over."

"Okay. Time check," Broker said, glancing at his wrist-watch. "I have two ten. Show should start in about twenty minutes, over."

Harry signed off by pressing the talk button twice. About a minute later Joey came on, slightly breathy. "Broker, Joey. Hadda stop and get out the radio."

"What's it look like out there?"

"Just normal traffic on the trails. I'm going to be doing short loops so I can stay near the lot. And I have a fix on your Detroit buddy and his girlfriend. I'll keep an eye out for any-body coming in through the trees. Over."

Broker smiled at the girlfriend remark. "Sounds good. Stay sharp. Out."

He rejoined Soap, who was sitting behind the wheel scan-ning this morning's *Pioneer Press*. As he opened the plug on a tall Stanley thermos, Soap said, "You didn't make the front page today; got bumped by the hostage stuff."

Broker said nothing as Soap produced a spare cup from the glove compartment, poured and handed him coffee.

"Don't matter. Point has been made. People think you and me are up to no good together. At least old Hector Garza does," Soap said.

"So what's Hector's story?"

"Exactly the kind of guy your cop buddies want you to be in the same room with. If you pass the sniff test," Soap said.

"Define 'sniff test,'" Broker said.

"Oh, he might bring some muscle to poke at you. See what you're made of. But you killed a cop. That's gold medaling with these guys."

"What's Hector into?"

"A lot of west side high rollers frequent his restaurant. I imagine if you got a pass to sit in there, you'd hear about mainly drugs and guns—that's what got Leper in hot water with them. Dumbass got hustled by some savvy old National Guard master sergeant who pawned off a lot of useless inventory. When Leper got the stuff to the Mexicans, they were expecting fully automatic M-16s and grenades. All the rifles had defective bolts and barrels, and the grenades were smoke grenades. Took a little doing to keep Leper's knees from being broken." Soap held up a hand, two fingers almost touching. "Hector was that close."

"Did you talk to Desmond this freely?"

Soap grinned. "You mean before I decided to pivot to respectability?"

"Rita showed me the picture in the lunch room of you and your buddies."

Soap nodded. "Me and Tommy and Jimmy. Ten mile runs through the Georgia pines singing 'Little Liza Jane.' Yeah, we went on quite a tear up and down the West Coast after the war." A flicker of nostalgia crossed his lips. "Not just Hell's Angels. I was getting drunk with a two-bit thief name of Neil Cassidy before he ever met Kerouac. Eventually we found our way back here with a stash of ill-gotten loot and bought the bar in St. Paul. Used the bar to launder cash. How I bankrolled the shop. But now Tommy's gone and Jimmy's got the heart condition. It takes a lot of energy to be a fucked-up outlaw. You get older, you decide to point the energy in a different direction. I meant what I said about being mostly straight." He looked out the window and laughed to himself, and the conversation ended.

Broker sipped his coffee and watched a father herd two preschoolers on stubby skis in from the trails toward a shiny new Jeep wagon. The slow, time-released snow continued to filter down. He glanced at his wristwatch: two twenty.

A white and tan Washington County squad car slowly turned into the lot and made a circuit. Broker eyed Soap. "Scheduled patrol loop, no sweat," Soap said. A moment later the squad exited the lot and continued north on the county road.

"And what about this Heywood dude?" Broker asked.

"Southside Disciple middle management, brought in from Chicago to ride honcho on product quality and distribution and to keep the St. Paul street sets in line. We really want to talk to his sister, Charlene. She may have been the last person to see Leper."

Ten minutes later a gleaming black Fleetwood limousine slowly prowled into the lot looking lost, like it had been separated from a funeral cortege. The passengers were unavailable behind tinted windows as it drove a slow circuit of the area before stopping its wide chrome grill directly in front Soap's Suburban, bumpers almost touching. It just sat there for a moment, making an elegantly menacing statement in a cloud of exhaust. Then the driver's side door swung open. A hefty man in an overcoat got out. With a porkpie hat topping his pitted face, he ignored Broker and Soap, walked past them to the ski trailhead, and took a moment to inspect the area, left and right. When he turned and studied the other vehicles in the lot, Broker lowered his window to get a better look. Apparently satisfied, the guy took a position where he could see the road, the lot, and the trails and woods. He folded his gloved hands together and rocked slightly on his heels before settling into a sentinel stance. When he rocked, Broker could hear the expensive leather of his shoes creak in the crisp, still air.

A second man exited the rear door on the driver's side. In contrast to the first man, he was lean and wore a short black leather car coat and no hat. His dark hair was pulled back in a ponytail. As he came around the back of the vehicle and opened the passenger side rear door, Broker noted the small black tarantula tattoo on the side of his neck. Taking his cue in this bodyguard ballet, Broker exited the Suburban and held the passenger door open.

Hector Garza heaved out of the Fleetwood's back seat, a heavyset man swaddled in an overstuffed, ribbed, white down parka and a white, rabbit-fur-lined Elmer Fudd cap with dangling ear flaps. As he approached, Broker laughed out loud.

"What?" Hector asked politely, then stopped and looked around. His face was smooth and round like his voice.

"You look like the Michelin Man in that rig," Broker said with a shrug.

Hector raised a gloved hand to stay his two men, who had started forward like alert Dobermans. He grinned at Soap through the open door. "So this is Broker? A comedian who shoots cops. I like that," he said.

"Relax, Hector. Grab a seat," Soap said.

With some difficulty Hector shoehorned into the passenger seat and removed his cap, revealing neatly barbered hair that smelled of talc and cologne. "I'm here as a courtesy," he said, "in this out-of-the-way place because I assume meeting in a more civilized venue might draw attention from your friends in St. Paul Narco, correct?"

"I am feeling some heat," Soap allowed.

Hector turned and looked pointedly at the three gun cases that leaned diagonally—in plain view—in the baggage area behind the rear seat. "Indeed, and now apparently you have acquired a rock star bodyguard," he said.

Broker opened the back door and climbed in behind Hector. Tarantula came in the opposite door and positioned himself behind Soap. As they settled in, Soap said, "So?"

"So," said Hector, steepling his pudgy fingers on his ample stomach, "you know Charlie the Pencil Man?"

"I do. Charlie talks to everyone in St. Paul, and everyone talks to him," Soap said. "Every cop in town thinks Charlie's their special snitch, but he's Hector's snitch too," Soap added over his shoulder to Broker.

"Yes, well, when it starts getting cold I bring Charlie in off the street, to keep him close. I let him sweep up and give him meals and a place to crash in the back. So last night—because I am your very good friend—I asked him about all the things suddenly missing in your life: that *maracon*, Travis, your truck, and the always exciting Annie O'Neil."

Hector paused, letting the anticipation build. Then he snapped his fingers. "Charlie's like Radar in *M.A.S.H*. He misses nothing. So he breaks it down. St. Paul narco was twisting arms to get a line on Annie dropping out of sight, maybe with some product that didn't belong to her. Just like you were. No mention of Leper. They came up empty. After Desmond got shot, the pressure eased. But Charlie hears that someone else is showing a lot of cash, real quiet like, and they were interested, the end of last week, in the same thing that you are now: a connection between Travis, your truck, and Annie. Now what do you make of that?"

Soap didn't fake the concern on his face. "Who are they? Feds?"

"Charlie doesn't think they're feds, at least not local feds. So I asked around. It's not my people and not the Disciples' franchise in St. Paul and not the bikers."

Hector slowly rotated his large head and regarded Soap with half-lidded eyes. "So you—and your new *pistolero*—aren't the only people looking for Travis. And a few days ago you were only looking for Annie. Some of us think you know more than you're letting on, Russell. Like why they both disappeared at the same time."

"What can I say, Hector? My truck came up missing, and Travis' car is in the lot in front of my shop." Soap tossed off the remark.

"Uh huh." Hector shifted on the seat, causing the Suburban to sway slightly, and studied Broker with brown Aztec eyes. "Be careful around old Russell here, my friend. He knows things."

"What things?" Broker asked.

Tarantula, sitting at Broker's side, feigned distraction, picking at a hangnail on his index finger.

"He knows secrets," Hector said with a jovial hush coming into his voice. "For instance, only he knows for sure whether Annie can really touch her nose with the tip of her tongue."

Soap looked straight ahead, a study in boredom. "That was a while ago, Hector. Memory fails," he said.

Tarantula continued worrying the hangnail. Broker engaged the flicker of intelligence that backlit Hector's now blasé brown eyes. He felt the spidery flicker of the big man's gaze scurry over his face.

Hector continued, "We could ask Joe Desmond, but he isn't here, is he? The question is—did he go away on purpose or by accident? What do you say, Russell? We all would love to know."

Soap, who continued to focus on a point in the snow-covered pines about eighty yards away, said nothing.

"See," said Hector, "secrets."

Broker found himself watching Soap just as carefully as Hector and thinking the same thing. *Secrets.*

Seconds ticked by. No one spoke. Just as the silence approached ominous proportions, Hector rumbled with laughter. "Just kidding with you, my friend," Hector said, pounding Soap on the shoulder. "Probably Charlie is just a lying sack of shit, *que?* Singing for his supper. Tabloid gossip rules the day. If Travis is never seen again, good riddance, and I suspect, like people say, Annie is in Vegas playing blackjack to avoid the publicity. As for your truck, you have a successful business. You can afford another truck."

"So that's it," Soap said, "no word on the street?"

Hector mulled it for a few beats, then said, "Oh, something is going on, for sure. Charlie isn't entirely full of shit. But it's more like a long shadow, a sudden coolness. Nothing we can pin down." Hector swung his gaze back to Broker. "You come from the woods up north? So what's it like when something big and unexpected comes into the forest? Scary maybe?"

Hector's eyes lingered on Broker's face. Then they twinkled, amused. "Tell you what. In appreciation for ridding us of that prick Desmond, I'll comp your meals at my restaurant, but—" the smile widened, "—not every night. And I recommend you upgrade your wardrobe."

With that Hector heaved forward in the seat. Tarantula immediately was out the door, circling the Suburban and opening the passenger door for his boss. The thickset guy in the overcoat marched in from the trailhead. A minute later they were gone.

As Broker watched the Fleetwood depart, he said, "There goes one depressing conversation."

"So there's money on the street," Soap muttered.

For a few moments a meditative silence filled the front seat; then Broker leaned into his parka and spoke into the Motorola. "Anything? Over."

Harry's voice came back. "Normal traffic on the road, no one turning into the lot. Nothing in the woods. Over."

"How's your teammate holding up?" Broker asked.

"Cool. We're discussing lyrics to Eagles songs, 'Hotel California,' mainly. Bet you didn't know she was at Woodstock. Wait one."

A few seconds later, Andrea's voice came on the radio. "Yeah, Broker?"

"You, at Woodstock?"

"Right after I got my bachelor's. I was the one with clothes on."

"So how are you holding up?"

"Reminds me of the time my dad took me ice fishing on Mille Lacs when I was in junior high. That time, at least, I caught some sunnies." After a moment she added, "Over."

"Hang in." He keyed the talk button twice, then tucked the radio deeper out of sight. He turned to Soap and asked, "So can Annie O'Neil really touch her nose with her tongue?"

"Could." Soap fingered the patch of hair under his lower lip. "Once upon a time."

"How's the food at Hector's restaurant?"

"Wouldn't know. Place is kind of dressy for me."

Over the next hour and a half Joey zipped by three times on his skis, showing excellent form. They finished the coffee. They used the facilities. Broker smoked. Soap read the newspaper. The cold, thin afternoon light accentuated fatigue coming off a string of mostly sleepless nights. Broker was starting to question his ad hoc plan to snare what he assumed were highly-trained phantoms.

He tossed a cigarette stub out the window and found himself staring at the butt of the Colt peeking out from Soap's jacket. "You doing okay?" he asked.

Soap's eyes tilted up from the newsprint. "How old did you say you were?"

"Thirty last March."

"Uh huh," Soap said as he went back to reading the sports section. A moment later he said, "Vikings play Tampa this Sunday." When Broker didn't respond, he said, "You know they beat Detroit last week."

"What?" Broker said absently as his eyes tracked the road and the tree lines. Nothing was happening except that the tempo of the snow had increased to a persistent trickle. Then the radio made a static hiccup in his jacket.

"We may have company," Harry said. "It's a blue Ford Escort, a '75 or '76. Look at ten o'clock off the nose of the Suburban." Nudging Soap with his knee, he looked. Sure enough, a blue compact was sitting on the shoulder of the county road just north of the park entrance, facing south. Harry continued. "At first I didn't pay attention because it was the first car behind you when you approached the park entrance. It just kept going. How copy, over?"

"Solid copy."

"Then he went by again, this time heading south, when you were talking to the guys in the Fleetwood. He just made his third appearance going north again, but this time he made a U-turn and parked on the shoulder. Could be he just followed you from the car shop."

"If that's true, he's pretty sloppy about it," Broker said.

"Or he's hiding in plain sight. I think it's two people in the front seat, but the light's bad, reflections on the windshield. Let's keep an eye on him. Harry out."

Soap folded and set aside his newspaper. "Just sitting there," he said, staring at the blue Ford that sat almost two hundred yards distant.

Before Broker could answer, the Escort started up and slowly trolled past the park and disappeared behind the trees to the south.

The radio chirped again and Joey came on. "I monitored your last. You want me to move in closer, over?"

"Negative. Stay where you can back up Harry."

Then Soap tapped Broker's knee, pointed his finger at the park entrance, and grinned. "Heads up. I'd know that car anywhere. We've worked on it enough."

The black and turquoise Coupe Deville took the turn into the lot a little too fast, and the rear end fishtailed before straightening out just in time to miss a couple slogging in from the trail with skis on their shoulders.

"Jesus," Broker said, sitting up. "Hector. This guy. What is it with Caddys?"

In a continuation of the spastic energy of his entry, the driver skidded to a stop diagonal to the Suburban and piled out from behind the wheel. Heywood was maybe twenty-five and clean cut, with a stingy moustache and short-cropped hair. Oblivious to the weather, he was dressed in a black and red tracksuit and high top tennis shoes. He could have been a varsity athlete, Broker thought, except for the absolutely merciless set to his brown eyes.

"Hey Soap, what is it with all this Nanook shit?" Heywood inquired as he sauntered up to the driver's side, where Soap had cranked down the window. "They got these things called buildings, you know, with heat."

"Yeah, yeah," said Soap. "C'mon, get in."

Broker had exited the truck and now held open the door. But first Heywood turned to his car and grabbed at air, vigorously summoning his passenger. "Charlene, shag your ass over here and talk to the man."

Charlene exited the Deville, all sleepy good looks in a long car coat, a wool tam, and winter boots with two-inch heels. Stepping carefully, she approached the Suburban, and Heywood took her arm and hurried her into the back seat. Then Heywood came around to where Broker was holding the door open for him.

"Well, well, well, the mystery man himself," Heywood said, pausing dramatically to scan the fading bruises and swelling on Broker's face. "You been in the papers and TV for capping Desmond's animal ass, and all kinds of bullshit's being hung on you. Looks like the pigs didn't thump you *that* bad. Now the gossip's sayin' you're working for old Soap Turrie. What's it all mean?"

"Means he's on the payroll as a handy man. He's going to work on rehabbing some property I own," Soap ad-libbed as Heywood got in the passenger seat. Broker resumed his position to Heywood's rear. The doors pulled shut. The heater fan whirred. Heywood took out a Salem, lit it up and cracked the window.

"Tell you what I don't know first," Heywood said without preamble. "I still got zip on Miss Annie O'Neil because her business and my business, they kinda pass like ships, you dig?

Only met the lady one or two times, socially. Folks are saying she split town because of the stuff in the news about her and Desmond. Only thing is, some snitches who work for narco came by hassling some of my street runners last Thursday, Friday; was asking about her coming into large amounts of something hot, cocaine maybe. Nobody had any idea what they were fishing for. It didn't make sense—anything big on the street, I'da heard. And as for your boy, Leper?"

Charlene spoke up. "Man's name is Travis."

Heywood whipped around and cut her with his eyes. "Charlene? Exactly when did that average white boy become a man?"

Charlene sniffed. "Well, he did have a man-size roll of hundred dollar bills in his pocket."

Heywood grinned. "I still don't believe that. You sure it wasn't a bunch of singles with a hundred wrapped around for show?"

Broker was half listening, preoccupied with the solid wall of trees to the south, behind the outbuilding. But the last exchange caught his attention. He held up his hand, warding off Heywood, and leaned toward Charlene. "You talk to any cops about him flashing money?" he asked.

Charlene batted her large eyes that came with long eyelashes. Heywood draped an arm over the seat, turned and patiently addressed Broker like he was instructing a difficult child how to tie his shoe. "Now why would they talk to Charlene? The cops were looking for Annie O'Neil. Nobody's looking for Leper except Soap here."

Broker noted that the young gangster appeared more earthbound than Hector. No mention of money on the street.

"Let her talk," said Soap, who had also turned in his seat.

"Last thing he was doing was flashing that money," she said. "He called me at the club around ten last Wednesday night. Had let himself in to my crib; he knows where the key is.

182

Said he needed to lay low for a while and could I score some blow. Said he was good for it. I get off around four in the morning, so that's into Thursday. When I get home, he's there with a lot of money. Five thousand in hundreds and change."

"You're sure about that?" Heywood pressed.

Charlene drew herself up. "Heywood, you got a lot of people thinking you're a badass, but you always gonna be my baby brother. Why was it you brought me here, to the sticks, from the South Side?"

"To keep count of my money." Heywood sagged slightly.

"Five thousand and change," Charlene repeated.

"And this money came from where?" Soap asked.

"Wouldn't say," Charlene said. "He just wanted to hide out and get high and come down off of being pretty shook up. He was like, on foot; didn't even have his car. So that's what we did."

"Like he turned a deal? Fenced something?" Broker asked.

Charlene shook her head. "Listen to me. He wasn't talking about it. Only thing he said this one time was he got in way the fuck over his head into something that involved a ton of money, and he laid it off and just wanted out." Charlene paused. "He was scared. So that's what we did; eat takeout, watch videos, get high and hide out."

"And then what happened?" Broker asked.

Charlene shrugged. "I come home Sunday morning after work and he was gone. No message at the club. No note. Just gone."

"A ton of money," Broker repeated.

"It's what you call a term of art," said Heywood. "I'm sure to Leper a couple thousand bucks would look like a ton of money."

"But where'd he get it?" Soap asked.

Heywood said, "No way Leper could turn a real deal on his own." He turned to Soap. "Soap, man, I hate to be the one to point out the obvious—but it is in Leper's nature to be a chronic thief. Could it be he stole your truck and sold it? You ever consider that?"

Soap and Broker looked at each other and couldn't suppress a spontaneous sputter of laughter.

"That's pretty good," Broker said. "We never thought of that."

"Oh yeah." Heywood turned and measured Broker with a pitiless stare. "If I'm so good, then why ain't I white?" Then he grinned. "Just fuckin' with you, Handyman." He turned to Soap. "We done here?"

Soap nodded. "Appreciate you going the extra mile, you and Charlene."

"No big thing. I appreciate the extra work you put into my ride." Then Soap and Heywood negotiated an elaborate, farewell thumb-lock hand dap, and Heywood and his sister got out of the car. Broker moved back to the passenger seat.

As they drove away, Broker said, "Handyman?"

"Rita's idea. She saw your tools," Soap said.

"Uh huh. In J.T.'s notes it said Leper's partner, Norman, spilled his guts around seven Saturday night."

"So they must have grabbed Leper at Charlene's early Sunday morning," Soap said.

"Tough kid, if they worked on him for two days. But what about the money part?" Broker was saying when the radio squawked and Harry's voice came through in a controlled low and slow tone that eliminated all the clutter and cinched Broker's guts into a familiar knot:

"Gooks in the open. I have movement coming your way. Two men. Inside the trees. Just off the trail to your south. A hundred yards and closing. They are definitely not here to ski."

Chapter Twenty-One

"Stay put," Broker advised Soap as he vaulted out the passenger door. "Things get sporty, stay behind the building." Then he slipped past the privy, the .45 out, cocked in his right hand and laid along his pants leg, the radio set pressed to his left ear. "Moving," he transmitted as he slipped into the trees behind the building.

Harry came back. "Roger that. I'm coming down the slope to cross the trail on your right. You thinking of talking to them?"

"For starters."

"Cool," Harry came back. "Give peace a chance. I'll cover you in case it doesn't work out."

After Harry signed off, Broker crouched, scanning an impenetrable thicket of mixed pines and hardwoods and brambles. He strained his hearing to separate out the sounds: faint voices from departing skiers loading their gear in the parking lot, a car passing on the road, the sound of a small gas engine in the distance. A chainsaw. He could actually see the air fill in, graying toward dusk and now spangled with thicker snowflakes. Then, shit! He keyed the Motorola. "Where's Andrea?"

"No sweat. Sent her north along the tree line to get clear. Told her to wait with her car running in the parking lot." Then silence. A bushy stand of low pines blocked Broker's vision of the trail to the west and north, the direction from which Harry was approaching.

The radio chirped and Joey came on. "I monitor. I'm down the state trail to the west. Where do you want me?"

Before Broker could answer, Harry came back on, breathing heavily, obviously jogging in snowshoes. "Stand down. I say again—stand down. These guys are goofy—some sort of civilians." Going slower now, his voice came easier. "They just moved back to the trail, and they're stumbling along in street shoes. One of them is carrying something." Harry's voice expelled a laugh. "And it's a camera."

Cautiously Broker started moving through the tree cover toward the trail. "Broker, Joey, over," the radio scratched.

"Stay put; could be a false alarm," Broker answered, now striding through foot-deep snow. The adrenaline spike retracted. He re-holstered the Colt but kept his hand on the butt inside his jacket. As he stepped from the tree cover onto the trail, his suppressed heartbeat started to pound. *Breathe.*

Ten yards away, two men stood flatfooted on the trail, staring first at him, then at Harry, who at thirty yards and closing covered ground in easy strides. His long duffel bag rode easily on a strap across his chest and tucked under his right arm. Harry was grinning. The two men were not. They shivered slightly, dressed for trips between the car and indoors.

The short one, who held the camera, wore a light winter jacket, jeans and low quarter regular shoes. Unruly hair sprouted from a purple Vikings stocking cap, and more hair formed an untidy beard on his pop-eyed frog face. But Broker's attention was drawn to the lanyard he wore around his neck, from which dangled several laminated cards. PRESS was prominently stamped on one of them.

The taller guy wore a tan overcoat and, hatless, his white hair was open to the weather. He held a spiral notebook and a pen in his hands. No gloves. No boots. His face was pouchy, but his eyes were hard and pointy, as was his tone of voice.

"Phil Broker, right? I'm John Lager from the *Pioneer Press.* I saw you earlier in the parking lot with Russell Turrie . . ."

"So what happened to journalism?" Broker took his time. "You're trading in melodrama and rumors."

"Now'd be the time to hear your side of the story." Lager spoke swiftly. "The shooting last Saturday is a story that tells itself. Yerbich, at Wash Co, showed me the range tape yesterday, on deep background. But the rumor mill links you to Turrie and a contract on Desmond. And here you are together? You care to comment?"

Then Lager paused because Harry had joined them, moving in tight, invading their personal space. His crazy grin and the sheer physical tension he exuded caused Lager and the photographer to instinctively shy closer together.

"Cool," Harry said with his best intense grin as he casually reached out a gloved hand and covered the lens of the news photographer's camera with his palm, just as the camera came up to focus on Broker. Making a show of being fascinated, he fondled the camera and said, "It's a Nikon F2, right? And that looks like the new super-fast telephoto lens, a 180."

Lager and the photographer exchanged wary glances and braced for trouble, not sure which way this was going. Now Broker stepped in, but easy, keeping his distance, and said to Lager, "Let's see some IDs, both of you, so I know you're who you say you are."

As the photographer fumbled with a picture ID hanging around his neck, Harry, who had removed his gloves, smoothly extracted the camera from the photog's hand and popped it open, exposing the film. "Oops, sorry about that. Was just curious what kind of film you're using for these light conditions," he said, his amiable voice at odds with his crazy grin.

"Ease off," Broker said to Harry. "They're just doing their jobs."

"And you're just doing yours?" Lager said, taking a step forward. "So just what exactly is your relationship with your new friend, Russell Turrie?"

Broker glanced at the picture ID Lager took out of his wallet and handed it back. "You think creeping through the woods making a blind approach is a smart way to get an interview with a guy who's been receiving threats on his life?" he asked.

Lager nodded. "Yerbich mentioned that, off the record, yesterday. So I was on my way to talk to Turrie, and we saw you leave his shop together and followed you. This is where you stopped." Lager's insistent voice accelerated, more aggressive, seeing the way Harry had crowded and then "disarmed" the photographer.

Then two things happened that changed the tenor of the testy confrontation. The darkening sky burst open like a winter jackpot and showered them in fat white flakes. Simultaneously, Soap's deep baritone boomed behind them: "What is this bullshit?" He stomped forward, staying to the left of the ski tracks, and turned to Harry. "Soap Turrie."

Harry freed his right hand. "Glad to meet you."

As they shook hands, the photographer tugged at his empty camera that remained stuck in Harry's firm left hand. Lager, determined in the face of obvious intimidation, turned his attention to Soap. "Mr. Turrie, how would you characterize your relationship with Mr. Broker after the events of last Saturday?" he asked.

"Sure," Soap said, adopting a more conversational tone, "be happy to help you out. Turns out Mr. Broker and I share a love of the outdoors and were thinking of going skiing." Then he glowered. "Except you and your asshole sidekick are standing in and trampling the groomed trails that my tax dollars pay for. And you can quote me directly on that."

Soap had to raise his voice to compete with the wind. The weather was doing a better job of discouraging the interloping newsies than the combined efforts of Harry and Soap. The snow now came with a sudden ferocity, thick and fast and so wet and sticky that it plastered, white on white, to Lager's bare head. From his cringing body language, it was clear that a winter storm trumped byline ambitions. For emphasis, Soap threw up his hands at the sky, tugged his windbreaker hood over his head, turned and demonstrated the proper human response by walking swiftly back toward the parking lot to seek shelter.

Gob-smacked by an infectious Minnesota moment, the four men stuttered with involuntary, absurd laughter. Then Broker, his face now obscure in his parka hood, suggested in a loud, reasonable tone, the words wrestling with the wind, "Maybe this isn't the best time to have this conversation given the way you two are dressed."

Lager screwed up his lips and stared with the resignation of an angler who felt a big fish slip off the hook.

Broker moved in closer to reassure him. "Look, Lager, how about a rain check? Perhaps after the holiday we could meet for coffee. You know, the normal way? A phone call setting an interview? Not this skulking around in the woods stuff. Maybe we could clear the air about all the silly things you've been saying about me."

"Yeah, right." Lager pulled his wallet out again and, shivering, handed Broker a business card.

"Thanks," said Broker. Then he cuffed Harry's arm, signaling him to release his hold on the photographer's camera.

The two journalists exchanged frustrated looks, then turned and retreated swiftly back down the trail. Thirty yards out, their shapes became indistinct.

"So what's with you playing good cop?" Harry asked.

"Why should the BCA guy, who put me in this, be the only one to play footsie with the press? Lager could be useful down the line." Broker shrugged. "C'mon, let's go check on Andrea." Then they walked back to the lot, where Soap was sitting behind the wheel of his truck, dusting snow off his hair.

As Harry removed his snowshoes, he chatted with Soap through the driver's side open window. Squinting through the storm-blur toward the shadow of the Audi on the far side of the lot, Broker took out the Motorola. He glanced up. The churning air looked like a wind tunnel full of crazy white moths. He pushed send. "Joey, nothing's happening except the storm. Time to wrap it up and go home." Joey just keyed the static twice in response.

Broker continued toward Andrea's car. "Wait a minute," he yelled as he jogged up to the Audi, swept snow off the windshield, and stared at the empty driver's seat. "Where's Andrea?"

"What?" Harry was right behind him. Soap, seeing the sudden movement, jumped out of the truck.

"She should be here, warming up in her car," Harry said in a too-calm voice.

"Maybe she got turned around in the woods?" Soap offered.

"Not likely. She'd be within sight of the lot the whole time." Broker's eyes locked on Harry's in the failing light. *We fucked up.* In another half hour it would be too dark to see.

He raised the radio and called Joey, who came back immediately. "We got a problem. We're missing Andrea." He looked at Soap as he spoke. "Keep your eyes open. Soap's coming your way down the state trail. Once you meet up, call me and we'll coordinate a search."

"Standing by," Joey said.

Broker turned to Soap. "You and Joey cover the south. Harry goes back and picks up her tracks. I'll cut in above you to work the north end. You both have flashlights?"

Harry patted his bag. "Got one in the truck," Soap said.

"Go," said Broker.

Chapter Twenty-Two

B roker ran in shin-deep drifts, slipping on hidden roots and branches. The rolling ground jerked in and out of focus. The remaining light spun into crepuscular, wind-blown cotton candy as frozen branches shuddered and creaked overhead. The dark trees were turning fuzzy, their edges bleeding into the air. Going to black.

Broker was all in his eyes and ears and his pounding heartbeat. No thoughts. His thoughts would shame him with the folly of what he'd done: potentially putting a desk-sitter in harm's way.

He skidded to a halt and listened. Nothing but the wind. He switched on his flashlight and surveyed the ground ahead that was a maze of fallen trees and tangles of deadfall. He was about a hundred yards in from the north end of the parking lot, heading west. He had the radio clutched in his left gloved hand, the long-handled, heavy-duty flashlight in his right.

Harry's voice leaped in static. He slammed the Motorola to his ear. "Broker, man, we been played. Looks like they were snooping us while we were snooping them." Harry was breathless, obviously running. "I found her snowshoes—where her tracks met with another set of tracks—snow's all messed up—found a light blood trail—two sets of tracks that go southwest—toward the state trail."

Jesus. Before Broker could respond, Harry gasped. "Angle south. Cut the trail. I'm going to run them down."

Then Harry was gone and Broker was trying to call Joey as he turned left and crashed straight through a thicket of deadfall. "Joey, Broker, you monitor?" More deadfall. More snapping dry branches. "Joey?"

Nothing came back. *Forget Soap and Joey. Move.*

Forty heartbeats later he found the trail smashed into the fresh snow. Three sets of boots. One set deeper than the others. Harry running. Dots of fresh blood. Heading south.

He broke into a sprint in the slightly more passable broken trail that lurched, seeking the easiest access among the hills and hummocks and deadfall. Instinctively he stowed the flashlight and pulled out the .45.

She may be resisting, which would slow down her captor.

Running flat out now. Breath burning. Vision going to sweat. *Can't keep this up for more than a minute, but* gotta try— *what Harry's doing. And he's carrying equipment.*

Don't think. Move.

Faint at first, wind playing tricks? No, those were snatches of voices. He could just make out that the tracks skirted to the right, around a low sloping hill. Broker's gut told him to go straight up the hill, and as he scrambled, falling, getting up, to the top, he distinctly heard Harry's challenge ring out sharp and clear and dead serious:

"HALT! TURN AROUND! LET HER GO! NOW!"

He topped the rise and blinked away sweat as he caught his breath. Twenty yards below him he made out three shadowy figures. Harry moved forward in a stalking crouch, his hands raised, the camera bag slung on his back. Something in his left hand? Broker pawed the snow from his eyes. He recognized Andrea by her hair that was flying in the wind. A man dressed in gray winter gear had his left hand tangled in that hair, pulling her in close to shield his body. As Broker's .45 came up in a two-handed grip, he noticed that she was gagged. Her hands were bound, crossed in front of her. The man wore a black ski mask and extended his right hand—*Gun!* Broker steadied the Colt. Sheer reflex. Point and shoot, but the target was hugging Andrea so close.

What! The sudden flare of illumination blinded him, but in the fading flash of light he heard two muffled pops. Blinking away stars, he made out that the man next to Andrea was down, dragging her with him as Harry darted forward. Bounding down the hill, Broker saw that Harry was carrying a camera body in his left hand with a flash attachment. *Where'd he get the silenced .22 in his right hand? Yanked it from the bag on his back? Jesus, Harry. Talk about pushing the edge. Shut your eyes. Trip the flash. Blind the other guy.* As he reached level ground, Andrea had rolled away from the prone figure, raised her bound hands and torn off the gag.

She scrambled in the snow, kicking at the body of her former captor to gain some distance. Broker heard her voice spike with rising hysteria as she saw him approach. "Jesus Christ!" she shouted.

He saw the problem: he and Harry were just two more threatening shadows in the gathering dark. He switched on the flashlight.

"Broker!"

Then he was kneeling to her. He stowed the Colt in his waistband and jammed the handle of the flashlight in the snow. He pulled off his gloves, removed a knife from his pocket, and flicked it open with his thumb.

"It's okay," he said as he cut through the duct tape that bound her wrists, then pocketed the knife. "Breathe."

"Breathe? Are you nuts? *Is he—dead?*" she shouted as a spasm of bone-deep shivers wracked her body. A normal person would have avoided her eyes.

Broker put a hand on her shoulder to steady her, then took a moment to inspect her face. Her nose was bleeding, and there was ugly swelling on her left cheek. She shied away when he touched the bruise lightly to test for broken bones.

"Came right up, smiling, never said a word. Grabbed me. I tried to fight and he hit me, put that gun to my head," she stammered through chattering teeth as she tore at sticky shards of the tape that still clung to her wrists, flinging them away like repulsive insects. Then she clasped her red, chapped hands together. "Lost my hat and gloves."

Then he turned to Harry, who, totally spent, had slumped to his knees next to the man he'd just shot in the left eye. Turning back to Andrea, Broker gently brushed fragments of the dead man's eye socket from Andrea's forehead—a wasted gesture. Now her forehead was streaked with more blood.

"Breathe through your nose. Do it," he commanded as he reached under his coat and ripped the hem of his fleece. "Pressure," he said as he held the ragged swatch of cloth to her nose. When she reached up and held the compress, he turned back to Harry.

Harry was shaking his head, trembling from holding it together till the end of the sprint. "What—the—hell just happened?" he gasped.

"I don't know. Yet," Broker answered.

"Cat didn't leave me any choice."

"I'm real glad you were here, man," Broker said.

All he could see in the gloom were the whites of Harry's eyes. "Was close, Phil; hadda go for it." Orienting quickly, Harry caught himself. "Well, we are now officially in the shit! Question is, whose shit?" He rifled the dead man's parka pockets and held up a small roll of duct tape that he tossed aside. Next he found a compact pair of Zeiss binoculars, which he threw to Broker. He completed the pocket search and said, "No radio." Then he plucked the dead man's pistol from the snow and held it up in his left hand, next to his own pistol in his right hand. Both .22s. Both silenced.

Andrea, who picked at stuff caught in her hair, jerked alert, confused when she heard the alien, tonal sounds of Vietnamese come from Harry's lips: *"Co le ang chang nay giong nhur chung toi."* Maybe this guy's like us.

Broker responded, *"Chung tai phai siu co lai gan."* We have to keep her close, he said, glancing toward Andrea, who had started to hyperventilate, panting through her mouth. *"Khong the de co ay noi chuyen voi canh sat."* Can't let her talk to the cops.

Harry nodded as he tossed the pistol in the snow next to the body. He withdrew the separate pieces of his Car 15 from his camera bag and swiftly assembled them. He slapped in a magazine and pulled the operating rod, and the bolt slammed home with a metal clash, arming the weapon. "Guys like this don't operate alone," he said, reverting back to English. "I'll get up there, on over watch." He jerked his head at the hill Broker had descended, the only high ground in the immediate area. "You check him."

"C'mon." Broker tugged Andrea's jacket, pulled her to a squatting position, and quietly, but firmly, commanded, "Breathe through your nose. You have to help me."

"What? WHAT?" she gasped as she fumbled the compress.

"C'mon," Broker repeated, pulling her toward the corpse. The world had become very tiny, just a body in a pool of flashlight beam. The two of them. Darkness and storm swirl closing in. When she hung back, he raised his voice. "Do your job," he said and cuffed her shoulder, hard. Which was just the simple lesson you learn in the killing fields—give her something immediate to focus on. Now it was a toss-up. Would the adrenaline flooding her veins swallow the shock and allow her to function? Numb, she rallied, and they hunkered over the body. Andrea balked and flexed her freezing hands. "Go through his pockets. Do it," Broker said in a firm voice as he reached up and pulled the ski mask from the man's head.

As Andrea tentatively started searching the inner pockets of the man's jacket, Broker crouched and played the flashlight across the dead man's face. Forty maybe, clean features, if you ignored what the hollow point had done to the left eye. With the prominent nose and a thick shock of black hair, the clotted features were handsome in a chiseled way. Even in the compromised electric light and furious snow, Broker saw facial features that suggested the Middle East.

"Nothing in the pockets," Andrea said. Her voice faltered, still shaky, but better.

"Take off his boots and socks. We're looking for anything," Broker said as he began stripping off the dead man's jacket, then his fleece and upper underwear.

The radio scritched in his jacket. Quickly, he had it out and keyed send. "Joey, where are you?"

"Good question," Soap's voice came back. "You find the woman?"

"We found her. She's—okay."

"Glad to hear, but I never found Joey. His skis, poles and pack with the radio and his pistol were laying along the side of the trail. His tracks cut into the woods to an access road and this little county equipment shed. There's tire tracks, something with big snow tires, and that's where Joey's tracks end."

Broker's heart plummeted. *Shit!* This thing didn't have a bottom. "Gather up Joey's stuff and meet us in the parking lot."

"We're not looking for him?"

"Soap, buddy. Listen to me. We just had a little dust-up in the woods." Broker stood up and walked several paces away, out of Andrea's hearing, then cupped his hand over his mouth as he spoke into the radio. "I'm pretty sure I'm looking at one of the guys who put Leper in your freezer. You copy?"

"Oh yeah, I copy. I'd like a few moments alone with him."

"Never happen. How do you hear?"

After a few seconds Soap just said, "Roger that."

"Head for the parking lot. We need to get those cars out of here before they draw attention. Now move. Fast," Broker said.

Soap, perhaps jolted back to his days in the snowy Ardennes, answered crisply. "Wilco." Will comply.

Then Broker stuffed the radio into his parka and turned back to checking the dead man's naked torso and arms. Andrea made a face as she pulled off the boots, then the socks. She paused, staring at snowflakes that stuck on the bare ankles. Broker swiped snow from his eyebrows to clear his vision and turned back to his body search. He was looking for an identifying mark, a scar, a tattoo, mole, birthmark? Anything. As he lifted the loose left arm, he shined the light below the bicep.

What the hell! He jerked, drew in a sharp breath, and rocked back on his heels. There was your normal shit and then there was deep, dark, dangerous shit! *Here we go.*

"Harry," he yelled up the hill, "they're professionals. Get down here. I got something you're going to want to photograph."

"Quiet down. I'm more worried about them coming back on us," Harry called back in a husky voice.

Broker didn't quiet down. "Whoever else was here is gone. For now. We have other problems. Just talked to Soap, and Joey's missing. Said his tracks ended where a vehicle had been parked along the trail."

"Great," Harry said as he scrambled down the hill. Hearing about Joey, Andrea's eyes glimmered, moist, in the pool of spill light coming off the flashlight. She scooted closer, on her knees in the snow. She was clutching herself in an effort to contain the shivers. But she held a business card between two of her fingers. "This was in his right sock; it's from a tobacco shop in St. Paul. There's a phone number on the back," she said. Then, leaning forward, she saw the tattoo in the light of Broker's flashlight, on the underside of the dead man's left arm. "What's that?" she inquired. Broker heard more curiosity than fear in her voice, and her bouncing back was maybe the only thing to feel good about in this whole downward spiral of events. Less good was the fact that the image scribed in the graying flesh was Harry's namesake.

"It's a winged griffin," Broker said softly.

Chapter Twenty-Three

"It's a Persian mythological beast: a winged lion, normally with the head of an eagle," Harry explained in a loud but calm voice, over the moan of the wind and the creaking branches overhead. Time was tight, so he quickly arranged the arm to get a good angle on the tattoo. Then he copied the number off the card into a notebook, put the notebook back in his bag, and placed the card, with the phone number up, next to the tattoo. He motioned Broker in to pin the card in place with his thumb, so it wouldn't fly away in the blowing snow. Harry raised his camera and focused, and the flash winked. Six, seven, eight pictures. Then he took several careful portraits of the dead man's face and his upper torso to include the tattooed arm.

"In this configuration it has the head of a Persian king from antiquity, Cyrus maybe," he said as he wiped snow from his camera, stowed it in the bag, and turned on his flashlight. He glanced at Broker.

With a slight grimace, Broker continued the narrative. "Which happens to be the icon on the official seal of the Saze-man, something or another, Amniyate Keshvar. I assume the script under the image is in Farsi—so what we're looking at is the insignia of an outfit better known by its acronym: SAVAK."

Harry's eyes were bottom-lit by the flashlights and entertained a witch's brew of amusement, doom, and fascination as he turned to Andrea and stated, "So if this is for real, what's a member of the former Iranian secret police doing pointing a gun at your head?"

Andrea's face misfired. "Here! In a rinky-dink park in Washington County, Minnesota?" She cleared her throat. "Broker," she said, her voice rising, "I don't think we're supposed to get *this involved!*"

"No shit," Broker said slowly as he appraised what his plan had come to: three people, shivering, their clothes soaked with sweat, huddled over a half-naked body in low beams of light. What the hell had Travis Diggs stumbled into? He was fresh out of insight. The machinery that had served him so well in the tropics was stuck in the cold.

Out of reflex he started redressing the body, first handing the card back to Andrea, who, learning fast, gingerly inserted it back in the sock on the corpse's right foot. Then she reached for the boots and replaced them. She paused to blow on and flex her freezing fingers. After she laced the boots, she stood up and dusted snow off her smarting hands. Harry handed her a spare set of gloves and a hat from his camera bag. As she pulled them on, she tilted her head. "Now what?" she asked in a more steady voice.

"We *di di mau*, man," Harry said. "We split as fast as we can."

"What are you getting me into here?" she blurted. "We're just going to leave a body lying in the woods?"

"Probably won't be laying here long. These kind of guys clean up after themselves," Harry said.

"Andrea," Broker said, putting more firmness in his tone than he was feeling at the moment, "we have other problems. Like where's Joey? We'll talk this through later. Right now we have to get out of here. Are we clear?"

Andrea took several deep breaths. "Clear," she said as her shoulders sagged, and she let Broker lead her from the shooting scene. Immediately they set off through the woods, flashlights doused, the storm forgotten. Broker read an east azimuth on the luminous dial of the compass that he always kept in his parka. Harry stalked a dozen paces ahead, careful heel and toe, pausing every eight to ten steps to listen as the short black rifle in his hands swung slowly from side to side.

Chapter Twenty-Four

Soap met them on the state trail and they hurried toward the parking lot, where three vehicles remained under a solitary sodium vapor lamp. When Harry added the dead Persian detail to the gunfight in the dark, Soap stared at Andrea's face, then stopped in his tracks. *An echo of losing Joey maybe,* Broker thought. But Soap quickly shook it off, joined the others, and got busy hot-wiring Joey's Bronco. Harry drove Andrea's Audi. Broker had the Suburban. They convoyed on Soap in the Bronco, who took the point. Forty-five bad minutes after the shooting, they limped into the questionable warmth of the repair shop lobby. Rita was waiting, fists on hips, with typical *sang froid.*

"So who the hell is this?" she asked, sizing up Andrea's blood-streaked face and bedraggled hair.

"She's with me," Harry offered.

"And who are you? The Detroit guy?" she said to Harry.

Broker dumped his gun cases in the corner. Harry helped Andrea to a seat, then dropped his camera bag. Utterly exhausted, they flopped on the couch and two chairs. Rita persisted, "Where's Joey?" Only then did she ask the operative question. "Hey, Dad? What the fuck happened?"

First Broker tried to collect his thoughts. When they failed to line up right, he stood up, abruptly stripped off his coat, and flung it aside. Seeing the wary expression come to Rita's face, he managed to moderate his voice. "Rita, can you show Andrea to the shower and find her something dry to wear?"

202

"Andrea, huh." Rita approached Andrea and appraised her thousand-yard stare. "What's up? I say again, where's Joey?"

"Just do it," Soap growled, coming forward on the couch. Then, in a devastated gesture, he lowered his face into his hands and his baritone cracked. "When you get her situated, come back here and we'll talk."

A chastised Rita motioned to Andrea and helped her up from her chair. "C'mon, hon; this way."

Soap moved to the front door, rested his hand on the handle of the Colt in his waistband, and stared into the snow. A guard, of sorts. To give him some space, Broker motioned Harry down the hall, past the shower room and up the stairs to the lunchroom. They pulled off their sweat-drenched underlayers and hung them to dry. Their eyes met and they agreed. Speaking would only undercut the murderous silence.

After they dug dry clothes out of Broker's duffel, they changed, and coming back down the stairs, they exchanged tight smiles. Their leg muscles still shook from the sprint through the snow. Harry stated the obvious: "Time, doncha think, for Soap Turrie to come clean about who we just tangled with!"

They entered the lobby and found Soap still staring out the thick glass door. When he turned, Broker wasn't sure which storm was more turbulent, the one outside or the one in Soap's eyes.

"You have some explaining to do," Broker said in a cold tone of voice—one Soap was hearing for the first time.

Soap removed his windbreaker. "I don't know who they are," he said, his big voice now uneasy.

"Then get a fucking clue." Harry's narrow face stripped down to ruthless edges and angles that echoed in his voice. "There's a dead Iranian goon laying out there in the snow, and he damn near killed Andrea." He paused, then shot some poison Broker's way. "Who shouldn't have been anywhere near this thing."

Broker shook off Harry's censure, but the sting stayed. *Joey's missing. Andrea's in the back, freaked out.* He didn't need the rational machinery to remind him that he was running a streak of bad calls.

"Dead Persians." Soap cleared his throat. "You want to talk about dead Persians? Care to connect some dots?" Walking heavily, he crossed the room, went behind the counter, and knelt to the small company safe. Only the top of his head showed over the counter as he moved items to the desk. He stood up and came back with an envelope and dumped the contents on the coffee table. "There's your dead Persian."

A pile of foreign currency scattered on the table. Broker perused the ornate beige and rust design, the notations in Farsi, and the bust of Shah Reza Pavlavi, brocade high collar, shoulder boards and all. There was even a prominent engraving of a winged griffin. "Iranian *rials*, from the old regime," he said, narrowing his eyes.

Soap nodded, crossed back to the counter, and leaned in to pick something off the desk. "But here's the thing," he stated as he tossed a shiny package about the size of a compact cereal box made out of Benjamin Franklin's enigmatic United States Treasury engraved smile endlessly repeated. Broker caught a brick of vacuum-sealed one hundred dollar bills.

"What do you think it weighs?" Soap asked.

Broker hefted it and handed it to Harry, who said, "About two pounds."

"One bill is one gram," Soap said.

"Four hundred fifty-four grams to the pound," said Broker.

"Okay, so, shit." Harry tipped his eyes up. "Add two zeros and a comma and . . ." He gestured with the brick. "Just whose ninety thousand bucks are we holding here? Iranians with a drug connection?"

Moisture pebbled Soap's forehead as he sagged into one of the leather chairs. "It's not dope that Leper blundered into.

Norman Bolin took the bicycle parts at face value. Leper dug deeper and found cash."

"Cash; not product?" Harry's forehead creased.

"Cash money," Soap said, turning to Broker. "I didn't really believe it until you first showed up. Once you were upstairs, asleep, Joey brought in *this* stuff. When he went up to check on Annie, she walked him through it. Broker, the box? It's packed full. Joey wouldn't lie."

"You're shitting us, right?" Harry asked, his eyes fixed on Soap's face.

"Joey wouldn't lie," Soap repeated and pointed at the *rials*. "He said *that* stuff was strewn on top of the currency. Maybe somebody's idea of a joke. Maybe not so funny now." Broker and Harry stared at him. "It's ten feet long. It's five feet on a side."

"Which is—one hundred and twenty-five cubic feet," said Broker, taking the cash brick back from Harry. "Mashed down like this?"

"Annie figures you can fit more than a million bucks in a cubic foot," Soap said.

"Annie figures?" Broker said.

"Correct," Soap said.

Harry inclined his head and hitched his eyebrows. "In a box? In the fucking woods?"

"Yes, sir," said Soap. "Chain of custody is Leper to Annie, who said it was just too damn much money to steal. So she called Desmond." Soap squinted his eyes and kneaded a couple thick fingers at the bridge of his nose. "And we all know how that turned out."

"So she called you," Broker said after a pause.

Soap nodded. "Last Wednesday night, from a pay phone on the road. After Desmond failed to show up,"

"So you played dumb all week, first with Desmond, then with Merriweather, and now with me and Harry. And what did you and Annie decide on the phone last Wednesday night?" Broker's voice coldly stacked the words.

"She'd fort up in the cabin. I'd nose around to see who might be missing a good-sized crate full of money. What Desmond was looking for, but different. Then I found Leper."

Harry winced, scrubbed his face in his palm, and proceeded to pace back and forth. "I love it! And along came Broker!" He bobbed his head from side to side as if to negate the doomed fascination in his eyes. "Last time it was a Chinook full of the CIA's fucking heroin. Now it's a dump truck full of what? The Shah's rainy day fund, that's drawing sharks with SAVAK tattoos?"

"We don't know whose it is, goddammit," Broker said. *But you had to admit—*

"Well, *somebody's* swimming pool full of cash got lost in the shuffle and wound up in *Minnesota*?" Harry shot back. "Broker, man, this is starting to get that heavy feeling. Swear to God, I think you *attract* this shit!" And he said it all without once dropping the bemused smile from his lips.

He lost the smile when he spun and pointed his finger at Soap. "You should have told us who we were up against. The *size* of the cargo should have *informed* you!" He set his coffee cup down on the table, went to his camera bag, and withdrew his short black rifle along with a tac rag. He wiped away moisture as he cleared the action, checked the magazine, reinserted the mag, and stowed the rag. Immediately he moved to the front door. His eyes darted back and forth across the parking lot. "We should move," he said. "This is *not* a defensible position."

Broker sank into the chair across from Soap. *Okay. The world is a little tilted. Time is skewed, and we're bouncing off walls in reaction mode. And Andrea's shock is getting a little contagious.*

"So you see why Annie ran for it. Who do you trust when you're throwing around those kinds of numbers?" Soap said.

"So you brought me in to clear a minefield," Broker said.

"What was I supposed to do?" Soap came forward in the chair, testy. "Go to my buddy Hector and say, 'Gee, I need some help with these bad dudes leaning on my guys and, oh yeah, Annie has their stuff, a hundred million bucks, give or take a few million, in a truck out there all alone in the fucking woods'? You met Hector. He's a career criminal. Bye bye, Soap and Annie. I thought maybe we could *manage* finding the guys who cut on Norman Bolin," Soap said. "Well, they found us trying to find them, and Boom, here we are."

"A ton of money," Broker said softly. "Like Leper told Charlene."

"Broker." Harry came over and enunciated. "You are not grasping the potential gravity here, man. We need to relocate, post haste."

Soap tensed, feeding off Harry. "They've got Joey. They could be cutting on him right now. And he knows where Annie is, with their—stuff."

Broker thought about it.

Soap's facial muscles clenched. "Too many people are dead or missing, and my wife and kid are at risk. You had your shot, Broker. You two?" He swung his eyes on Broker and Harry. "You get to ride off into the sunset. Me?" He thumped his chest. "I have to bury Leper, and now maybe Joey!"

"Slow down," Broker said.

"Fuck you, slow down." Soap's voice rose. "I'm calling it. Have Andrea phone Cantrell; then we lock and load and head for Hinckley and pray that Annie's still there in one piece. If she is, we set up a perimeter and wait for the cavalry. Fuck a bunch of undercover bullshit!"

"We make a run for Annie, they could follow us," Broker said.

Soap rose from the chair in a crouch. His right hand chopped the air, driving home his words. "*Then get us an escort. They. Have. Joey!*"

Broker continued to think about it as he fingered a battered Lucky from his jeans and thumbed his Zippo. He took a calming drag, expelled a lungful of smoke, and watched it twist arabesques in the uneasy air. It was just a feeling, an unexpected intuition, like a piece of Detroit appearing on a wall in a small Minnesota river town. But he went with it. *Thing about smoke. Why the Vietnamese burn all that incense. They believe their ancestors can only read smoke coming off the joss sticks. Smoke is a prayer.*

"It's time to make the call," Soap finished.

"Not yet. Did you actually see someone take Joey?" Broker asked.

"I saw the goddamn tracks, man." Soap was on the verge of throwing his coffee cup at the wall. "What? You're playing with people's lives now?" he yelled.

Broker peered into the black bottom of his coffee cup. When he looked up, he saw Rita standing in the ajar door that led to the back of the shop. There was a slight bloom of steam drifting in the doorway, the faint background drip of a shower someone hadn't turned all the way off.

"How long have you been standing there?" he thought out loud as an edgy silence filled the lobby and they stared into each other's eyes across the wreckage of the day.

"Long enough, and Andrea told me some." She walked into the room and stood in front of Broker. "And I don't think she should be alone right now." Then she faced her father. "So, does this go all the way back to greasing the skids on psycho Uncle Danny's dope operation and sticking him in prison? Is it a question of calling the cops?" She paused and looked directly, first at Broker and then at Harry. "Or are the cops already here?"

When no one responded, a cynical grin spread across her freckled face. "Right, I get it. It's complicated." She jerked her head back at the doorway. "So what does it mean, have Andrea make the call? Is she the cop?"

"She's a psychologist, actually," Harry said.

"Uh huh, right," Rita said. "Goldilocks is a psychologist. *With blood on her face.*" She inhaled, held the breath for a thoughtful moment, then expelled it. "Okay, here's the deal. I don't know about tons of money and this undercover I Spy bullshit. But I'm betting on Joey. He's not exactly a kid. So let's not count him out yet."

Huh! Broker showed an affirmative grimace.

All eyes turned to Soap, who bridled his lips and threw up his hands. "Just sit here and do nothing?"

"We watch the phone," Broker said.

"And wait?"

"Maybe they're back on their heels, just like us," Broker said, still riding his smoky hunch. "Harry, you said it—they didn't have radios. Why's that? You really think a platoon of Iranians is going to get on line and assault across the parking lot in a winter storm? They don't need more drama now. They've got their hands full."

Harry squinted, weighing it. "The guy not having commo was off. So you're saying we can't confirm they've got Joey. And they do have a body to dispose of. So maybe they need to regroup, listen to a police scanner, see if anyone has reported a shooting. Which could buy us some time." He paused. "But hey, Phil?" he said. "This will not end well."

With that off his chest, he slung his rifle over his shoulder and briefly assessed the other faces in the room. Then he went to his camera bag, removed a camera, and tapped a button to rewind the film. When the Nikon stopped whirring, he opened it, removed the roll and held it up. "Darkroom," he said to Rita.

Rita's voice was steady, but her eyes were still riding the rapids of the last few minutes. "Tommy Lynum, guy I dated in high school. He lives on the north hill, five minutes away. He's standing by. He works in a bank, but his hobby is environmental photography. Has a set-up in his basement you can use. No questions asked, if, ah, Dad agrees to fix his car for free for the next year."

Soap grumbled. Broker appreciated how Harry was moving in fast to fill the depressing vacuum with busy work. He said, "So you drive Harry over there. No detours, point to point. Leave us a number, and call the minute you arrive."

"I can do that," Rita said as she walked around the counter, grabbed a pen, and wrote two numbers on the blotter, then printed PAGER under one of them. Then she picked up the phone receiver and dialed. After several beats she said, "Yeah, Tommy, it's Rita. That thing we talked about. It's happening now. Okay. See you in a few."

As she put the receiver back in the cradle, Harry removed the notebook from his bag and slapped it down on the service counter. "So does Andrea call her friend and discreetly run that number? Or do we sit on it? Be nice to know where it rings and who answers it. Just the number, not what we left back there in the woods. Can she handle that?"

"Her friend, huh?" Rita snorted, eyes rolling up. "You guys."

"I'll talk to her, see where she's at," Broker said, looking toward the doorway that led to the back of the building and the shower room.

"Cool," Harry said. "And while you're at it, explain to her that she's on the bus or off the bus from now on. If she balks, we may have to sit on her until it plays out."

"Great." Soap managed a chuckle. "So we add kidnapping to not reporting a shooting and leaving a body in the woods. That's federal. Why don't we just rob a bank while we're at it?"

"I'll talk to her," Broker repeated, picking up the notebook and tucking the brick of cash under his arm.

Rita reached behind the counter for her coat, then said, "Dad, Jimmy Briggs called. Number's on the blotter." She motioned to Harry. "C'mon, Motown, I'm in the Trans Am in the lot." After she pulled on her jacket, she leaned over and switched on the desk radio to the public radio classical station and said, "How about everybody chill out?" She turned to Harry, who draped his parka over his shoulders like a shawl, concealing the short Car 15. "Okay. Wow, I guess," she said as they went out the door into the blowing snow.

Soap heaved to his feet, came around the counter, and sat heavily in the chair. "I'll watch the phone and the parking lot," he said, glum. He turned the radio dial to Waylon and Willie on a country western station, then stared at the number Rita had left for him on the blotter.

Chapter Twenty-Five

His cramped leg muscles smarted as Broker followed the damp footprints up the stairs and into the converted lunchroom to where Andrea sat on a cot in a jumble of blankets with her hair turbaned in a towel. She wore the same terrycloth robe that Rita had worn earlier in the day. Her wool socks, fleece and long underwear hung, drying, off the top of a cupboard, alongside Broker's and Harry's. There was a stack of clean, neatly-folded clothing on the cot next to her: a sweat suit, socks, some underthings. She picked up a big-toothed plastic comb that sat on the clothing as he lowered himself down on a cot across from her and placed the notebook, number showing, and the package at his side.

"She's something, Rita Turrie," Andrea said in a disembodied voice without raising her eyes. "Heard the yelling downstairs. What's up? Dissention in the ranks? Any word on Joey?" Then she saw what Broker had placed on the cot. She stared at the notebook on the rumpled blankets and spotted the lump of money smothered in plastic wrap like a greenback pot roast.

"What is *that*?" She pointed with the comb and blinked, losing the fog. "I mean, I know what it is, *but what is it*?"

Broker hunched his shoulders as a bitter smile rippled on his lips. "The yelling downstairs was Soap filling in the back story. Turns out everything we know is wrong. It isn't dope. It's smugglers and a literal *ton* of hundred dollar bills. One dead Persian doesn't prove it came out of Iran when the regime collapsed. But there's a drift in that direction. Anyone's guess how it landed in a warehouse in St. Paul."

First her vision clears up, now here comes the personality, Broker thought as he watched the hot Gypsy eyes surge to hex levels. "Broker, *you sonofabitch!* What did you get me into?" The effort drained her, and the heat sputtered in her eyes.

"It *was* a negotiation. *Now,* after what happened in the woods—looks like we're in a fight," he said.

She'd collapsed back into numb. With sleepy motions she methodically removed the towel from her head, shook out her hair, and raised the comb. Each movement was scripted, tightly controlled. Her pupils yawned, dilated. "And Joey?" she asked.

"We're waiting."

"Really. For what?"

"It's unclear. Possibly they didn't snatch him."

"After they failed to snatch me?" She pursed her lips, then spoke in a very metered, taut voice. "You know, when we left the car in the lot to head into the woods, Harry told me to leave my ID in the glove compartment. I assume he wasn't carrying any. And now it occurs to me that if things had taken a different bounce out there, and I'd kept my wallet in my jacket—that someone could be rifling the clothing on my dead body, just like I did to that guy. And they would have found Cantrell's business card, with the contact number written on the back." She took a deep breath, then let it out. "That occurred to me." Her gaze wandered, helplessly, back to the money. "How much is that?"

"A lot. So how are you doing?" Broker asked, carefully watching her face.

She trembled, hugged herself with both arms, and jerked a weak grin. "Are you fucking kidding! Christ. Look at us. *You're* assessing *me* for shock!"

"Answer the question," Broker said quietly.

"How am I doing? How about I'm having some trouble processing. As a general rule I tend to keep my emotions pretty locked down. But I'm pretty shook up. The hot shower helped. A lot. A whole lot, in fact."

"And?"

"Now's the time when I say 'Gee, too bad about the other guy, but it's sure great to be alive, huh?'" She raised her hand to the right side of her face and laid the fingers along her temple. "His head was touching mine when the bullet hit. I felt it." She shivered. "I heard it. A few minutes ago I watched little pieces of his skull wash around my bare toes and go down the shower drain, stuff that was matted with blood in my hair." Another deep breath, another exhale. "Harry's real good. I never thanked him for . . ."

"Not the way it works," Broker said. "He was there for you, and now . . ."

Andrea dropped her eyes and drew the comb through her damp hair. One stroke, then another. Her voice fell into a dirge-like cadence. "So it's jailyard rules. Now I repay the gesture by being there for him, and for you and for Turrie and his family?" For several heartbeats she stared into the middle distance, then continued, "Which takes priority over being there for Cantrell and the state crime bureau? Is that how it works?"

"We need your help, Andrea," Broker said simply.

"You need my fucking silence," she said.

"We need your silence. For a while." A muscle jumped in Broker's cheek.

Her wobbly smile curved downward, and her eyes did a bank shot off the money package. It took several seconds for her to compose a response in that deliberate voice.

"So the way it works is, I can stick to the reporting rules I'm sworn to uphold—harm to self or others. Or I can keep faith with the guy who saved my life. Wow. Some trauma seminar you're running here, Mr. Broker."

"Does that mean—" Broker began.

She raised a hand to silence him. "You, and your crazy pal, you're not just out-of-work Samurai. Who the hell are you?" She was trying to rally, trying to recharge the full frontal eyes.

Broker rubbed his forehead, reached for his Luckies, saw her extend her hand. "Didn't know you smoked," he said, shaking out two cigarettes. He put them to his lips and lit them with the Zippo.

She accepted the cigarette and took an experimental drag. "Just once in a while. Like now," she said. Calmer, she was waiting for his answer.

He watched the smoke seep from their lips and mingle in the space between them. No prayers this time. Just smoke. Like what comes off wreckage, like the usually reliable machinery that was mashed into a lump in his chest. He flexed his jaw muscles and just shrugged. "Sorry."

"So you think you can shitcan the past like that tattoo on your arm? What's that leave you? One big scar?" she asked.

Broker thought about it. He was asking a lot from her, so he had to give her something. He said, "Not all the out-of-step dreamers were marching in the street." Broker couldn't suppress an absurd laugh. "You ever see that little cartoon trailer from back in the sixties—*Bambi Meets Godzilla*?"

"Yeah, I remember." She forced a fragile smile, more at ease, doing that lift and tuck with her bare legs, resettling on the cot.

"Suffice it to say that, in the geo-political scheme of things, me and Harry—we were Bambi. So, we kinda got stomped by all sides."

Andrea absorbed his words, then raised the cigarette to her lips, made a face, and held it at arm's length. Broker got up, searched the room, and found an ashtray. As they stubbed out their smokes, she said in an amazed voice, "An hour ago I had some guy's optic nerve tangled in my hair, and now we're sitting here smiling?"

Broker fixed on her eyes that were stronger now. "You survive the worst thing in the world. Can't imagine being more shook. Then some time passes, and you realize you need to eat, go to the bathroom, sleep."

"Guess you can't beat some clichés. So can I go home now?"

"'Fraid not."

"So who was that guy who grabbed me?"

"Not sure yet."

"Right. Bullshit." She sat erect and folded her arms across her chest. "I was there, listening to you and Harry talk in what—Vietnamese—to keep me out of the loop. You have an idea, don't you?"

"You work with cops. You know that intuitions—suspicions —aren't evidence."

"Oh, c'mon. I've just been through the fucking looking glass. You want me to play cat and mouse, you have to level with me."

"You won't like it," Broker said.

"Try me," she said.

For a beat his mind slipped, and he wondered if she'd ever been married.

"Well?" she prodded.

He caught himself. "We said we got a feeling off that guy that reminded us of us—what we were. Covert operators."

"Jesus. You're right." she said. "I don't like it. Doesn't mean I'm going to curl up in a fetal position." She set her jaw.

"What's the arrangement with Cantrell?" Broker asked.

"I have his pager number. I call it, he calls back. But I doubt he's staring at his pager waiting for it to buzz. Tomorrow's Thanksgiving. Even Cantrell probably has someplace to go to dinner." Andrea tilted her head and continued to draw Rita's comb through her hair, working out tangles, the strokes surer now. "How much of that is there?" She pointed with the comb again.

"Too much to steal, according to Annie O'Neil," Broker said. "You were saying?"

"Cantrell, right. Not like he's suited up in a garage with a task force ready to roll out the minute the phone rings. This was a shot in the dark, remember?" Her lips bridled. "Bad word choice," she said in a more subdued voice.

Broker leaned forward. "Bringing in Cantrell is tricky until we know who we're dealing with. We'd like to know who answers this number." He lifted the notebook. "But, if you reach out too soon, it could tip them, blow my cover, and make Soap's problem worse. And now Joey's whereabouts are up in the air." Then more carefully Broker said, "And we'd have to involve Cantrell and BCA on a selective basis."

"You mean I lie," she stated.

"Omit certain information," Broker said.

"About a body in the woods."

"Andrea." Broker came further forward and leaned his elbows on his knees. "That was the *second* body."

"Jesus." Andrea put down the comb, repositioned, and swung her feet to the floor so that now she also leaned forward, elbows on knees. "You have to make the call, bring in Cantrell."

"No big-footed war elephants, not yet," Broker said firmly. Then he collected the notebook and the increasingly malignant chunk of cash and stood up. "Okay, tough guy," he said. "Get dressed for outside. We're taking a walk. I'll be in the lobby."

Downstairs the gloom was palpable in the stuffy air. Soap was hanging up the phone. "Rita called. They're developing the film. And that was Jimmy Briggs, my real estate partner, also a graybeard elder with visiting rights to the Castaways. Only person I trusted to get Jan out of here. Jimmy says that an hour ago a guy was showing lots of money in the Bucket of Blood.

That's a biker joint in North St. Paul. This guy was all business, very fit and squared away, and not the least bit impressed with all the leather and tattoos. He was willing to pay for information about me and Annie, like, way back when we were in the game running stolen goods, did we have a love nest/stash house."

"Like Hector said," Broker said.

Soap nodded. "Jimmy said everybody was cool and blew the guy off, thinking he was a fed. So they're going to move Jan and put some more guys with her. That could be a weak spot if enough money gets flashed. They get a line on my wife?" Soap bit his lip. "Rolling the dice with Joey is one thing; Jan is another."

"Slow it down," Broker said. "If they have Joey, why would they be spreading money around?"

"You're reaching."

"Yep. Meanwhile, we have to bring Andrea all the way on board. That means filling her in about Leper. So I need the keys for out back."

Soap sagged, shaking his head.

"Soap, when the time comes, we need her to finesse liaison with BCA. So we let her in on everything."

"You think?" Soap was dubious. "Some straight arrow college professor *shrink*?"

The strained, low-pitched laugh of a woman who works with men preceded Andrea, who entered the lobby wearing her parka over a maroon Minnesota Gophers tracksuit. "Not like you have a choice, Mr. Turrie. I'm in too fucking deep." She nodded at Broker. "And he won't turn me loose."

"Jesus," Soap grumbled, pulling open a drawer and digging in a pile of keys. "You put on Rita's old warmup and now you're talking like her." He slammed a key ring on the counter and pointed. "Gate. Garage. Freezer. And cut the Mr. Turrie stuff. It's Soap."

"Soap it is," Andrea said, pausing briefly to note that Soap had uncased Broker's shotgun and his assault rifle. The two weapons now leaned against a file cabinet next to two more shotguns.

They exited the shop, heading for the back lot along the chain-link fence, and Broker's facial muscles relaxed as he registered the silence. No wind. No snow. The storm had paused. Their breath preceded them in the clean, cold air as, all around, white sequins sparkled and smoothed out sharp edges, like a childhood vision of Christmas. They unlocked and passed through the gate; then Broker opened the Quonset door, reached around and switched on the overhead lights. Their boots crunched on the frozen trap rock as they walked down the aisle of building materials and earthmoving equipment. Broker stopped in front of the freezer. Last key. Last lock. Last secret. He lifted the lid.

Andrea grunted, a sound between gagging and clearing her throat, and leaned into Broker's shoulder and squeezed his arm with gloved hands. Then she quickly recovered, and Broker watched her galvanize her newly augmented coping skills to rinse all emotion from her eyes until nothing was left but focused attention.

"Travis Diggs," Broker said. "Worked for Soap."

"I read the file," Andrea said.

"So you know he was a harmless little thief who stole the wrong crate, popped the lid, freaked out, and passed it on to Annie O'Neil."

"How long have you known about this?" Andrea asked.

Broker composed his face in his best date-with-the-hangman grin. "Since about an hour before I called you last night. Suddenly it was a whole new ballgame."

"I guess." Andrea drew in a deep breath, let it out and swallowed. Steeling her voice, she said, "What—happened to his hands?"

"Torture. You saw the note. Soap coughs up the missing crate or Rita and his wife are next. The deadline was Friday noon. Now I got a feeling all bets are off."

"Jesus." She wrapped her arms across her chest and hugged herself. "Those claw marks on the side?"

"Yeah," Broker said. "Now you have an idea who we're dealing with."

Andrea took a few beats to let it sink in. "What else didn't you tell me?"

"Since this started, Soap has known where Annie is hiding with the cargo. Unfortunately, he sent Joey to check on her. This cabin in the woods near Hinckley."

"So if they have Joey?" Andrea's words made cryptic puffs in the chill air. She was still staring into the freezer, her eyes brimming with her second close-up look, in the last two hours, at unfiltered, violent death.

"We are currently hanging by a thread," Broker said without enthusiasm.

Then she drew herself up and pulled her gaze away from the contorted icicle that had been Travis Diggs. Turning, she said, "So what're the odds that me keeping my mouth shut will get you out of the hole you've dug for yourself? What exactly are you trying to prove, taking this on all alone?"

Broker reached for something to brace on, but the machinery had stalled cold in the woods. Cornered, his answer came out blunt, no padding. "I—my folks—need the money, dammit. And because I haven't had a real job *going on four fucking years! I can do this.*"

Before he could finish the thought, they both jumped at the anomalous sound of a horn blaring just outside the building. Immediately he shut the freezer lid, snapped the lock shut, and pocketed the keys. Then he motioned Andrea to shelter behind the thick wheel of the nearby front loader and, with his .45 out and feeling the way forward in a two-handed grip, he cautiously approached the door through which they had entered.

What the hell?

The horn continued to honk. He braced himself, then quick-peeked around the door jamb. The tension totally collapsed when he saw Soap's Suburban parked just ten yards from the doorway, the horn now playing at Morse code: three short bleats, then a longer one. Da da da Daaaaa. *Okay,* Broker cocked a shaggy eyebrow. The grace notes from Beethoven transformed into dots and dashes—V for Victory.

The driver's side door swung open, and Soap jumped out and waved his arms. "C'mon. *Joey just called,*" he yelled.

"What? WHAT?" Broker shouted, shielding his eyes against the high beams, stepping forward. Now he could hear Andrea's quick footsteps behind him on the stiff gravel.

"Joey called," Soap repeated, his face loose and easy with relief.

"Where?" Broker shook his head as he stowed the automatic in his holster.

"From the pay phone at Pine Point Park. Sounded real cold and real pissed off. Like he wanted to know where his car was. C'mon." Soap made shooing motions to Broker and Andrea to get in the Suburban. When they were inside and the doors slammed, the Suburban threw ice and gravel fishtailing through a turn. As he lurched through the gate, Soap chortled with a sideways grin. "Fucking Joey. He found their hangout. That vehicle, the tire tracks I spotted near the trail, where Joey's tracks stopped? They didn't *take* him. He *hitched* a ride."

"How?" Broker cocked his head. Andrea, sitting in back, pitched forward between the seats, all eyes. Broker kept blinking, attempting to clear his mind. He was experiencing a rare sensation somewhere between bewilderment and giddy relief.

"I'll let him tell the story. It's a good story," Soap crowed. He stepped on the gas, and they plunged into the dark.

Chapter Twenty-Six

B ut before Joey could tell his story, his teeth had to stop chattering and he had to crack the ice off his whiskers, which he did on a shivering ride from the park back to the shop, where Harry and Rita were back with developed pictures. Rita was the one with the "told you so" smile.

"It was a white van, big-ass V8, Ford Econoline. Not long after you called me about Andrea, I saw this guy booking out of the woods, so I kicked off my skis and dropped the pack, trying to keep low and follow him. Dumb, I know; shoulda kept the radio and the pistol, but it was happening so fast." Joey had shed his stiff, icy clothing and now sat on the couch in the shop lobby, wrapped in a blanket. Andrea and Rita were sandwiched on either side with their arms draped over his shoulders for warmth. He held a big mug of coffee in his still-shaking hands. He seemed unaware when the steaming liquid slopped on his trembling fingers. Bits of ice still clung to his flaring white mutton chop whiskers, and his bare feet were ankle deep in a clean oil pan that was filled with lukewarm water. Harry knelt, alternately massaging and inspecting Joey's toes that were a little too inflamed for his liking. Harry was being quiet about it, but Broker knew he was assessing the chances of onset frostbite. Cross-country ski boots weren't exactly snow-pack Sorels, and Joey had done a fair amount of winter hiking tonight in below freezing temperatures and foot-deep snow.

Harry pressed his thumbnail into the big toenail on Joey's right foot. When he released the pressure, a faint pink effusion crept back into the pressure-whitened nail. "Capillary circula-tion," he said. "I think you'll survive." Harry got up and stepped back, wiping his hand on a towel.

Soap leaned across the counter with an expansive expres-sion on his lined face. For the moment he was happy, like all of them, except for Harry, who had returned to the front door to scan the parking lot, the street, the snow on the rooftops.

Seeing Broker staring at him, Joey's square face twitched. "What?" he said.

"I never caught your last name," Broker said. Like every-one present, he knew that *Gotterdammerung* could descend on them at any minute. Harry had Joey's .45 tucked in his belt. Soap and Broker both had Colts within easy reach. Harry's and Broker's assault rifles leaned, locked and loaded, on either side of the front door, along with two shotguns. So it was less than ideal conditions for a welcome home party, but even Broker, whose experience with waves of relief had been stingy at best, wore the contagious grin on his face.

"Tikkonin," Joey said.

Finns. Winter War. Best ski troops in the world. "Go on," Broker said.

"Then I saw the van pulled off by this equipment shed, and clearly that was where the guy was headed. So I used the van for cover and came in on the blind side. Well, he kind of fit the profile of who we were looking for: black ski mask. Little black pistol in his hand. Way he was swiveling his head, in a real hurry." He turned to Soap. "That Ford is huge anyway, and it had real serious snow tires, big suckers, so I figured there was extra room—freeboard—between the undercarriage and the road."

Soap just shook his head, marveling. "Fuckin' Joey, man."

"So, what the hell? Job was to get a fix on these dudes, right? So I scooted underneath, hooked my heels on the rear axle, sucked in my gut, and cinched my belt to the cross member, made sure I didn't get my feet between the leaf springs and the frame, and, you know, held on."

Joey paused to squirm away from Rita, who planted a big wet kiss on his cheek.

"Lucky for me, we didn't go all that far," Joey said. "Rundown old farmhouse out all by itself off Highway 7, going toward Square Lake."

"Sonofabitch," Soap grumbled, "they've been set up just north of town? How'd—?" Broker waved him to be quiet.

Joey continued. "When the van stopped, I waited till the driver got out and hurried toward the house; then I rolled out from under and found some cover. Oh, ah—" He held up his left forearm, where he'd scrawled BZX 539 in faint ballpoint. "License on the van," Joey said. "There was a blue Buick Century station wagon, but I didn't get close enough to see the plate number."

Broker immediately crossed to the counter and flipped open the manila file folder he'd started. It contained the note that Soap's midnight visitors had left, along with the still tacky, black-and-white photos Harry and Rita had just brought, fresh from the developing bath. He wrote the license number in the bottom margin of the picture that showed the dead man's tattoo and the card with the phone number.

Then he picked up the currency brick from the desk and held it up for Joey's inspection. "For the record?" he asked.

"It's for real, Broker." Joey glanced at Soap and lowered his eyes briefly. "I saw the whole damn crateful."

"You get a look at them?" Broker put the money down.

"I saw four guys; three came out of the house. They had this fast confab on the porch with the driver. Two of them went in, got on their coats, and left with the driver in the van. Couldn't tell exactly what they were carrying—a coil of rope, maybe. Could be they went back to the park to police up the stiff you told me about on the way in," Joey said matter-of-factly.

"Didn't think we were alone out there," Harry said, glancing at Broker. Then he turned back to Joey and asked, "Can you describe them? Any of them look *foreign*?"

Joey shook his head. "Best I could tell they were white dudes, mid-to-late thirties. It was more the way they moved. Didn't look like any rough trade from around here, or in Miami, for that matter."

Harry and Broker made fast eye contact. "Explain," Broker said.

Joey shrugged. "Like guys I've seen before, loading on choppers when I was on the *Ticonderoga* off the coast of Nam. Force Recon and Navy SEAL types: low key, efficient. You know. Snake eaters. Had a military vibe to them."

"Not good, when you put them together with the dead Persian and a ton of money." *But the dead Persian didn't have a radio?* Broker exhaled as he watched the party balloon deflate to silence and they all went back to being afraid in their separate ways. Rita, being youngest, covered fear with a game smirk. Joey opted for a placid calm. Andrea was exploring it. Harry and Soap, like Broker, employed the veteran trick of using it to sharpen an edge.

The machinery reappeared. *Okay to be a little scared; not okay to hesitate.*

"So now what, guys?" Andrea, leaning on Joey's shoulder, finally asked with a jerky smile. "Bodies are piling up."

"Oh, bullshit," Joey sighed as he gently disentangled himself from Rita and Andrea. "This is getting old, sitting here with my feet in a pail of water." He stood up, tucked the blanket monk-fashion around his shoulders, stepped from his foot bath, and approached Harry. "May I?" he said, slowly removing his .45 pistol from Harry's belt. He joined Soap, placed the automatic on the counter, and said, "There's only four of them."

Broker polled the eyes in the room. Harry, predictably, said in his best merry, doomed voice, "At least we have a target."

Rita said, "Why aren't we stacking sandbags, getting ready for when they storm through the front door?"

"We're hoping they're too busy right now, like disposing of their buddy," Harry said. Then he drifted back to the front of the lobby and continued his scan of the snow-covered streets.

Broker said, "We go back to the park. We see if the body's still there. That'll tell us something."

"Now we're ghouls," Rita said with a tight smile.

"It'll tell us how professional they are," Harry said as he eased over to Broker, ushered him aside and lowered his voice. "We need to regroup, Phil, because everybody here is *beaucoup* strung out. Including us."

"So are they," Broker said evenly.

Headlights swept the parking lot, causing Broker, Harry, and Joey to reach for pistols and rifles. Soap turned off the lobby lights. Rita turned them back on and made a production of doing scary fingers and big Betty Boop eyes. "Now what? The Mafia? The dreaded Chi? Nope. It's Domino's Pizza," she said, going out the door.

A moment later she was back with four steaming flat boxes. "Early Thanksgiving dinner. Let's eat," she said.

Soap pulled up a cooler full of soda. Joey, Rita and Andrea joined him around the coffee table. Broker and Harry visited the pizza boxes but stayed by the door, discussing whether to post someone outside.

The pizza seemed to have a sedative effect, so Broker drifted back and asked Joey, "What about the house, the surrounding area?"

"With all the snow, it woulda been kind of hard to creep the place without tracking it up, so I hid next to a collapsed barn. I got the basic layout. Then I figured I'd better boogie. Worked around across this pasture in back, then cut through the woods to get to the road. Had to walk all the way back to Pine Point."

"Think you could sketch it out?"

"Sure. Give me something to write on, and I'll put it down." He experimentally flexed his crabbed fingers and said, "In a minute or so."

Soap turned to Broker. "So what do you think? Between Wild Bill Hickok over there—" He nodded to Harry, who flipped him the bird. "—and Joey finding their nest, you think we have an opportunity here?"

Broker nodded. "We move fast, maybe we can finish what we started. We get pictures, faces, license plates, an address. We discreetly turn them over to BCA, then make ourselves scarce. If they are high-end military contractors, let BCA go to the party."

"So we call the cops," Rita said, resigned.

Broker raised his can of Coke in a benighted gesture. "Here's to Annie. If we can isolate the guys who are hunting her, she can surface. And then we just point her in the direction she was headed in the first place when she called Desmond. So you see, Rita, we don't call the cops."

"Annie does," Rita said slowly. "And then what?"

"The Bureau of Criminal Apprehension will figure something out," Andrea said. Then she turned to Broker. "Which still leaves the bodies."

"We're in deal territory." Soap wagered with his fingers. "Merriweather and Cantrell will be generous if we hook them up to a fucking whale."

"Might work." Harry thought about it. "They could say a patrol officer spotted suspicious activity at a deserted farm. They bring in surveillance, they invent some probable cause and go in with a warrant and bring those bad boys in for questioning. They get a forensic team in that house, they might find something."

"You mean Leper's blood," Rita said soberly.

"They might find something," Harry repeated, then sagged. "Which still raises the question of Leper's body."

"One body at a time," Broker said. "Joey, can we get in close enough to the house to stay hidden and snap these guys? Like in the morning?"

Joey shook off his hood. "Yeah, I think so. Soap? We're going to need a road map of northern Washington County. Just give me a minute to shower and clean up and put on some clothes." He left the grease-stained carnage of the pizza boxes and headed toward the back stairs.

While Soap searched for a map, they cleaned off the table. Harry put on his coat and hat, tucked his rifle in close to his side, and opened the door. "I'll be outside. Find me a comforta-ble shadow," he said. Andrea motioned to Broker, and they stepped through the side door into the cool, hollow silence of a garage bay.

Amid the dangling chain hoists and drums of oil, with Rita's mural coiled, unseen, in the darkness, Andrea said, "So you caught a break."

"I could kiss Joey," Broker said.

"No more shooting?"

"Hope not."

"And you think we can deal our way clear of this?"

"Ask me tomorrow. Right now I don't know," Broker answered honestly.

He was trying to gauge her eyes, but they were just pockets, hidden in shadow. So he could only go by her voice and her body language: the way she knit her brows in con-centration and plucked self-consciously at her lank hair. With her bruised cheek, wearing an old college tracksuit, she had the aspect of a newly homeless person.

"I see what you're doing," she started slowly. "You want to steer BCA onto the bad guys and still protect your under-cover status. And Soap's reputation, which is part of that cover."

Hearing the rational cadence creep into her voice, Broker said, "But you still have issues with erasing what happened this afternoon."

"I have *issues* with getting almost shot by para-military types with God knows what kind of connections. And so should you." She reached into the kangaroo pocket on the sweat suit, removed her wallet, and fingered out a business card. Broker took it and angled around to catch streetlight coming in through the window panels in the garage doors. *Harold J. Cantrell, Special Investigator, Minnesota State Bureau of Criminal Apprehension.*

"It's on you. The pager number's on the back," she said.

Broker put the card in his pocket and listened to his heart beat, slow and steady, for several moments. The machinery that had jump-started at Joey's resurrection told him he was good.

"You found who you were looking for. You did your job. Quit while you're ahead, Broker," she said. "Make the call. You give Cantrell first dibs on confiscating that loot, and I think we'll come out of this with immunity. I mean, I could. Not you, because you've decided to live a third of your life *as a fucking ghost.*" She took a step forward, and all the good old Serbian anger was alive in her voice. "Undercover is another word for *hiding*, Broker."

"I don't need this shit right now," Broker said, his eyebrows in a bunch. "I *do* need another day. If we call in the cavalry right now, procedure will set in; they'll need to tool up, hold meetings, and tie the laces on their fancy SWAT boots, and by then the guys in that house could be gone."

"Oh, c'mon," she protested, placing her hands on her hips. "You're trying to relive something. To prove something. And for what? *To be a night watchman in Cook County? Jesus!*"

"Look, Andrea," Broker said, "I've just met Cantrell and company. I've just met you, for that matter, and Soap and Joey and Rita. I *know* Harry. We can do this." He stepped forward and cupped his hands on her shoulders to reassure her. "We call in the cavalry too soon, and somebody in this building is going to get hurt. I need one more day," he said.

She pushed his hands away. "Don't patronize me," she said in a level voice. "I left ethical parlor talk back in the woods. Now it's survival rules." She cocked her head and searched for his face in the shadows. "I'm just trying to be practical."

"We're all scared, Andrea. It goes with the territory," Broker said.

Andrea looked away. "There's just too many loose ends. Stuff that will come out."

"Andrea, c'mon, you said yourself. If we hook Cantrell a whale, he'll cut us some slack."

"But what happens when we bring it in for a landing? It's unlikely that people who know me—I mean colleagues—would believe I was a candidate for Stockholm Syndrome and captive bonding. If I tell it straight, it means that I admit that I made a choice to go along because you basically dared me to." She shook her head. "If that gets out, it's a career-ender for sure."

"It's just one more day and we're clear; don't over-think it," he said.

Andrea threw her hands in the air. "Who can think?" She stopped pacing, turned, reached up and lightly touched his cheek. Then she withdrew her fingers and cautiously explored the still raw swelling on her face. "You know, when this started you were the only one with bruises on your face."

For a moment Broker could smell the cheap soap from the shower lingering from her warm fingers. "You'll be okay. Either way you go, I'll back you up," he said.

"Christ," she muttered under her breath, "I *am* living in a fucking Hardy Boys novel."

"What?" Broker leaned in a little closer.

"Nothing. Okay." She raised her hands in a steadying gesture. "One more day." Her voice was forced, upbeat. "I'm still a little off balance. I think I'll go up and sleep for a few minutes.

Until the next crisis." Andrea composed her lips in a game smile. But Broker was back where he couldn't tell if the smile was real.

When they reentered the lobby, Rita, who was now stuffing pizza boxes in the trash can, perused them with slightly lidded eyes. As Andrea went through the back doorway toward the stairs, Rita swung up next to Broker.

"So you and Andrea, you ah . . ." She waffled her palm back and forth.

"You have to be kidding. I just got here," Broker protested —obviously too much, judging by the look in Rita's eyes.

"So you trust her?"

"Not as much as I trust you. Is there a phone upstairs?"

She bobbed her head. "In the front office."

"Could you go up, quiet-like, and unplug it and bring it down here?"

"I can do that," Rita said. She kept her lips in a noncommittal straight line, but her eyes were cautiously smiling.

Chapter Twenty-Seven

Thursday

The upstairs office opposite the lunchroom was now a staging area. Soap produced two duffels from the office closet that contained his old stash of winter camo and bow-hunting gear. Broker picked through the clothing: a parka for him, bib overalls and a smock for Harry. The vial of Black Dex sat on the table, and Harry had popped two of them. Broker decided to hold off. And now the pills had added a chatty dimension to Harry's normally gruesome humor.

"Those four guys out there? If Joey's accurate? Hell, man, we could know people in common." His percussive laugh snapped like castanets. "We coulda got shit-faced with them at the Green Door in Hue City." He sat at the desk with the shop's first aid kit propped open, ripping irregular strips of white adhesive tape that he used to break up the black silhouettes of first his and then Broker's rifle. Just in case.

"Yeah," Harry continued, "too bad we can't pay them back for Andrea, snatch one of them, get them to talk." The speed cranked up the intensity in his eyes—except for the dead places. "But you don't do shit like that anymore since you re-invented yourself as a Boy Scout working on his cop merit badge."

"Harry, man, you're speeding, and we're going to the field," Broker chided.

"Negative," said Harry. "We are going to *a* field in the Kingdom of Oz with a pick-up team. Off to see the Wizard. That'd be the mythical Annie, who's behind the curtain in the Emerald City, locally known as Hinckley. You ever see her? I never seen her. And we're going into battle with an aging Tin Man, Joey the Un-cowardly Lion, Andrea the reluctant straw shrink, and Rita the rad tomboy. All we're missing is the fucking dog."

Broker grinned. "You are so full of shit. We're not that rusty. We'll be in and out. Worst case, we freeze our ass."

Harry deliberately decelerated the amphetamine boost of his voice. "Just saying . . . the loose end we're tugging on? Could be the tail of a very large reptile."

Broker attempted to stare down Harry's speed-merry eyes and failed. Was the speed a mistake? Was Harry indulging his penchant for saying what other people were reluctant to say? *Focus*, the machinery counseled. His gaze wandered out the open office door toward the closed lunchroom door, behind which Andrea was trying to rest.

"Uh huh, the longer this drags on—" Harry read his mind.

"The longer she has to think about the potential consequences." Broker finished the thought. "In fact, she's already there. She wants me to call in the locals."

"Bad idea right now. So we have to keep her close in hand. Period." Harry went back to his tape.

Broker nodded and then said, "I'll take Rita with me when I check for your dead Persian in the park. See if she'll open up about her dad. I worry that Soap always has one more thing to tell me."

"Watch yourself," Harry said. "Blind man can see she runs deeper than her salty tomboy act. She's got more in her pocket than brass knucks and a dead frog. She could have an open manhole in there where men just disappear."

Broker turned toward the mural that was a wall away in the dark. "You could be right," he said. "Remind me, on the other side, to show you something."

Harry laughed soundlessly and shook his head. "Sure. But Phil? I hope you know what you're doing, because we don't really know these people." More serious, he pointed his finger. "I'm *working*. *You* are starting to *like* these guys. I say again, watch yourself."

"Knock it off. We do know what happens if we screw up," Broker said.

Harry tapped the pill bottle up and down on the desk top. "And I know what happens if you don't *gas up*, because I've been watching you, man, and *you are burned out*."

Broker looked away and turned back to sorting hand warmers into two piles. The chatter ended and they became silent. Harry went back to his winter camouflage, and they worked quietly, side by side, as they'd done a hundred times before. Harry replaced the batteries in the Motorolas and ran his checks. Then he did the same for his cameras and packed them, along with the compact mirror lens and the tripod, in his long camera bag. Then he added his and Broker's disassembled rifles and eight loaded magazines. They sorted the leftovers from Soap's hunting season into two piles: energy bars, chemical hand and foot warmers. They pulled on fresh long underwear and clean, dry wool socks, put on the hunting gear, and laced up their boots.

Rita appeared, bringing canteens of water. "I checked on Goldi—ah—Andrea," she said with the faintest hook of conspiracy in her tone, enough to make Broker's and Harry's eyes click.

Downstairs Joey and Soap were refining their understanding of the county road net that surrounded the target house and planning the approach. As Rita paused on a turnaround from one of her trips up and down the stairs, Broker reminded her to tell her dad that they had probably IDed Soap's Suburban and Joey's Bronco from the park fiasco.

"So we'll need different wheels," Rita said, "and we have four or five candidates sitting in the lot over the holiday that haven't been picked up yet." She headed back down the stairs.

Ten minutes later she returned. "Dad will drive you and Harry to the drop-off point in a Land Cruiser that belongs to Dr. Flodin, our dentist." She smiled, showing even teeth. "Joey will follow in a Dodge pickup with Andrea and me."

Broker frowned at her. "Hey. Take it down a notch. This isn't fun. Okay? Now go tell Andrea to get squared away to spend the rest of the night hanging out in a car. So if anybody needs to use the head, now'd be the time."

After she left, Harry commented quietly, "Might be a good idea to keep those two in separate cars."

Then he and Harry went down the stairs and saw Soap and Joey poring over the detailed map of the farmhouse and immediate area. Broker smiled. Like they were casing a job.

Joey's diagram showed a house set back from the axis of an east/west county road marked County EE. A rectangle representing a collapsed barn sat to the east of the house, fronted by fenced pasture. A vertical, north-south county road T-boned into the first road just east of the house. Broker concentrated on the rough drawing and turned off the questions that naturally popped up in his mind—about how they'd managed to be installed in such a convenient location on such short notice. But that was work for Cantrell and Merriweather. His job was to get in, get pictures, and get out with Harry, undetected.

"It's fenced pasture on three sides with a lot of dead elms," Joey said. He tapped the intersection of the two roads. "Thick brush and new tree growth along the fence line on this north-south road, and I saw a huge tangle of deadfall where three of those elms tipped over. Here, in the pasture just east of the driveway—that might be the best vantage, best cover. It'd give you a view of the house and the vehicles." He indicated the tree line along the ditch. "If we come in from the north and drop you a quarter mile up the road, you should be able to move along the tree line into the deadfall."

Harry nodded. "Feel our way going in, make adjustments if we have to."

Broker leaned forward and lowered his voice for emphasis. "After you drop us off, it's important to keep Andrea with you at all times. No straying to a convenience store or gas station to use the john."

"You think she might jump the gun and call her cop friend?" Soap asked, confirming that he'd been comparing notes with his daughter.

"Don't think so," Broker said. "But let's not give her a chance to be tempted." Then he added, "And keep Rita and Andrea in separate cars, out of each other's hair."

A little after one in the morning Thanksgiving Day, Broker and Harry were ready, layered in enough white tree-bark camo to look like late season hunters getting an early start to a bow stand. They'd left the upstairs lights on, as well as those in the lobby. The three cars they'd used at Pine Point were parked in the lot. The Land Cruiser and the truck were warming up inside a garage bay.

"There's four of them, and they have two vehicles that we can recognize. We think." Broker cuffed Joey affectionately on his thick shoulder. "They've had a bad day, so let's hope they're all in that house right now sleeping it off. Maybe waiting for orders."

Harry disapproved of this sugarcoating with a downward glance, but Broker figured Soap and company had been through a lot, and he just wanted to keep them out of the way.

Rita worked fast at the Mr. Coffee on the sideboard, stopping up a fresh thermos and measuring out grounds and water for two more pots. She hit the on button, then doled out the filled thermoses, one each for Broker and Harry and one for the rest of the crew. "We only have three thermoses. Tony probably has the fourth one. At some point we're going to need a coffee resupply," she shot Broker a sidelong glance, "because *you* guys are hogging all the speed, and nothing's open."

Broker looked at Harry, who rolled his eyes and shrugged. "If we see both cars on site. If they're tucked in. If everything's dead quiet. Main thing is, we need you to be close if we have to get out fast."

"Use common sense. Don't split up. And be in range for radio checks," Broker said.

Rita nodded and joined the group, and they stood in a semi-circle around Broker, dressed and ready. The silver ring on Rita's hand flashed as she pulled her hair tight and fixed it into a ponytail. Then she pulled a wool cap down to the level of her combative eyes. Joey had had augmented his ski clothes with fresh wool trousers and snow pack boots. His eyes were still a bit red from the cold, but steady. Soap kept his face neutral, but he wore a red bandit bandana fixed tight over his head that suggested this was not his first war party.

Andrea stood a little bit to the side and made an effort to look involved, but she couldn't quite disguise the aura of an indoors-type professional who wasn't one hundred percent sure she should have signed up for the Outward Bound Survival Course. She cleared her throat. "For the record, I just want to point out that everybody here is completely exhausted."

"Duly noted," Broker said. "But this is real simple and should go down easy. We get pictures, hopefully before noon. We ease our way out and get them developed. We pass them to the cops. We break open that money brick that's in the safe and pay ourselves enough to lay low in a hotel far from here that's got a swimming pool and a sauna, till the dust settles. Once they're in hand, we bring in Annie."

Everyone but Andrea chuckled in the affirmative.

"So where do you want us?" Soap asked.

"We need you close when we go in and when we come out. Once the sun's up, you guys fall back and stay out of sight.

Radio checks every thirty minutes. Planning range on these sets is a mile at best."

"Every thirty minutes," Rita repeated as she tossed ballsy mid-twenties eyes toward Joey.

"Stick together. No solo acts," Broker said.

"Let's do it," Rita said.

Harry, Soap, Andrea and Broker pulled out first in the Cruiser and roamed the town to see if a white van or a blue Buick wagon appeared. Joey and Rita left ten minutes later. Coordinating on the radios, Joey trailed them as a second set of eyes. After half an hour trolling the deserted streets, they decided it was clear. Next stop was the park. Broker had already informed Rita that she'd accompany him on Ghoul Patrol.

The rest of the crew sat in warm vehicles parked off the county road near Pine Point. Broker was back in the inky woods on a jerky slog with Rita, backtracking the faint trail that he, Andrea and Harry had created when they walked out this afternoon. Several inches of new snow had blurred their boot prints, but the path was still readable.

They were plodding in silence, getting a feel for their footing in the low-swinging surreptitious flashlight beam, when Rita said, "You're a pretty locked-up guy, trucking around in all that armor, aren't you?" Two steps later, she added, "So is there a key? Or are you just another crispy critter like your pal, Motown?"

Her tone carried an intimate undertone: out here, alone with him, in the spooky old woods, on their way to the spot where a man had been killed less than ten hours ago.

"I don't really know you." Broker huffed in the icy air. "Or your father, who's a little hard to figure himself." After a few snow-shuffling steps he added, "Just saying—I'm not quite sure why he allowed me in his life."

She'd thrown a scarf loosely around her mouth and nose. The hem of her wool cap was pulled down to her brow. All he could see in the bouncing glow of the flashlight was the gleam of her eyes. "You're my first cop, you know that?"

"I'm not a cop."

"But you're trying to get me to fink on my dad?" She almost laughed.

Broker thought he saw a sparkle in her hooded eyes. Or it could have been a trick of the low artificial light on the snow. He lurched to a halt and said, "Look. I'm on your side." It came out in compact bursts of white, crystallized breath. Rita remained silent with her head cocked. Her visored eyes were unavailable in the dark.

Broker balked and thrust his gloved hands up in an indignant pantomime, a little annoyed by the growing realization that Rita had this funky, pretend-outlaw, yet *clean* energy coming off her, and it had started to itch under his skin. *Watch it,* the machinery echoed Harry. *Not only still waters run deep.* "Ah . . ." He pawed the air, turned, and continued walking in the faint tracks.

"Hey, Broker? When was the last time you were really scared?" she called out, unmoving.

He turned off the flashlight and faced her in the dark. Without the flashlight beam, she made a shadowy pillar against the night-washed snow. Overhead, a gust of wind set up a rattle of dry oak leaves.

"Dad's scared," she said. "I've never seen him really scared before. He's been investing in real estate: broken-down old mansions, like the house he was born in. Farmland along Highway 36. Like he's trying to make amends or trying to reclaim something. And he goes out of his way to take in strays. Joey. Leper." She paused. "You maybe."

Their frozen breath curled off to black. "Now he's lost Leper," Rita said. "He almost lost Joey, and he's worried about me, Mom and everything he's worked for. Just before we left, he told me the dope world was kid stuff compared to this." Rita tilted her head. "This is different. For sure, he doesn't trust his old crook buddies with it. Or the cops. Who's that leave?" The question hung between them, unanswered. Staring straight at him, she went on.

"But mainly he worries that the guys in that farmhouse represent people who are bigger than the cops—I mean, if it is a hunk of the Iranian treasury, how'd it wind up in Hinckley, Minnesota? So you tell me: what's scarier than dope and bigger than the cops and involves dead Persians?" Rita turned, started up the trail, and threw the words over her shoulder. "It's not that hard to figure what has my father shook up."

Five minutes later the tracks ended, and Broker played the flashlight beam to the right, up the slight hill he'd clambered over. Then he brought it back to the patch of trampled snow in front of them.

"The boot cleats are still distinct," Rita said in a steady voice.

Broker pulled out the Motorola and pushed send. "Harry, Broker."

Harry tapped squelch twice in acknowledgment.

"Next round at The Alcove is on me. I have negative for a body. I have positive for a drag trail. I say again, no dead Persian. How's it look on your end?"

"Dead quiet. We're out here all alone."

"Okay. Heading back."

They walked swiftly on the return trip, saving their breath. As they came up on the county road, Rita tugged his sleeve. "Up north, those tools in your cabin. How good are you with them?" she asked.

"Rough to finish, like I told you, I do okay. Why?"

"Nothing, just thinking," Rita said.

"While you're thinking, I'd appreciate it if you'd lighten up on Andrea. We need her," Broker said.

"I can do that," Rita said, showing her teeth in a tight smile. "After all, she probably was valedictorian *and* prom queen."

Chapter Twenty-Eight

Outside the thermometer read fourteen degrees and still falling, and the featureless overcast floated on a cushion of mist. Northern Washington County spread out in an Amish quilt of hazy white fields stitched together with a dark fretwork of barren tree lines. Random sentinel yard lights marked farmhouses in the distance. One closer light established the target house perhaps half a mile across a pasture spiked with towering dead elm trees.

Inside the Land Cruiser it was warm. The seats oozed a rich leather fit and finish. The dash lights sparkled on Andrea's concerned face. They all tensed as the radio squawked.

"Broker, Joey. How do you hear?"

"Got you four by four," Broker said into the Motorola.

"Both cars in the driveway. One white van and one blue Buick on site." Joey, lights off, was doing a drive by of the house.

"Roger that. Meet Soap back up the road after he drops us off."

The tension dissipated in the Cruiser. Broker exhaled and looked at Harry's darkened profile. No big deal. So far so good. In a minute they were out of the truck, had shouldered their gear and were checking each other. Nothing flashes. Nothing jingles.

Through the driver's side windshield Broker watched Andrea's lips move. *Be careful.* Then he rapped his gloved knuckles on the glass. Soap cranked it open. "Nobody sleeps," Broker said. "Once we're in, you ease off but drift back within radio range every thirty minutes."

Soap nodded and closed the window. Broker pointed north, up the county road. Lights out, the Cruiser executed a U turn and slowly drove away.

Without speaking, Broker and Harry waded across a snow-plow drift, then a shallow ditch and slipped into the frosted thickets and tall dry sedge that skirted the road. Harry took the point, moving in his patient step, step, stop, look and listen ballet. They covered ground slowly, easing through the snow-clotted brush, carefully placing their feet in the knee-deep drifts. The snail's pace was out of caution, but also to avoid too much exertion that would sweat up their clothing. They could have a long, freezing wait ahead of them.

Harry stopped, raised his hand, and then pointed a gloved finger to his wristwatch. Half an hour. Radio check. They knelt as Broker made the muffled call. "Joey, Broker. Five hundred yards to the house. How's your end?"

"Dead quiet. Empty roads. Happy Thanksgiving."

Now they were within direct line of sight of the house: a two-story, peeling clapboard. They got a whiff of wood smoke from the chimney and saw the tangle of dead elms in the pasture. Harry nodded at the yard light that burned out front and whispered, "That's sloppy. Makes it harder to see from the house in snow conditions." Faint illumination came from a window in an addition off the back, the kitchen maybe. Like Joey had said, the two vehicles were parked in the turnaround in front of the house.

Now it was boonie walk time, modified for snow. They plotted a serpentine vector through patches of cover that would permit them—with luck—to sneak out in daylight. Thirty slow minutes later they had gained the crunch of fallen elms that created a corridor in which they could move forward unseen. The cold made an insistent argument that started to batter down the layers of Broker's clothing. The snow-furred branches loomed in front of them like dirty twisted ivory. Like dinosaur bones.

"Two hundred yards. Moving into position. Both vehicles on site. Get comfy. Could be a long time before we get movement."

Joey came back. "Understood."

They picked and squirmed their way into the obstacle course of jammed, broken trunks and branches and crept close enough to see the frost forming on the van windows. For several minutes they gave the lighted rear window their full attention until they were satisfied that no one was moving inside.

Harry selected a shebang of mangled branches that was protected by an angle of tree trunk, where he had adequate sight lines to set up the tripod lens. Broker estimated the distance to the front porch at just over a hundred yards. The collapsed barn, on slightly higher ground, to their right front was the ideal location. But it stood out alone, too exposed, and was surrounded by pristine snow. Tracks going in and out would give them away.

As they hunkered in, Harry began opening, shaking, and then dropping more chemical heat pads into his camera duffel. Then he stuffed his gloves into his pockets to squeeze already activated hand warmers. "I'd like to give it a few minutes to warm up before we have to take our gloves off and assemble the rifles," he said.

"But we might as well slap them together now, just in case," Broker grunted. Next thing Harry was handing him the upper and lower receiver parts of his rifle. He removed his gloves, reflex took over, and his fingers raced the cold: Pop the cotter pin at the end of the lower receiver, forward of the magazine well. Lock the barrel in place; snap the pin home. Check operating rod, bolt carrier and firing pin. Re-slot them in place, slide them back into the breach. Ease the disjointed rifle into one rigid assembly. Secure with pin on the neck of the stock above the pistol grip. Insert a magazine of eighteen rounds, because they'd learned the hard way that the feeder spring could fail with a max load of twenty. There. Locked but not loaded for now. He leaned the adhesive-striped rifle against the tree trunk. Plastic piece of shit. Never cared for the M-16. *Miss the wood next to my cheek.*

Harry sidled closer, produced a tin of Copenhagen Long Cut from his pocket, and pried it open. Broker could make out his lips, jerked in a crazy smile. "Can't smoke, so this'll smooth some of the jitters outa my jit-jit optics."

Broker passed on the chew. Harry removed his glove and inserted a pinch between thumb and forefinger. "What is it till legal shooting?" he asked.

Broker nudged up his cuff and checked his watch. "Almost three hours."

"Hope these assholes wake up early," Harry said. "I'll set the camera up just before first light. But it's not so bad, actually." He crossed his arms and hugged himself. "November of seventy-four, hunting in the Upper Peninsula, you remember? Yeah, you remember. That was cold, man. This is tolerable. Okay, this here *is* a little nuts. Usually when I do this I'm catching somebody cheating on their spouse." He pondered. "Thing is, I'm okay with nuts. But, Phil, buddy, I don't think you've figured that part out in your head yet." Speed rapping.

"Working on it," Broker mumbled, his eyelids sagging.

"Cool. So the sun comes up, we get some snaps, and we scoot real careful out of here, and we're done."

Broker nodded and tried to get comfortable with his back nestled into the tree trunk, sitting cross-legged with his arms folded. The cold minutes and Harry's hushed words piled up. Broker's eyelids continued to flutter. Now motionless after the hike and the tense approach, he felt his body heat leaking away.

When the wall of fatigue ambushed him, it was soft and seductive, and he slowly pancaked and faded out.

His eyes popped open. Harry was shaking his sleeve. He'd been dozing. "How long was I out?" he whispered.

"Almost two hours. Don't sweat it. Nothing's happening." Harry emitted a hollow speedy cackle. "Nobody is up in this whole dreary white-bread state."

Broker roused, shivered, looked around. "Radio checks?"

"Like clockwork. They ran out of coffee an hour ago. Soap said they drove around, nothing's open, like Rita said, so they're doing a fast run back to the shop."

"Like Rita said," Broker exhaled. "Shit."

"Soap said they'll be back for the next radio check." Harry shrugged. "Lost the edge when we decided they were tucked in for the night." The speed couldn't restrain a yawn. "Shit, *I'm* losing my edge."

"I hear you," Broker said. "What did Soap say, exactly?"

"They figured everything's quiet and locked down, so first Rita and Joey went for coffee, then Soap decided they probably shouldn't split up, and it's less than thirty minutes, max, round trip. So he called it in from the road."

Broker rubbed his eyes. "Rita doesn't like being ordered around. And Joey's got the hot hand right now."

"Invincible youth. They'll be back. Don't mean a thing." Harry cackled. "Everything is backwards. Especially you. *I* have a valid Michigan PI license. *You?* You've been on some kind of trampoline since I hit this drop zone. Gotta admit, it's weird after all we been through that I wind up being the adult who's tasked with keeping you out of trouble."

Broker pointed a gloved finger. "You're fucking ripped."

"Hey," Harry protested, "I'm not the one who fell asleep. Or tried to pull this off with a bunch of civilians off the street." He opened an ungloved hand that contained two of the black pills and thrust it forward. "Time to gas up. One to finish your term paper, two to get a grip."

Broker swallowed the pills with a sip of coffee from his thermos. They settled back and strung the cold minutes together. Broker focused inward, waiting for the drug to ignite. Then he and Harry jerked alert as they both heard the barest jingle of a telephone in the dark house. Broker held his breath, then raised his hand and soberly pointed. Lights came on in the house and created buttery rectangles in which the shadows of moving men appeared. "You gotta be kidding me." An icy sensation tiptoed in his chest.

"It's too dark for cameras," Harry whispered back.

Broker leaned forward into the branches. "Five in the morning?"

Distinctly, in the ice-chime air, they heard the front door slam and saw a shadow walk to the van. He got in, started it up, got out, and vigorously began to scrape freezing snow from the windshield. They pulled their caps above their ears to catch faint snatches from two other shadows who stood talking on the porch. Too far. Then one shadow came down the steps and joined the first shadow in the van. Shadow number three still stood on the porch. No one else came out of the house.

"I count three." Broker whispered.

"Not four—not four that we can see," Harry whispered back. "I hope this isn't here-we-go because, buddy, we are fucking stranded." The van started to move.

Broker leaned to the radio. "Soap, Broker, come back." Static. Nothing. Shit. They froze in place as the turning headlights swept their cranny of dead timber. The lights passed and the van exited the property and turned west. The night crowded in and had grown teeth. The third shadow reentered the house. All the lights stayed on. Harry nudged Broker's shoulder. "Could be anything. But if that guy's in there alone, now'd be the time to grab him."

Broker blinked several times as he sensed the amphetamine bomblets exploding softly in his bloodstream. Waiting on the boost, he slowly shook his head. "Big if. Don't start, Harry. Job is to find and fix them." Broker gritted his teeth. "And now Soap and the gang are out there wandering around." He raised the radio. "Soap, Broker."

Just static. *Prototype piece of crap.* More static and then something, broken, garbled. He keyed send. "Broker, say again?"

Broker and Harry grumbled, antsy, back and forth, listening to the blank crackle of radio waves until—Broker pitched forward and pressed the set to his ear. Soap's usually forceful voice came cottony through the static. "Broker, Soap. Yeah, couldn't hear, had to stop and turn and go for high ground. What's up?"

"The van just left the property, going west with two guys. We only see *one* other guy at the house so far. How far ahead of you is Joey?"

"Three four minutes. Jesus. Understood." The signal garbled, a sound like a gunning engine, then Soap came back on. "I'd feel better if you guys pulled out of there."

"Soap, it's all about getting pictures."

"Okay. But it only takes one guy to run a camera."

Broker exhaled and stared at the lighted windows in the farmhouse. "Calm down. One of us will pull back to the road."

"Meet me where I dropped you off. Be there in thirty minutes flat." Soap clicked the squelch and was gone.

Broker turned to Harry. "You get all that?"

"Pretty much. Soap's feeling lonely all of a sudden. Let's hope it's just a fit of nerves," Harry muttered. They both turned toward the house, then back to each other. "Could be a coincidence," Harry added. "Have to wait and see." Huddled, their near-whispers made fragile white tatters in the dark. "You go hold his hand. I'm here to take-a da pictures. Which was the point."

Broker muttered, "You're right about the pictures. So check me out on the camera and take a hike. Be on the road when Soap gets back."

"I say again, fuck that," Harry guffawed. "I'm not going anywhere. You jerked me out of a pool game I was winning, and here I am. You want pictures or not? We can be done with this by noon. All I need is a half-reliable radio link and wheels to flee on." Harry's chemical-assisted grin leered in the gray snow dark. "Now get. Whip the troopies in line and sit your ass in a warm car, you wus."

"You know we're both a little bit cranked," Broker said.

"Hey. We've been out in a lot colder weather than this. And you know what Robert Capa said?"

The world was possibly ending, but Broker almost smiled. "If your shots are bad, you're not close enough."

Harry jerked his head toward the pile of collapsed barn lumber forty yards closer to the house. "Kinda cramped in here, so I'll set up in there, close enough to see the color of their eyes. Trust me. I won't leave tracks they can see from the house, and I can use the terrain to wriggle back to the tree line."

He was right, of course. It all depended on the pictures. "Okay, man. But no more hero shit. You've already exceeded your limit."

"Yeah, yeah." Then, "Here." Harry removed his gloves and swiftly popped open the pill bottle. "Keep two for me." He carefully pocketed the pills, recapped the vial, and handed it to Broker. "Go on. You'll feel better knowing I don't have it."

Broker didn't argue. He stowed the pills and handed over the radio. "When they pick me up, I'll call and fill you in, then I'll hang around as back-up. You might be stuck here for a while. What about the cold and the cameras?"

Harry dug a handful of warmers from his pocket and held them up. "Take off," he said. "Ain't nothin'."

Chapter Twenty-Nine

As he wormed his way back to the road, the Dexedrine really kicked in and goosed Broker's heartbeat and hardwired his vision and exaggerated his inner ear, and he could almost hear the night's departing grays acquire a broken glass edge and slice the still air to ribbons. He felt pressure in his eyeballs, and his breath tasted like a Formaldehyde chaser. He blinked, and the hollow, spun-glass sensation in his chest informed him that he should have stuck to just one of those black capsules because they were shifting the contour of his thoughts.

Never should have scored the speed. Now Harry is seeing big lizards everywhere. Guy is an addict. Addicted to booze and to drugs and to women.

And to danger and to not making tactical mistakes in the field, the machinery reminded him, humming on the amphetamine tune-up.

Harry's crazy, everybody says so.

If he's the crazy one, why is it always you that drags him into crazy shit? the machinery commented.

I can still do this, dammit. It's a simple stakeout.

The machinery remained silent.

He gained the road, and the eastern horizon stacked up glorious as all hell and frigid and gleaming with inlaid mother-of-pearl shot with fiery pinks and magenta. It was a breathtaking shift in the weather that was totally wasted on Broker, who was keeping low in the tall weeds next to the road, dressed in the winter camo and trying not to show the white-taped assault rifle in his hands. Talk about lurking in the daylight. *Feel like a vampire who missed morning curfew.*

The joke curdled in his gut when he saw the Land Cruiser creep in, too slow, from the north, pull to the top of a slight rise, then ease back down the gentle slope, using the roll of the ground to keep out of sight. Broker took a moment to clear his head, then rose to his feet and glanced back once. The hilly pasture only gave him a view of the top of the house. Of lazy morning chimney smoke. *Hang in, buddy.* He turned and jogged over the hill.

"Andrea?"

Seeing her *alone* behind the wheel, he jerked alert. And that was the ice cold spider that scampered over his heart. Then he opened the passenger door and absorbed the bloodless expression on her face. Her hands were clamped, knuckles blanched ivory, on the steering wheel.

"How bad?" His words thudded, tone deaf. It was all there in her harsh but disciplined eyes.

"Pretty bad. One of them was waiting. Jumped Joey and clubbed him. I guess they regrouped quicker than we thought."

"No sleep. And the speed. It's on me." Broker exhaled.

"Bullshit. It's on all of us. We're *all* strung out." Andrea paused to compose herself, then went on. "The truck was in the lot, running, lights on. After they hit Joey, they cornered Rita in the office. Looked like quite a fight." She sagged behind the wheel. "They took her, Broker." She paused for a breath. "They left one of her fingers behind and wrote a message in her blood."

"Radio," Broker hissed between clenched teeth. She produced a Motorola from inside her jacket. He seized it and pushed send. "Harry?"

Even over the shaky radio reception, Broker didn't like the sound of Harry's voice. "I'm ahead of you," he said. Too calm.

Harry, calm, meant he was getting all the way inside the dead places in his eyes. A calm Harry was a very dangerous Harry. "The van pulled in a few minutes ago. They walked Rita in, one on each elbow. Her left arm was in a sling, and she was stumble-footed, drugged. I didn't have a play. All I could do was watch. Tried a few pictures. Light wasn't good enough." Static, garbled moment, then, "Joey said four. I count all four of them on site."

"Now she's trading material." Broker slumped. Flat. Stating a fact. *All you guys want is one thing these days*—crystal clear recall.

"Be advised: they ain't off-balance anymore. They'll make contact now to settle up. We got us a rescue situation, and we don't have much of a window. So go assess the damage. Tell Soap I'm on the job for his kid. And, Phil, it's time to go look in the mirror and seriously *unfuck* yourself. Think of it as therapy. Figure something, man. Or I will. Griffin out."

Broker lowered the radio. Andrea watched him with Medusa eyes. "Harry is officially pissed. And you're alone," he said.

"Don't worry," she said through barely moving lips. "I drove past all the phone booths. I convinced Soap to stay back with Joey." She said it tight and practical.

"*You* convinced *them?*" Broker said as he tossed his gear in the back and climbed into the front seat.

"Dr. Sabic's first rule when you find yourself ass-deep in FUBAR is don't do anything to make it worse." Her eyes clicked on his face. "They were in no shape to come out here. They'd rush the damn house." She put the Cruiser in gear.

Broker understood that what he called "the machinery" amounted to his personal cocktail of psychological survival mechanisms: mix two parts selective compartmentalization with one part dissociation. He'd learned to take it neat, stirred not shaken, to overcome fear and panic. Then it refined to coax calm reactions in the middle of impossible situations. And, of course, it required the ruthless suppression of empathy.

As Andrea stepped on the gas and ate up the snowy county road, he confronted, head on, something he usually avoided, something that she would probably rattle off the top of her head.

The machinery was there to deny and evade pain. Not the kind you feel in your head. This was the stuff that hits you smack in the chest.

"What did the message say?"

"'No more games. No cops. Stay put. We'll call,'" Andrea recited. Another mile passed under the tires. She said, "It was her little finger, the one with the ring."

The streets leading up to the shop were deserted and innocently at peace. More Christmas wreaths out. Turkey getting ready for the oven. The sun peeked out of a patch of clear blue sky.

Soap sat behind the counter on a low file cabinet. He stared straight ahead and still wore his wool cap and gloves and windbreaker. Joey's usually stolid face was a puddle of pain, anger and shame. He slouched forward in a chair, holding ice cubes wrapped in a bloody towel to his head. Seeing Broker, he put down the ice pack and stood up. Blood streaked his wool shirt. He clasped and unclasped his powerful fingers. Unlike Harry, he didn't know how to calm and refine the murder in his blue eyes.

"Joey." Broker went to him and grabbed him by his wide shoulders. "Doesn't matter. Don't think of *anything* except a way to help me beat these fuckers. You got that?"

Joey nodded. Broker continued his inspection. Chaotic footprints smeared spilled coffee on the linoleum, along with shards of broken glass and plastic from a Mr. Coffee decanter. Furniture all askew.

Broker walked around to the rear of the counter and had his turn. A slender silver ring enclosed a severed human digit that curled like butcher's scraps in a splash of still bright blood on the desk blotter. The message Andrea had recited was scrawled on the blotter paper, casual, streaky and smeared, but legible.

When Soap broke the silence, his voice was low and unexpectedly steady and coldly centered. Different from his reaction yesterday, when they feared Joey had been taken. Rita's abduction had stripped him down to a scary core, and Broker thought he might be hearing a killer's voice from 1944. "I was waiting for you to see it," he said. Then he nodded to Joey, who came forward, gently detached the ring, and then wrapped the finger in a piece of paper towel, taking care to neatly fold the edges. He stooped to the small refrigerator behind the counter and tucked the package into the freezer compartment. Then he handed the ring to Soap, who absently eased it into his pocket.

"She's in that house, Soap. Harry saw them bring her in after I headed back to the road," Broker said.

Joey, Andrea, and Broker stood in a loose semicircle. Soap continued to sit. They were all very aware of the phone sitting on the desk and the dots of blood that stippled the push buttons. The air in the office was hard to breathe. Tinder-dry and ready to ignite.

Soap held up a restraining hand and spoke in the too-calm voice. "We'll take blame and get pissed later. I imagine the bastards will take their time calling. To let it sink in. If we're going to do something, we better do it quick." His wintry gaze shifted to Broker. "We still have our hole card."

"Harry has eyes on the house where they feel safe. We have to rely on the radios." Broker winced slightly.

"So how do we play that card?" Soap asked. "Because if we screw it up, they'll deal the next one face up. Rita's face." Then he turned his eyes, as did Broker and Joey, toward Andrea.

Put onstage, the color returned to her high cheeks. Very deliberately she faced Soap and said, "You want me to make the call now, I will. You want me to make it later, fine. *You prefer that I don't make the call at all, I can abide with that, too."*

Okaaay. Broker nodded slightly. After rubbing shoulders with excitement, fear, and shock, she'd bellied up and taken a slug of the hard stuff: cold, payback anger.

"You sure?" Soap asked.

"I'm still here, aren't I?" She took a step forward. "We were lax out there. Maybe because the main worry was keeping me from slipping off. Oh yeah. So I own a piece of this."

Soap slowly appraised Andrea. "You know what we could be talking here?"

Broker moved forward, thinking they might need another private consultation in the garage bay. Andrea raised a cautioning hand and said in a clear, level voice, "Hold it right there before you step on broken glass and track coffee all over." Then she asked Soap, "So where's the mop and the broom and dust pan?"

Broker and Soap locked eyes for the briefest moment. Dr. Sabic was on the job, diffusing the tension.

After Joey returned with the broom and a mop and pail, he inclined his head at the blood on the desk. "You, ah, want me to . . ."

"No," Soap said. "Leave it for now. To work an edge."

Broker approached Joey, who said. "Didn't see it coming. He was on me fast. He was pretty good. Scary good."

Of course he was. They're Shadows. "What about the radio?" Broker asked.

"Out in the truck. They missed it. They were focused on Rita."

Don't care about our radios. Leave the yard light on. They think we're jokes with all our sneaking around. Broker's mind raced. The air he took in reeked of pure adrenal exhaust. The fatigue was familiar. The dread wasn't. For all their anger and miles logged and scar tissue, they moved like sleepwalking actors attempting normal things. They cleaned up the room, rearranged the furniture, doled out coffee from the remaining decanter, and settled slowly into seats. Soap's eyes wandered out the window, across the parking lot, and cursed the anonymous apartment units. "Bastards."

They sipped their coffee in silence for a full minute, during which they all turned tense eyes in the direction of the desk phone at least twice.

"So?" Soap said, finally. Their eyes shifted to Broker, who rubbed his thumb and forefinger across his eyebrows.

"It's too big, too much money, too damn many moving pieces, and now they have Rita." Broker shook his head. "I'm trying to square a circle," he said, looking from face to face. "If we go totally on our own, hit them hard and fast, like Harry wants to do, we risk Rita and some of us. We call in the troops, we still risk Rita, plus everything we've been through is in the street."

"Where's that leave us? We hand the whole game over to the Washington County Patrol Division? They might shoot the house into Swiss cheese." Soap glowered.

Andrea said, "They get a sniff of all that money . . ."

"Be like what happens at the end of a car chase," Joey agreed. "Nothing good."

Broker made an erasing motion with his hand. *Do something.* He stood up. "We play for time. They call. We insist on proof she's alive. We buy time. Whichever way this goes, we need time."

"Jesus." Soap shook his head.

"They need her, Soap. She's their lock on you, but you're the path to their box. Remember, we have something they want, too. We have room to bargain," Broker said. "They call. We play for time." He glanced at the desk, where the phone almost ticked like a live grenade. "I need a minute," he said.

Then he went into the washroom, ran the tap, and threw a handful of cold water on his face. Looking at his drawn, unshaven features in the mirror, he flashed on Harry, out there hunkered down in the snow.

Unfuck yourself.

Harry doesn't think this is about cops and robbers. Not now. More like cops and spooks. And that's a game we know how to play. The trick being to do the dirty without leaving a trace.

Not what Merriweather and Cantrell had in mind at all.

So why would you tell them?

See, the machinery whispered, *how easy it comes back.*

Broker stared back into the mirror and said, "I'm working on it." Then he dried his face with a paper towel and opened the door and saw Joey standing there holding the ice compress to his matted hair. The mechanic cocked his square, whiskered face, collecting his thoughts, and said, "I was just thinking. Like you said. When I was up north, I saw some stuff Soap dumped that might interest you. From one of Leper's failed jobs."

"What kind of stuff?"

Joey told him.

Broker pointed to the garage bay. "Let's talk."

For the next half hour Andrea and Soap divided their attention between watching the phone and following Broker and Joey through the window as they paced back and forth in the lighted garage bay, in front of Rita's mural that Andrea was seeing for the first time.

The door opened, and Broker and Joey came back in. Joey shrugged. "Gonna be like Rita said."

"We're going to fight them." Broker's lips curved in a downward smile. Harry would be pleased. "We're going to hand them their asses, indirectly."

"I'm listening," said Soap, who'd set the thermometer on his cool eyes about a degree above ice cold.

"What if Annie never had a box or went to Hinckley? What if Leper drove it up there and stashed it? What if Leper has the last word in this?"

Andrea and Soap stared at him.

"We have to lure them to the cabin," Broker said to Soap.

"No cops up front," Soap said.

"No cops up front." Broker looked over at Andrea and saw no hesitation there.

"So let's hear it," she said.

They huddled, talking, for thirty minutes. Soap made a few brief phone calls to tell his two trusted mechanics that it was all hands on deck. Joey slapped a band-aid on his scalp and left through the back to hug the snow-clogged evergreens along the landscaping lot fence, then work his stealthy way up to the 36 frontage road. Tony—who'd walked away from Thanksgiving prep after Soap's call—was waiting in his truck. They'd drive through a jigsaw that would hopefully end with Joey, undetected, in radio contact with Harry. Soap was making another pot of coffee when the phone rang. Crossing to the counter, he and Broker checked each other.

"A touch desperate," Broker reminded him.

"And a lot pissed off," agreed Soap.

Chapter Thirty

Soap Turrie took rapid breaths after the first ring, continued them through the second, and picked up after the third ring with a shaky challenge. "What?" He listened for a moment, caught Broker's eye, and nodded in the affirmative. Then he deftly employed the transparent macho-technique of masking fear with anger and yelled into the phone. "Now you listen to me. Nothing happens until I know she's all right, all right as she can be missing her goddamn finger."

He listened for another few seconds, furrowed his brow, and held out the phone. "They want to talk to you," he said.

Broker's eyes narrowed. He took the phone. "Yeah?"

The shadow's voice was smooth, but schooling couldn't entirely disguise a slight twang from somewhere between Texas and the Mountain West. It rang familiar bells from a dozen military and clandestine training courses and old missions.

"I've been reading your press clippings in the local paper," the shadow said. "Too bad this columnist, Lager, doesn't know the right phone numbers to call."

When Broker made a point of clearing his throat, the shadow said, "What's-a-matter, cat got your tongue? Broker, Phillip Andrew?" He then read Broker's Army serial number. "Enlisted October sixty-six, Duluth, Minnesota. You were seventeen. Your dad signed off on it."

Broker motioned for Soap to step away from the desk as he lowered himself into the chair and stared at Rita's drying blood. "Shit," he muttered under his breath.

"No need to be modest," the shadow said. "Lot here to be proud of. Basic at Knox, AIT at Leonard Wood. Jump school—then the One Oh Worst in good old Vietnam. Bag full of medals. Came back your second tour, assigned MACV with the Hac Bao Company, 1st ARVN Division in Hue. Field promotion to lieutenant. Should I go on?"

"Can you?" Broker said in a tense voice that he had to fight to maintain so as not to lapse into a looser tone. A wave of pressure lifted, and the contortions he'd tied himself into trying to play by Cantrell's rules untangled. For the first time since the whole ball of knots started rolling, he knew exactly where he was. The world had become a very small place, and he was talking shop with a man he planned to destroy. Put another way, Detective Harold J. Cantrell didn't get to investigate dead spooks.

"My pleasure," the shadow said easily. "Now the dirty stuff. Somewhere there in Hue City, before Tet, you fell in with some opium-smoking, pinko ratfucks who regrettably were running the Hue Station for the outfit, and they recruited your dumb, young ass. Looks like you got around: the Aussie Jungle School at Carungra, Queensland, the SF crash course on Okie, and even a stint with a Hong Kong special branch unit."

"Where are you getting this?" Broker asked

"From the top, my friend. From the Big City. Okay. Pretty soon, the aforementioned ratfucks had you creeping around doing all sorts of nasty stuff, to include meeting with the fucking enemy. And you all kept in touch after you got out. They convinced you to go back in April seventy-five, where—blah-blah—the refugee thing. Basically, you stole something that didn't belong to you, and then it all disappears in a puff of smoke." The shadow took an extra-long pause for effect, then continued. "Let's make this simple. You're a smart guy. If you didn't already know that you and Turrie are in way over your head, you know it now. But maybe we can work this out. So,

Broker, tell me: do you ever wish you had your life back? It can be arranged, you know, with a sizable bonus."

"Proof of life," Broker rasped. "My eyes on Rita Turrie! Then we talk!" He slammed the phone down on the cradle and flopped back in the chair. Joey and Andrea were leaning in, arms on the counter, intensely watching his face. The sweat on it. Soap stood to the side, stooped slightly, to listen.

"So how'd I do?" Broker asked.

"Sounded pretty conflicted to me," Andrea said.

"No lie there," Broker said as he fingered his shirt pocket, then his jeans, looking for a cigarette. Remembered he was out. Soap quickly rummaged in a drawer and found a pack of Rita's Marlboros. After Broker lit up, he blew a stream of smoke, eased back in the chair, engaged Andrea's inquiring eyes, tossed off a thin smile, and said, "Could be *déjà vu* all over again."

Andrea, who was adept at tracking context, selected a quote from memory and said, simply, "Godzilla."

Soap moved in closer. "Define Godzilla, exactly?"

Broker was very aware of all their eyes, watching the way he'd eerily relaxed. He took a drag, exhaled, and thought about the dead reading smoke. "Goddamn Harry, I hate it when he's right before I am. I don't know if it's sanctioned or off the books or rogue, but I'll bet my ass I just talked to an asset from the Agency or Defense Intelligence. Someone way down in the tank, with access to classified files."

"So what'd he say?" Soap asked.

"He read me my expunged biography. It's a dangle to get me to switch sides, to shop your ass. He offered to give me my life back, with extras," Broker said.

Soap squinted, jutted his chin, and stroked his throat. "So do you want your life back?"

Broker took a moment to inspect, in granular detail, the carnage on the desk blotter. His eyes wound up on the shattered picture frame of the family portrait. Soap in the Hawaiian shirt. The wife in the bikini. Rita grinning through her braces.

"Not as much as I want some other things," he said.

So now the silent phone had transformed, for Broker, from live grenade into full blown Sphinx. This time when it rang, they all three jumped. But it was Joey, calling from a convenience store pay phone near the target house, reporting on his radio communication with Harry. What passed for good news was Harry had pictures of all four faces, the cars and the house number. It came as no surprise to Broker that he had elected to stay in place.

"He wants me and Tony to hang close by, in radio contact, for support in case they move her," Joey said.

"Do that," Broker said. "Tell him we're trying to set up a proof of life meet."

"Okay. I told him we're working on making some lemonade. No details."

"Right. And, Joey, be careful getting in radio range."

They went back to waiting and phone watching. Duke dutifully showed up and sat sentry in his truck in the parking lot. While Soap brooded on the couch sipping coffee, Broker and Andrea cleaned up the desk. Andrea picked up the pack of Marlboros that sat on the counter. Broker gave her his lighter. She lit the cigarette and walked to the front window. The sky had only been flirting with blue and now closed cloudy ranks. Broker joined her.

"They won't recruit you over the phone," she said.

"Nope. He sounded arrogant, sure of himself. He'll want to personally break me. There'll be a meet. And I'll go in with a reasonable case to make a deal. So he'll look for handles. You know. Triggers. Vices, debts, secrets, insecurities. Personal stuff that makes me easy to manipulate."

"And you have a big handle."

"I do. Cantrell spotted it and gave it a twist. I needed a work history. They're offering to make me a legitimate person. I'm curious if they'll have more to show than just talk." Her watchful silence shouted a question, so he admitted, "Not all handles are negative. Yours are boldness and a certain idealism."

"Broker, you can kiss my ass," she said. Then, after an interval: "You'll play hard to get."

"I will. But then I'll grudgingly come around and opt to live my silly little life, at the price of yours and Soap's and Joey's and Rita's."

"You've been here before."

"Similar."

"Were you doing the recruiting then?"

Broker smiled. "Were you really at Woodstock?"

Andrea backed off. "I was. I had a peace symbol on my cheek in magic marker. The music was great."

They both looked out the window and watched the overcast slowly steal the light until the air thickened to drab and then to somber and collapsed the shadows. Out there, people were sitting down to turkey and mashed potatoes and cranberry sauce, were getting ready to watch the Bears-Cowboys game.

Andrea understood that Broker needed some room to prepare, so she took refuge in being efficient. She looked in the small refrigerator behind the counter, then said to Soap, "We're going to need some food around here."

Soap gestured to Broker and did some fast pidgin sign language as to Broker's input. "Send Duke with her," Broker said.

"Put on your coat and hat. I'll get Duke to run you to the ma and pa on Owen and Myrtle. They should be open till noon," Soap said.

As Andrea got ready, Soap waved in the burly, bearded Duke and explained the errand. As she approached the door, he said, "Len's has a good deli counter. Best load up on sandwiches and goodies." He started toward the cash drawer under the counter. She waved him off and went out to Duke's waiting truck.

Soap followed her and watched the truck leave, then raised a hand and gave the finger, in general, to the apartments across the road. "Life's little rituals. Guess you have to eat," he said.

"What?" Broker looked up from lighting a fresh cigarette off the butt of the last one.

Turning from the door, Soap muttered, "I said I've lost a lot of people, but I never lost a kid." He flopped into a chair.

Broker waited a moment, then asked, "How secluded is this cabin?"

A memory smiled in Soap's eyes. "Before this started, only three of us knew about the place. Annie, myself and Jimmy Briggs. And, used to be, her husband, Tommy."

"But it has to exist on somebody's map. County taxes? A fire department?"

"Not true. Belongs to a guy who thought it was fun to go slumming with us in the old days. He gifted it, in appreciation, I guess you'd call it. He lives in Florida now. He's a beneficiary of a family trust. His granddad was a timber cruiser, bought up huge lots of land east of Hinckley. It's this old hunting shack with a pole barn, sits all alone on a section of land. Nobody knows about it. The trust pays the taxes. Strictly four-wheel-drive getting in. No direct county road access. No telephone line, no electric, no fire number. We used to warehouse certain items there. After we got too old and straight to jump high, we'd use it for hunting."

"How many ways in and out?" Broker asked.

Andrea returned with two full shopping bags. She tossed Broker a pack of Luckies, then stacked three more on the desk. As she stowed groceries in the small refrigerator behind the counter, she said, "Lady behind the cash register told me there's a hell of a winter storm rolling in across the Dakotas. Could be a blizzard. Going to hit in the morning. Maybe we should turn on the radio."

Broker jerked a smile. Blizzards were a pain, but on the up side, they obliterated tracks and made the world brand new. His smile twitched because he found himself coming in for a crash landing as the speed flamed out. And he did need to look suitably open to suggestion if he had his audience with the Shadow. So he tossed down two more Dexedrine, chased them with a bottle of water, poured another coffee, and proceeded to chain-smoke his way through a fresh pack of Luckies.

Joey called. Nothing new from Harry, who was still on Ice Station Zebra, freezing his ass. And then.

Soap answered after the second ring and started out with an icy growl, "You fuckers!" and held the anger decibel for several sentences. "I thought we were going to talk on Friday and sort this out. Why'd you start shooting at people and kidnap my kid!" Then he put his hand over the receiver and motioned to Broker. "It's your big lizard friend. I don't think he wants to meet me, so you're up."

Broker came to the phone. The Shadow said, "You seem to like Pine Point Park, so have someone drop you off at least a quarter mile south of it on the county road and walk in. Go to the shithouse and lock the door. When there's no civilians around, a vehicle will pull up, and someone will rap on the door three times fast, three times slow. Unlock the door, face the wall, and have a ski mask turned backwards, over your eyes. Any tricks and the girl pays. Understand?"

"I understand," Broker said.

"The clock is running," the Shadow said and hung up.

"It's on," Broker said. Soap nodded as he shut the door on his company safe. He plunked the cash brick on the desk next to the pictures of the dead Persian and his tattoo. Then he reached in a drawer and pulled out a Scotch tape dispenser.

Chapter Thirty-One

Forty minutes later, pale late afternoon light striped Broker's face like quiet war paint. It filtered through the shutters on the small, high window of the restroom in almost-deserted Pine Point Park. Two guys, working off the tryptophan, were playing winter frisbee in the parking lot. Their laughter subsided, a car started, and they left Broker alone, waiting for it to begin. All he had to work with was the flat loaf of cash, some pictures, a certain amount of balls, and a reputation for tactical agility in the midst of chaos. He took a deep breath of piss-sour outhouse air and made no effort to throttle down the uppers that fried his veins into hot red wires. *Okay. Check your dance card.* Andrea and Duke were on phone duty at the shop while Soap had sped him to the drop-off point. Harry was still in position. Joey was with Tony up the road someplace. Then, out of reflex, he lapsed into counting. He'd seen men freeze, piss their pants, and pray, waiting for it to start. He'd joined the silent bench. In his silence—senses topped off and hair-trigger ready —he counted. *One. Two. Three. Four.* Over and over. Sometimes faster, sometimes slower.

He counted so he wouldn't think about the men who waited for him. Worst case, they'd be tier-one special operators. Seasoned senior NCOs. Some could be dead-eyed ciphers who drank too much. What Harry might be in a few years. Some would have wives and kids. And some would attend church. What they shared was a proven willingness to instantly kill whoever's name was on the target list.

Best case, they were sweepings from the clandestine services. Bums who couldn't cut the discipline.

Count, counseled the machinery. *One. Two. Three. Four.*

Tires crunched in the snow. Then he heard the knocks on the door. Broker freed the latch, pulled down the reversed ski mask over his eyes, raised the cash brick in both hands, and faced the wall. The door opened.

"Keep facing the wall," ordered a neutral military/law enforcement voice. All Broker could read in it was male, fit, trained. The package was snatched away. "Put your hands behind your back." He placed his hands behind his back and felt cold metal snap his wrists. Brusque hands frisked him, then deftly added a heavier elastic blindfold over his knit mask.

"We're going outside and getting into a car," the neutral voice said. They waited for almost a minute until another curt voice called from outside. "Clear." A no-nonsense grip on his elbow marched him out into the snow. An opposite touch guided his head—police reflex style—below the door jamb as he clambered, blind, into what felt like the back seat of a—station wagon?

Broker figured they'd drive a pretzel route to disorient him, and they did, for thirty minutes. So there were two of them, one in the seat next to him, one driving. Silent men without real names, with fake ID. Who just disappeared when they died. Shadows.

Then the road sound changed from compacted snow on pavement to snow on gravel, occasional shards of which banged up into the wheel wells. A few minutes later, the vehicle stopped.

He was helped out, and as his boots crunched through the snow—if it was the same location—he calculated that Harry was watching him, no more than sixty yards distant, hidden in the collapsed barn. *Patience, Harry, patience.* "Steps," said the one who'd cuffed him, whom Broker had christened "Neutral Shadow," based on the controlled meter of his voice. Broker climbed the steps, heard a door open, and entered a musty warmth of scalded iron tinged with smoke. The air smelled of dust. Unlived in.

He counted steps. Six, until he was stopped and steered left. A skirling sound, cheap runners on some kind of rod. Neutral Shadow said, "I'm going to remove your mask. Continue to face forward."

Rita appeared by the harsh light of an unshaded bulb that hung from the ceiling. Her left hand appeared to be professionally bandaged, and an IV ran from her arm to a bag tacked to garish floral wallpaper over the chipped bedstead. Eyes closed, she was clearly more than asleep. Another Shadow wearing a winter camo windbreaker sat on the bed next to Rita. Her boots had been removed, the top button of her Levi's was unfastened, and a cushion had been placed to elevate her feet. *As if to say, See, we're not all bad; we've patched her up and given her standard treatment for shock.*

The one sitting on the bed also wore a ski mask and held two things in his hands. One was Rita's right hand, palm turned up. The other was a thick-bladed fighting knife. With the precision of a manicurist, he used the sharp tip of the knife to clean under Rita's fingernails. In doing so, the jacket cuff on his right wrist rode up enough for Broker to glimpse what looked like the tailing calligraphy of a tattoo. Broker marked him as Fool Shadow, because he'd shown himself with the knife.

Neutral Shadow said, "Her injury has been cleaned, sutured and treated by a qualified medic. She's been given antibiotics, the saline drip to keep her hydrated, and a sedative."

They'd tried to tidy her ponytail, but several dark strands crossed her face like cracks. Lips parted, she breathed through her mouth, slightly labored, like a kid struggling with a cold. Fool Shadow put his knife away, and as he lowered Rita's good hand to the wrinkled sheet that served as a mattress cover, Broker saw the active bruising and swelling and scabs forming on her knuckles, painted with iodine. Not defensive wounds.

The mask was pulled back down over his eyes, the blindfold adjusted, the curtain rod snickered, and he was rotated about face and urged left, then forward. Spongy carpet. A skitter of static to his right. Neutral Shadow said, "He had this."

"Wonderful," said another voice that sounded like the asshole on the phone. The static stopped. So one to the right, add Driver, Neutral Shadow and Fool Shadow. All four of them were in the house. *No more dicking around. This is showdown time.*

Six more steps. Then he tripped when the floor level pitched up an inch and the temperature cooled. He was entering an addition, the rear room, perhaps. He smelled fresh brewed coffee.

Neutral Shadow said, "I'm going to remove your handcuffs. Then you take off the mask. You'll see a table and a chair. Sit in the chair and place your hands on the table. Keep facing straight ahead. If you turn around, we will render you unconscious and hurt the girl. Signify by saying 'yes.'"

"Yes," said Broker. And then it was click and snap and the cutting metal pressure released from his wrists. He brought his tingling hands to the front and briefly massaged them together. Then he slowly raised them and removed the mask and the blindfold.

He stood in a small kitchen in front of a short plank table with two chairs. As he stepped forward, he saw that the linoleum on the floor had buckled and the Formica countertops were mostly peeled away. The electric stove looked used. The refrigerator was dead, but the sink had a scrubbed, lived-in feel. Tenting cobwebs occupied the ceiling corners and sprouted from floor to baseboard. His eyes stopped on an overturned cat bowl, where the cobwebs were matted with tufts of animal fur. And that wasn't the first time he'd seen signs of feral cats quarreling over what they'd found in an abandoned house.

As Broker carefully lowered himself to the chair and placed the mask and blindfold on the table, he saw the percolator on the counter behind a roomy plastic cooler. Strictly temporary digs, he thought as he slowly placed his hands on the table. From the corner of his left eye he saw an ajar door that revealed a slice or workbench, a vice, tools and, he speculated, some rusty barbed wire. Maybe the echoes of Leper's screams. The kind of house you keep around in case nobody needed no place to go.

Steps sounded to the right, and a lanky, six-foot man sauntered along the counter. He wore a lightweight black ski mask and a heavily-woven, gray Peter Storm wool sweater with leather elbow patches. His tan cargo trousers had lots of pockets, and the serrated grip of a short, black automatic pistol was jammed in the one on his right hip. A stack of newspapers was tucked under his left arm, and he held up the cash brick in his right hand, with the picture of the dead Persian taped on top. "Goddamn," he said, "but you are a pain in the ass. What's this? A lame attempt at insurance or blackmail? Why am I not surprised you figured out a way to kill a cop?" he said as he put the papers, along with the money, on the table. Same smooth voice, the faint twang now marbled with insouciant humor. Broker put him in his mid-forties, effortlessly fronting a good imitation of being relaxed and confident. So this was Shadow Number One.

The Shadow removed a cup from the cupboard, briefly inspected it, then placed it on the counter and poured coffee. He picked it up, turned and paused to study Broker's hands on the table that fidgeted slightly and then willed themselves still.

Broker let the machinery crank down on the minor meteor storm that surged in his blood, tingling right down to the capillaries in his fingertips. He pulled it in deeper so he projected a faint oscillation of trapped, and therefore unpredictable, menace. The Shadow placed the cup down on the table in front of Broker and took the opposite chair.

The ski mask was hooded, so Broker couldn't see the color of the eyes, only dots of light. The dots continued to study him. Broker's mouth was dry and his heartbeat was accelerated. His pupils were dilated, his hair was askew, and his bruised face was unshaven.

"Jeez, man, look at you." The Shadow moved his hooded head from side to side in a sad little shake. "There you were, taking the backwoods, minimum-wage cure, and this happens." He patted the top issue of the *Pioneer Press.* "And you wind up playing bodyguard for an aging ex-bad guy? We don't quite believe that."

"Yet here we are," said Broker. "And fuck you." He leaned forward slightly, so as not to excite the goon to his rear. "And I'm not a bodyguard," Broker said. "I was hired to find *you.* And to have this sit down. At first we thought *that,*" he said, pointing at the cash, "belonged to some hotshot Colombian dope dealer. But then we met the guy in the woods who stupidly took a shot at me, and suddenly it didn't look like dope anymore."

"Thanks for the dance. Now show me some leg." The Shadow opened his hands.

"Ten percent finder's fee. And the pictures disappear," Broker said. "Travis Diggs was a thief, and that involves risk, and you guys are just excessive, I guess. But Soap Turrie didn't *take* anything. He just got caught in the middle. *You* lost your goddamn box. *He* found it." Broker shrugged. "Anything else happens to the girl, or to Turrie, or to me—those pictures go public."

"So what? A picture of a dead guy laying in the snow. That could be anywhere in the world."

"Right," said Broker. "Except it shows enough of his arm to identify the tattoo. And if you look at the other picture that's taped to the bottom, you see the detail on the tattoo, along with the little card with a phone number. That's a local exchange. So, when an enterprising reporter calls that number, who picks up? Maybe someone who knows you?"

"Jesus, so now you're a degenerate fixer?" The Shadow thought out loud.

"Just telling you how it is. But for kicks, let's call that number and see who answers. You have a phone in here, right?"

The Shadow exhaled. "Russell Turrie's band of ruffian mechanics, hiding in the trees." He glanced at the photo taped to the money. "With cameras?"

Broker started looking for gaps. *Unless it was intentional omission, asshole here didn't ID Harry by name. Or Andrea. Maybe he only IDed me because I was in the paper. Slow down, man. He knew who to call.*

"You started shooting," Broker said.

"You were getting tricky, guys hiding in the trees with their little toy radios," the Shadow said. "What happened next created a problem."

Maybe they didn't see the shooting? Just the aftermath, and the guy who reported back had Joey for a passenger? Are they partially in the dark, too? As Broker processed this possibility, he said, "A problem your man started." He jerked his head back in the direction of the room where Rita lay unconscious. "So why her?"

"We had to send a message. Turrie's a scumbag who associates openly with known criminals. So it had to be crude enough for him to understand."

"I think he got the message when he opened that meat freezer. He was shook up. When he got a look at what was inside that box, he called me in. And there's him." He pointed at the photo. "Plus the Shah's in New York getting chemo. Soap Turrie couldn't conceive of telling *that* story to the police." Broker turned—screw the guard—and pointed toward the hallway. "Until you *did that* to his *kid*."

"Okay, Broker, calm down. Let's work this out." The Shadow picked up the cash brick and placed on the table between them.

"He thinks you'll kill her, and him, to cover your tracks," Broker said. "So what's he got to lose? He *was* scared. Now he's *mad*. The shop's turning into an armed camp. Just saying, this could get official. Property will be seized."

"What's your angle?"

"There's only one angle," Broker said. "You sight along a line that starts with some hungover forklift driver in Duluth loading the wrong box on the wrong truck. Enter you guys. It gets unexpectedly messy. Now you're looking for a way to tidy up the battlefield. Maybe the only smart thing that *you did* was dig up my bio. How'd you do that, anyway?"

"Finder's fee." The Shadow mulled it, no longer pretending to be relaxed. "So he didn't call the cops because he thought he could make a deal. Or did you figure out a way to benefit from this cluster and give him a nudge?" He briefly balled his fists, then thought better of it. "That man you left out in the snow? One of the guys was at his daughter's christening —or whatever they call it over there. You tell Turrie we were pretty restrained with that fuckin' wildcat, under the circumstances."

Broker heard a crackle of radio traffic behind him, some cop ten-code mixed in.

"Don't hear that, Broker. You know the drill. Like they told you in the old days? *We're not here.*"

"Oh yeah?" Broker pointed to the picture. "I have plenty of copies, just not with me."

"Really. I have some copies too." The Shadow reached down, for a cargo pocket probably. His hand came up holding a folded sheet of paper. He passed it to Broker, who opened it and didn't fake the jolt in his throat, because he was looking at his DD214 discharge paper. Or rather, half a copy—a somewhat muddied-in-transmission copy—of the right hand portion of the form, showing his Social and Army service number. *Place of entry into current active duty: Duluth, Minnesota.*

"They didn't *destroy* your records. They *pulled* them. Welcome half-way home, soldier boy," the Shadow said.

And now all the cards were on the table. Broker slowly shifted some facial muscles and let his bargaining facade recalibrate from bluff to sober. He pointed to his chest pocket. "I'm going to light a cigarette," he said. Which he did. A minute passed in a jerky nicotine meditation. He raised the coffee cup, took a sip, and doused the smoke in the cup. His eyes never moved off the discharge fragment.

"It means they can be put back." The Shadow canted forward. "So where's the fucking truck, Broker?"

"At a secure location, up in the woods. Turrie won't say where," Broker recited.

"Bullshit."

Broker shrugged. "Then you talk to him."

He started to get up, and the Shadow raised a cautioning hand. "Cool your jets. It's with the O'Neil woman?"

Broker resumed his seat. "No, man, Turrie says that's a crock. She's shacked up with an old boyfriend somewhere."

"So how did the truck get up in the woods?"

"I don't know. Ask Travis Diggs. I do know this only ends one way. Ten percent and Rita doesn't get more unhealthy." Broker pointed to the picture taped to the cash. "Or that shows up on the evening news."

The Shadow snorted. "Maybe you can stay here with her, hold her good hand." After dismissive humor came a glum reflection. "Sonofabitch. You took fucking pictures?"

"Was too good to pass up," Broker said.

"You'll be on certain people's radar if I do this."

"I'm already on their radar. I say again, how did you access my records?"

"What records? Last I heard, you didn't have any records." The Shadow cocked his hood. "Pay you off, to make it all go away?"

All Broker could see was the flicker of the hooded eyes. Without a face to go with the eyes, it was like talking to an effigy. Slowly, grudgingly, the Shadow pointed to the partial discharge. "If you want to see the other half of that, you will get Turrie to listen to reason. And I'll go *five percent*."

"Eight."

"Seven," the Shadow grumbled. "You make that work, you get your records restored. After the transfer. And I get the pictures and all the negatives."

Broker shook his head. "Never happen. I do that, and who's to say I don't get hit by a car, or hang myself, or drown while I'm out kayaking like William Colby? Nope. I hang on to the pictures."

The Shadow said, "We'll come back to that, but the seven percent is final."

Broker could see no further movement across the table. He pretended to think about it, but he was working up to the main play. The Shadow wasn't a free agent; he was under some kind of discipline. And it sounded like the guidance recommended making it go away as quietly as possible. He exhaled. "Okay."

"So we work out the exchange."

Broker lit another cigarette to stretch the negotiation. He took a drag and peered into the hidden eyes. *So are you a good sheep dog? Obedient to orders? Good boy, table scraps, sleep by the fire?* He said, "Soap can have it in town later tonight. We agree on a swap site. You bring Rita. We trade straight up and count our money and everybody goes home. We could start it in motion in an hour—"

"Right," the Shadow snorted. "Meet in a dark, empty field? Everybody with safeties off and on edge. That's a recipe for the OK Corral. Don't think so. No more moving that truck."

Broker made a production of thinking about what he was willing to happen. *C'mon, boy. Follow the bread crumbs into the woods. Good Fido.*

Seeing Broker balk, the Shadow tried to sound reasonable. "If he's the only one knows where it is, he can prove it by taking us to it. Him alone. And you guarantee all you want about the girl. But he's got one shot. One tiny thing looks out of place—any step along the way—the girl is gone. And we have much better radio communications than you do."

Yeah, maybe baby, but I kind of fucking doubt it. "Just get him to go alone," Broker said, like he was reading contract language.

"Just him, by himself, in that big gray Suburban. Tomorrow morning. And we'll follow along. But no tricks, because we'll be here, too." The Shadow inclined his head toward the front of the house. "With her."

"If he agrees, he'll go armed," Broker said.

"Wonderful. We'll have target practice in the woods."

The Shadow extended a blunt manicured finger. "And you stand clear, along with Turrie's pitchfork-wielding mechanics. If we see you anywhere around this thing after tonight, the girl disappears. You pull any more games, the girl disappears. And forget restoring your records. Sorry—more crude stuff—but we know where your folks live. You won't see it coming. Acknowledge."

Broker stifled a visceral grunt in his throat. "Got it. And no one else gets hurt," he said, knowing it was code for "everybody else gets hurt except maybe me." But down in sub paragraph B somewhere, the fine print stipulated that Broker got hurt too.

"Nobody else gets hurt. Turrie gets his kid back and some hush money. You walk away and go home with your cut and your background," the Shadow said.

"In the morning?"

"We'll call in two hours with specific instructions. If he can't decide by then, we'll put the kid on the phone and see how long he can stand hearing her scream." The Shadow picked up the half photocopy of Broker's discharge, produced a Bic lighter, and set the paper aflame. As Broker watched it curl into ash on the table top, the Shadow said, "Think about it. You have two hours." Then he picked up the money brick and tossed it to Broker. "You work for pay. Consider this an advance. Now earn it."

They told Broker to stand up and put his hands behind his back. They pulled the ski mask over his eyes. They stuffed the cash brick down the front of his jeans. As they led him away in cuffs, past the unseen room where Rita lay in limbo, Broker was sure that the Shadow had been contemptuously toying with him, like a mouse he wouldn't kill until he'd served a purpose. And, of course, the feeling was mutual. Broker had already made up his mind to feed this smug fucker his karma for lunch.

Chapter Thirty-Two

"She's asleep, drugged for sure. She's received competent medical attention. Antibiotics, they said. I did see a saline IV," Broker told Soap when he climbed into the front seat of the Suburban at the empty park. They'd dropped him off, blindfolded, on the road. He'd walked to Pine Point and called from the pay phone.

"And?"

"Sorry, Soap," Broker said, flicking his lips, "but they threatened to go after my folks, so I have no choice but to betray your ass. The phone number got his attention. He agreed to seven percent. But he's just practicing his social skills. If we think we have a deal, we're more manageable as they lead us to slaughter. When I told him you had the only line on the truck, he liked the idea of you leading them in solo. His idea."

"Bingo," Soap said with a grim, satisfied smile.

Broker nodded, then held up the cash brick. "My advance. To convince you to go alone. Once he gets the box, he'll deal with me as a side issue."

"So nothing new. They plan to kill us all." Soap's voice was fatalistic, iron in it.

"Looks that way. Couldn't get a read on their local resources. Anyone can buy a scanner, but someone had to help them track down the box and get into that farmhouse on short notice."

"So did he give anything away?"

"He dropped watercooler stuff, inside Agency lingo. He suggested a prior relationship with the SAVAK guy Harry shot in the woods. But that doesn't prove they smuggled money out of Tehran. We just don't know. They could be sworn officers from a clandestine service who caught a shitty detail on a shoestring time line. Or they could be contractor scum who went in business for themselves. Maybe they're just thieves with powerful friends. Maybe they're all three." Broker thought about it. "But I don't think he really knows what happened in the woods when they lost their Persian buddy. Could be his arrogance is a cover for insecurity." Broker faced Soap. "Could be they're as desperate as we are."

"Someone else will have to figure all that out some other time," Soap said as he put the truck in gear and started to drive.

Yeah, like me, Broker thought. But he said, "The idea we'd try to turn an advantage, to bargain for a percentage? That's a play they can understand." Broker paused. "He showed me a partial copy of my DD214, and I didn't fake my reaction to seeing that." He smiled tightly. "That's a real hook."

"And you were tempted." Soap's tone probed.

"I sure as hell *looked* tempted." Broker thought about it and added, "But not as much as you think." *Just be going back to a whole lot of bad history, and I'm starting to like this. Where I'm at now.* He waved a hand. "It's just bullshit. They're betting that having Rita as their ace trumps all our wiggle room. And on you knowing for certain they will kill her, without hesitation, if you deviate from the plan. But Harry is *our* hole card. So we have to get him in to warm up, develop film, and be ready to get back in position."

Soap nodded. "And I called Jimmy Briggs. He's on his way." Without taking his eyes off the high beams making a tunnel in the early evening, he tapped his teeth together and said, "But she's okay, considering?"

"She's not okay, Soap. But she's alive."

"Good enough. You think they're still watching the shop?"

"Who cares? I told them you'd gone to the mattresses, had troops coming and going."

"Threatened your folks, huh? And your dad was in the second battalion at Bastogne." Soap chewed on that for a few beats, then rumbled, "I don't know, man. Second bat was a bunch of pussies."

Broker grinned. "I'll let you sort that out with him someday. But as a dutiful son, it leaves me no choice. After I convince you to take a solo drive, I make a discreet exit. Joey and I will slip out the back, like he did with Tony." He paused and stared at Soap. "There's getting to be a lot of people tacked on to this thing. Briggs. Your mechanics."

"That's right, along with Annie." Soap raised a hand and his fingers turned an invisible key in his lips. "And ten-twelve years ago we were what your cop pals would call a gang." He stepped on the gas and growled, "Trick is not to think about everything that can go wrong."

When they walked in, Andrea was behind the desk, watching the phone and talking to a natty guy, Soap's age, who had closely barbered silver hair and a matching moustache and chin beard and who went with the shiny new El Dorado in the lot. In addition to slacks and dress leather shoes, he wore a trim, black leather vest over a starched Oxford shirt, like a sanitized memento of rougher times. And that was Jimmy Briggs, Soap's partner in local real estate and jumping into Normandy.

Andrea said, "Joey called from the phone at the convenience store. Harry saw them taking you in and out. He says all four of them are on site."

Broker turned to Soap. "They're betting it all on Rita to get you in that truck tomorrow."

Soap nodded and went behind the counter to lock up the cash brick. Then he called Broker over, introduced Briggs, and they talked low, heads close. Then Soap went to the desk, uncovered the folded-over blotter sheets from yesterday, and found the number Rita had left for Tommy Lynum's pager. "Guy works in a bank, something to do with computer systems, so he's on call 24 hours a day, even on Thanksgiving." Soap picked up the phone and called the number.

They all looked at the wall clock, which read 7:26 p.m. Broker wanted to be on the road to Hinckley with Joey no later than nine. After Briggs left, Soap assembled a small satchel of tools for Joey. Broker went upstairs and checked his weapons cache. The assault rifle and .45 for him, Harry's rifle for Joey, when it became available. Then he laid out the now-dry winter camo outfit he'd worn in the tangle of fallen elms.

One Two Three Four.

Soap opened a garage door when Tony wheeled his truck into the lot. Joey hopped out and then assisted Harry, who staggered into the lobby and shed his camera bag, rifle, boots, and frost-stiffened outer clothing. He trailed used hand and foot warmers. "If I ever meet the guy who invented heating pads, I'll gladly blow him on the spot," he muttered. Then he took a roll of film from the waistband of his underwear and placed it on the counter. "Shower," he croaked, limping toward the back of the shop.

When Broker came back downstairs, a subdued Soap was talking on the phone. He hung up and announced, "Contact. I drive to my death at eight a.m." Harry, somewhat revived and pink-cheeked from a hot shower, was seated on the couch wrapped in a wool blanket. He'd reversed roles with Joey, who now knelt and vigorously massaged his feet. Seeing Broker approach, Joey got up and went to pack some deli sandwiches and water canteens. As Andrea brought Harry a fresh cup of coffee, Broker sat down next to him.

Harry took a draught of hot coffee, saluted Andrea with the cup, and said, "As a medical professional, doesn't it make you worry that none of us are thinking of *stealing* the money? I'd say that's odd."

Andrea smiled, raised her middle finger, and withdrew.

Harry placed his coffee on the side table and turned to Broker. "Joey told me on the way in. Figured you'd hit your stride eventually. So we've been unleashed, huh?"

They slammed their palms together, locking thumbs in a death grip.

"Life number nine is the charm," Broker said.

"Fuckin' A," said Harry.

"Lot could go wrong. You going to be okay without me to hold your hand?" Broker asked.

Mugging his best Detroit Harry grin, Harry answered, "No sweat. All I need to do is stay focused on breaking the seal on a fifth of Jack Daniel's, right here, twenty-four hours from now." The grin vanished and, all business, Harry said, "Now tell me what you remember about the inside of that house."

At nine sharp Broker, in winter camo, and Joey, in his snowmobile suit, shouldered their gear and eased out the back and into the thick snow tunnel of evergreens. Tony's truck was waiting for them on the frontage road. After positioning the truck, Duke and Tony were tracking down Tommy Lynum to get the film developed.

Joey drove random jigsaws around Stillwater for half an hour, rolling past flickering windows lit by TV campfires where people gathered to digest too much turkey. Satisfied they weren't being followed, he turned the truck north, away from holiday visions of peace.

Chapter Thirty-Three

"A winter storm warning is in effect for the Twin Cities starting at midnight and extending until 9 p.m. tomorrow. Eight to twelve inches of snow are expected, with blowing snow and winds gusting to fifty miles an hour," the radio voice said.

Joey turned off the broadcast and aimed his latest vehicle, Tony's Dodge pickup that was outfitted with snow tires, north on 35E. The wind had already picked up from the west, and it funneled ridges of snow snakes across the highway in the open spots.

Broker told himself that he had a pretty good plan. Harry had pronounced it an okay plan for a trained team with state-of-the-art comms and a chopper on call to yank them out—but what the hell.

He knew they were rolling the dice. There could be more of them. A lot *could* go wrong. Talking about it would only be a distraction, because the plan had three moving parts and each of them had to be independently executed, with little or no co-ordination. *You think about it, you vividly see Rita on that bed. You picture Soap, Andrea and Harry going their separate ways into danger. So don't think about it. The job now is to execute it.* He repeated this simple tactical mantra over and over as he patiently tried to steer his full-blown speed run to a less intense, slower outer track.

Joey, who instinctively understood all of this, had turned meditative behind the wheel, ruminating, to eat up the miles.

"We just don't know, do we?" he said, peering into the night full of wind-blown snow. "Thirteen billion years ago there was nothing; then something goes bang, and all this is the result? What's the difference between that and the book of Genesis, where it says 'Let there be light'?" He turned to Broker. "You ever think about shit like that?"

"All the goddamned time," said Broker.

An hour later, they turned off the back roads east of Hinckley and left the truck in a foot of snow on a logging trail that was overgrown with almost impenetrable brambles. Shouldering their gear, they plodded into the woods, relying on Broker's compass, Soap's hand-drawn map, and Joey's previous visit to bring them in the back way to the cabin.

They traversed rolling hills thick with walnut, oak and maple that were frequently obscured by clouds of shifting snow. They found no sign of Joey's previous tracks. Fresh snow blanketed the ground and created an untouched monotony that might have been last seen by an Ojibwe hunter three hundred years ago. Overhead, the outriders of the coming storm thrashed in the upper branches of the bare canopy. Hunched beneath their packs and rifles, Broker and Joey set a brisk pace, without flashlights, in a spectral dimness that refracted and glowed off the crystals underfoot.

A quarter-hour later, working along a low ridge, they smelled wood smoke. A few minutes later they saw the faint glow of candlelight framed in a window. They paused on a hillside overlooking the cabin and the adjoining pole barn to let their breath return to normal.

"I best go ahead alone," Joey said. "She brought a pistol, and there's an old .45-70 that was in the cabin."

Broker nodded assent and watched Joey trudge down the hill in his white snowmobile suit and backpack, billy goat whiskers whipping in the wind.

As Joey made his approach, Broker, whose eyes had adjusted to the gloom, mentally mapped the ground below. The cabin had been built at the end of a shallow, flat depression between two slopes. A rough track ran through an overgrown ravine behind the house and connected with an old logging road: Soap's escape route, with the help of tire chains. At the opposite end of the clearing, a notch in the tree line was obvious even in these light conditions. And that was the crude road they'd come in on.

He estimated the distance from the front of the pole barn to the road to be just under two hundred yards. The shed was simple, corrugated tin, but large enough to accommodate two pieces of farm equipment. And that was where the famous truck was hidden, along with the woman who'd started this whole mess.

He turned his attention back to the cabin and made out slab sides fashioned from bark-on oak. The tin roof was rusted, and the smoking chimney pipe tilted.

Down below, Joey was now standing on the porch in a flicker of saffron candlelight that poked through the open door. "All clear," he hallooed up the hill. "C'mon down and meet Miss Annie O'Neil."

As he approached the cabin, Broker confirmed his suspicion that he would meet no boring personalities on this outing. He mounted the sagging steps and got his first look at Annie O'Neil, who bore a passing resemblance to a burnt out—but still smoldering—fireball. Her low-slung hips filled out tight jeans like a thirty-year-old's. But the candlelight spilling through the door delineated the lines on her face that put her closer to fifty. Her untidy faux-blonde hair had yielded to dark russet roots, an inch of ash was built up on the Pall Mall in her lips, and the old, heavy caliber, lever action rifle hung at arm's length in her hands.

"You took long enough getting back here. So who's he again?" A husky, combustible voice. She smelled like wood smoke and nicotine and worry and unwashed clothes.

"Phil. New guy, works for Soap," Joey said diplomatically.

"Oh yeah, Phil who?"

Broker and Joey exchanged glances.

"C'mon, boys, lighten up. We are only standing here in the close fucking shadow of death. Phil who?" Annie repeated.

"Broker, Phil Broker."

"Uh huh. You know I parked Soap's truck in that barn," Annie said. "And in that truck—besides a hundred million in cold cash—is a pretty good radio. So I've been regularly following the news, to include an interview on public radio with that St. Paul columnist, Johnny Lager. Your name came up enough." She took a step forward and studied Broker's face in the flickering light. Broker responded by putting out a finger to move the muzzle of the rifle out of line with his nose. Annie slowly shook her head. "I was waiting for Desmond, to give him the damn truck, and he never showed. Now who's standing in front of me? The fucking guy who shot him."

She had managed to say all this without removing the cigarette from her full lips or spilling a dot of the built-up ash. Now that he was standing closer, Broker could make out her high-voltage brown eyes. No beauty, she'd never launch a thousand ships. But she'd sure as hell get a few more men killed before it was over.

Joey cleared his throat. "Like I said, new guy that works for Soap."

"And?" Annie asked as she finally took the cigarette from her mouth and flipped it into the snow.

"And we're going to get you out of here. In fact, you were never here in the first place," Broker said. "But right now we have some work to do, because, Annie, that shadow you mentioned? It's for real. Leper is dead. We already shot one of them, and they took Rita and are holding her hostage to get their box back."

"Cut off her little finger," said Joey.

"So what are you going to do about it?" Annie said after a moment, eyeing the rifles on their shoulders.

"Prepare a surprise," Broker said.

"Big time," Joey said.

"All right, then." She indicated for them to enter the cabin with a toss of her head. "C'mon in. All I have left is tea or coffee."

Inside were threadbare hooked rugs on rough pine floors, Goodwill furniture, and lots of candles. A large tea kettle steamed on the roaring woodstove. Right after they doffed their gear and jackets, Joey led Broker to the back of the cabin, where a door opened on a large storeroom. Their flashlights revealed stacks of vintage stereos, TVs and kitchen appliances, all still in their dusty, unopened boxes. Joey set up one of his battery-powered work lights.

"What the—?" Broker stared at a whole rack of M-16 rifles. Fully automatic M-16s—he could see the forward assist on the side that was standard military issue.

"Soap ever mention Leper's famous gun deal that went south?" Joey said. "Not one of those pieces will function. Hector Garza damn near cut Leper's nuts off when he showed up with those junkers. Soap didn't know what to do with it all, so he socked it away up here." Joey pushed aside a pile of boxes, then manhandled out a cardboard container that was almost as tall as he was. "Stuff's in here."

Annie appeared in the doorway with two mugs of tea. "Morning Thunder. It's got a red buffalo on the box with lightning shooting out of its ass. You guys don't strike me as the Sleepy Time type." She handed out the cups, then settled her smoky eyes on Broker. "So? If I'm not here, where am I?"

Broker sipped the bracing tea. "Thanks, this is good." Then he told Annie her end, straight up. "In the morning Soap will drive through in a hurry, hopefully with a world of hurt on his tail. Not your problem. He'll collect you on the fly, drive out the back, and hook up on the highway with Jimmy Briggs. Soap tells me you and Jimmy go back a ways."

"I know Jimmy," Annie said.

"He'll take you to the condo he keeps on Superior, north of Duluth. You'll be seen clubbing together, and word will get out how he gallantly stepped in and gave you a place to lay low, away from public scrutiny. So you're off the hook and out of the loop."

Annie knew a good thing and adjusted effortlessly. "I get it. Anything else?"

"Clean everything out of this place that can put you here. And the keys?"

"In the truck," said Annie, pirouetting in the doorway. As she left, Joey reached into the box again and pulled out an olive drab canister.

"Smoke grenade," said Broker, impatient.

"Yeah, except Leper promised Hector frag grenades."

"I thought you said—" Broker began.

Joey waved him closer. "C'mere. Help me tip this beast over." When they had the box on the floor, Joey got on his hands and knees and pawed inside, pulling out cardboard cylinders that contained more smoke grenades. Then he called out, "Jackpot." This time he pulled out a gray canister topped by a fuse and a grenade pin pull ring.

"Thermite grenade. Okaay . . ." Broker said, inspecting it in his hand.

"Musta been packed by accident, along with some other stuff, huh?" Then Joey wiggled back in the box, dug around, and tossed something out. The horizontal, convex, olive-green plastic panel skittered on the rough floorboards. "And that's what else I found up here," he said with pride of ownership.

When it came to rest, Broker read the raised letters on the curved surface: FRONT TOWARD ENEMY. "Okay, I'm a believer." He reached up and scratched the speed bugs in his hair. "Leper must have wound up with some real sloppy supply sergeant's junk box. So how many?" he asked.

"Six Claymores. Five thermites. Plastic's cracked on all of the Claymores, and they're missing the hell boxes and cord, and the detonator ports are mostly busted off," Joey said.

"But," Broker said, hefting the thermite grenade.

"But that bad boy burns at four thousand degrees Fahrenheit," Joey said, smiling.

Chapter Thirty-Four

"You ready for this?" Joey said as they played their flashlights over the truck in the shed. "One each, seventy-eight Ford F-four-fifty dumper with a one-ton, extended box. Overloaded. Probably shot the springs." *Yards by Soap* was stenciled on the white, mud-streaked driver's side door, along with a street address and phone number.

Broker swept the flashlight beam over maybe a hundred flat, oblong cardboard packages that were neatly stacked along one tin wall. The brand name *Pegoretti* was printed on the sides. One of them had been opened, and a chrome bicycle fork was displayed on top of the pile.

They climbed into the bed of the truck. Like Soap had said, the crate was almost ten feet long and five feet by five feet. The lid had been removed to reveal that it was absolutely jam-tight with rank on rank of sealed, stuffed plastic bags. Several were shuffled around, and on one of them that stuck up, Benjamin Franklin's inexplicable green smile set Broker's senses dancing. *Enough cash to fill Scrooge McDuck's fucking swimming pool.*

"So, piece of cake," Joey said. "I reroute the hydraulic pump that lifts the box. Disconnect the power take off cable from the control lever in the cab, rewire the lift lever to the transmission so it's engaged, and tie it off on a mounting bolt. I can adjust the wire to set the dump box to lift at a certain rate once you turn the key and start the truck. We'll need to play with the tension to get the right rate of rise." Joey shrugged. "Put it in neutral, drop the tailgate, start the truck, the box goes up. Nobody needs to be in the cab. The crate will slide out."

Broker thought about it as his flashlight continued to explore the inky interior of the shed. The light stopped on a cache of five-gallon cans of gasoline, then moved to a neatly stacked cord of dry, split oak. Then he went to the sliding tin door, braced and shoved it open on creaking, rusty runners.

"Not here," Broker said to Joey, who was taking a tool satchel and two large battery-powered work lights from his backpack. "We pull the truck out . . ." His voice trailed off as he picked up a work light, turned it on, and walked from the shed into the snowy field. About forty yards out he paused to assess the sight lines and the distance to the access road. He set the light down in the snow. "Here," he said. "We park the truck here."

For the second time in as many days, Broker was in the pitch black woods working by artificial light. The wind turned on divots, blocking out moments of silence in which he heard the yip of prowling coyotes. Joey had repositioned the truck, and now Annie had been drafted to sit behind the wheel. Broker was perched on the side of the truck bed and Joey sprawled underneath, working in the illumination of two emergency lanterns.

"Now try," Joey's muffled voice sounded out.

"Start 'er up," Broker called to Annie.

The engine turned over, and Broker gauged the rate of the rising truck bed. At around fifteen degrees the huge box started to inch down the inclined plane. There was only a foot or so between the end of the box and the tailgate, and that was their practice margin.

"Turn it off," he called to Annie. The engine died, and the truck bed lowered to level. "A little more lift," he called to Joey.

They repeated the exercise again and again until Broker was satisfied; then Joey jogged back to the cabin. Annie climbed down from the front seat and came around to the back, where they'd used an old toboggan to haul a pile of firewood and all but one of the gas cans from the pole barn. Broker was piling the split oak in a semicircle around the back end of the truck. Then he dropped the tailgate, climbed into the truck, and proceeded to smash out the rear end of the crate with a splitting maul. As the wood siding fell away, the packed bundles of currency spilled out, showering down on his woodpile.

"Don't mind me," Annie said, peering over her Pall Mall. "Just go ahead. You wouldn't believe some of the weird shit I've seen in my life."

Broker straightened up and arched his back. "You're the one who said it was too much money to steal."

"Yep. So fuck 'em if they can't take a joke," said Annie as the work lanterns projected their huge, grotesque shadows toward the trees.

Broker raised his arm and pointed. "They'll come in through that notch, following Soap, who'll blast through, grab you, and head out the back. We hope. So they'll be on guard. We think it'll be three of them," he said. "Normally what guys like this would do is shake out one man along each ridge," he said, sweeping his arm at the hills, "to either side, to scope out the truck and the buildings, then approach real slow. The third man will stay back with their vehicle. They'll be linked by some kind of walkie-talkie radios."

"So?" Annie asked.

"So we need them to violate protocol and all three rush the truck." Broker toed the pile of oak. "I'm operating on the assumption that men usually run from fire," he paused, "unless there's millions of dollars burning in it."

They heard footsteps crunching in the snow, and Joey appeared with his backpack. Then he and Broker climbed into the truck bed and removed the Thermite grenades and the antipersonnel mines from the pack, along with a coil of fishing leader and a roll of duct tape.

While Annie held a lantern, they dug out bundles of hundreds and created a pocket at the back end of the crate. Next Joey took out a hammer and a fistful of ten-penny nails and pounded them into the freed-up inner wooden wall. Each hammer blow echoed, hollow, in the wind and faded into the surrounding hills. Then they used the nails as anchors to secure four of the grenades across the back of the crate with thick bands of the tape. They'd use the last one to fire the cabin on the way out, where a can of gas had been positioned in the storeroom. While Joey carefully knotted the thin filament to each grenade pin, Broker hauled five-gallon cans of gas and placed them in the space behind the crate. Then he positioned the six mines, business end facing out, on a bed of currency in front of the grenades. Joey methodically fastened the loose ends of the trip wires to the cross brace at the top end of the truck bed, pinching off the slack in one hand, testing each knot with the other. They'd already topped off the truck's gas tank.

They were ready. Annie was packed. Broker glanced at the luminous dial of his wristwatch. Four forty-three a.m. Then he stared into the black, spiky trees and listened to the rising wind. The naked branches rattled like sparring antlers.

Now it depended on Soap and Harry and Andrea.

Chapter Thirty-Five

Friday

D r. Andrea Sabic sat behind the wheel of a '74 Dodge Ram Charger that belonged to Duke, Soap's other mechanic. The truck idled on the north-south axis road, nestled in a dip about half a mile from a target house that she had never seen. The sun, a smear in the overcast, had come up, and so had the wind. The Dodge's chassis shuddered, and a green ground cloth, held in place by cinder blocks, flapped behind her in the truck bed. The tailgate, which was down, clattered in gusts of wind. One of the Motorolas sat on the dashboard. The other lay in Harry's lap. They'd been up all night completing various tasks, and she had taken half of one of the black capsules to stay awake. As far as she could tell, Harry was operating out of some kind of hang-time zone and hadn't swallowed any more amphetamines.

"Ask you something?" she said.

"Shoot. We have some time."

"That scar on Broker's arm, where he had a tattoo removed. What was it?"

"He'll tell you it was a military tat. When we were doing cross border stuff in sixty-nine, seventy, we had identifying marks removed."

"But you know different."

Harry exhaled. "Yeah, and I owe you that much because it appears you're taking him on as a project, right? Well, good luck." His eyes drifted over the distant pasture to bare wisps of smoke leaking from the target house chimney. "June sixth, nineteen sixty, his older sister Katie was driving him to a friend's surprise party. She was a high school senior, just got her license. Load of pulp wood came loose on the truck ahead of them. She swerved to avoid the logs and went off the road, over an incline, crashed down on this cobble beach, and slammed into a boulder. She was thrown against the steering column and killed instantly, and Broker, who was hunkered in the passenger seat, was catapulted through the windshield. He wound up on his back in a pool of lake water, hemmed in by rocks, unable to move. He doesn't know how long he lay there, choking on his blood, until help arrived. He survived by regulating his breathing to stay afloat." After a moment, Harry added, "The tattoo was three sixes; sixth month, sixth day, sixth hour."

Andrea exhaled and took a moment. "Now there's some scary numbers to draw to. And that was how his personality was formed."

"Pretty much learned how the world works right there," Harry said. "He gets to the war, and the first bad night when everybody is losing their shit and running in circles, he calms right down and regulates his breathing."

"So why lie about it?"

Harry turned in the seat and appraised her, then spoke with unexpected gentleness. "People have secrets that bind them together. You don't steal from your friends, Andrea. And sometimes, you lie for them."

They sat in a silence for a few moments; then Harry made sure the other radio was securely tucked into the inner pocket of his wind jacket. Today he was stripped down to basics, just the radio and Joey's .45 caliber Army Colt. "Ready?" he asked.

"Ready," she said. She was anything but, because it was all happening too fast.

"Okay, give me half an hour to get in position in the old barn. Then I'll call for a radio check. We good?"

"We're good," Andrea gulped as she extended her arm and touched his shoulder. She didn't say, "Take care," because care was the furthest thing from the concentration calibrated in Harry's eyes. Eyes the color of over-steeped tea. Very cold tea.

"You'll be fine." He squeezed her arm. And then the door opened and he was out, loping into the pasture, using the folds of ground to mask his approach.

She fingered one of Rita's Marlboros from the pack on the seat and used book matches to light up. Then she glanced at her wristwatch. Six fifty-three a.m. The electric sky raced in ranks of burnished clouds that were backstopped to the west by a darkening horizon. To her right front, in the pasture behind the target house—where Harry had now disappeared—a wind gust splintered a branch off a tall dead elm, and she watched it silently crash to earth.

If a tree falls in the forest and no one hears . . .? Question of physics. If no one sees a certified psychologist aid and abet . . .

She gripped the steering wheel and stared straight ahead, keeping the image of Rita, lying in the house, suffering, front and center in her thoughts. *Maybe, a little bit, because of me.*

She wore a winter camo smock over her wind suit, the same coverlet that Harry had worn on Wednesday night. Her hair was twisted up into a matching hunting cap. Broker had left it up to Harry as to how they were going to get Rita out of that house. And Andrea was hoping like hell that she was getting the "brilliant" Harry. Not the erratic one. He'd laid it out in simple, common sense terms. "Too chancy, rushing the place," he'd explained. "Best way is to get them to come out. And that's your job."

Andrea puffed on the unaccustomed cigarette and stared straight ahead.

Do your job. Jesus.

She looked at her watch.

Seven-oh-nine.

She finished the cigarette and tossed it out the window. Looked again.

Seven-twelve.

She jumped when the Motorola came alive. Harry's voice crackled in the static: "Three getting into the van. I say again, three getting into the van. Two of them are carrying long gun cases. One left standing on the porch. Make the call and contact me when you're back in position."

Andrea put the truck in gear, drove north, then east, on back roads, then turned south and came out near the convenience store with the pay phone on Highway 7. She parked the truck, got out, walked to the phone booth, picked up the receiver, and dropped the dime in the slot.

Soap listened, then placed the shop phone back on the cradle. He stood up and pulled on his denim jacket and his windbreaker. He took a moment to chat with the family dentist when he walked through the door to pick up his Cruiser after the holiday. "All set. Changed the oil and antifreeze and rotated the tires," Soap said. He nodded to his mechanic, who now sat behind the counter. "Tony will fix you up."

Then Soap went outside and looked up at the storm-charged sky and marked the rising wind. Killing time, he walked around his big Suburban, eyeballing the tires before he threw a look in the cargo compartment at the heap of heavy tire chains. He got in the cab, turned the key, adjusted the heater, hit the radio dial, and listened for a weather report. When he heard the forecaster say "potential blizzard conditions," he turned the radio off.

Ten minutes later he spotted the white Ford van lingering on Curve Crest, west of the shop parking lot. Patiently, he waited another ten minutes before he switched his headlights on and off twice. Then he put the truck in gear and drove slowly from the lot.

In the lobby, Tony saw Soap's lights blink twice and then watched his boss drive away. He picked up the phone and called the general number for the Washington County Sheriff's Department. He knew the call would pick up in the county comm center.

"Hey, hello. This is Tony Kizer at Soap's Shop in Stillwater. No, this isn't about people phoning in threats. I want to report a vehicle that went missing from our lot . . . No, ah, it's not a customer. It's one of ours. I mean, it's a dump truck we use in the landscaping business . . . Yeah, sure, got it all right here. It's a white Ford four-fifty, one-ton dump truck. License number is TDN two-seven-two. I also have the VIN—no, that's fine; when a city officer or county deputy drops by, I can show him all the paperwork."

Tony paused, listening, then said, "Well, it's been gone for more than a week. A guy who works here part time borrowed it, week ago Tuesday night. And we can't find him either. Hasn't come into work, and he doesn't answer his phone. And his car has been sitting here all that time . . . Sure. Name's Travis Diggs. Age twenty-seven, dark hair, has this purple birthmark on his left cheek . . . Okay, got all that, Social Security, address, all on his employment file. I can show it to the officer when he comes around to take the report . . . No problem. We're open till six."

Tony hung up the phone and smiled at the middle-aged woman who stood at the counter. "Yes, ma'am," he said, "now how can we help you?"

Ten miles northeast of where Tony was sitting, Andrea was back in position on the north-south county road. She took a deep breath, checked her watch that read seven-forty-six, then picked up the radio and keyed the transmit button. "Harry, Andrea. All set. I'm back."

"This is it. Just remember, they feel safe here," Harry said in a too-calm voice. "Go."

Andrea swallowed and put the truck in gear. Just like that. Her life was tumbling like icons on a slot machine, and it had turned into an affair of clichés: *Life goes on. This is it.*

As she accelerated, she reflected that the most stressful thing she'd dealt with in the last six months—before the shooting in the woods—was breaking up with an attorney she'd been dating. Certainly, horror shows regularly came through her office, but they appeared in the form of sterile clinical language that attached to subdued people sitting across from her in a chair.

Coming up to the turn now, she could clearly see the gray clapboard house to her right, the pile of collapsed elms, the wreckage of the barn, the blue station wagon parked in front.

Heart pounding, cotton mouthed, she took the turn too fast and skidded onto the east-west road. A few seconds later, she also made the turn into the driveway too fast. Her fingers were damp with sweat inside her gloves. She gripped the wheel. She panted, open-mouthed.

So what else do you say at a moment like this?

Hard to beat *This is it!*

As she mashed to a halt between two stunted oaks that were still speckled with shuddering bronze leaves, she immediately started pounding on the horn: long, insistent blasts. Then, swirling a scarf loosely around her face, she jumped from the cab and screamed at the top of her lungs. "Help! Please! My husband's hurt. Out bow hunting!" She ran up the front steps and pounded on the door. "I need to use a phone." She slammed her fist on the door like a panic trip hammer. "PLEASE! PLEASE! OPEN THE DOOR!"

When no one answered she staggered briefly, then ran back to the truck, reached in through the open door, and leaned on the horn. As it blared, she shouted as loud as she could, "HELP! SOMEONE PLEASE HELP!"

She paused to catch her breath and stared at the motionless door. Okay then, she figured that one of three things was going to happen: the cops would show up, the battery was going to give out, or that sonofabitch was going to open that door. Andrea pressed the horn and went back to yelling.

The horn made a steady, plaintive bleat long after her voice quit. She kept it going, manic, beyond all reason, and so, finally, the door cracked and a skinny man leaned out, shot looks in either direction, then yelled, "Ma'am, could you knock that off? We don't have a phone here." Only snatches of it carried in the whipping wind.

Andrea stalled for a beat, a little electrified that she was actually *seeing* one of them. But then her eyes narrowed as she remembered that he was the *second* one of them she'd seen. So she leaned back on the horn, found her voice and raised a scream, actually enjoying the catharsis of near hysteria. The man was coming down the steps now, visibly agitated, furious at the insistent horn. He wore dark cargo pants and a blue fleece. The haft of a knife protruded from the top of his left boot.

He swung his eyes as he walked, knees slightly bent, one hand poised behind his back. He cocked an ear to the persistent skitter of stubborn oak leaves overhead. Then, abruptly, he turned around to check the rear. He made the turn a fraction of a second after Andrea saw Harry duck behind the blue Buick that was parked not ten yards away.

"Hey, hey," he barked as he reached in past her and seized her wrists away from the steering wheel. "Knock it off. Just stop!"

A narrow, sandblasted face, dehydrated, pale blue eyes, and close-trimmed corn stubble hair. She thought he might have sand in his heart. The desert eyes darted, hot and cold, and in them, Andrea—who had been prepared for a shot of mortal terror coming face to face with one of them—saw a conflicted mix of wariness, anger and exasperation. Her visceral blip of fear was short-lived, because Harry was in motion, and she learned that "This is it" can happen way faster than in the movies.

Harry didn't believe in a lot of things. But cutting the timing close was one of them. And he trusted the wind barreling, cicada-like, through the oak leaves to diffuse sound and cover his footfalls. He reversed the .45 so he held it by the barrel when he covered the last yard. The guy heard the footfalls too late. He tensed alert, released Andrea and spun, reaching—ha—not for the gun, but for the fighting knife in his boot, which he raised halfway up before the Colt steel club crashed into his temple. Twice.

Andrea shifted from foot to foot in the snow, thinking she was going in that house, goddammit, to find Rita. But Harry raised a hand. "Wait, something's off. This was . . . too easy." He stared at the house. "So one thing at a time. First him." He nodded at the stunned man curled on his side in the snow. "Then I go in, check Rita, and clear the place. Then you come in." Quickly, he stuck his pistol in his belt. Eyes darting at the surrounding snowfields, he adjusted his light tactical gloves, stooped and rolled the man over face down. He removed the automatic from the back waistband. Then he bound the guy's hands behind his back with duct tape, then looped his ankles tight and slapped a final strip across his mouth.

"I was afraid he'd never open the door," Andrea said, clasping and unclasping her gloved fingers.

Harry allowed a crooked grin. "I have this theory that if a car horn honks long enough, it'll drive you nuts and cause some guys to forget their programming and just want to make it stop." His eyes continued to track the surrounding countryside. "Just didn't expect him to come straight out the front. That didn't make sense." Rising to a crouch, he fiddled for a minute with the pistol he'd just acquired, then handed it to Andrea. "That's hot; you pull the trigger, it'll fire. So be very careful, just in case I can't be everywhere at once." With that he seized the now-stirring man by the collar and sat him up against a truck tire. Moving fast, he yanked a blue bandana from his pocket, packed a handful of snow into it, and tied it around the man's forehead to staunch the bleeding. Then he frisked him again, carefully. "No radio," he said under his breath. He stared at the house again. "No fancy solid state Agency radio."

He turned to Andrea. "Wait here. Keep your gloves on. Don't touch anything when I call you in." Then he dragged his "prisoner" across the snow, up the steps, through the cluttered porch, and into the main room. After he dropped the man on the carpet, as he stalked past the woodstove, he spotted the room walled off by the curtain and immediately ducked in his head. Rita lay on the bed, partially nude, but breathing. *Be right back.* He stepped back out and noted that the stove door was swung open. Inside he saw a bed of ash and a thin layer of coals. Looking down the narrow hallway, he saw the kitchen at the end. *Just like Broker described. And that's a stairway that Broker didn't see.*

As he raised the .45, he stood absolutely still and listened, eyes tilted toward the ceiling, and only heard the creak of the wind. He cautiously mounted the stairs, checked the upstairs, and came back down and waved Andrea in. "Room behind the curtain," he said. He had taken two steps into the hall toward the kitchen when he heard Andrea cry out behind him. Not alarm. Anger.

In a few fast steps he intercepted her coming out of the curtained side room. She was headed for their prisoner, whose eyes blinked, disoriented, below the rag tied around his head.

"There's no medical kit," Andrea snarled. "There's a filthy bandage on her hand, and you smell that? She's shivering in a puddle of urine."

The prisoner's foggy eyes focused, and he violently shook his head and kicked his bound feet in obvious frustration.

Harry cocked his head. "Not exactly the response they teach you in survival school," he thought out loud. He gripped her arm, pried the pistol from her hand, clicked on the safety, and stuck it in his waistband. Then he turned her around and said, "What'd you expect, the Red Cross?" He stepped past the curtain and saw Rita curled, trembling, on her side. Her eyes fluttered and her breath rasped, shallow and drugged. The bandage on her left hand was soiled, not filthy. She lay with her torso and bare legs positioned around a piss-smelling stain on the bare mattress, and she wore a baggy pair of men's clean white boxer shorts. A sodden sheet, along with her wet, tangled jeans and twisted underpants, was crumpled on the nappy carpet. A pan filled with soapy water sat on a side table along with a washcloth and towel.

"Look around." Harry nodded into the living room at wires and parts of a police scanner stuffed in a cardboard box on the table next to the telephone. "Stove's going out. They were packing up." He went to the box, dug around, and held up a bulky rectangular device. "Christ, a TRC two-hundred. That's off-the-shelf garbage." Harry shook his head. "No fancy radios." Then he spun because Andrea was yelling.

"You sonofabitch! And you were just waiting for the phone to ring." Andrea glared at the bound man on the floor, who glared back and continued to shake his head.

"Cool it," Harry told Andrea. He jerked his head at the prisoner. "That guy was *cleaning her up.* That means something. Now, get her off the bed and wrap her up." He pointed to a pile of bedding on the floor. "If he looks cross-eyed at you, yell. I'll be right back." Harry padded into the hall.

When he returned a minute later, Andrea had moved Rita to the floor and had rolled her into a raggy blanket and was crouched next to her, holding her good hand. Harry yanked the wet sheet off the floor and spent a moment wiping down the bedstead and frame and anything else Rita might have inadvertently touched. Then he wrapped Rita's soiled clothes in the sheet, bundled it up, and gave it to Andrea. He scooped Rita up and carried her outside and put her in the front seat of the truck. Andrea got behind the wheel, stowed the dirty laundry behind the seat, turned the key, and cranked up the heater. Harry went back in, checked the bound man's pockets and left his wallet and pocket change, but kept the car keys with the Buick fob. Then he dragged the feebly resisting man out the front door and through the snow, lifted him, and heaved him in the truck bed on top of the flapping tarp.

He climbed in, kicked aside a cinder block, and pulled the fluttering ground cloth away. His prisoner's eyes enlarged when he saw Leper's graying face twisted next to his, the purple lips stretched back over the waxy gums and gaping teeth.

"Looks like they left you holding the shitty end of the stick, pal," Harry said as he swiftly used floor ties to cinch the man in place. "That workroom off the kitchen? There's a mop and pail and scrub brush in there, along with a bottle of bleach. But I bet you didn't get all the blood stains off the dirty-ass cement floor. And I saw a rusty roll of barbed wire in there too." Harry covered the thrashing man with the tarp, then positioned several of the blocks to hold it in place. He patted the convulsing lump under the tarp made by the prisoner's head.

Then he leaned back against the cab and spent half a minute smoking a Camel, all the while watching the empty road and wind-beaten fields as the tarp rustled and emitted the rising, nasal protests of a gagged man. He flicked out the ash, field-stripped the smoke, tore it into tatters, and let it dissolve into the wind. Then he came down to the passenger side, opened the door, and took out a small camera bag. He snapped a couple shots of the station wagon on approach before using the keys to open the door. Then he took out a spiral notebook from his bag and opened it to the page on which he'd written the number from the card Andrea had found in the dead Persian's sock. He placed the notebook, number up, on the passenger seat, closed and locked the door, and took several shots through the window.

Then he acted as ground guide and directed Andrea to drive around the station wagon and then to back up, close to the barn wreckage. Satisfied, he looked around one more time, whipped the tarp back and, easing Leper's rigor-stiff body as gently as he could, he transferred it to the lip of a collapsed silo base next to the barn lumber. Six feet below, he made out the skeleton of bedsprings and other rusty shapes that peeked through the snow. "Sorry," Harry muttered as he lowered and then released the body.

Then he came back to the truck, checked the restraints on his passenger, and said, "You don't get off so easy, pal. You and me are gonna have a talk."

Harry covered the wide-eyed prisoner with the tarp and securely weighted it down with the blocks. Then he came around and got behind the wheel. Andrea had moved to the passenger side with a sweaty, gray-faced Rita huddled into her shoulder. She laid the inside of her wrist on Rita's forehead and announced, "She's burning up."

"Won't be long now," Harry said as he wheeled the truck around and headed up the driveway.

"What did you mean about the radios?"

"Phil and I were worried they'd have some space age shit from NASA or something. I didn't find anything in there except a regular phone line and an inferior, commercial walkie-talkie. Maybe these guys are reduced to using pay phones, same as us."

Harry squinted up at the sky that was now spitting the first tiny snowflakes and briefly imagined Broker, up north, staring into the same swift storm clouds. He grinned and turned to Andrea. "General Winter's on our side. Gonna cover our tracks." He paused at the driveway, looked once toward the north, then turned west onto the county road and found his way to Highway 7. He drove into thickening snow until he came to the intersection of County Road 55, where a brown van sat on the shoulder. Soap had called in a favor, no questions asked, and Hector Garza's man, the one Broker called Tarantula, was right on time. Another man, who didn't fit the gangster profile, slid back the side door and briskly got out to help transfer Rita. He was the West Side physician whom Hector owned.

Chapter Thirty-Six

The dump truck sat, stranded, all alone in a field of snow. The tailgate hung down, the crate in plain sight. Behind it, wood smoke fretted from the cabin chimney. Phil Broker squatted on his haunches next to the woodpile he'd assembled in back of the truck. A dull plastic glitter marked the cascade of money packages that overflowed the shattered crate and scattered among the split oak. A single five-gallon gas can sat at his side. With his arms loosely resting on his knees, he watched the clouds roil above the tilted trees. The first snowflakes spun giddy in the wind, probing ahead of the coming storm. He checked his watch. Nine fifty-nine. His eyes tracked across the open space that ended in the notch of trees. He shifted on his heels and settled back down. Getting close.

He hoped Soap was out there right now, methodically fixing the tire chains that would give him an edge when he came balls out across the field. He pushed aside an image of Soap, screaming, held down while they carved on his finger joints. Instead, he visualized Soap fixing the chains to his tires on some turnoff from a back road. With luck, the talkative Shadow One would be in a vehicle not far behind. They'd come in slow and cautious, to watch what Soap would do.

He didn't question it anymore. It was happening.

Annie was packed, suitcase and travel bag. She stood just behind the cabin, near the ravine. Joey sat in the truck cab. Their rifles and packs were cached against the rear cabin wall, close at hand for their dash into the hills to retrace their steps back to Tony's truck.

Joey was whistling a tune from the early sixties. The lilt of "Sukiyaki" insinuated, pure and haunting, before being swallowed by the wind.

Broker hummed along with the juke song that he'd listened to in a hundred Army beer halls. He was aware that he'd spent a lot of years learning to ignore his thoughts at moments like this. Anxiety, ideas, arguments, resentments, his own history: they were just so many printed pages, scattering away.

He'd eventually learned that *think fast* didn't mean *think*.

Joey stopped whistling.

The sound of a powerful engine gunning it in low gear growled in the distant trees.

A dying snake tail of Black Dex lashed once in Broker's cheek.

The incoming growl changed, accelerating, shifting into higher gear. Broker stood up and glanced over his shoulder. Joey turned, peered out the cab's rear window, and graced Broker with the last thing in the world that Broker ever thought he'd witness on Joey's stoic face: a wink.

Wearing a fatalistic smile that was worthy of Harry Griffin, Broker turned around, reached in his pocket, and curled his fingers around his knife. He touched the shape of the Zeiss binoculars in his other pocket. He checked the gas can. The cap was unscrewed and hung by a chain.

Danger forward!

The gray Suburban burst from the tree line, lurching, tire chains flashing, throwing huge clods of snow and dirt, picking up speed. The lights blinked three times. Three of them.

Broker tensed on the balls of his feet. *Okay. Here goes.* Rita was out by now or it had all gone to shit. He reached for the gas can and held it up, tilted, not quite spilling. He could see the mass of Soap's head and shoulders in the racing Suburban, then the details of his furrowed forehead, the set of his jaw. Without even so much as casting a sideways glance, Soap slewed past, throwing a splatter of frozen earth.

The white van rocked out of the tree line and wallowed, fighting for and then grabbing traction, in Soap's tracks. Broker lifted the gas can. The van slowed and then stopped. Broker poured some gasoline on the wood and put down the can. Both van doors opened. Two men got out. The figure on the driver's side lifted both hands to his face.

A horn sounded on the far side of the cabin. Soap saying farewell, Annie in tow, with three short bleeps and a long blast. Da da da Daaaaah.

Broker stooped, palmed his Zippo, and shielding the wind with his body, flicked the wheel. A whoosh of flame leaped from the woodpile. Back on his feet, Broker brought out his knife, thumbed open the blade, reached over, picked up a money pack, slit it open, and shook the currency into the flames. Then he took out his own binoculars and raised them.

And there you are in your fancy gray sweater. Shadow One came into focus, momentarily lowering his binocs. He wasn't wearing a mask, and so Broker could make out his blond hair and the moustache over his gaping mouth. And the bruise on his cheek. *Rita's work, I hope.* Figuring they were locked on to each other, Broker held the binocs in one hand and swept more bundles into the flames with his other.

Then Broker shifted the focus and saw that the man on the other side was pulling a scoped rifle out of a case. Shadow One still had his binoculars trained, so Broker lifted his right hand in a slow, palm-open wave. *Hi. Bye.*

Along with a cold promise: Sin loy, *motherfucker. You thought you weren't here? Well, we weren't here first!*

Now it came down to fractions of seconds and whether the guy unlimbering the rifle moved away from the van and slipped into the trees.

"GO!" Broker shouted. "Go! GO! GO!"

The motor coughed, caught and purred. The truck bed began to lift, and the crate audibly groaned. Broker kicked the gas can into the fire and then darted around the side of the truck, hoping the gush of black smoke would cover him.

Fast glance over his shoulder to confirm that both men who had left the car were now getting back in. Fast.

"Run like hell," Broker yelled at Joey, who made a ridiculous figure, sprinting ahead in the giant white Li'l Abner boots. They could hear the engine running, the hydraulics straining. "They're driving, not shooting. But keep the truck between us and them."

They made it around the corner of the cabin and crouched, panting. Broker immediately leaned his upper body out to train his Zeiss. "Bed just went all the way up!"

"One thousand one," Joey intoned.

"Three of them out of the van."

"One thousand two."

"Kicking at the fire."

"One thousand three."

Broker stepped out into the open to see better. "One of them's . . ."

"One thousand four."

Broker and Joey locked eyes. Broker jumped for the corner with Joey pulling on him. They rolled over in the snow and came up staring at each other. Reflex. Open mouth to equalize pressure—*OH SHIT!*

The shock wave came a microsecond before the blast, and Broker filed it in the place where he kept all his other shock waves. Then *Holy Shit*! Broker maybe heard the front cabin windows shatter just before his ears popped and the dirt and debris engulfed them.

Triple clap explosion. The first was sharp, nasty and propulsive as hundreds of ball bearings flayed the field. Then the gas tank on the truck cooked off. A fraction later the van blew up. Broker and Joey struggled to their feet. Joey smashed the surviving storeroom window with his rifle butt, pulled the pin on the last thermite, and lobbed it in. Then they ran at a right angle to Soap's tire-chain tracks. Packs grabbed in one hand, rifles in the other, they scrambled up the slope they'd come in on. Soot bombs of frozen dirt fell all around and splashed black smudges in the virgin snow. Other debris was raining down: branches, rocks. The storeroom erupted in a whoosh of flame.

"Ow." Broker reached up and felt his shoulder, where—

"I do not believe this shit!" Joey gasped as he reached down into the snow and pulled up a singed, shrink-wrapped brick stuffed with hundred dollar bills.

Money packs were falling all around, some bouncing off tree trunks. Broker blinked, then raised his hand and pointed toward the fuming column of black smoke beyond the trees on the far side of the cabin. "That," he gasped, "was too much money to steal."

"True," said Joey. "But—"

"But this shit is falling out of the fuckin' sky!" In a spasm of giddy hilarity, they scurried, grabbing packets and stuffing them in their packs. Abruptly, the manic moment passed, and they soberly shouldered the now-heavier packs and slogged higher on the ridge to a vantage where Broker had an unobstructed view of the explosion site. A wide, magnificent swirl of hundreds detached from a rising column of smoke, caught the wind like thousands and thousands of tiny sails, and fluttered due east toward Danbury, Wisconsin.

The bones of the dump truck were obscured by smoke and flame, so Broker focused on the burning van that was twisted on its side. He steadied on a sprung front door that jutted up, wavering in the wind, but remained in place long enough for him to dial in the focus and see the dense shrapnel pattern that had spiked the black scalded door panel. And that pretty much said it.

He couldn't make out definite forms in the smoky, shredded debris field, where crooked tongues of gasoline still burned at the outer radius.

Broker put away the binoculars, glanced up as icy snowflakes stung his face, and blew a kiss to the Minnesota sky for the gift of snow. "C'mon," he said, "let's get the hell out of here."

A few minutes later Joey turned for another look and saw that the black smoke rising above the trees had to fight for definition against the driving snow. As he turned back to the slog, he shook his head. "Hey, Broker, you ever read *The Magic Christian?*"

Broker, who had paused to tighten a boot, cupped a hand to his ringing ear. "What?"

"You ever read *The Magic Christian?*" Joey enunciated, louder.

Broker winced, reached in memory and found it. "Yeah, sort of. Terry Southern."

"Remember the scene where he fills a swimming pool with millions of dollars mixed in with hot steaming shit?"

"To see who'd jump in," Broker said as they resumed trudging.

Joey glanced back one more time and said, "Yeah."

Forty minutes later they stumbled on a tunnel of brambles, consulted the hand-drawn map, and followed it until they saw the shape of Tony's truck materialize out of the storm.

As they got in, kicking snow off their boots, Joey said, "People are going to say that Leper did this from his fucking grave."

Broker nodded. "And they'll be right."

"Go Leper," Joey said softly as he turned the key.

Chapter Thirty-Seven

Broker hunched over the pay phone outside a Standard station near the Hinckley 35E on/off ramp. Snow battered the sides of the booth as furtive cars crept, lights on, through a white-out, darkness at noon. The ringing in his ears had dialed down to a tolerable buzz.

When Tony answered the shop phone and said, "Rita's okay," the fright spider that had been spinning a dense ice web in Broker's chest since yesterday morning melted and washed away, and the release made his knees wobble. "Here's Andrea," Tony said.

"Hey Broker." Andrea came on the line, her voice thready with excitement and fatigue. "Tony told you. She's receiving medical attention, off the grid, in West St. Paul. We already developed the film. Soap's still on the road. Weather's got everybody jammed up." Her voice tensed. "How'd it go?"

"We're good," he said. "All accounted for. To quote Joey, 'Leper's had his revenge.'"

"I see. Okay, then come on home, because we took a 'prisoner,' I guess you'd call it. Harry's got him out back, says he's 'tenderizing' him. And we have to get our stories straight so I can call Cantrell."

"On the way," said Broker. He hung up the phone, exited the shelter of the booth, and walked with a lighter step through the whipping snow toward Tony's truck. He raised his hand to Joey, gave a thumbs up and grinned.

Harry took a prisoner.

*   *   *

It was two in the afternoon when Broker and Joey finally wheeled in through the pelting snow and returned Tony's truck to its slot in Soap's parking lot. The gray Suburban was parked in front of the office. And Andrea was sitting in her Audi, windshield wipers going, obviously waiting.

Joey headed into the office. Broker jogged over as she rolled down the window. "Sorry. Roads were bad, standstill in places."

He jammed his hands in his pockets and drew in his shoulders against the blowing snow. "So we're good?" he asked.

"We're good. She's going to be okay. And a deputy came around before noon, wrote up a formal report on a missing vehicle, looked over Leper's car in the lot, then took his description and vitals. Annie's in Duluth unless they're stuck on the road." She leaned over and pushed open the passenger door. "C'mon, get in."

As he climbed into the passenger seat, she perused his clothing, all grubby and torn from the dash through the woods. "You look terrible," she said. Then she held up a folder. "Check these guys. Real sweethearts."

Broker opened the folder and studied ten black-and-white photos that showed four men moving between a white van, a Buick Century wagon, and the front of the house. He saw hard faces, dead eyes, and humorless competence.

In some shots the license plates were clearly visible. In another it was the house number. Three pictures showed the Buick and the phone number on the note pad sitting on the seat. Two envelopes paper-clipped to the folder contained strips of negatives. He thumbed back and pointed to the guy with the moustache, not the least surprised that he took a self-important candid picture.

"He's the one I talked to," he said.

Andrea tapped a narrow face. "And that's the one Harry has out back with a good-sized knot on his head. So does he come under the heading of loose end?"

Broker, whose eyelids felt like lead, leaned back. "Andrea, we'll get him to talk. I'll figure something out. Could get a little harsh, but we'll stop short of . . ."

Andrea stared at him. When he didn't flinch, she hunched her shoulders. "Okay. Harry says we might have got lucky with this one."

Methodically he went through the group pictures and removed the one that most legibly showed Harry's prisoner's narrow face and tucked it inside his jacket. It took a little longer to identify the matching negative. He used his knife to cleanly excise it from the black strip. After putting his complete set of negatives in his pocket, he handed the folder of edited pictures and negatives back to Andrea. Those were for Cantrell. He looked up and said, "Lucky?"

"What he said. Don't want to know anything about it." She skipped ahead. "I'm going back to my place. When you're *done* here, call me with a time line. Once I page Cantrell and tell him about the pictures and the house and give him the phone number from the car seat, he'll want a face to face."

"You'll tell him I copied it before I took the picture."

"And that you located Annie O'Neil." She nodded and their eyes met, and they erupted in spontaneous, nervous laughter. "Yeah, we're still all here." She grinned, raised on the seat, and inspected her face in the rear view mirror. "Christ, I look like a total wipe. My hair's gone to seed, and the circles under my eyes are permanent." She turned to him. "You can find my place, right?"

Broker nodded. "I'll have Joey's truck."

"Well, don't take too long. And bring your clothes bag. We're going to suggest that you spent last night with me." She seemed to take genuine pleasure in the way she arched her eyebrows. "Cantrell won't be able to resist being thrown off by the notion, not after the months he spent trying to get into the bed—" she paused and smiled, "—that you slept in last night." She leaned over and kissed Broker softly on the cheek, then drew back. "That'll have to be my wedding night for the time being. I get the feeling Rita has first dibs, and besides, we still have work to do, you and I." She raised her arm and wrinkled her nose. "And first on the list is a bath."

"You sure about this?" Broker massaged her shoulder.

Andrea cocked her head. "I don't know all the ins and outs of crime in spook world. But back here, in the ordinary crime world, people like us need these things called alibis."

*   *   *

After quick, congratulatory handshakes, Broker huddled with Soap and Joey and was informed that Harry was way ahead of them and had already made stops at an office supply shop and a liquor store. So Broker gave them time to get in place, then came around back, entered the Quonset, and walked down the gauntlet of earth movers toward the lighted office at the other end as the storm set up a racket against the tin walls like a flock of suicidal birds. He had an understanding with Soap to take the long view, but when he saw him actually standing there slapping a three-foot-long, chrome tractor wrench into the palm of his leathery hand . . .

The stage was set with folding chairs and a fold-out banquet table on which a stack of blankets was arranged, along with a wallet, some bills and change, and a set of car keys. A Weber grill, heaped with glowing coals, made the chilly air rhumba. Joey sat at the table—compact, glacial—projecting his own micro-climate of murderous calm. The stuffed backpacks they'd carried out of the woods lay next to his feet. Joey looked tired. So did Soap. And Broker had a hollow, empty flap going in his chest. Out of gas. Auto-rotating. Harry, who was thawing brats set around the edge of the grill with a long-handled fork, looked totally relaxed and alert. Two fifths of Jack Daniel's sat on the table, along with a stack of tall plastic cups. Harry had about three inches of Jack in the cup in his hand.

"Glad you could join us," he said, raising an eyebrow.

"Three down. Confirmed," Broker said.

"So when can we ask this piece of shit why he cut off my daughter's finger and killed Leper?" Soap brought the wrench down with a vicious chop that left a sizable dent in the freezer and echoed off the shuddering tin walls. The freezer trembled. Broker heard a hollow thump, then another.

Harry indicated the wallet opened on the table, a license and credit card pulled out. "George Lohmer, it says. Lives in Red Wing, Minnesota, it says. Mastercard issued in the same name."

"What about comms?" Broker asked.

"Zilch. I think we had better radios than they did," Harry said as he walked over to the freezer, yanked open the top, and probed down with the red hot tips of the grilling fork. "You catch a chill in there? You want me to warm you up? You best not piss all over Soap Turrie's venison, hear?" He slammed the lid shut, muffling the renewed thrashing. He walked back to Broker and smiled. "He ain't been in there *that* long." The smile expanded. "Out at the house, I lashed him down in a truck bed next to Leper for a while." He raised the cup and took a long drink. "That got his attention."

"So what do you think?" Broker asked.

"He's hard core, but when we got there he was literally giving her a sponge bath after she'd peed the bed."

Broker cocked his head. "So not exactly ready to snuff her out."

Harry shook his head. "There it is, Phil. It went down too easy. My gut tells me he's a bit shook, plenty tough, but also

317

plenty pissed off. He was protesting about something through the gag, even before I put him with Leper." Quickly Harry explained the circumstances in which they'd found Rita. "What if they left him back to kill her and when it got right down to it, he couldn't? Maybe he was looking for a way out. Why else barge through the front door after Andrea? We would have gone out the back, circled around."

"So let's unpack him and see what he has to say," Broker said, then nodded to Joey.

Joey stood up, went to the freezer, flipped open the top, reached in and pulled the gasping, shivering man out, and pitched him on the crushed trap rock. He squirmed, raising his head, eyes bulging, trying to adjust to the enclosed gloom. The rattling sheet metal walls. The shadowy machines. The dangerous men in winter coats.

Broker saw he was lean, mid-forties, wearing dark tactical pants, a blue fleece, and black leather boots. Beneath the cock-eyed blue bandana tied around his head, his gagged face was a smear of blood, snot and frost. His lips had worked desperate impressions in the fraying strip of duct tape over his mouth.

Broker said, "Sit him in a chair."

Joey moved a folding chair from the table, picked up the shaking man, and roughly positioned him on it. Broker picked up the driver's license off the table, took another chair, and swung it around so he sat forward, resting his forearms on the back. He glanced at the license. Even beat down and shaking, the guy exuded the low-key snap and buckle of a senior NCO. Thinking he might relate to structure, Broker tried some honcho smoke.

"So George," he began, "I'm going to make this real simple. You're the guy who goes on jobs? I'm the guy who plans jobs. And your pals, all three of them . . ."

Harry leaned in and, shaking the ice in the amber bottom of his cup in one hand, wiggled the fingers of the other in a walking pantomime. "We see many tracks going into the woods. We see none coming out."

George blinked rapidly, shooting looks back and forth between Broker and Harry.

"Fuck him," Soap rumbled, striding up and thrusting the long wrench into George's chest and knocking him off the chair.

Joey made a convincing display of backing Soap off.

Broker got up, hooked his hands in George's armpits, lifted him, and placed him back on the chair.

"So it's like this," Broker said, resuming his seat. "Look around. There's no phone call. Nobody's coming. It's just us. Now, you don't know who I really am. But I think *you* were mixed up with the Iranian secret police as a trainer, some kind of bullshit consultant, maybe?" Broker reached down and opened his fanny pack. "So what we're going to do is show you some pictures." He got up, took a folder from his pack, and spread photos on the table. "Now I'm going to remove the tape on your mouth, and you'll have five seconds to convince me not to let this man," he turned toward Soap, "beat your brains out with that wrench because you cut off his daughter's finger and murdered one of his employees. But he won't kill you. He'll leave just enough for the cops to find. You ready?"

George's Adam's apple bobbed.

Broker ripped off the tape.

George blurted, eyes straight ahead, the words gummy from the adhesive, "Wasn't supposed to get this rough, and I never cut nobody."

"Uh huh," said Broker, who wasn't moved by the blank expression that George put on his face, belied by the sly lifer wrinkles that framed his eyes. He held up the photo with the tattoo and phone number. "When that number rings, who answers it?" he asked.

George shook his head and stared at the gravel. His lips worked soundlessly, and his narrow face strained as it contemplated a personal void.

Broker nodded to Joey, who opened a buck knife and stepped forward, leaned down and cut through the tape that bound his hands. Then he came around, knelt and freed his legs.

"Show him we aren't kidding," Broker said.

Joey picked up the two packs and upended them at George's feet. More than two dozen of the plastic bundles spilled on the ground. Most showed the seared effects of blast and fire.

Broker turned to Harry. "Pour him a drink. Looks like he could use one."

Harry walked over to a nearby front loader, reached up and broke a fist full of icicles off the bucket, crunched them in his hand, and dumped them in a cup. He added a generous splash of bourbon and handed it over.

"Smoke?" Harry asked, bringing out a pack of Camels.

George accepted the cigarette and a light, and he drained most of the drink. Joey picked one of the blankets off the table, unfolded it, and then draped it over George's shoulders. He unfolded the second blanket and stepped back.

Broker picked up a bundle, brought out his knife, flicked it open, and sliced through the plastic. He withdrew a thick wad of currency, then tossed the rest of the bundle on George's lap. When he shied away, Soap stepped in and tapped him on the forehead with the end of the long wrench. "Pay attention," Soap said.

George sat up straight as Broker deposited more bundles in his lap and arranged the rest of the money packs around his boots, taking care to display the ones with blast damage. As Soap and Joey stretched out the second blanket and held it as an anonymous backdrop behind George, Harry took a camera from his bag and adjusted the lens.

Broker removed the cigarette from George's left hand and moved it up to his mouth. Then he spread the sheaf of hundreds into a fan and inserted it in George's fingers. He rolled up the sweater sleeve on George's forearm to reveal a dragon tattoo that tailed calligraphy, some of which he had glimpsed last night at the farmhouse.

"We don't cut people, George. We take pictures," Broker said.

"Hold the drink a little lower so I can see the tat," Harry said, tipping forward in his shooter's crouch, looking through the viewfinder. "Now let's have a smile."

"Huh." George's jaw trembled.

Soap was holding one end of the blanket taut with his right hand. He reached around with his left and swatted George along the side of his head with the wrench a second time. "Smile, the man said."

George's smile was bell-ringer tight, but his teeth were showing. "Relax. Pretend I'm not here." Harry grinned as the Nikon snickered in sync with the flash attachment.

When Harry finished, George squinted to clear the stars from his watery eyes, shuddered, drained his drink, and held out the cup, into which Broker poured a stiff couple of shots. George watched Harry stow his camera and then take a flat, rectangular, hinged metal pad from the bag.

"What?" George reacted as Harry put the pad on the table along with several sheets of high-gloss white paper, some paper towels, and a plastic container of antiseptic alcohol.

Broker dragged George and his chair up to the table, in front of the spread pictures. Then Broker poured his own hefty shot of bourbon and fell heavily into the adjoining seat. "We're going to take your fingerprints. After we develop the film in that camera, you'll be the poster boy for this cluster fuck. We'll release the pictures of you and the money, with your prints, to the press. Not right away. In a couple days. When the media is in high ape shit over what's littering the fields and snow banks east of Hinckley, Minnesota."

"We weren't funning with you, George," Harry said, arranging his ad hoc fingerprinting kit. "The money and your friends got seriously blown to shit, man. Turns out Travis Diggs was not the guy to mess with, because he booby-trapped that truck ten different ways."

Broker leaned in. "So let's be clear. You go the Omerta route—first you get the wrench, then the cops find you in an alley. The pictures get distributed. Along with the ones we just snapped."

Harry added, "Pictures showing you going into that house. They'll find what's in the silo. You with me so far?"

George slowly bobbed his head up and down.

"On the other hand, you get smart, we let you go. But we hear that you've mentioned anything to anyone, we will publish the pictures." Broker paused. "You will give us a reliable address. You will keep us informed of your whereabouts. If we contact you at a later date and if you refuse to cooperate, we will publish the pictures."

"Listen to you." Harry chuckled again. "You're starting to sound like a fucking case officer."

"*Du ma!*" Broker quipped, then turned to George. "So you ready to look at some pictures?"

Options, short of coma by bludgeon, seemed to revive George, who finished his second drink, asked for refill, along with another cigarette, and then bellied up to the table.

Chapter Thirty-Eight

B roker took a sip of bourbon, and the whiskey stoked a deceptively cheerful campfire that soothed the Black Dex vacuum in his chest. He saluted Harry, who had the eye to spot George's flaw, or salvation. And so Harry truly was fucking brilliant when he wasn't truly fucking erratic.

Now came the tricky part of the job that called for a balance between cynicism and empathy, because you had watched your enemy—a phantom shadow—materialize into a person who had a real name and a story with a beginning and a middle and a mother. "George" was, in fact, Kyle Shipper, who retired from the Marines as a master sergeant and took a job with St. Louis PD until some old crotch buddies recruited him for the freelance market, and he eventually wound up as an advisor to the Shah's secret police.

Broker took a strong pull of the whiskey and reflected that there are a number of men like Shipper on the market after a war, and most of them responded to seeing history made up close by acquiring a few exaggerated growth rings and moving on. But some get caught in the switches and can't abide the Mickey Mouse and the chicken shit and all the stumbling civilians who look like sleepwalking TV commercials. They make lousy citizens. They drink, they get high, they beat their women, they eat their guns. Maybe they think they're slick enough to run drugs or rob a bank. People like Andrea dashed back and forth on the edge of the drop-off like Holden Caulfield, trying to salvage a few.

And some, like Shipper, just continue to work. They practice violence with the attention to detail you'd expect in a journeyman plumber or electrician. And so Broker watched Shipper, like a seasoned, skilled tradesman, make the correct decision about the terms of a transaction that offered him his life in exchange for information.

Shipper took a moment to collect himself, then tapped the dead Persian's photo. "I was an advisor with SAVAK, and a year ago—when the politics over there started looking shaky—my counterpart, Major Mostafa Jobrani, and I were recruited by an American philanthropist who wanted to preserve Iranian antiquities." He took a sip of whiskey. "Our end was to come up with the loot, which was easy because we were security officers. We shook down the black market, hit museums and private residences." His cool, dry eyes briefly inspected Broker's face. "We had a good thing going, a couple of well-paid smugglers."

He thumped his knuckle down on the photo of Mr. Moustache and his hard-ass friends. "When the regime started falling apart, these guys showed up and threatened to expose us. They blackmailed our client and took over our smuggling route and used it for a load of cash."

Broker and Harry exchanged measured looks.

Shipper went on. "I don't know where they got the money. Draining the Iranian treasury comes to mind. I don't know where it was supposed to go after the pickup or whose brainchild it was. But this guy does." He pointed to the picture that showed the number on the card next to the tattoo on Mostafa's arm. "He set up the smuggling route and arranged for the Italian bike parts cover. The stuff went out on a slow boat to Duluth, where he took possession. Call that number, you get Stuart Klunder, the in-house attorney for the St. Paul Maston Foundation."

Soap cleared his throat. "As in the Maston Bank of St. Paul? As in Maston County?" He glanced at Broker.

Shipper hunched his shoulders in a cautious shrug. "I wouldn't really know because I don't live here. What I do know is that the guy Klunder works for has one hell of a collection of antique Persian art objects."

Broker smiled, quietly intrigued. The Mastons were one of Minnesota's oldest families, already established in timber and fishing before statehood. The narrow county that bore their name lay south of Duluth.

Shipper fingered another Camel from Harry's pack that lay on the table. Broker gave him a light. Shipper blew a stream of smoke and engaged the curiosity in everyone's eyes.

"I'll bite," Harry said. "So what happened?"

"Since we knew Klunder, Mostafa and I would shepherd the box and each get a million bucks to keep our mouths shut. Mostafa would get asylum. Asshole and his bad-asses were waiting with a rental truck for the exchange."

"But the box was misrouted and got lost in the stacks," Soap said.

Shipper nodded. "For want of a nail, huh? So Asshole freaks, and we were off to the races. Suddenly Mostafa and I are important, because we've met Klunder, we know the guy."

"What's Asshole's name?" Broker asked.

"Was a no-name asshole, very into being a—" Shipper made air quotes with his fingers. " '—clandestine asset.' Told us to call him 'Mace.' I always called him Asshole. We didn't get along."

"And the other two?"

Shipper managed a smirk. "Number One and Number Two. I shit you not." He flicked the cigarette ash on the gravel. "Asshole came prepared for a simple pickup. So we scrambled, no real gear." He turned to Harry. "You saw the crap we had."

"So how'd you track down the box to the warehouse in St. Paul?" Broker asked.

"Mostafa called Klunder. His people traced it. Asshole was blackmailing him, anyway. When we figured out that someone had stolen his box, he really freaked and started cutting on people." Shipper smiled contemptuously. "Like he learned in Nam when he worked in your shop, huh?" His shoulders slumped. "I thought he was going to kill this old bag who had an apartment across from the car shop. We wound up giving her plane fare and enough for a week in Miami Beach."

"So you had an observation post. What else?" Broker asked.

"Just the two vehicles, the police scanner, the shit radios. Klunder got us into the foreclosed farmhouse through the bank. Got the lights turned on."

"Bullshit," Broker said. "If you didn't have a pot to piss in, how'd Asshole get ahold of my classified records?"

"He was for real. He had that fake ID whipped up in nothing flat. He was always on the phone," Shipper protested. "He had a lot of juice going in. Once the box went missing, all the back-up got cold feet, and we were on our own. They'd find the records for him, to maybe turn you. They wouldn't commit any resources."

"Why go after us in the park?" Broker asked.

"Ratchet up the pressure. Grab one of you. After Mostafa got it, Asshole decided to go after the girl."

"What happened to Mostafa?" Broker asked.

"Sleeping with the muskies. Logging chains. Dumped him in the St. Croix River." Shipper turned to Broker, and you could find more sympathy in a column of numbers than in his dry blue eyes. "But all that doesn't matter, does it? What the little fish do to each other."

"No, it doesn't," said Broker.

Shipper laughed softly to himself. "You guys are all the same. Cops? Feds? Spooks? The Cartels? I've worked for all you fuckers one time or another, and you always want the same thing: to trade up."

Broker turned to Harry. "What do you think?"

"Worth a chance," Harry said.

Broker stood up and nodded to Joey, who tossed one of the burned money bundles. Broker caught it and slapped it on the table in front of Shipper. "You know why you're still breathing?" he asked.

"Fuck you." Shipper made an attempt to draw himself up. "I didn't cut on anybody. Not the dispatcher, not Travis Diggs. And not the girl. I did two tours with Force Recon. I picked up two Purple Hearts, and I have two ex-wives bleeding me for alimony and child support. I got dirty over money, but I don't kill girls."

"But you were there," Broker said. "Was it loud, what they did to Diggs? Where were you when they put him in the ice-box?"

Shipper turned away.

"Look at me!" Broker raised his voice. Shipper did. "Peel back the scabs on that bundle and there should be enough to get you to St. Louis and then some. Stay off the radar for the immediate future, Kyle. Your ass belongs to us, but we won't crowd you. Don't do anything to get yourself famous. And I hope to hell, for your sake, you didn't leave fingerprints all over that house. You understand?"

"Sure, I understand," said Shipper. "So what am I now? Bait?"

Broker stood up, turned his back on Kyle Shipper, stepped away from the table, and summoned Harry to join him. "Get his prints and an address and clean up his face and fix him up with a hat and coat. Then you and Joey dump him at the nearest Greyhound station."

Harry looked around. "So I guess you won't leave this at three bodies and a blown-up truck, huh?" He toed the strewn bundles of cash. "And it appears you've found funding for your project."

"Soap will give you a bundle as a retainer. Maybe, if you survive the binge I suspect you're planning, you could swing by St. Louis and look in on Shipper to keep him honest."

"Cool. I'll do that. After I get back from Vegas, huh? Joey says I can get a train in St. Paul that has a well-stocked lounge car."

They embraced, and Harry said, "Always a pleasure, Phil."

Soap came over and gripped Harry's hand. His eyes moistened. "Thanks—for Rita."

"Ah . . ." Harry shook it off. "Just tell her, next trip, I get a picture with her in front of that wall in there." Then he turned to Broker and said, "Keep an eye on him, Soap. He tends to take the bit in his teeth. He requires a steadying hand." Harry ambled back to the table to fingerprint Shipper, who sat bolt upright like a reprieved death row inmate, with Joey looming over him.

Broker walked down the equipment aisle, exited the Quonset, and went into the yard. Ignoring the snow, he stopped in front of the pile of stacked shingles and took a deep breath of pure cold air. A moment later Soap joined him. "We'll stash the money with Annie, wash it through the bar in easy stages. Tony and Duke should get something, and you take whatever you need for operating expenses. I'll check if Leper had family."

Broker nodded. "Harry gets a bundle up front, to keep him on call for contingencies."

Soap said, "Will do. So now you bring in the cops, and it gets official. We go white knuckle until it plays out. Jan's coming in from Chicago. I wanted to collect her before I check in on Rita. But with this weather, the flight's delayed." After a moment, he added, "Joey's taking Harry round the local bars, after they send that shit bird on his way. You really think he gave Rita a break?"

"Yeah, I think he did. He's an ex-jarhead lifer. No matter how covered in shit he gets, he'll always have trouble killing if he isn't wearing a uniform." Broker rubbed the scruff of stubble on his chin. "Tell Rita . . ." The words failed. "It'll be a while."

Soap chuckled. "She'll understand. You still have work to do. So where are you taking this, Broker?"

"Don't know. Yet. Job security, maybe. I'll drop the photo kit and location on Cantrell and see what he does."

"Don't get your hopes up about that phone number. The Mastons are Minnesota royalty. I'll be real surprised if they get dragged into this. Everybody will tell Cantrell he's out over his skis—chances are that number won't even show up in evidence."

"Uh huh. Might take a nudge. This Klunder guy? You think Joey could get his running pattern: residence, work, where he eats lunch?"

"We can do that."

Broker slipped out his wallet, extracted a card, and squinted at Johnny Lager's work number in the swaying yard light. "Couple nudges, actually," he said. Then he turned back toward the Quonset to call Andrea and tell her to call Cantrell.

Chapter Thirty-Nine

"Shower," Andrea commanded when he trudged in the back door and dropped his duffel and fanny pack on her kitchen floor. Then he placed Harry's Nikon on the table. As he removed his snow-caked boots, he noted that she hadn't taken that bath yet. The kitchen smelled of tobacco smoke, and two of Rita's Marlboros were stubbed out in a saucer on the table. Her eyes were still bloodshot and raccooned with dark circles; her hair looked like straw combed with a rake. But she was moving with purpose, not to say tenacity. His mind wandered, and she reminded him of Irene's baseline: that women were routinely required to master pain, stress, and fatigue, in order to get through childbirth and generally put up with men.

And going there was a gauge of just how slaphappy he was; Jack Daniel's poured into an amphetamine crater on an empty stomach while going on three full days with little sleep. And an explosion. And three more dead men. And the weight lifting, knowing Rita was safe.

"In a minute." Broker blinked several times as he lowered himself to a kitchen chair.

"So what happened with that guy?" she asked.

"We set him up and then we let him go, with a bundle of cash and a leash around his neck." After a moment, Broker added, "And there's a real possibility he spared Rita." He rubbed his eyes. "He's source material now, and a potential witness." Broker looked up with a weary smile. "Paradoxically, it's called the Intelligence Game."

"I guess." Andrea folded her arms across her chest and watched him closely.

Broker pointed to the empty chair across the table. "Now that you've been on the wild side and made your bones, I need your help identifying the local flora and fauna. The number you found in the dead Persian's sock—whose name was Mostafa, by the way—and we came by that without resorting to blood. That you planted at the house?"

"Yes?" Andrea took the facing chair.

"It rings on the desk of a guy named Stuart Klunder."

"No way!" Andrea sat up straight and sputtered an absurd laugh. "I've met Stuart Klunder. He's the legal gun at the Maston Foundation in St. Paul. He helped me get a grant approved."

"So is he a snake?"

Andrea shook her head. "The opposite. Save the Whales." After a pause, her brow arched. "No shit?"

"Got it straight from Harry's 'lucky' guy, who smuggled antiquities for him. The money could have been someone else's idea."

"So those guys had his number, and now so does Cantrell."

"How'd it go?"

Andrea's head bobbed along with her singsong reply. "I did the beeper thing, and he calls me and I tell him you located Annie O'Neil, but no box. How you spotted the guys eyeing Turrie and followed them to this farmhouse north of Stillwater. How you crawled in with a camera and took some pictures, which I described in a general way. That you crashed here last night and took off today to get film developed."

"And you gave him the number."

Andrea nodded. "Few minutes ago he called again, and now he wants to talk to you. I said you stepped out for NyQuil, and he said he'll be here at five, with Merriweather, who's sort of between jobs at the moment." Andrea slid a Marlboro out of

331

the pack on the table and rotated it briefly, then put it back in the pack and pushed it aside.

"So he ran the number."

"Could be. Second time he called he wanted the location on the house. But Jesus, Broker! Tying those guys in the woods to the Maston Foundation?" She threw her hands in the air, describing an upheaval. "I don't see that happening anytime soon."

"People keep saying that."

"With reason." She huffed a breath that chased a wandering strand of hair from her eyes and switched to practical. "Right now, let's get you cleaned up and into a bed for a couple hours so you don't look like you've been out blowing up shit."

Broker was directed down the hall into a bathroom that sparkled and smelled otherworldly after the last three days. Holy almost. She closed the door behind him.

Women's strange bathrooms, or was it strange women's bathrooms? He fumbled out of his filthy, sweat-moldy clothes and started the water, fiddling with the unfamiliar shower controls. Broker had grown up with basic box store soap, stuff on sale, followed by a military downgrade. She had emollients, shampoos, and conditioners to choose from, in tall beige containers with French names in black cursive. And she had these big fluffy towels. After drying off, too tired to shave, he wrapped one of them around his waist and stepped into the hall, mildly delirious from hot water.

She was waiting for him, standing there with his fanny pack slung over her shoulder.

"I thought you'd have more hair on your chest," she said absently.

"Huh?"

"Nothing, but, hey—you remember? You told me when this is over, you'd tell me about that?" She pointed at the scarring on his left forearm.

"Oh yeah." He shrugged. "Was a pair of jump wings. Certain jobs they didn't want any identifying marks. They took it off." Without missing a beat, he pointed to his temple. "Had a big mole here. Same, same." Then he added, "And it ain't over yet."

"Uh huh," she said, and Broker totally missed the full frontal flash of her eyes. Seeing him teeter slightly, she pointed to the doorway on his left.

He went through and stood for a moment, embracing the idea of the queen-sized bed stretched beneath him like a fluffy white cloud. She eased up beside him and whistled softly. "I don't know, Broker. I just opened this pack, and there's fingerprints in here, pictures, negatives? What are you doing, starting your own case file?"

Broker turned to her and blinked, glassy-eyed. "Well, I dunno either. We'll see. Nobody else takes a look, maybe I'll snoop this foundation bunch, you know, to see who's really behind you getting almost shot, Rita losing her finger, and Travis Diggs getting murdered."

Then he turned, gave it up and pitched forward, hugging the fresh bedspread and the plump white pillow. When he collapsed on the bed, the towel unfurled, and Andrea took a moment to appreciate the scars on his back, along with his high, tight ass, which she patted affectionately. "We have work to do, my fugitive boy," she said softly before she covered him with a blanket.

Broker began to snore, which he only did when he felt safe. Maybe he heard the machinery whisper. *You can do this.*

* * *

"Get up. They're early. They're coming up the stairs!"

Broker instinctively did the drill, rolled over and placed his bare feet firmly on the carpet. *Up.*

333

"Quick, put these on," Andrea said, and as she materialized in his sleepy vision, he noted that she'd been into her stash of bathroom vanities and acquired an improved face and looked less like a wired co-conspirator and more like a tired professional woman who had a cold. Pedal pushers, a comfy flannel shirt, and bedroom slippers completed the picture. She handed him some folded clothes, which he shook out and . . .

"You've got to be kidding." The extra-large, gray T-shirt had a feminist symbol on the front over bold type that proclaimed: I DIDN'T COME FROM YOUR RIB, BUT YOU CAME FROM MY VAGINA. In his other hand he held a pair of men's purple pajama bottoms at arm's length. They were decorated with little orange sail boats.

Andrea shrugged. "What can I say. I'm not a nun. Men leave stuff. They dribble. On the toilet seat and various items left in closets."

"Some men," Broker grumbled.

Cantrell had finally met his match and came through the door wearing a hat that was covered in snow. It was not a proper Minnesota hat, but this rakishly curled, dark fedora.

He didn't even blink when he saw Broker come down the hall in bare feet, the baggy shirt, and the ridiculous pajamas. "Andrea said you have pictures," he said.

"Hey, Broker, sounds like you been busy, man," said J.T., shaking off snow right behind Cantrell.

Andrea had arranged the props. The folder of pictures lay open on the coffee table in the living room next to Harry's Nikon, a bottle of NyQuil, and a box of Kleenex. His funky clothes were strewn in the hallway, still looking rode hard and put away wet. She set down the percolator and a tray containing cups. When she and Cantrell briefly locked eyes, she gave him a tight, all purpose, but very honest smile: *like there I was doing a favor for you state crime boys, and it took a fast, dirty little bounce.*

They did not sit down. They did not remove their coats. J.T. spied the phone on a long cord, sitting on a low table with the stereo and TV, and brought it over, if needed.

Cantrell kept a police radio in his hand as he paged through the photos, stopping on the one through the car window with the notebook. The usual smart-ass shifts were absent from his eyes, replaced by intense curiosity. "How?" he said.

Broker, who did sit down on the couch and help himself to the coffee, pawed at his unruly sleep hair and said, "We located Annie, right? She was hiding out with an old boyfriend, buddy of Soap's, up in Duluth."

"That's sweet," said Cantrell, handing the photos to J.T. "So how'd you get these pictures?"

"You told me to look out for Soap Turrie, right? So I spotted these guys following him around. Long story, but I tailed this white van—the one in the pictures—and followed it back to this not-quite-abandoned farmhouse in north Washington County. Went in with the camera yesterday, before sunup. Couldn't get all of them until the afternoon. Had to wait for dark to get out. Called Andrea and came straight here."

Without mentioning Annie O'Neil, Cantrell pulled a map of Washington County out of his trench coat pocket and unfolded it on the table. "Show me," he said.

Broker held up his hand. Cantrell immediately offered a pen. He made an X at the intersection of the county roads north of Highway 7. Then he drew a rough diagram, labeling the house, the tree deadfall, and the collapsed barn. Lastly, he pointed to the house number in one of the pictures. "It's right there: eleven seventy-three County Road double-E."

Cantrell repeated the address into the radio. "Mike, get John Eisenhower at Washington County . . . Yeah, he's in Patrol. Ask him to run a car by that address. Tell him it's a favor. Concoct something he can live with, like we see vehicles, activity and lights at an abandoned house. Then call

Yerbich, tell him we have a line on the box . . . no, he'll know what I mean. See if he'll wire a judge. We're going to need a warrant to get in there." Cantrell turned back to Broker. "How'd you go in?"

"If you come in along this tree line, on the north-south road, you can creep into this deadfall. The barn is better. That's where I took the pictures. Stuck my neck out, approaching that Buick in broad daylight."

Cantrell looked at J.T. "We need a rendezvous point to assemble a team to stake out this place till we get paper."

Broker said, "There's a convenience store, gas station here." He scribed a circle on the highway about a mile east of the target house.

Cantrell nodded, then raised his radio again. "I hope you guys packed cold weather gear, 'cause you're going to need it. There's this . . ."

As Cantrell talked, J.T. motioned Broker aside. They stepped into the office alcove. "So what did Annie O'Neil say when you found her?" he asked.

"I didn't find her; Soap did. She's in Duluth. He told me she just saw the truck. She was trying to hook Diggs up with Desmond, who didn't show, and Diggs got super paranoid and drove away. You'll have to get the rest from Soap, or her. But looks like she caught a whiff of the gossip headed her way and boogied. But, you know, she's okay."

J.T. now directed some serious detective X-ray vision Broker's way. "But Travis Diggs isn't okay, is he? Because somebody called from Soap's garage this morning and reported a dump truck and an employee missing."

"I wasn't there for that," Broker said in all candor. Then he asked, "Why's Cantrell all jacked up? I didn't actually see those guys do anything."

"He ran the phone number," J.T. said ambiguously. They moved back into the living room next to Cantrell.

"Wait one," Cantrell said to the radio, then faced J.T. "Time to bring Norman Bolin in out of the cold and cut a deal. You'll have to work that out with Turrie. I want him to look at these pictures."

Broker interrupted. "Check the pictures again. Those guys look like they can handle themselves."

"So can we," said Cantrell. Then he went back to the radio. "Okay, J.T. and I will meet you at the ma and pa on Seven." He stuck the radio in his pocket. "It's the fucking phone number that's weird," Cantrell speculated as his facial muscles twitched back and forth between puzzled and intrigued. "I don't want to get ahead of myself, but—if they're who you think they are, we need to get a handle on them, fast as we can." Then, almost under his breath, "But what's that phone number doing in a car with guys chasing a load of lost dope? Guys who cut on Norman, the dispatcher."

Broker scratched the stubble on his chin and stared, which was just part of the job they'd designed for him. "Go under cover," they'd said. *Never said how far.*

Cantrell squeezed Broker's arm. "Not your problem. We'll take it from here. Not bad, Broker. There'll be something extra in your stocking. Now take a break. You ain't looking so hot." Only then, at end of business, did Cantrell grace them with an easy, creeping smile and add, "Both of you." J.T. couldn't suppress a modest grin. Andrea was not enjoying the fun and jerked a fake-hostile thumb, showing them the door. But she touched them each on the shoulder as they filed past.

With unexpected grace, Cantrell turned and executed a slight, but courtly, bow, which caused melting snow to drip from his hat brim. Then he and J.T. exited the apartment.

When they heard the downstairs door pull shut, Broker and Andrea faced each other. She spoke first. "Can't be sure with Cantrell. He's a tricky guy . . ."

Then they muttered at the same time: "Weather report." Andrea went to kitchen radio and searched the AM frequencies for weather news. They found what they were looking for on the fifth try:

"On top of forty-mile-an-hour winds and road closings— get this," the broadcaster said. "We have unconfirmed reports coming in from eastern Pine County that several people have found hundred dollar bills blowing in their yards. Yep. That's what they said."

Broker could tell she was feeling the same rush of visceral release. It was all there in the macabre victory dance in their eyes.

"You know," Andrea breathed, eyes alight.

But the emotional relief also sprung a sharp jolt of libido that Broker could damn well feel zig-zag in the close air between them.

So he excused himself and got dressed in his driest clothes, finished lacing his boots, then said, "I think I'll take Cantrell's advice and go home for a late Thanksgiving."

Andrea rolled her eyes. Arms crossed firmly, she said, "You're not serious, driving up north in this? Tired as you are?"

"I know a little about a lot of things," Broker said. "One thing I know a lot about is driving in the snow. Joey's truck has new snow tires, and . . ." He held up the vial of amphetamines. "I have my little friends."

As Broker pulled on his jacket, she remained insistent. "You should hit the sack, wait till it clears."

"Look," he said, "we need rest. You've just lived a whole lifetime in three days. There's a fire hose of crazy stuff blowing through our heads. Your bed's in there. Nice bed. Mine's in Devil's Rock. I need a break. Andrea, it's time to step back and let it unfold."

Her gray eyes blazed briefly, lighting candles from clinical all the way to carnal. "You're making a mistake," she said.

Broker was aware that they were standing almost in the exact spot where they'd been standing the first night—when the Shazam had thrust them closer together. But he caught himself being drawn forward. The timing was off.

He drew back and said, "Dr. Sabic, I don't know about you, but right now I'm too damned weak to handle even a weak moment."

He shouldered his packs and walked out the back door.

"Asshole," Andrea called after him. Then she smiled.

*   *   *

Okay. It was a white lie. Broker stared into sparse but cautious traffic feeling its way up North 35E and finally churning east onto Highway 36 into gusting whiteouts. It was not the time to explore possibilities with Andrea Sabic because he had a previous engagement.

Perkins was a lonely lighted igloo on the outskirts of Stillwater with a few cars gathering snow in the lot. Johnny Lager's white hair was easy to spot among the three widely spaced customers. Parka unzipped, he hunched forward in a booth with a tall glass of soda.

When he saw Broker approach, he held up his hands. "Your rules. Nothing written down or recorded. No notebook, no tape recorder."

Broker sat down across from Lager, and as he dusted snow off his cap, he took a moment to study the columnist. The fact that he'd shown up, no questions asked, here in the boonies, in a blizzard, spoke to his willingness to run out the grounders. He noted that Lager didn't take care of himself; a Snickers wrapper lay next to his soda, and he had inflamed, chewed cuticles. Then Broker keyed on the relentless focus he saw in Lager's constantly moving eyes. Maybe just a touch of hunter-killer instinct.

"And I don't need to explain what happens if any of this comes back on me?" Broker asked.

"I get it. Don't help me to get you pissed off."

"None of this deep background stuff."

"Broker. I'm not here, man. So what have you got?"

"Call it a test. To see how good you are. And I'm curious about what guys like you leave in and take out of the story. Same with the cops. Down the line, this could get dangerous. So maybe I get to see how well you function when you're scared shitless."

That got Lager's attention, so Broker pulled a napkin from the table dispenser and placed it between them. A slow motion waitress appeared, and Broker ordered a large black coffee to go. When she departed, he took out a pen and plunked it on the napkin. "Write down this address," he said: "Eleven seventy-three County Road double E. That's just north of Highway Seven, maybe ten miles from where we're sitting. BCA's getting ready to move on this abandoned farmhouse. Don't go straight in; work the edges at the start. Could get interesting."

Lager narrowed his eyes. His fingers fidgeted and started to tear at the bottom of the napkin. "That's it?"

Broker got to his feet. "Oh yeah," he said, casually. "You might call whoever does the police checks in the newsroom and have them ring up the Pine County Sheriff's Department and ask them if anything unusual is going on."

An inky light cranked up in Lager's eyes, searching for the code between the lines. He said, "How do I get in touch with you?"

"In a week or so I'm starting a job here in Stillwater. Comes with a place to stay, so I'll let you know." Then he waved to get the waitress's attention and pointed to the cashier, where he collected and paid for his coffee. As he left the restaurant, Lager was hunched over the pay phone, no doubt rousing some poor, unsuspecting photographer from a holiday stupor.

*   *   *

And now you let it all play out. Broker sat in Joey's Bronco and watched Lager jog out and get into a station wagon and then slip and slide off north into the storm. He ran up the heater controls. He took out the container of Black Dex—one more time—and contemplated all the bare wires lying dormant in the tiny vial that were ready to snap, crackle and pop. But he had just soldiered though amphetamine crash world and now thought it best to go the rest of the way on his own fatigue. So he rolled down the window and dumped the pills into the snow.

He took a sip of coffee and meditated briefly on six hours of the worst driving he could imagine, to just get north of Duluth. And then the real fun would start. But it's *okay*, the machinery told him. *Don't need an artificial boost to get us through another rough night.*

Forget a rough night. Broker put the truck in gear. He didn't want to be anywhere near the Twin Cities for the next week. As he started for home, the machinery hummed, happy.

Working again.

Chapter Forty

Broker slept for most of two days. When he got up and felt half right, he picked up the phone and called the shop in Stillwater. A low, mature female voice answered, and that was Janet Turrie, back from Illinois. "Rita is fine," she said. "She's resting at home. Do you want the number?"

"No, tell her I'll see her next week when I get back."

"And Phil?"

"Yes, ma'am?"

"Thank you."

Next, Broker drove to Grand Marais and left his shaggy persona on the barber shop floor. Now he went with a high, tight trim and scaled-back eyebrows. He'd missed the turkey, but he helped Irene make a soup out of the carcass while his dad bitched from the sidelines about restrictions the docs had put on his activity. Broker Senior still had cancer, but it was staged low grade and treatable.

Broker spent a day scooting around on cabin roofs, checking the tarp job that Davey had rigged to make it through the winter. The old man was improving, so they all moved easier around the house, respecting territory, especially the papered-over vacancy that memory could evoke.

And so, from one of the remotest corners in Minnesota, Broker watched and read and listened as a media wet dream seduced the entire state and just became, happily, messier and messier. MONEY IS BLOWING ON THE WIND IN PINE

COUNTY! All three TV networks were there within hours to join the thronging local newsies. The state patrol and emergency services in Pine and adjoining counties struggled to deal with hundreds and then thousands of obsessed treasure hunters who waded into the snowbanks and woodlots east of Hinckley intent on finding Ben Franklin's elusive smile.

Johnny Lager owned the story from the second he broke the news that BCA had discovered a frozen body on an abandoned farmstead in Washington County. A birthmark connected the body to a missing person's report on a Travis Diggs. Ahead of the BCA, he was on the scene when Pine County deputies and volunteer firefighters led him to the black, twisted wreckage of the truck that Travis Diggs had gone missing with. A *Pioneer Press* shooter snapped the money shot of the truck at the epicenter of a deadly explosion that claimed three lives and explained why all those burnt, shredded, but sometimes intact, hundred dollar bills were scattered from hell to Wisconsin. There was no estimate as yet about how many tens of millions in U.S. currency was scattered in the ashes.

The FBI traveled to Pine County along with ATF, DEA and Treasury. Rumors flew. Colombians? The Tri-Lateral Commission? Nixon's hidden re-election fund? Broker's favorite had it that the millions had been hidden in the basement of the Congdon Mansion in Duluth. The coverage churned on as BCA ran the plates on the car at the farm and on a van that had been destroyed at the blast site. The plates had been lifted from long-term parking at the airport. Not a trace of identification could be found on the remains at the explosion, or much in the way of fingerprints or dental work.

Then about four days in, the outlines of a narrative began to emerge from all the hype. Lager received a tip that a Norman Bolin had negotiated a plea agreement with the Ramsey County Attorney and confessed to helping Travis Diggs steal a shipping crate from the St. Paul warehouse where he worked as a dispatcher. Soon the reading and viewing public were treated to pictures of his mutilated, stitched fingers. Word leaked from the Washington County coroner's office that extensive, similar wounds were plainly in evidence on the Travis Diggs cadaver. The BCA lab was rushing tests to determine if the blood traces they'd discovered in the farmhouse matched a sample from Diggs' slowly thawing body.

Soap called. "Rita's still recovering at home, out of public view. And God bless the dimwits and the dopers. They're turning Leper into a local legend. But foxy old Hector Garza is piecing it together, so I suspect we just gained some quiet, serious street cred in West St. Paul."

Broker told Soap he'd see him in a couple days, when he came back to the Cities. He hung up the phone and smiled.

Leper lives!

There was even a buried sidebar about Annie O'Neil surfacing in St. Paul. But in the tsunami of reporting, Broker neither saw nor heard nor read a single peep about a phone number. *Cantrell might have a real good reason for keeping it quiet. Or he might not.*

*   *   *

Broker inventoried his closet and found one good black marrying-burying suit and not much else besides rough-neck work clothes. He chose an old vanity purchase, this black Café Racer motorcycle jacket that, coupled with his winning personality and his new hair, just might project a subtle touch of menace. He finished packing and threw a light shine on a pair of low-quarter Chukka boots.

Early the next morning, seeing him in fresh jeans, a dark shirt and the leather jacket, Irene gave a wistful sigh over her coffee cup. "A tad sinister, just a tad."

"Won't even ask," said Broker Senior.

Just after dawn he drove south with all of his woodworking tools packed in the back of Joey's Bronco. Once he got past the cobble beach south of Devil's Rock, he rode easy.

In fact, as the miles turned on the odometer, he actually looked forward to having a real job, along with his unreal job. But first . . .

He tried to time the squall of snow approaching St. Paul from the west as he was coming in from the north, and they met on North Robert Street. *Make a note, you hick: learn the street map of the capital city in your state.* He crept along, getting his directions straight. Lonely cars turned on their lights as the town emptied to a snow-blown winter wasteland at street level. But one story up, warmly-lit walkways connected the buildings, and he saw people strolling in shirtsleeves. St. Paul, he decided, could pass, today, for a base in the Antarctic.

He found a meter, plugged it, picked up an old leather briefcase he'd borrowed from home, and hit the unfamiliar streets. After a couple of wrong turns, he located the west entrance to Park Square Court, where a clean-shaven, closely barbered, new Joey was waiting in a quiet, gray leather car coat that was so expensive it looked plain.

"Look at you, *Sportin' Life,*" Broker said, shaking off snow.

"You should talk. Hey, these are just my street threads for when I sneak and peek. I still turn wrenches."

"Yeah, right; not cool to flash the money, Joey."

Joey thumbed his lapels. "You are so wrong. It's from Miami. Back before I broadened my perspective." He pointed at Broker's new hair.

Broker shifted his shoulders, deadpan. "My dad told me to get a haircut before I had to climb a tree to take a shit."

They laughed easily together as the lunch crowd swirled around them, filling the food court.

"Must be a hair vibe going around." Joey edged closer, with a folded newspaper tucked under his arm. "Way it works is, Charlie Manson cancelled out Woodstock, then *you* lost the war and the Beatles split up. Now we're seeing a lot of him." He pointed at California Governor Ronald Reagan, whose picture had equal billing with the Pine County Gold Rush on the front page displayed in a *Pioneer Press* sales box. "The sixties are definitely over."

They kept up the joking banter as Joey used the folded newspaper to smoothly slip a crispy, mostly burned, bundle of the money into Broker's open briefcase.

"He's this way," Joey said, leading him through the eating court and into the skyway system. A few minutes later they were standing on a walkway across from the *Pioneer Press* building. "Any minute now," Joey said. "He comes this way to the Athletic Club side door for lunch."

And then, "There he is."

"Which one?"

"The pear-shaped Nebbish in the horn rims and the lawyer suit."

Stuart Klunder shuffled, totally absorbed in reading the front page of *The New York Times*. He was indeed pear shaped, to include his face that was anchored in a wide, dour jaw and matching lips that pursed in consternation when, quite suddenly, a tall, hard-looking young man with dark military hair was standing in front of him. The man wore a kind of leather jacket in a certain way that raised the lawyer's street hackles. As did the solemn green eyes and the fake smile. Klunder did appreciate the beautifully weathered briefcase the man held open in his hands.

Broker nodded. "Mr. Klunder, Phil Broker. I heard that a shipment you were expecting went missing." He opened the briefcase wider and allowed Klunder to see the burned package and behind it a glimpse of Mostafa Rhobani's stark, dead face.

Stuart Klunder put on his best lawyerly blank stare as Broker closed the satchel and said, "Nice to meet you." He plucked the newspaper from Klunder's hand and palmed a pen. "You're a busy man, so I'll just leave an address." Broker wrote his name and his new Stillwater street address on the paper and handed it back. Then he nodded and walked away.

A few paces on, Joey turned. "So is he the next job?"

"Could be," said Broker.

Chapter Forty-One

Six twenty-four North Fourth Street commanded an elevated lot on Stillwater's north hill. People called it the Old Turrie House. Broker checked the street number when he saw the building hunched against the sky like a gloomy, gabled ghost. It may have started in the 1890s as an elegant, turreted, double decker Queen Anne mansion, but now weather and neglect had chewed deep into the siding and shingles and gingerbread trim. Nothing looks more forlorn than a cast-off refrigerator sitting in the snow. Broker counted two of them marooned on the wrap-around porch.

A driveway in the back led to an apron on which Rita Turrie's black Trans Am was parked in front of a large, double-door, high-peaked garage. As Broker got out of the truck, he saw Rita come out the garage doorway looking a little gaunt and pale and haunted, like she'd just stepped off a tarot card. She wore jeans, tennis shoes, and a blue hoodie. Her dark hair swung free. A leather driving glove covered her left hand; above the hem, several strips of adhesive tailed up her wrist.

"Jesus, Eyebrows!" She rallied and cocked her head. "You got a haircut? You look like a fuckin' narc."

Encouraged by the spunk in her tone, Broker said, "Starting a new job; figured I should clean up my act." He stepped in closer. "You mind if a narc gives you a hug?"

"I can do that," said Rita, her lips slowly composing a smile.

When Broker wrapped his arms around her he felt not so much electricity as the tug of something older and more elemental, gravity maybe.

She drew back and nodded at the Bronco. "You bring your tools?"

"In the back."

"Good. Once we get set up, there's lots of work to do. We're in the middle of a historic preservation frenzy, don'cha know? C'mon inside," she said. When he just stared at her, her voice turned serious. "I intend to talk to you about every bit of it, just not yet." When she held up her gloved hand, Broker noticed that she'd stuffed something, tissue probably, into the empty glove finger to give it body. "When people get around to asking, I'll tell them I injured myself in my studio. They'll understand that." She tossed her head. "C'mon."

Okaaay. The interior walls were sheet-rocked and insulated, and a fire was going in a wood stove. The floor space was two-thirds workshop, one-third living space behind a low partition. An overhead steel girder had been installed and ran the length of the room, supporting a chain hoist. Several large ventilation ducts snaked along the walls. Below the dangling chains—

Sonofabitch. Lookit that! The heavy, wire, skeletal frame was seven feet tall and sketched the fluid shape of an eagle poised, wings flared, like he'd just landed on an *engine block.* Meticulously shaped metal feathers, overlapping black on white, were welded to parts of the wings. A ruff woven out of spark plugs circled the statue's neck. Broker came closer to inspect the block that served as the pedestal for the metal sculpture in progress. A chunk had been literally ripped out. Looking up, he saw it clamped in the gleaming beak. He reached up and tapped the copper beak, then questioned her with a look.

"Expansion tank from a '65 T-Bird. Braze it and shape it, and it shines up like a new penny," Rita said, then added, "I think I'm in an artistic rut."

"Uh huh." Broker pointed at the missing hunk of engine block. "How in the hell did you do that?"

Rita flashed her old kinky smile that Broker absorbed like crooked sunshine. "It's cast iron, right? So I rigged a gandy-dancer hook to the block, lifted it on the hoist, and used a torch. Just before it got molten, the part between the hooks tore out." She raised her eyebrows.

"I guess." Broker walked a quick circuit of the work area. Benches lined two of the walls and held an eight-inch bench shear and a bead roller. Butcher paper sketches were tacked to the pegboard over the bench. Black and white car doors and trunk lids were stacked against one of the walls. Clumps of solder and shards of snipped metal crunched under his boots. An industrial-sized MIG welder sat under the bench. A welder's hood hung on a wheeled dolly with an acetylene torch. Wooden bins held spark plugs, copper tubing and machine parts. Some of the bins were filled with metal strips that had been cut from the door panels. Several of them lay on the bench next to a pair of heavy duty, aviation tin snips. He picked up the snips, tested the tension, and figured she used the snips to fine-tune the metal strips into feathers. Broker smiled. *Now I know where you got that grip.*

Carefully calibrating her tone, Rita easily pulled off being poised and offhand. "Yeah, I know. You liked me better as a biker bimbo." She shrugged. "What you see is what you get, and I got my master's in studio arts at the U of M a year ago."

Broker cleared his throat, took a moment to estimate the height of the sculpture, then sized up the dimensions of the two-car garage door. "You'll never get it out that door," he said.

"So we tear out a wall and build an addition. Looks like I'm going to need a carpenter, huh?"

Despite her wounded hand, and the insane events of the last two weeks, they spontaneously broke into laughter.

"So where's it going to wind up?" he asked.

"On the corner where you turn into Dad's shop. Screaming Eagles and all that good shit."

After laughing, Broker found himself flat-footed and tongue-tied. "Rita, I never meant . . ."

She closed the distance and laid a cool index finger to his lips. "Shhhh. C'mon, I have this funky student apartment set up behind the partition. Used to be a carriage house room."

Her space consisted of a small gas range, refrigerator and sink. Oriental carpets covered a raised plank floor. The commode sat behind a folding Japanese screen. A table and chairs was piled with stuff from the workshop: wings, bent tubing, piles of heavily annotated sketches. The bed was a rumple of heavily woven Andean ponchos and pillows. On the wall over the bed, a tall poster showed a smiling naked woman squatting in scattered human bones beside a grinning skull. Andrea would appreciate the caption: *He asked me to eat him so I did.*

She poured coffee from the pot on the stove and handed him a cup. "I also minored in interior design, so I'm in charge of the restoration of Granddad's house next door." She pinned him with a sidelong glance. "Plan to take it down to the bones and put it back the way it was. Maybe you could pitch in. We haven't drawn up a contract yet, but Dad says you can work as much or as little as you want, so as not to interfere with your, ah, other job. This is the only functional stove on the premises at the moment, so maybe we can negotiate visiting privileges. You have your pick of the rooms in the house. There's heat, sometimes." Rita finished with a genuine freckled grin. "Hope you don't have a problem working for a woman."

Broker didn't smile a lot, so his facial muscles were starting to cramp.

The one easy chair was stacked with metal wings, so she guided him to the bed, and they sat down side by side. Two plastic prescription vials sat on the bed table. One contained pills. She opened the other one and held up a joint.

Still smiling, Broker shook his head. "It's a little early for me."

"You sure?" She produced a butane lighter, fired it up, took a hit, held it, and let it out with an achingly sweet sigh. "You sure?" she repeated, setting the reefer aside. "Because I have this theory that certain plants are looking to hook up with certain people. Like people who get all turned around in the world and come back in steel cages and aren't sure where they fit in." She removed the coffee cup from his hand and placed it on the side table along with her own.

Broker took a deep breath. And, for sure, she knew his eyes were running all over her face, trying to take her all in at once. This sensation gripped him. If he was, in fact, locked in a cage, then who would be the best person to set him free? Andrea was dedicated to measurements and picking locks. Rita lived in Vulcan's workshop and conjured eagles with tools that burned and bent steel.

"And I do have a definite idea where you'll fit in." Rita nibbled his ear.

Broker ever so gently ran his hands over her back and waist and eased her in close, careful of the glove. He heard her whisper, "You know, I'm a lot better at this when I have both my hands."

"Here," he said, "takes two."

Acknowledgements

Special thanks to Happy Thomsen, who founded Happy's Stillwater Automotive in 1989.

Dennis P. Moriarty, Commander, Washington County Sheriff's Department (ret.), also a snappy Army codebreaker back when people did it, not computers.

John Bolger, Sergeant, Minneapolis Police Department (ret.), Senior Special Agent, Minnesota Bureau of Criminal Apprehension (ret.), who shared some insight from his forty-one years on the job.

Pete Orput, Washington County attorney, Washington County, Minnesota.

Tony Kizer, automotive technician at Happy's Stillwater Automotive; also the creator of unique metal miniatures made from used auto parts.

Chris Valen and Jenifer LeClair at Conquill Press, for their very helpful editorial comments.

Jennifer Adkins, for wielding a sharp red pen.

CPSIA information can be obtained
at www.ICGtesting.com
Printed in the USA
LVOW08s0810270117
522345LV00001B/1/

31192021180664